# AMORAN

## Book One of the Amoran Chronicles

Debra Koehler

~ Crescent Place Press ~

Cover Design: Ebooklaunch.com
Edited by: Raquel Brown Editing Services

ISBN: Paperback — 979-8-9907429-0-1

ISBN: ebook — 979-8-9907429-1-8

~ Crescent Place Press ~

## Praise for *Amoran*, Book One of the Amoran Chronicles

"*Amoran* begins in a perfectly ordinary New England household and expands into an extraordinary multiverse. Koehler weaves in classic fantasy motifs, but grounds them in modern emotional realism. It's this juxtaposition, heroism amid domestic practicality, that makes *Amoran* stand out in a crowded genre."
— *Jessica Fahey, San Francisco Book Review*

"Original, deftly crafted, and a fun read from cover to cover. With a genuine flair for the kind of imaginative and humor laced storytelling that will appeal to fans of fantasy, romance, and unlikely heroines drafted to save the universe."
— *Midwest Book Review*

". . . feel-good portal fantasy. Readers looking for a fun, comforting story with an enjoyable heroine, a warm tone, and light romantic tension will likely have a great time here."
— *Fantasy Book Critic, Self-Published Fantasy Blog-Off*

". . . a heroine's journey in the best sense. We travel with Kerrin as she navigates a world so beautifully described, I want to vacation there."
— *Marlene Cullen, The Write Spot*

". . . Debra Koehler does a great job showing us both worlds and how Kerrin gradually comes to terms with her place in each of them. The story engaged me to the point I finished it in two days."
— *Sheri McGuinn, Author & Screenwriter*

To Chris Baty and the founders of NaNoWriMo

*Without you this book would have remained a vague idea
jotted on a scrap of paper—and then forgotten.*

# PROLOGUE

A shimmering twister of light spiraled out of the Seventh Vortex, shot to the floor with a *whoosh*, then snapped back through the hole in the ceiling. The opening closed up, and the suburban home returned to its former state.

Except for the otherworld traveler standing in the family room.

Arrien held his breath, listening in the predawn darkness. He'd misjudged his timing before and nearly been caught. Now, satisfied that the family remained asleep, he lessened his grip on the special letter prepared by the Vortex Guardians. The fate of Earth and Amoran depended on Kerrin absorbing the information energetically encoded within each word. Thirty days from now, the memory activators would complete their job, enabling Kerrin to recall her true purpose.

Arrien shivered. *And what's in store for her.*

How to deliver the letter safely was a challenge. The dimensional differences between the two worlds required Kerrin to read and assimilate the contents before anyone from Amoran could directly contact her. To do otherwise risked deadly consequences.

Moonlight drifted in through the picture window, illuminating a book on the coffee table. He'd seen Kerrin borrow this book from the library yesterday during his undercover observation of her. Judging by the placeholder, she was already a third of the way through. Arrien smiled. *She does love a good mystery,* he reflected, then froze as hurried footsteps sounded on the uncarpeted stairs. On impulse, he snatched the bookmark from the novel and replaced it with the letter.

He barely managed to shield himself before the light flipped on.

# CHAPTER 1

"Kiley," I bellowed up the stairwell to my daughter. "Downstairs now or you're grounded. The bus will be here any—"

I groaned as the vehicle in question rumbled past our house. The driver hadn't even bothered to downshift. Only three weeks into the school year and he already knew better.

"Problems?" my husband asked as he rounded the corner and grabbed his computer case.

"No more than usual," I grumbled under my breath. "Not that you'd know."

John hiked up an eyebrow. "Fascinating. Negative emotion aimed at me. I will attempt a mind-meld to learn the reason." Fingers splayed, he reached for my head.

After fourteen years of marriage, John not only knew which buttons to push, but all the dials, knobs, and levers that made the Kerrin Scott machine run. I wound up laughing, which is what he'd counted on.

"Much better," he said, dropping the Spockisms. "Now what's got you snarlin' darlin'?"

"You mean, besides the fact that we hardly see each other anymore?" The new job he'd taken a year ago had turned into a time suck nightmare.

John lifted both eyebrows this time. "Really? You can say that after last night?"

I smiled, remembering how we'd celebrated his homecoming from an extended business trip. "You know what I'm talking about."

He pulled me into his arms. "I don't like this schedule either, but I'm committed to the job-from-hell through next summer. Can you hold on for one more year?"

When he punctuated his query with puppy dog eyes, I forfeited all hope of a serious conversation, and answered him with a kiss.

"*Ew.* Do you have to do that in front of me?" Kiley, who finally deigned to grace us with her presence, considered an outward show of affection between grown-ups tantamount to child abuse. In a rare display of sibling support, her older brother agreed.

"Yeah, get a room," Ryan said as he breezed by us. In a blur of dark hair and navy backpack, he was out the front door to catch his carpool ride to the junior high.

John shook his head. "Where do they get this stuff? Must be your side of the family."

I narrowed my eyes at him, which only made him smile. "Okay. What's my penance?"

"Don your chauffeur's hat and take our darling daughter to school."

Kiley ignored us as she jammed books into her backpack, complaining nonstop about the plight of poor, overworked waifs forced into scholarly servitude for six hours a day.

John rolled his eyes. "Quit the Dickens routine, Kiley. Let's go."

She gave her long blond hair an exaggerated flip, then gifted him with The Look.

"Whatever you do," she ordered as they headed out, "*don't* drop me off in the parking lot. Pull over on the street, and—" The slamming door cut her off mid-decree.

Savoring the sudden, delicious quiet, I made my way to the family room to retrieve the latest edition of my favorite mystery series. Tucking the book under one arm, I paused to appreciate nature's masterpiece on display through the picture window. Backlit by the morning sun, the birch, maple, and oak trees behind my house glowed like an incandescent mosaic of autumn colors. So completely was my attention captured that when my cell phone vibrated, my overactive startle reflex kicked in. I flinched and dropped the book, which hit the floor with a page-crunching thud.

Shoot. That was a library book I'd just injured.

I fumbled the phone out of my pocket, checked caller ID, and pressed the talk button.

"I'm not officially late until Tom asks where I am," I greeted my coworker, Megan.

"You're rarely late, period, although how you manage that while living with the Tardy Teen Titan is nothing short of miraculous."

I laughed. "Don't rush it. I've got two years to go before she's a teenager. And God help me when that day arrives."

"Amen to that. Can you pick up some tea and scones? You and I are going to need the fortification today."

"And the occasion is . . . ?"

"You'll see," she sing-songed, then hung up before I could pump her for details.

I stuffed the phone back into my pocket. My poor book lay spread-eagled in front of the sofa. I smoothed out the bent pages, then scanned the floor for the grocery list I'd used last night as a bookmark, but it was nowhere in sight. Crouching down, I slid my hand beneath the low-slung couch, trying to ignore the crusty feel of the sofa's underworld. Out came the instructions to a game, Ryan's math homework from two weeks ago—he really had done it after all—an empty bag of chips, and a playing card, the King of Hearts. "You've always been my favorite," I told the royal face smiling up at me. "But you should have ditched that hard-boiled queen long ago. Look what she did to poor Alice."

I pressed my face to the floor and peered under the couch. A single item remained. It had to be my grocery list, but how had it managed to travel that far back?

Stretching my arm as far as I could, I teased out my list.

Except, it wasn't.

I stared at the pink paper clenched in my hand. The texture was similar to parchment, yet it was as thin as wrapping tissue, while at the same time, felt surprisingly durable, like Mylar. Folded in thirds, my name was printed on the outer flap in a precise cursive, the kind often used by mass marketers to make you think you were receiving a special, handwritten invitation—typically to part with large sums of money. They'd piqued my interest with the unusual texture, though, and I unfolded the page as I rose to my feet.

*"Dear Kerrin,"* the solicitation began. *"You were once known to us by another—"*

"Oh," I exclaimed. The room grayed out as a rush of dizziness brought me to my knees. I have low blood pressure, so I'm not a stranger to this kind of thing. I'd simply stood up too fast. I leaned on the coffee table for support, still clutching the letter in front of me. It took longer than usual for my vision to clear, and by the time the world came back into focus, another call rang through.

"Bring your extra set of office keys," Megan said without preamble. "Dave misplaced his again. And hurry up. I'm hungry. And excited." *Click.*

I sighed. When would my life not entail hurrying?

Distracted by Megan's hints at a surprise, I shoved the letter into my tote bag along with my book, and was halfway out the door when I remembered the keys Dave needed. I grabbed them from my desk in the den and got as far as the driveway when the nagging feeling that I'd forgotten something else drove me back inside. A loud *whoosh*, like running water, reached my ears when I stepped through the doorway. Then the sound abruptly stopped. Hoping we weren't headed for a plumbing nightmare in our hundred-year-old home, I checked the faucets in our only bathroom and the kitchen. Nothing wrong there. Still plagued by a vague uneasiness, I scrambled through the house, making sure all locks were locked, the coffee pot was switched off, and that I hadn't left the clothes dryer running.

As far as I could tell, everything was as it should be.

So why did I suddenly feel like nothing was as it should be?

---

I entered the renovated Victorian that housed the Tea Leaf Café and took my place at the end of a long line. To kill time—the thing I never seemed to have enough of—I admired the rows of pastries waiting behind the rounded glass case front. "Some of you will be leaving with me," I called softly to them.

The woman ahead of me, her arms nearly wrenched from their sockets by a squirming toddler on one hand, and a whining preschooler on the other, regarded me with calculating eyes.

*Note to self: Keep thoughts in head where they belong. Conversing with baked goods is not indicative of sound mental health.*

But the woman hadn't been measuring me for a straitjacket after all.

"I'm engaged to the chocolate croissants," she said with a conspiratorial smile. "But you can have that raspberry Danish; I'm through with his crap."

I laughed, thankful I wasn't the only oddball living in Glenwood Falls. "That's okay. I've been seeing the blueberry scones on the side, but I think my husband is getting suspicious."

"Let him. It keeps the mystery alive." The girls were swiftly transforming their mother into a maypole. She rolled her eyes at me. "Do you have kids?"

I nodded. "Eleven and thirteen."

Maypole Mom registered a faraway look as the toddler dove between her legs. "Is it true about how fast they grow up?" she asked, pulling the little girl back. "Cuz I am really trying to appreciate this phase."

As if on cue, the toddler let out a screech of frustration. I crossed my eyes and blew a raspberry at her. She stopped mid-wail and giggled. Kids.

I looked back at the mom and shook my head, remembering. "It's hard to believe, but one minute you're in the middle of diapers and daycare. Then suddenly, you're chauffeuring them to Scouts, soccer, karate, and dance lessons. There were days I couldn't wait for my kids to be older. But now that it's here . . ."

I trailed off, gripped by the strangest sensation that my life was about to radically change. I couldn't imagine why; nothing much ever happened to me. Then again, Ryan was a brand-new teenager and Kiley already acted like one. And teenagers spelled CHANGE with capital letters.

The woman's attention was diverted back to the little girls—that had been their diabolical plan all along—and we advanced to the order station without further conversation.

I left the café with my purchases and drove to work. In my decade-long tenure, I'd done everything from general office work to writing promotional materials at Pierson & Todd—the office design business that my childhood friend, Tom Pierson, started with his life partner, David Todd. This wasn't what I'd pictured doing with a degree in English, but I still counted myself fortunate. I worked with a great group of people in the small New England town I'd grown up in, the pay was decent, and my three-day work week accommodated my family life. Especially now, with John playing the role of absentee husband.

Megan was finishing up a call as I carried our breakfast into her office and set it on the desk. She plunked the handset down and pumped her arm. "Woohoo! It's official. The owner of that vacant building on Main Street agreed to sell."

As if that explained everything. When Megan was excited, important details were often left out as her mind leapfrogged past her mouth.

"Megan? I flunked my mind reading course."

She laughed. "Sorry. A developer would like to convert the building into a mini-mall of vintage stores. They want to hire Pierson & Todd to design the internal common areas."

"That's great," I said. Work had been slow enough lately that the specter of layoffs hung over our heads.

"Get ready for the onslaught," Megan added. "This project is just the tip of the iceberg."

That gave me pause. "What do you mean?"

"You know that saying, 'feast or famine'? We're gonna get stuffed to the gills."

Before I could press for an explanation, Tom stopped by to announce an emergency staff meeting that would run until lunch. When I congratulated him for landing the plum account, he smiled affectionately while giving his partner the credit. "You know Dave. The developer now believes we can walk on water while turning it into wine. Let's go. We've got some serious planning to do."

---

I refused to let the growing wind and graying sky deter me as I settled onto my favorite park bench at noon. The morning-long meeting had given me a headache and I hoped the fresh air would do me some good.

When I reached into my tote bag for my sandwich, my hand closed over the letter I'd found earlier. I pushed it aside and dug around for my lunch, but it was like the letter kept gluing itself to me. Questioning why I'd bothered to keep it, I took it out for another look. Sheesh. The entire page was filled with rows of that fake cursive. *Hmm. Should I find out what the Pink Paper People are selling? Or crumple this into a ball and pitch it into the recycling can?*

I didn't get to do either. My headache ramped up, bringing with it the nausea and dizziness that herald a full-blown migraine.

"Boo," a voice called from behind.

And there went my overactive startle reflex. I yelped, loosening my grip on the letter just in time for a gust of wind to drive it across the grass. Like I was out to save the Dead Sea Scrolls, I bolted from the bench and galloped in pursuit, catching up with it on the other side of the park. I doubled over, gasping for air as my friend, Rebecca, covered the distance at a more reasonable pace. With all that had gone on at work, I'd spaced out our lunch date.

She pointed at the pink paper. "I hope that was worth the effort."

Was it? "I don't know why I ran like that. I'm pretty sure this is just a piece of junk mail. It's weird, though. I had a budding migraine a moment ago, but now it's gone."

"Lucky you. Exercise just makes my headaches worse."

"Yeah, me too. Usually."

We returned to the bench, where I pushed the letter to the bottom of my tote bag, got out my lunch, and filled Rebecca in on the newest developments at Pierson & Todd.

---

My part-time schedule allowed me to leave the office at three o'clock on Monday, Tuesday, and Wednesday, my official workdays. And today, I really needed to get the hell out of Dodge. In order to land the mini-mall account, Dave had agreed that Pierson & Todd could help the developers with several of their other office design projects on a rush basis. Tom and Dave had asked me to work as many extra hours as I could, but I'd hedged on my answer. I'd been trying for years to get back to writing, aching to pen my own cozy mystery series. But life always seemed to muscle in and arm wrestle that dream aside. No more! I'd made a promise to myself to partake in a writing contest this November that I hoped would jumpstart my creative life, and I couldn't afford to give away my free time now as I prepared for it.

I picked up the kids from their respective schools (Kiley only took the bus on my workday mornings), then proceeded to do my least favorite dance: the after-school-activities-shuffle. When we arrived home, cooking dinner was the last thing I felt like doing. Not that I ever did. The kids and I debated the merits of heating up leftovers or breaking open a box of macaroni and cheese. Agreeing in the end that having a pizza delivered was an even better idea, Ryan phoned in our order while I put the kitchen back to rights from the morning madness. I was loading the last of the breakfast dishes into the dishwasher when the phone rang.

"Hi," John said, in a voice that spelled doom.

I groaned. "How long will you be?"

"Midnight, if I'm lucky."

"Better not make it any later than that, or you won't be."

"Won't be what? Oh. Ha ha. Very funny. I thought you might be mad at me again."

"Again? Have I stopped?"

That brought a chuckle. "You are a hard woman, Kerrin Scott."

I smiled to myself. "Yeah, but you love me anyway."

"Always and forever," he said, and rang off.

---

Midnight arrived and still no sign of John. The kids were in bed, but I'd had too much caffeine after dinner and opted to put my chemically induced insomnia to good use with a leisurely bath and some quality reading time.

Late September air, unseasonably warm and fragrant with the musky scent of dried leaves, drifted in through the open window next to the sink. I filled the tub, then went to my bedroom to get my book. I reached into my tote bag, surprised to find that the junk mail letter had somehow worked its way to the top again. I hadn't thought about it since lunchtime, but now it seemed strangely alive, almost as if it were summoning me. Shaking my head at the fanciful notion, I smoothed out the crumpled paper and read:

*"Dear Kerrin,*

*"You were once known to us—"*

My stomach somersaulted as the room danced around. Praying the pizza wasn't to blame, I shut my eyes and gritted my teeth. Thankfully, the queasiness passed quickly, and I continued reading.

*"—by another name, but since you have been living on—"*

"Oh!" It was much worse this time. I ran to the bathroom, dropped the letter onto the counter, and hunched over the toilet. A few seconds later, the nausea and dizziness were gone. I was pleased to deny the porcelain Goddess her sacrifice, but something didn't seem right.

I thought back over my day. Then I questioned my sanity. Unless I was mistaken, it seemed that each time I had tried to read the letter, I'd felt dizzy or sick to my stomach—or both—a reaction that grew stronger with every attempt.

*Get a grip, Kerrin! A piece of paper cannot make a person ill.*

Determined to prove myself right, I gave reading the letter another shot. I could only manage *"—living on Earth for the past—"* when the words vibrated and spun to the left. I clamped my hand over my mouth and looked away.

When my stomach settled again, I tried mind-over-matter to keep going. But I could not get past that first line without feeling like I was in the passenger seat on a winding mountain road. A strange trembling set up in my body as my inability to read the letter sparked a fierce determination to do just that. But how was I going to access this roller coaster of a message when I couldn't even ride a merry-go-round without feeling sick? Or go on a long car trip without my motion sickness pills?

None of that mattered, though. It made no sense, but I knew, deep in my bones, that I needed whatever information that letter contained. I had to find a way. Had to.

I peeked at the innocent looking pink sheet resting on the counter. And nearly passed out.

*Uhhh. I can't even look at it now without feeling like I'm going to die?* This was way worse than motion sickness.

Motion sickness! I had a mental-head-slap moment. My motion sickness pills were good for quelling nausea and dizziness. Worth a try.

I rooted through our large, cluttered medicine cabinet, hunting for those little red pills with the same intensity I searched for chocolate during a certain time of the month.

And came up empty.

A throbbing pressure began to pound inside my head. *Oh, dear God. Make this stop.* I knew relief would only come when I could read that damn letter. Where the hell were those pills?

Doubling my effort, I pawed miscellaneous tubes, packets, and bottles out of the way—half of them expired—until I finally found the small white container hiding behind an empty box of Band-Aids. Hands shaking with frustration, I worked to line up the opposing triangles on the cap and bottle. I succeeded at last, but then I couldn't pry the lid free. I was ready to get a hammer and smash the stupid thing open when the top popped off and rolled behind the toilet.

As if the letter were trying to communicate with me, the urgency surrounding it grew. I scooped out a pill, then dashed to the kitchen for a drink. One talent I did not possess was the ability to take pills without water. And I mean a *lot* of water.

I had just swallowed the pill when I heard someone using the bathroom sink. The same sink with the counter on which I'd carelessly tossed that strange letter.

I bounded up the stairs, burst past Kiley on her way out of the bathroom, and exclaimed in relief. My letter lay precisely where I'd left it. I'd been lucky this time. Recalling how I'd had to chase it across the park earlier, I reached up to close the window so a random breeze wouldn't waft it into the tub. That's when Kiley lumbered back into the bathroom and did something I would have kissed her for on any other day.

"Sorry. I forgot," she mumbled, and flushed our low-flow toilet.

A wave of panic had me lunging for the letter—but the sleeve of Kiley's robe got to it first as she turned to go, knocking it into the bowl at the peak of suction. In a blur of pink, the tissue-thin paper whirled in a circle and disappeared around the bend.

Mere seconds had elapsed from flush to finish. Oblivious to what had transpired, Kiley was already back in her room. Me? I stared into the now clear, peaceful water, engulfed by an inexplicable sense of loss.

———————

The letter's demise haunted me for several days until I came to my senses and accepted that I'd let my imagination run wild. My various symptoms merely coincided with the letter; they weren't caused by it. Lack of sleep from the previous night when John came home early from his business trip (well worth the sacrifice of those ZZZs) had affected my blood pressure the following morning when I first found the letter. And it was increased work stress that gave me a budding migraine when I tried to read it again at lunchtime. Finally, too much caffeine late in the day, topped off by a questionable pizza—Kiley and Ryan both said they had stomachaches that night—sealed the deal.

With that explanation firmly in place, the letter dropped off my radar while I spent the next four weeks keeping up with the frantic pace at work while flying mostly solo at home.

As the end of October approached, I focused on the writing contest. Every participant who could pen fifty thousand words of a new novel in the month of November was considered a winner. Fifty thousand? I'd be thrilled if I got past the first chapter, something I hadn't been able to do when I started a novel fresh out of college. Since I couldn't begin my book until the official start date of November first, I tried a few writing exercises to get in shape. Encouraged by how easily the words flowed, I congratulated myself with smug satisfaction.

Then I read my brilliant literary contribution back to myself. Complete and utter dreck.

I slammed the keyboard into its hidey-hole, dragged myself to the kitchen and brewed a whole pot of Earl Grey tea—it promised to be a long afternoon. I filled a mug, set the teapot on a warmer, then scratched away at a crossword puzzle. But even those words tormented me, their innuendoes and double entendres escaping my mental grasp.

I was rescued from further word-related disgrace when the house phone rang. We still had a landline since cell reception in our location at the base of a mountain was often spotty.

"Hey. How's it going?" asked the man on the other end.

"Listen, buster," I hissed. "I'm on the Do Not Call list and I'd love to sue you for the hefty fine." I waited a beat. "Then again, your voice sounds kind of familiar. Do I know you?"

"Such a wit," John said. "Or do I mean a half-wit?"

I snorted. "Oh. Wait. Let me write that funny line down so I can include it in my book."

"No need to be sarcastic. Besides, I haven't been gone that much."

"I beg to disagree, ghost-of-a-husband. And for your information, I could use a few good lines. And talent. And ideas. I'm ready to call it quits before the contest even starts. I'll never be able to do this."

"You can't quit," John said. "You've been looking forward to this for months."

"Yeah. Too bad I need this stupid thing called a plot. On the bright side, we'll be able to host Thanksgiving if I'm not using up precious holiday hours to achieve the impossible."

John jumped into cheerleader mode, waving verbal pom-poms.

"Don't throw in the towel yet. You can write a novel *and* we can host Thanksgiving dinner. Never say never. You can always pull a rabbit out of a hat."

With an exaggerated groan, I bid good day to the King of Clichés.

Rabbit out of a hat. What a dork. A geeky dork, at that. But he was my geeky dork and I loved him. I had to agree, though, that running a household, managing four people's schedules, and holding down a job made me very good at pulling rabbits out of a hat—so to speak.

*Hmm. What if I give up on people and write about rabbits? Talking rabbits. Talking white rabbits that drink tea and live in magical black hats with secret tunnels that lead . . .*

I turned around and screeched at the sight before me.

This was no rabbit.

# Chapter 2

"**A**re you ready to go?" said the little man that I had to be hallucinating.

*I'm not crazy. I'm not—*

"Well?" He jammed pudgy hands on his hips and glared at me.

*I fell asleep standing up. Horses do it all the time. I just need to wake up.*

I pinched myself. Twice. It did no good. The hairy little guy was still there.

"We don't have all day," he barked.

Quite the demanding hairy little guy. I stepped back—I didn't know if he'd had his shots—and took in the whole picture. Dark eyes skewered me from beneath a sea of wild brown hair. A massive beard tumbled to his stomach, obscuring most of his orange and red striped shirt. Polka dot suspenders in visually painful hues of neon blue and yellow held up garish plaid pants. He stood only as high as my chin and looked like an escaped dwarf from a Disney movie. Except furrier.

"Are you through staring at me?" he growled. "We have to go."

"Go where?" I demanded, wondering why the hell I wasn't calling 9-1-1 to report a stranger who had appeared in my kitchen out of nowhere. And yet . . . something about him seemed familiar.

"Don't be obtuse. The letter explained everything."

"The letter?"

"Yes. The . . . let . . . ter." He enunciated each syllable like I was a moron.

I didn't connect the dots right away, but when I did, I swallowed hard, amazed that I was about to seek confirmation of my growing insanity from a delusion I was having—the only explanation that made sense for what was happening.

"I found a letter . . . about a month ago. Pink paper? Really nice handwriting?"

He nodded impatiently. "Yes, yes. The letter's activation only required thirty days to be complete, so you must know why I am here."

"Not really. I never got to read it."

"You didn't . . . you didn't . . . *read it?* What is the matter with you?"

"Nothing a stay in a rubber room couldn't cure," I said under my breath.

Arms flailing, he paced across my kitchen floor, moaning and groaning about the end of the world. Hallucination or not, I'd had enough.

"Calm down, will you? I tried to read your stupid letter, but my daughter flushed it down the toilet before I could get past the first line."

He stopped like he'd been shot and did a white-knuckle grip on the edge of the counter. If he was a cartoon character, his eyes would have been spinning in circles.

"Where . . . is . . . the . . . let . . . ter . . . now?"

That supercilious pronunciation was back. I wanted to slap him.

"It's . . . gone. . . Ein . . . stein. What part of 'down the toilet' don't you get?"

What little I could see of his face went decidedly white. "Without the activation contained in that letter, your memories and abilities will not return and the entire Reparention is doomed!"

My head started to ache. "What the hell are you talking about?"

"Thanks to your incompetence, the destruction of both our planets!"

"And that's my fault?" Remarkably, I took the fact that he was allegedly from another world in stride. It was being made responsible for yet another person's well-being that did me in. I didn't know if I was having an honest-to-God close encounter or a psychotic break, but I took a stab at finding out, and I don't mean symbolically. I poked him in the ribs to see if he was solid.

"Ow," he cried, as if the tiny jab had hurt him.

"Ow is right. You're still here."

I hadn't proven anything. Don't people hallucinating believe their experience is real? At a loss for a better idea, I opted to make the most of what had to be a nervous breakdown. Besides, if I'd made him up, I must have done so for a reason. Might as well find out why.

I waved at a chair. "Have a seat. I'm sure we can come to a meeting of the minds." *Provided I haven't already lost mine.*

The dwarf continued to glower.

"Oh, come on," I said. "How about some tea and cookies? A snack always puts me in a better mood. And I have lots of cookies to choose from. Kiley's Girl Scout troop didn't get the top seller award for nothing."

I opened a cupboard filled with neatly stacked, colorful boxes. Grumpy regarded them with such a thoughtful expression, I snickered to myself. *Probably doesn't know what a Girl Scout is. Do they even have cookies on Planet of the Dwarves?*

"Trefoils," he announced. "And some Thin Mints, too—they're my favorite."

My diminutive delusion had a favorite Girl Scout cookie? I'd gone bonkers for sure.

He plunked himself down and drummed his fingers on my kitchen table, glaring the entire time it took me to refill my mug, pour a fresh cup for him, and arrange a small plate of cookies.

I ferried our repast to the table, took the seat catty-corner to him, and let out a sigh.

"Look. I consider myself to be a sensible, rational person. Yet here I am having a tea party with one of the Seven Dwarves. That's pretty certifiable."

Grumpy ignored me. He removed the Trefoils and most of the Thin Mints from the plate and dipped them one by one into his tea before devouring the soggy mess. Not a pretty sight. I'd seen babies eat with more decorum.

After gobbling the last Trefoil, he finally made eye contact and mellowed his voice for the first time.

"You don't remember my name?"

I shook my head.

He frowned. "You recall nothing about why I am here today?"

I just stared at him.

It was his turn to exhale a huge sigh. "My name is Danaeus," he said, studying me with a disturbing intensity. "I am a Guardian from the planet Amoran, which is linked to Earth by an energy vortex. I came here today to bring you back . . ." He paused, searching my face. "To bring you to your . . ." His lips pursed as his porcupine eyebrows drew closer together. "Oh, dear Light. What do you feel right now?"

"Apart from this nagging concern about my mental health?"

He leaned closer. "When I told you my name just now, you didn't experience anything . . . unusual?"

"Was I supposed to?"

"Yes!" He slumped back. "This changes everything. I don't know how to . . . I cannot bring you to Amoran now, it's too risky . . ."

He trailed off and began fidgeting with his napkin while grumbling to himself, things like, "I shouldn't have to be the one. What am I supposed to do now?" and something about an elf. To fortify myself in case he totally lost it, I reached for one of the few remaining cookies.

That got his attention. With a longing look at the Thin Mint I stuffed into my mouth, he said, "I must go on regardless."

"Have at it," I mumbled around the chocolate bits.

"It is critical that vortex energy remain balanced. The most recent imbalance nearly destroyed both our worlds, and we cannot let that happen again!"

He stared at me like he expected a reply, so I obliged him. It's the pleaser in me.

"Can you get to the point? I have to pick my kids up soon."

"This is unbelievable," Danaeus roared.

"You got that right."

He thrust forward so we were nose to nose. I cringed as his hot breath hit my face.

"A massive imbalance is developing in the vortex. Without correction, the vortex will implode a few months from now, and Earth and Amoran will be sucked inside and destroyed!"

A kaleidoscope of images tumbled through my brain. An enormous spiral of rainbow-colored light. Roiling black clouds. A glowing aqua cloak. All . . . vaguely familiar.

Shaken by what I'd just "seen," I exclaimed, "Why are you telling *me* this?"

He banged his fist on the table. "I am telling you because we need your help to repair the vortex and prevent this disaster!"

"My help?" I burst out laughing, then glanced around. "Okay. Where's the hidden camera?"

Danaeus leapt out of his chair, red splotches dotting his cheeks. "Enough of this. Be ready for transport at nine tonight."

I was about to tell him precisely where he could stuff his transport when a blond-haired guy dressed in blue jeans and a T-shirt smiled at me from the other side of the table. Since he'd appeared out of nowhere, I yelled in surprise.

"Wow," the newcomer said as he snatched the last two Thin Mints from the plate. "I don't remember you being so jumpy before, M—"

"Mrs. Scott!" Danaeus shouted over him.

Blond Guy's mouth opened as he turned to the dwarf. That's when I noticed the pointy ears.

Seriously? An elf and a dwarf? All we needed now were a wizard and a pack of hobbits.

"She never read the letter," Danaeus squeezed out.

The cookie-pincher paled. "But I saw—" He cut himself off and stared at me. "You didn't read it?" I shook my head. His face went even whiter. "Oh, no. This is a nightmare."

"I certainly hope so," I muttered.

Danaeus swiped a cookie from his companion, then shot me a warning look. "We have to figure out what to do with this mess. Nine tonight. Be ready. Be waiting."

"Waiting? Waiting where? For what?"

They vanished without answering.

---

I waited all right. I waited at Kiley's school for an extra ten minutes because her class had misbehaved on their museum field trip. I waited again at the junior high for Ryan to finish his makeup PE class and explain to his math teacher why his homework was missing—again.

Then we did the Thursday activities marathon while I tried to forget about an energy imbalance capable of inhaling whole worlds. Despite a valiant effort at repression, my denial mechanisms were losing ground. By nightfall I was convinced something had to be seriously wrong with me. What else could explain my visitors from the Twilight Zone? Maybe low blood pressure was robbing my brain of oxygen. I thought about consulting my family doctor, then nixed the idea. How smart would it be to tell him I'd fed tea and cookies to a dwarf from another world? A dwarf who insisted I was needed to help save the planet. No, wait. Make that two planets. Talk about delusional.

My internal debate was squelched by a blast of wind that rattled the windows. Rain, which began around five o'clock as a steady drizzle, now rammed the house like an army of little bulldozers. Kiley had fallen asleep early and Ryan was in the den using the computer. I could hear the low murmur of his voice as he talked on the phone with his cousin Robert while they played a game online. At one point, Ryan raised his voice. "No. Forget the ogre. Get the dwarf."

*Yes. Please get the dwarf. I'll even help you.*

In need of distraction, I got out my cookbooks to get a head start on planning the menu for Thanksgiving. Cooking isn't my strong suit, but I love preparing Thanksgiving dinner for my family and friends on that quiet, contemplative day before the madness of the holiday season begins—a madness that seems to arrive earlier each year.

An hour later, Ryan mumbled "good night" and went upstairs. As I tacked my Thanksgiving shopping list to the bulletin board in the kitchen, John blew through the back door.

"We really need a garage connected to the house," he complained.

"I vote for a second bathroom instead." John gave me a look. "Hey . . . just sayin'." I helped him out of his soggy jacket. "How come you're home so early?"

He glanced at the clock. "It's nearly nine. Hard to believe that now qualifies as early. But I lucked out. The vendor's tech wizard showed up and offered to stay until this latest problem is fixed. You know, so I could hurry home to my pretty wife."

"Uh-huh," was my response. John's lopsided grin told me I wasn't the only reason he'd rushed home. I mentally thanked the unnamed techie while watching my husband, waiting for the rest.

"And," John batted his long lashes and smiled, "*The Prisoner* finally arrived today at my office—the original show, not that terrible remake. Great watching on a rainy night—with my pretty wife, of course."

"Ah. You really know how to win a girl's heart." And I meant that. The Patrick McGoohan version is a favorite of mine. "Why don't you warm up with a shower? I'll make popcorn."

"Real popcorn?" he asked.

"Of course."

"You're on." And he squished up the stairs.

I measured out a third of a cup of corn kernels and set them aside. Next, I poured a few tablespoons of oil into a large, heavy-bottomed pan. I was about to turn on the burner when I heard a sound like running water coming from the family room. Hoping the roof hadn't sprung a leak, I went to investigate, relieved to find the room toasty warm and perfectly dry. But the sound of running water persisted.

I looked up and gasped.

I didn't have to worry about the roof leaking. It was no longer there.

# CHAPTER 3

A tornado of blue light barreled through the hole in my ceiling and yanked me skyward as I screeched and clawed at the spinning air like a madwoman. When I felt something solid, I clamped on for dear life.

"Let go," someone yelled through the whirling haze.

It took me a moment to place the voice.

"Danaeus? Help me!"

Danaeus tried to pry my hands from his arm, but I dug my fingers in deeper. This was all his fault; no way was I letting him go.

We soared straight up, then slowed to a stop. The blue twister whooshed away, affording a clear view of our surroundings. Too bad there weren't any.

"Oh my God," I shouted, dancing my feet around like a frenzied marionette as we dangled mid-air in a white-walled tunnel of light. "How—"

"Shut your mouth."

"Shut my—hey! Go to hell."

Danaeus pulled his arm free. "I mean keep your mouth closed. It eases the transition."

"What transition?"

A yellow funnel cloud snatched us up. Our ascent was so rapid, and the pressure so intense, I must have lost consciousness. The next thing I knew, I was lying on a hill carpeted with lush grass. Below me, a small lake glistened, its azure surface dotted by an occasional lily pad. Willow trees danced along the shoreline, their long, graceful limbs stretching out over the water's edge. A passel of flowers plucked straight from a Monet painting congregated to my left, and at the end of the valley beyond, snow-capped mountains rose high into the air. The setting was picture-perfect.

Almost too perfect. "Where are we?" I asked.

Danaeus shook his head like he was addressing the village idiot. "The Transition Space."

"Right. Stupid of me not to know that, considering I've never been here before."

His dark brown eyes smoldered. Guess the sarcasm wasn't lost on him. Score a point for the Earth-girl. At least he'd abandoned the cartoon look for a two-piece outfit that might have been at home in a yoga studio.

"So, what happens now?"

He grimaced. "We wait for the portal to open."

"The portal?"

"Yes, the portal. How irritating. Do you always repeat what you hear?"

"*I'm* irritating? You abduct me from my family room, whisk me away to God-knows-where, and you have the nerve to complain that I repeat things?"

"Now," he bellowed.

"Now *what?*"

The ground below us opened up and we plummeted down through a spiraling column of brilliant light in all the hues of a rainbow. Wide bands of radiant color swirled around us, but never touched our bodies. In fact, the only thing I felt—other than sheer wonder—was a slight pressure, not unlike being in a rapidly descending elevator.

While the view was certainly breathtaking, the speed of our fall *literally* took my breath away. I managed to pull some air into my lungs as we exited the rainbow tunnel and our descent slowed. The shimmering blue light returned, supporting us like a luminescent pillow until we reached the bottom where it spread out to cover the floor.

We'd touched down in a large, domed chamber that looked like it had been scooped out of stone. The rounded walls had seven tunnel openings, equidistant from each other with one exception—a span of wall where an eighth tunnel could have symmetrically fit. Several stories above us, glowing golden mist swirled in lazy revolutions beneath the ceiling. Soft, yellow light illuminated the remaining space, but I couldn't detect its source.

After the whirlwind psychedelic ride through the vortex, the place we'd landed in seem a bit plain by comparison. At least, that's what I thought until the blue mist rolled away from us with a delicate *swoosh*, and I gasped.

We stood in the center of a gleaming golden circle about ten feet in diameter. Beyond it, an enormous mandala decorated the rest of the floor. Thousands of tiny tiles in a dazzling array of colors made the sheer magnitude of the artwork overwhelming. I rubbed a hand over my eyes, unable to imagine how long it had taken to create.

Danaeus cleared his throat in that phony way people do when they're trying to make a point. He seemed fine after our tumultuous journey, but I wasn't faring so well. My legs were wobbly, a dull ache pulsed at the base of my skull, and my insides were—well, at least they were still inside me.

"Where are we now?" I asked, hoping the ground would stay put.

Danaeus puffed out his chest and managed to look down his nose at me while staring up into my face. "We are within the Sacred Mountain," he pontificated, "in the Main Chamber of the Guardian Sanctuary, Protected Space of the Guardians of the Seventh Vortex, presided over by the Master Guardian."

He lifted his eyebrows in a way that suggested I should be impressed.

How right he was. "Danny, you are such a drama queen."

He sputtered in protest, but I ignored him. The guy needed a serious attitude adjustment. I was about to stick my fingers in my ears and hum to drown him out, when someone called my name. Unaccountably, the deep, yet gentle voice resonated in my rib cage like I was the one who had spoken. Chills—the good kind—rolled up my spine in response. I turned, but gripped by a sudden bout of shyness, I couldn't seem to tear my eyes from the ground.

Footsteps whispered toward me. The bottom of a floor-length garment entered my field of vision, its aqua fabric shining with a faint light.

Startled and intrigued by that, I overcame my reticence and looked up at the man now standing before me.

Snowy hair fell in straight, silken lines to his shoulders, framing a smooth face the color of light bronze. Brilliant eyes—the same intense aqua as his glowing, hooded cloak—regarded me with an unreadable expression. Age? Hard to determine. Yet the overall feeling emanating from him was at once young and old and timelessly wise. I don't normally describe a man's looks this way, but in short, he was beautiful.

"Who are you?" I whispered.

"I am the Master Guardian," he replied, with a hint of wistfulness I found puzzling. He glanced at Danaeus. "Thank you. That will be all." The dwarf stalked across the chamber, grumbling the whole way, and disappeared down one of the tunnels.

The Master Guardian settled his unwavering gaze on me. "You seem to have traversed the vortex with no ill effects. Interdimensional travel is quite trying, though, and you must rest before we can converse further. An Assistant will take you to your room."

A young man entered the Main Chamber and headed our way.

Rest? Here? *Now*? I shook my head. "Oh, no. I can't stay."

The Master Guardian continued to stare at me. I began trembling, but whether from trepidation or excitement, I wasn't certain. Maybe both.

"I really can't," I babbled. "I'm making popcorn for my husband . . . back on Earth . . . where I live. On the outside chance I'm not dreaming, I need to go home before he notices I'm gone."

The Master Guardian's penetrating gaze seemed to dig inside my brain as he said, "You will be back on Earth before your husband can miss you. You have my word."

"How is that possible?"

Before he could answer, my trembling legs buckled and I started to go down. The Master Guardian reached out and grasped my arms to keep me from falling. The strength he packed in that slender build of his was surprising enough, but it was the soothing, yet restorative energy that poured from his hands and traveled throughout my body that had me regarding him with unabashed awe.

His expression? Never wavered. "It is imperative that you rest." He handed me over to the Assistant and strode away.

The energy infusion helped. Able to stay upright now, I decided to take the Master Guardian's advice and followed the Assistant across the colorful tiles to one of the seven tunnels. He wore the same type of outfit as Danaeus; a pale ecru top that fell to his mid-thigh, paired with matching leggings. Wavy auburn hair hung below his shoulders and covered his golden-brown face in a full beard and mustache. He was as easy on the eyes as the Master Guardian, but even less communicative. My attempts at conversation garnered only silence as he led me down countless gray-brown passageways in a mind-boggling series of twists and turns. At long last, he stopped, waved a hand, and a section of the stone wall in front of us just . . . vanished.

I gaped at the arched opening. "How did you do that?"

The Assistant pointed at the doorway, indicating that I should enter. And like the village idiot Danaeus seemed to think I was, I moseyed on through. Where was my common sense? Wasn't this the part in movies where the audience starts screaming, "No, you moron. Run!"

Too late for that. The Assistant waved his hand from the corridor and disappeared behind a barrier of stone. Heart pounding, I flung myself against the wall and dug at the smooth surface, looking for a seam I could wedge my fingers into and pry the stone apart. When that failed, I waved my hands like the Assistant had done. The stone wall remained stubbornly in place.

There had to be another way out! I whipped around and scanned the room.

And was struck, once again, by that nebulous sense of familiarity I'd experienced when Danaeus visited me earlier today. Surprisingly, the feeling of recognition began to calm my racing heart, and I took a few moments to more slowly take in my surroundings.

The generous space held a table, chairs, and a raised stone slab a little larger than a twin bed. A counter ran the length of the back wall, with dozens of multi-sized drawers nestled beneath, and cabinets above. Tapestries in soft, restful hues covered nearly every bit of wall space, in some cases reaching to the floor. The cloth emitted a faint glowing light, like I'd observed in the Master Guardian's cloak.

I tiptoed toward one of the tapestries. When I got within a few inches of it, the color and pattern changed from a succession of blue lines to muted green spirals. I backed away, and the tapestry returned to its original design. I advanced to the next wall hanging, which produced a series of orange and rust triangles. I checked out several more tapestries. Each had a unique response to my presence, almost as if the cloth were alive. Curious as to how it worked, I peered behind one, but there were no wires, bulbs, or any other indication of a power source.

On my way to inspect the odd assortment of drawers under the counter, I passed by the raised stone slab. Another group of panels descended slowly from the ceiling, coming to a stop a few feet above the slab, surrounding it like short bed curtains. Wavelike patterns rippled across the translucent fabric, which fluttered as if in a light breeze.

I brushed one of the panels with my fingertips. Threads of gold and silver light snaked through the waves. I sat on the edge of the stone to view them from inside the canopy and got another surprise. Instead of being hard as rock, the slab was as pliant as memory foam.

Suddenly exhausted, I lay back and closed my eyes.

---

I felt like I'd been asleep for hours when the now-you-see-it, now-you-don't doorway opened. A young woman with violet eyes, and skin and hair the color of India ink, beckoned me to follow her. Like her predecessor, she did not address me as we traversed another confusing array of corridors. At length, she stopped, opened a doorway, and left.

I crossed the threshold into a room that was larger, but otherwise not much different than the one where I'd taken my rest. Glowing, colorful tapestries covered the walls. A raised stone slab—was that really their idea of a bed?—rested slightly right of center in the floor space. The table, just beyond and to the left of the stone bed, was set with an interesting array of what I assumed was food. The Master Guardian sat facing the doorway as he filled two ceramic goblets with an amber liquid, then motioned me to sit opposite him.

When I'd deposited myself onto the wooden chair, he passed a goblet to me and raised his cup in a gesture of toasting. "In honor of your return."

My return? Confused by that, I set the goblet down without sampling the contents.

"Is something wrong?" he asked.

"You've made a big mistake. I've never been here before."

His shoulders lifted with a sigh. "We have made no mistake, Kerrin, something you would not doubt had you read our letter."

"I really tried," I said, unclear why it felt important to let him know that. "But each time I did, I felt sick and dizzy."

He seemed surprised. "It made you ill?" I nodded. "In all our calculations and preparations, we did not plan for that possibility." He gave a dismayed shake of his head. "Nor did we anticipate its potential loss. It is a terrible misfortune that the letter was destroyed before you could absorb what it contained."

That was a weird way to put it. Not sure how to respond, I relied on weak humor. "Next time, send me an email. It's faster, easier on the stomach, and can't get flushed down a toilet."

The Master Guardian allowed a small smile, which had me wondering. Did he know what email was? Or computers? I hadn't really expected him to get the cyberspace reference, but they must have some form of technology. How else could they light rooms without wires or bulbs and make whole sections of walls disappear? And the panels over my stone bed—I'd fallen asleep so fast, it was like they had a sleep aid in them. Had I been medicated somehow? That was a disturbing thought.

I frowned and pushed the goblet away.

The Master Guardian's expression turned impassive. "It will not harm you." He took a generous drink from his cup as if to prove the point.

"I'm not thirsty," I lied. No way was I touching the contents of that goblet. "Why was the letter so important? Why not just tell me what you needed me to know?"

He set his cup down and regarded me thoughtfully. "Due to the dimensional differences between Earth and Amoran, interaction with your world is limited. What contact we do have must be handled with great care. That letter took months for us to prepare, and it was the only way we could transfer certain energy values and knowledge to you while you are on Earth in an Earth body."

"Through a piece of paper?"

"A very special piece of paper," he clarified, "which we embedded with a type of energy key. As you read the letter, the words would have unlocked the doorway to your consciousness."

I didn't hide my skepticism. "Just by reading a bunch of words?"

He leaned forward and pressed his palms to the table. "Have you ever heard music that moved you so deeply, you experienced it physically? As if the vibrations of the musical instruments could reach inside you and pluck the strings of your heart?"

I was sideswiped by a rush of emotion as the sound of his voice, and the words he spoke, did exactly that.

"Yes," I said quietly. "I know the feeling."

"Good. That was how the key was designed to work. The physical resonance of the words, combined with the energetic coding in the key, would have awakened memories that lay dormant within you—most importantly the memory of your true identity. There would have been ample time for you to integrate the phenomenal changes the key initiated before Danaeus arrived to bring you back to Amoran."

*Phenomenal changes?* Like what—growing a few extra arms? Transforming into a blob of purple sludge? My throat went so dry, I was overtaken by a coughing fit. The Master Guardian's only offer of help was to point at the goblet. In desperation, I drank, hoping that whatever was in the cup wouldn't make me grow taller or shrink me down to nothing. But I got a much pleasanter surprise than Alice did. A soothing warmth radiated up my legs and throughout my body.

"It's backwards," I exclaimed, referring to how the heat of an alcoholic drink works its way south. I took another swig. "And delicious. A little like apples and honey, but without the excessive sweetness. What is it?"

"Fairybee wine. It does not intoxicate like the wine you consume on Earth, but does provide a pleasurable relaxation." He grabbed my wrists and pierced me with those brilliant eyes of his. "It is one of your favorite things."

And just like that, I was standing in an apple orchard so real I felt the warm sun on my face. Thousands of tiny bees with brightly colored wings buzzed in and out of an enormous tree. A man cradled a bee in his hands. He seemed to be talking to it. When he faced me and smiled, my heart swelled with an unexplainable affection. "They say to have patience," a younger Master Guardian said. "It will take longer to gather the nectar this year, but will be worth the wait."

The scene faded, and I had to push past sadness that bordered on grief before I could talk.

"I . . . I don't understand," I whispered. "What just happened?"

The Master Guardian gave my hands a gentle squeeze, then released me.

"You experienced physical recall of a time which meant a great deal to you. I am sorry if that upset you, but it was necessary for me to do."

He pointed at my cup. Since I was visibly shaking, I figured I could do with some relaxation and took another drink—a long one.

"While you rested," he said, "the sleeping cloths initiated the changes I spoke of earlier. Unfortunately, we do not know the effect it will have on you and must proceed with great caution lest we damage you in the process."

"Damage me? What do you mean by—?"

"You must eat now. Food will help balance you for the trip back to Earth."

"But what about this damage you—"

"Please." His expression softened. "Eat."

My grandmother had always called food "grounding." I decided to see if her theory held interdimensionally as I surveyed the strange assortment of colors, textures, and shapes, then gingerly sampled something brown and lumpy that looked like solidified oatmeal. "Wow. This is good, too. But please don't tell me it was a favorite of mine, or that I ran a lumpy-brown-food farm. I've had enough surprises for one night. If it's still night."

Apparently, I'd said something humorous. His laughter burrowed into me, evoking the same feeling I'd had as a kid on Christmas morning. I didn't know why he had such a profound effect on me. I found it unsettling, yet nice.

"The lumpy brown food is *monzennez*. And only a few minutes have passed on Earth since you left."

"That's all?" I mumbled around the wad in my mouth. "How does that work?"

"Through a process called time-stretching." He added more fairybee wine to our goblets. "Within the confines of Guardian Lands, we are able to control the speed with which time passes, extending it substantially when necessary."

"So that's how I'll have enough time to make popcorn when I return. That's incredible, not to mention incredibly handy." I was thinking about Kiley and her lateness.

"We find it useful." He shrugged as if treating time like a rubber band was an everyday occurrence. "Earth and Amoran exist in the same physical space, but at different dimensional levels of expression. Because of their disparate vibrational frequencies, they are invisible to each other. The vortex is our only link between the two worlds."

I didn't know what all that meant, but it reminded me of something Danaeus had said. "Is that why energy in the vortex has to stay balanced?"

The Master Guardian nodded. "Two thousand years ago, there occurred a radical shift in dimensional energy. The vortex escaped destruction, but the imbalance compressed the vortex portals, limiting interdimensional travel. The elf who accompanied Danaeus to Earth can pass through the vortex with relative ease. The rest of us must limit our exposure, as it is much harder for our bodies to make the transition from one dimension to the other. There are exceptions, however; individuals who are able to cross at will. But very few Vibrationals are left in either dimension, and those who have the ability are often unaware of it."

Thanks to the pointed stare he directed my way, I didn't need to be the sharpest tool in the shed to know where this was going. We locked eyes for a moment, then I lowered mine. I didn't have a clue what a Vibrational was, but if the way my heart began to thump was any indication, I didn't want any part of it.

"You are who you are," the Master Guardian said, gauging my feelings with remarkable precision. "Nothing can change that."

He spoke as if I had no choice in the matter, and it rankled. What gave him the right to decide for me who I am? And yet, I also experienced relief, as if some part of me had been waiting to be recognized. Torn between the two reactions, I stared at my plate. Silence stretched between us until a dish with large red berries wrapped in fuzzy green leaves slid into my line of sight. "Try this," he said.

I bit into one of the wrapped berries, savoring its unique sweet and sour taste. For the rest of our meal we kept to a safe topic—food. The Master Guardian slowly loosened up, although he never stopped searching my face like he was looking for something he'd lost. When I'd eaten enough to satisfy him, I braved another question.

"Danaeus said you need my help with the vortex. Why me?"

The Master Guardian's gaze drilled into me with a determination that had my head aching. As intrusive as it was, when he broke contact, I felt like I'd been orphaned.

"You must return to Earth now," he said tonelessly.

The abrupt dismissal threw me. "Already? Can't I stay longer?" The pleading in my voice embarrassed me, and the way his expression grew distant in response only made me feel worse.

"Perhaps when you return," he replied, with a vagueness that promised nothing.

"But . . . I thought there was this urgent . . . I mean . . . what about this impending disaster?"

Leaving my questions unanswered, he pointed at the open doorway. The message was clear. Time for me to go.

We made our way to the Main Chamber in silence, the Master Guardian seeming lost in thought. At the edge of the giant mandala, he took my hands and held them to his chest.

"You should not discuss Amoran with anyone on Earth. Amoran must remain . . . ." He paused, brows furrowing as though the appropriate word eluded him.

I couldn't help laughing at the idea of trying to explain to John what I'd just experienced.

"Not to worry. No one would believe it anyway. I'm not sure I believe it."

We walked to the center of the chamber where Danaeus and the blond-haired elf were waiting for me. "Everything has changed now," the Master Guardian said. "For you and for us. We will contact you when we have decided how best to proceed."

"Not another letter, I hope." But he'd already turned to go and didn't reply.

Danaeus moved his hands up and out in a wide arc as the elf said to me, "We have to send you back alone and don't have time to teach you the breathing technique for safe transport through the vortex. For now, you can substitute the breathing patterns you used for childbirth."

"Why?" I asked, wondering what an elf from Amoran knew about my birth experiences. "I didn't do any special breathing on the way here."

He seemed oblivious to Danaeus's constant grumbling. "You had one of us with you then. Birth breathing won't be perfect, but it will do in a pinch." He smiled and winked at me as hazy blue light rotated down from the top of the chamber.

I smiled back. "What's your name?"

His expression froze, then he drew his lips between his teeth and looked away. Clearly, I had touched a nerve, although I couldn't imagine why. Before I could pursue it, the swirling light sped up its revolutions and engulfed me, constricting my body with a sudden, intense pressure that was way more than what I'd encountered in the vortex. Frightened, I reacted the same way I had when the first strong labor pain hit me during Ryan's birth—only I'm pretty sure it wasn't what the elf was aiming for. I yelled, then breathed so fast and hard I hyperventilated and passed out.

# Chapter 4

I came to in a face-plant on the throw rug next to the coffee table. I waited for a dizzy spell to pass, then eased upright and checked the time. Unless the clock on our media player was broken, only ten minutes had elapsed since I'd followed the sound of running water into my family room.

I struggled up and stumbled to the kitchen. The corn kernels were on the counter, right where I'd left them. I don't know why that surprised me. I'd gone somewhere, not them.

*Really?* snapped my Voice of Reason. *Maybe you just fainted and had a bizarre dream.*

I turned the burner on to heat the oil.

Is that all it was? A dream? The idea dismayed and relieved me in equal measure. Unsure which feeling to go with, I ignored both by force-feeding myself a steady diet of mundane thoughts. *Melt the butter, fix some drinks, wine would be nice.*

My brain made the short hop from wine to fairybee wine. The Master Guardian said it was one of my favorite things. When had I been there?

*Never,* countered Reason. *Not before. And not tonight.*

I liquefied a tablespoon of butter in the microwave and set it aside. When the oil was hot enough, I added the kernels, covered the pot, and began the near-constant shaking necessary to keep the popcorn from burning. *That's it, Kerrin. Stay on task.* Shake. Shake. *Now for the wine.* Shake. Shake. *Merlot or Chablis?* Shake. Shake. Above the rising crescendo of popping corn, I heard rain battering the house. *It's a cold, wet night. Make it red.*

I opened the merlot with my fast, fancy corkscrew and filled two glasses with ruby liquid.

And found myself wishing it was fairybee wine instead.

*There's no such thing,* Rationality argued. *It was a dream, or you're nuts. Take your pick.*

When the kernels finished popping, I added salt and the melted butter, and poured it into a plastic bowl. Impulsively, I hugged the bowl to my chest, deriving an odd sense of comfort from the normalcy of popcorn.

"Do I need to be jealous?" John whispered in my ear.

The bowl flew out of my hands and hit the floor. "Don't do that," I scolded.

He tried, unsuccessfully, to stifle a grin. "Are you okay? You look like you've seen a ghost."

"I'm fine," I grumbled, bending to clean up the mess. "You know better than to sneak up on me."

"I'm sorry. I'll take care of that. Go get the first disk ready while I make another batch."

Still rattled, I accepted his offer. Wine glass in hand, I stopped in the doorway to the family room to check the ceiling, but no blue twister shot down from above. Relieved, I let out the breath I was holding and took a healthy sip of merlot. My tolerance for alcohol is no better than for caffeine, but I decided my present state of mind—or lack of it—required medicinal strength consumption. I gulped half the glass, popped the first disk out of its case, and slipped it into the media player. Then I went in search of that rare, elusive beast, the remote control.

John came in a few minutes later with a fresh bowl of popcorn.

"Did you load the disk?"

"Yup. Now I'm trying to solve the Mystery of the Missing Remote."

John stared at the silver device in plain view on the shelf above the TV, then at my now-empty wineglass, and rolled his eyes. Ever the adult, I stuck my tongue out at him.

He laughed. "Totter on over here, you wine wimp." Pressing play, he added, "The popcorn's ready and we have a favorite show to watch. What more do we need on a dark and stormy night?"

He fake-cringed at the cliché. I made pretend gagging noises, then joined him on the couch. As the opening credits rolled, John hummed the theme song, nudging me to join in. I gave it a half-hearted effort while scanning the room. There wasn't a shred of evidence anywhere that a blue tornado had dragged me away to another dimension. I was inclined to agree with the voice in my head that my soirée to another world had been a dream. It was better than the alternative—that Amoran might be one big hallucination, making me a bona fide nutcase.

Dream or delusion? Either way, I felt wiped out. Yawning, I snuggled closer to my wonderfully sane husband, who said, "By the way, where did you go earlier?"

My eyelids were already drooping. "Hmm?"

"I came downstairs to get a clean towel from the laundry room before I showered, and I couldn't find you. It was like you'd disappeared into thin air."

My mouth refused to work for a moment. "I . . . um . . . forgot my purse in the car."

I'm a terrible liar. The storm was still raging. If I had gone outside, I'd be soaking wet. But already caught up in the troubles of Number Six, John didn't respond.

---

John's assertion that I'd disappeared battled every ounce of logic I possessed; logic that argued my trip to Amoran couldn't be real. The next morning, I called a temporary truce between the warring sides of my mind via a swift return to the State of Denial, where my life in all its ordinary trappings trudged ever forward. And that life included copious errand running.

After stops at the discount outlet on the highway, the drycleaners, the hardware store, and the pharmacy, I ducked into the Tea Leaf Café for a late morning break. I settled in with my notebook and a pot of Scottish Breakfast, and optimistically went to work on an outline for my novel. John was right. I'd waited a long time for this. I shouldn't give up before I'd even tried.

I'd completed a few pages when I had the strangest feeling I was being watched. I glanced up to find an old man across the room studying me from under the brim of a gray fedora. Most people who get caught in the act avert their eyes, but this guy stared straight at me before shifting his gaze. I tried to shrug it off, but when I went back to my notes, I felt him watching me again.

This time when I looked up, I glared at him. His response? A smirk.

There was no way I could concentrate now. I packed up my things and swooped by his table on my way out. "Take a picture, it lasts longer," I hissed. I banged through the door, wishing his head was caught in the backswing.

I drove to the library and headed for the mystery section, where I walked the aisles searching for a book that would interest me as well as provide inspiration for my own writing. At the end of the last row was a large white paperback propped up like it was on display. A spiraling rainbow decorated the front cover, but the title, *Light Reading*, didn't sound like a mystery. I picked it up and my heart nearly stopped. Peering through a gap in the bookshelves was the fedora-topped ogler from the café.

"Hey!" I bolted around the corner, but he was already gone.

Bug-eyed, I ran the few yards to the main desk. "Where did that man go?"

The new desk clerk eyed me warily. "What man?"

"The one who came out of the row ahead of me." My pulse raced. Was this guy stalking me? "Didn't any of you see him?" I asked the people waiting in line.

The kinder souls merely shook their heads. The less kind souls snickered, and one man actually pointed at his temple and made little circle movements with his index finger.

"Oh, come on. You must have seen him," I said to the clerk. "You looked right at me after I shouted, and the end of the row is in plain sight."

She stiffened. "I most certainly did look at you. At my old library, visitors didn't yell for no reason, then accuse the staff of lying. Do I need to call security?"

Oh, brother. "I wasn't accusing you of lying. It's just that—"

"Just what?" Rebecca said from behind me.

It's nice to have friends in high places. In addition to being my occasional lunch-in-the-park partner, Rebecca was director of the library.

"Boy, am I glad to see you," I said. "I think I'm losing my mind."

I could tell by the desk clerk's expression that the two of us finally agreed on something.

"Let's talk in private," Rebecca said. She took the rainbow book from me and set it on the counter. "Marjorie, please check this out for Kerrin when you have a chance. You can get her number from the computer. Last name is Scott."

Too frazzled to correct Rebecca's assumption that I wanted the book, I trailed after her to her office. When she asked me what was wrong, I hesitated. I couldn't tell her the truth without sounding like a candidate for a padded cell, so I focused on my increasingly hectic job, my pathetic attempts at writing and how tired I'd become lately. So tired, I was afraid I was seeing things that weren't really there. She listened without comment until I told her about the man from the Tea Leaf who I thought had followed me to the library. "But no one else saw him, so it must have been my imagination."

"Maybe not," she said thoughtfully. "I noticed you in the mystery stacks and was on my way to say hello. When you yelled, I swear I saw a guy in the next row. A second later, the aisle was clear and you came charging around the corner looking madder than hell."

"Did you see what he looked like?"

Rebecca shook her head. "It happened too fast, like the flash of a camera."

"Well, at least you saw him, too. I'm not totally off my rocker."

I gazed out the window at the birch trees swaying back and forth against a graying sky. The beautiful day was giving way to the darkness of another storm front.

"If you see him again, call Dan," Rebecca said.

John and I had been close friends with Rebecca and her husband, Dan, since they moved to Glenwood Falls five years ago when Dan left "big city" law enforcement for a job with the our local department.

"I will. And thanks for listening."

She smiled. "I do believe that's what friends are for."

Rebecca accompanied me to the library exit, stopping as we passed by the counter to pick up the rainbow book. We were so busy talking, I didn't comment when she tucked it inside my tote bag. The snippy desk clerk was nowhere in sight.

At home, I fixed a sandwich and poured a glass of milk. I'd planned on reading a new mystery novel while I ate lunch, but the only book I'd brought home from the library was the one with the rainbow cover. Figuring it was better than nothing, I pulled it out of my bag.

The first odd thing I noticed was the absence of library markings on the spine. I turned the book over. The library barcode was also missing. In its place was a small Post-it that read, *Not one of ours.* The note was initialed MJ—a.k.a. Snippy Desk Clerk.

I opened the book, blinked, then fanned the pages in disbelief. Microscopic print, impossible to decipher, completely filled each page. The title, *Light Reading,* had to be a joke. I turned to the cover page and nearly choked at the inscription.

*Property of the Wizard of Amoran. Please return promptly.*

I slammed the book shut and gave it a good shove. It sailed over the edge of the table and landed on the floor, spine poking up. "I'm not reading you," I called out, sending it the evil eye as I ate my sandwich. "*War and Peace* would be faster."

I finished my lunch and straightened up the kitchen, stubbornly stepping around the book. Defeated in the end by my own love of a mystery, I picked it up for another look. A small scrap of paper fell from between the pages. *Tomorrow, noon. Trust your instincts,* it read.

Oh, my God. Were these people nuts? This was the new plan? A book I couldn't read, left for me to find by chance? Hadn't they learned a lesson with the letter? My teeth ground together as I balled up the note and aimed for the recycling basket. My only other "instinct" was to toss the incomprehensible tome in after it. But my inner bibliophile wouldn't allow me to throw out a book, not even this one. At the very least, it was tangible proof that something unusual was going on in my life. I placed the book on the sideboard, then bundled up and went for a walk to clear my head before I had to pick up the kids from school.

———————

John surprised me by walking in the door at five thirty, which meant we got to have dinner as a family for a change. After we ate, he lit a fire in the family room fireplace and we had a board game marathon. It was past eleven when Kiley and Ryan went up to bed, arguing over who won the most games.

John followed me into the kitchen and picked up *Light Reading* from the sideboard.

"New journal?" he asked, flipping through the pages.

"Hardly. It's some weird book I got from the library."

"Uh . . . define weird."

I took the open book from him. "Well, for one thing, the teeny-tiny print is impossible to—" I stopped, stared in confusion, then flipped through the pages myself. Every one of them was blank. "I don't get it. It was filled with printing before, and the rainbow on the front—" I turned to the cover, which was now completely white.

"Are we talking about the same book?"

"I don't know anymore," I said. "I'm not sure *what* I know anymore."

"Well, that sure looks like a journal to me." John yawned. "I'm going to bed; I'm beat."

"Okay," I mumbled. "I'll be up in a bit."

I carried the book into the family room and flopped onto the couch. The note inside had advised me to trust my instincts. *What instincts,* I thought grumpily. I tossed it onto the coffee table, but instead of landing flat, the book perched upright on its spine, then fell open. In a pretty, scrolling script were the words, *"To call the vortex from your family room portal, proceed as follows:"*

I turned to the next page. Nothing. I flipped through a few more pages. All blank. Mystified, I fanned the entire book again. It was completely barren of print, including the page I'd just read.

"Now what?" I whined. I tossed the book back onto the coffee table. It landed flat. I picked it up and dropped it again, spine down, hoping to duplicate the conditions by which the previous message arrived. Maybe the binding was like an on/off button.

The book hit the table with a thud and opened to reveal more scrolling script.

*"Ouch."*

Ouch? As I stared at the word, willing it to change into something more useful, I remembered a game my college friends and I had played with a volume of inspirational readings. I felt silly doing it now, but I placed the book on its spine, asked it if it had a message for me, then let it fall open.

I was graced with a whopping two words.

*"Much better."*

Cute. I balanced the book on its spine and let go.

*"Step One. Always enter the portal with a clear mind and a clear breath.*

*"To do both at once is expeditious."*

"I guess that means to use breathing to clear my mind." I spoke to the book as if it could hear me. "Is that all?" Hoping the instructions wouldn't all be in riddle form, I tried again.

*"Step Two. When you feel like you cannot breathe, do so twice.*

*"When you feel like you must breathe, do not breathe at all."*

Not trusting myself to remember everything, I grabbed a pen and some paper, and continued to let the pages fall open, copying down the information that scrolled across each one. I knew I'd learned all the book was prepared to tell me about vortex travel when the pretty script was replaced by bold, block letters that asked, *"WHAT MORE DO YOU WANT?"*

I smiled. I was looking forward to meeting the wizard with a sense of humor.

I reread the instructions until I had them memorized. Then, to ensure that no one in my family could accidentally learn how to "call the vortex," I tossed my notes onto the fire's dying embers. When the paper transformed into a flaky, ashen mess, I climbed the stairs and hid the book in my bottom dresser drawer under a pile of old T-shirts. The adrenaline rush of playing information roulette had subsided, replaced by a head-on slam of fatigue. I crawled into bed without even brushing my teeth.

———————

*I was in deep space, surrounded by thousands of stars. Light burst from the center of my chest, transforming my body into a brilliant, buzzing energy. In another explosion of light, the energy thrust out from where my body had been. I tried to control the energy, afraid that if it kept going, I would lose myself forever.*

*"Draw an imaginary line around where you believe your body should be,"* a man's voice said. *"Hold that line firmly in your mind. It eases the transition."*

*"What transition?"* I cried.

I woke up covered in sweat.

---

A biting rain was falling by breakfast, but there was still no snow in the forecast. The kids, always impatient for the first snowfall, acted out their frustration by irritating each other nonstop. John—bless him—offered to take them to a movie. "Hard for them to snipe at each other with a mouth full of popcorn," he said. "Maybe you can work on your book while we're gone."

My reply was a weak smile. I had no intention of spending the next few hours writing, especially since John's generous offer meant I could sashay to Amoran without having to explain my absence. Or the presence of a blue tornado in the family room.

John and the kids left at eleven thirty for the first matinee at the theater in the next town. I estimated I had until three o'clock before they returned. *Plenty of opportunity for interdimensional travel,* I thought blithely as I brought my freshly made tea to the kitchen table.

I tried to read the newspaper, but nervous anticipation made concentration impossible. Unable to sit still, I wandered from room to room doing minor pickup, amazed as always at the amount of stuff that dotted the Scott family landscape. Just shy of twelve o'clock, I parked myself in the family room. My unfinished tea had grown cold, but I decided not to warm it up since I didn't know when I'd be back.

In fact, there was a lot I didn't know about what was coming.

*In fact*—I rubbed sweaty palms on my jeans—*why am I even doing this?* This wizard guy seemed pretty sure I would toddle on over to his side of the vortex at a time of his choosing. What if I had been busy today at noon?

*But you aren't busy today at noon, are you? You are unusually free, almost as though—*

My pulse quickened. How could these people know so much about me? What if I refused to go back?

*But you won't refuse, will you? You didn't want to leave him in the first place.*

Him. The beautiful man in blue.

The wall clock's ticking fell into the deafening quiet like rocks dropped on concrete. I gulped cold tea to combat the dryness in my mouth.

At last, the chimes rang out that zero hour had arrived. I set my mug down and waited.

And waited.

And then, I waited some more.

Serious doubt crept in. One of the book's messages implied that the portal would be opened for me this time. Had I misunderstood that?

At seven past noon, I went upstairs to get the book and ask it what to do. Maybe noon meant something different on their world.

When I left the bedroom, I heard the sound of running water on the first floor. One important fact I'd learned from last night's vanishing verbiage—the portal only remained open for a few seconds. I bounded down the steps and executed a mad dash into the family room, dropping the book as I leapt into the center of the gyrating blue light.

That's when it all went so wrong.

A putrid green wind blasted the blue light away and dragged me into a storming vortex that made a Category 5 tornado look like a summer breeze. Thundering air wrenched me in several directions at once, as if every part of the vortex wanted a part of me. Until that moment, the kind of pain that could make a person blackout had only been a theoretical concept to me. I was living it now, catapulting past the point of endurance when the howling wind stilled and the pain thankfully left me. At least, that's what I thought had happened until I looked down. Hard to feel pain when you have no body, and mine was missing in action.

Freed of its physical constraint, my mind plummeted toward an area of turbulent black clouds far below me. I knew instinctively that great danger lay that way, but the closer I got to the dark clouds, the colder I became, and the colder I became, the less will I had to free myself. Before long, an utter hopelessness permeated me to my core. And the cold. So . . . so . . . *cold.*

My frozen brain teetered on the cusp of consciousness as a dozen white rabbits hopped out of a huge black hat and danced around me, chanting, "Trust your instincts . . . Don't give up . . . Hold the line . . . Trust your instincts . . . Don't give up . . . Hold the line . . . Hold the line . . . Hold the—"

*Hold the line?* That was from my dream!

With what little sense I had left, I mentally drew a line around myself. My body reappeared just in time for me to feel the full impact of it hitting the floor of the Main Chamber.

The blond elf commanded me to keep still. I tried to say something, but he shook his head.

"Don't move. Don't even blink."

A bearded, dark-haired man strode forward. "What happened?" he demanded.

The elf babbled about portal variations and energy inversions, but I fixated on the man's face. Forgetting the elf's caution to be still, I sat up to get a better look.

Wrong move. The chamber spun feverishly, and I pitched forward, pummeled by waves of pain.

The man dropped to my side. "You were told to keep still!"

Our eyes met, and it was like a jolt of electricity spiked through me before he jerked his head away. I gaped in astonishment. I'd never met anyone else with eyes that matched my unique shade of emerald green. Yet it was the sense of recognition, of *history*, that was most perplexing.

I am not a barfly, but all I could think to say before losing consciousness was—

"Don't I know you?"

# Chapter 5

I woke from a strange dream about talking rabbits and treacherous winds. Coaxing my reluctant eyelids open, I stared up at a ceiling made of stone.

*Wait. Stone? Where am I?*

The answer came in a rush of images, sensations, and feelings.

*The vortex. Killer winds. Amoran.*

So it wasn't a dream. I tried to sit up, only to discover that my arms and legs were completely numb.

"Oh, God! I can't move," I shouted over the sound of my heart thumping in my ears. When I turned my head to the side, looking for anyone who could help me, pain knifed through my skull. I cried out and struggled to move back, but now my head was stuck in place like it had been put in a vice.

"I told you before to keep still," the green-eyed man barked from somewhere behind me.

"Please. Do something. This pain is killing me."

"That is not what will end your life," he grumbled, as if he knew what would. "I will reposition you now, then stay put. And this time, listen."

Every muscle in my body tensed in anticipation of more agony. He cradled my head, then gently turned it so I faced the ceiling again. But instead of pain, all discomfort vanished, replaced by a sense of well-being that edged into euphoria. I was still numb from the neck down, but in the span of three seconds, I'd gone from panic to having not a care in the world.

"What *was* that?" I asked as he continued to hold my head.

"You encountered an energy inversion in the vortex which nearly tore you apart."

I giggled. "Not that, silly. I mean what you just did to me."

"Why are you laughing? There is nothing funny about an energy inversion."

"You're right. I'm sure it's bad." I chortled, hiccupped to a stop, and made a valiant attempt to suppress another outburst. But it was like trying to cap an erupting volcano of unadulterated glee. The longer he touched me, the better I felt. And I was in no hurry for it to end.

"It *is* bad," he snapped, sounding a wee bit testy. "If I do not correct the imbalance in your energy field, your next trip through the vortex *will* kill you."

Clearly this was no laughing matter, which made the way I guffawed in response hard to defend. "Kill me? Ha ha. Just keep doing that hand thing, Green Eyes. I want to marry you and have your babies."

He mumbled something about my Earth body and an odd reaction, and took his hands away.

"Hey! Come back here with those magic fingers."

I wound up being glad he didn't. The euphoria had grown so intense it felt like being tickled too much, and I was actually relieved when the well of well-being dried up.

In soft, urgent tones, a woman registered disapproval over a course of action, but my Huffy Healer outranked her. "I will do whatever it takes to make her well." He placed two fingertips on my breastbone and gasped. "I must perform the healing now or we will lose her."

"But your health," the woman protested.

"If she does not survive, my health will not matter, will it?"

It must have been a rhetorical question, because she didn't answer.

Green Eyes held my shoulders from behind. "Follow my commands precisely. Your life depends on it." He touched his forehead to mine, whispered something that sounded like a prayer, then said, "Administer the first draft now, Vianna."

Vianna turned out to be the same Assistant with dark skin and violet eyes who'd led me to the Master Guardian's room on my last visit. She propped me up, helped me to drink a small goblet of something sour, then lowered me back to the stone.

*Crack!* A noise like a gunshot exploded between my ears and my vision went dark. Abject terror would have paralyzed me if I wasn't already incapable of movement . . . or breathing. Even my lips were now numb.

"Dear Light," Vianna cried. "She is suffocating."

"Then I have no choice," the man exclaimed. "I must infuse her."

Vianna didn't like that either, but Green Eyes ignored her. "Kerrin, I am giving you a special kind of energy now." A fluid-like warmth seeped into the center of my chest. "Wherever I touch you, physical sensation will be restored for a short time."

Unlike the euphoria with its uncomfortable intensity, this was like liquefied love. It must have been good for him too, because he exhaled a blissful moan.

"Stay present," Vianna warned. "Do not sink too deeply into her energy field."

Whatever he was doing worked like a charm. I pulled in a lungful of air.

"Excellent. Keep breathing like that." He was all business now, shooting commands. My part was simple enough. I had to breathe at designated times as he moved energy throughout my body—the same body I couldn't feel except where he touched me. Simple as it was, I quickly became exhausted. And based on Green Eyes' ragged breathing and wheezed instructions, his role in this process was physically taxing for him, too. It seemed like we'd been doing this dance for hours when he rasped, "A goblet will be . . . brought to your mouth. You must drink . . . all of it. I cannot . . . use my hands to help you now."

I tried to picture where my mouth was, to imagine drinking and swallowing, but it was no use. Without his touch, I was a brain without a body.

*"I can't do it,"* I cried into the confines of my mind.

I was shocked when his answer sounded inside my head. *"You must. You can."*

*"No! I can't feel anything without you."*

Suddenly, it was like our emotions mingled. I felt his hesitation, then his fear. And I knew when he'd made his decision.

"Integration . . . Link," he choked out.

"I refuse," Vianna shouted. "You could die.

"Hand me that potion now or we will *all* die."

The dire prediction must have convinced her. He inhaled a drink with three loud gulps, coughed like he was going to be sick, then cupped his hands on my cheekbones.

As if we had all the time in the world, an exquisite sensation slithered its way through me, coating me from the inside out. The "special energy" he'd given me before had been beautiful, yet somehow neutral. But this? Somehow, I knew it was his personal energy, filling me up, saturating me like I was a thirsty sponge. The heavenly sweetness of it stung my eyes with tears—tears I could feel as the numbness finally left my body.

I was able to drink now. Vianna tilted my head, placed another cup at my lips, and I forced myself to swallow the bitter liquid. By some strange alchemy, when the potion hit my stomach it ignited into flames of pure emotion. Fire roared up my spine as every feeling I had ever experienced seemed hell-bent on escaping through the top of my head. I tried to call out to Green Eyes, but I couldn't make a sound. So I yelled at him with my thoughts.

*"Stop! Those are my feelings. You can't take them from me."*

No answer this time. I reached out with my mind—the only part of me I seemed to have any real control over—and tried to rescue my emotions, to "think" them back. But whatever was happening was far too strong. The harder I worked to keep my feelings, the faster they left.

And then they were gone. Every last one of them. I drifted for a while . . . peaceful . . . detached . . . empty. The whole experience was quite restful. Truly sublime.

Right up until the moment my lost emotions thundered back in with another deafening *crack!* All those feelings, all at once? Terrifying in their potency. Slamming into me with no mercy. My body buzzed and vibrated like I was a giant smacked funny bone.

*"Don't leave me alone with this,"* I cried mentally.

He didn't. He stayed until the worst of it passed, then his sweet energy withdrew.

Vianna wiped my face with a cool cloth, then held a third drink to my mouth, this one syrupy sweet. I'd barely taken a few sips when a luscious sleepiness inched its way through me.

"Say nothing about the Integration Link," Green Eyes said to his helper. "I must find the right way to tell them. Now get some rest. I will take care of her."

Vianna shook her head. "But who will take care of you?"

He didn't respond and she left without further comment.

My mystery man came around where I could get a good look at him. His dark brown hair dusted the shoulders of a white, floor-length caftan. A close-cropped beard and mustache set off the emerald eyes, which were trained on a goblet that he emptied in two fierce gulps.

"I had to realign your entire energy spectrum," he said. "It is a dangerous procedure, one that is inadvisable on someone from Earth. But you have done remarkably well."

That last potion freed my tongue, but slowed my thoughts. Getting the words out took effort.

"All . . . I did . . . was lie here."

We must have consumed the same nightcap. His gaze never left his empty cup, but his speech began to slur. "You . . . have done . . . more than . . . you realize."

I stared at those eyes, so like my own, wishing he'd look directly at me so I could see them better. "Who . . . who are you?"

He grimaced. "You may . . . call me . . . the wizard."

He said it like he hated the idea, like he was a civil servant unhappy with a new job title. I smiled at the thought of it, although my mouth went lopsided from the drink. He took in my goofy grin and his frown transformed into a small smile of his own. Holding my hands with something akin to reverence, he stroked my palms with his thumbs. The gentle, intimate gesture moved me. I wanted to thank him for all he'd done, but I was going down too fast. And so was he. He slumped into the chair beside me as I slipped into dreamland.

————————

I opened my eyes to find Vianna scrutinizing my face. She grunted with apparent satisfaction, helped me sit up and handed me a goblet filled with blue liquid.

I wasn't sure I wanted any more of their drinks. "What is it?"

"Morning beverage."

That didn't sound too bad. Maybe it was their kind of coffee, or more to my liking, tea. I took a sip. The minty taste was delicious and refreshing, but the drink had no noticeable effect.

The room appeared to be the same one I'd taken a nap in during my previous visit. When I questioned Vianna about it, she gave a brief nod and relieved me of the goblet.

"You were brought to your private quarters from the Healing Room last night so you could awaken here."

"This is *my* room?"

Her eyebrows lifted. "Of course. Where else would you be?" She pushed clothing into my arms. "You must wear this while you are on Amoran. Your Earth clothes are on the counter."

I looked down at the flimsy white caftan draping my body.

Vianna followed my gaze. "That is worn only for healing."

I should hope so.

"The wizard took many risks for you," she continued, narrowing her eyes at me, her unspoken reproach clear: *too many risks.* "He is still recovering in the Healing Room."

"I'm sorry he's not well. Will he be all right?"

"Yes." Her flat, no-nonsense tone indicated further inquiries about the wizard's health were not an option. That was okay. I had other questions.

"Does this . . . wizard . . . have a name?"

The simple query earned me a blank stare.

I tried again. "A name. Like you and I have?"

She blinked. Figuring I might be dealing with a language barrier, I elaborated.

"Your name is Vianna, mine is Kerrin, and his would be—"

"You must change," she said abruptly. "I will show you the ancillary."

I didn't know what an ancillary was, or why I'd want to see one, but I decided to drop the matter of the wizard's name for now. In a normal universe, requesting that information shouldn't be an issue. But this wasn't a normal universe, I reminded myself, at least not my kind of normal. Here, time stretched, and people not only got under your skin, but completely inside of you.

I flushed, recalling the exquisite sweetness of having Green Eyes' energy co-mingling with mine. "Do the wizard's hands always work like that?" I blurted out.

She frowned. "That type of energy was only available to him during your healing."

*There's a good reason for getting sick,* I thought, on the heels of which came guilt, as if by wanting more of that sweet energy I was somehow cheating on John.

Vianna stood to the left of where the invisible doorway to my room was located. With a wave of her hand, a different opening appeared. I hopped off the stone bed and followed her into a small room containing a stone counter and a stone bench. Lots of stone in this place.

She walked to the back of the small room and waved her hand again. A black cylinder, two feet high and roughly shaped like an hourglass, rose up out of the floor. Contrasting bands of dark gray spiraled up from the base, then flattened over the top, forming a solid disc. It reminded me of an art deco sculpture I'd seen in a museum.

Vianna turned her palm up and the top vanished, revealing a hollowed-out receptacle. I wondered if this was Amoran's version of a toilet.

"Take care of your needs, then put the tunic on," she said, and returned to the other room.

Yep. Toilet. I dropped the tunic onto the stone bench and "took care of my needs." In the absence of tissue paper, the apparatus functioned like a bidet that used warm air and light instead of water. When I stood up, the potty disappeared into the floor and an oval basin pushed out from the wall above the counter. I placed my hands inside and waited for the water to turn on.

More light sprayed from the sides.

I yanked my hands back and looked around. I didn't see anything else that would qualify as a sink, so I eased my hands into the basin again and let the warm, white light wash over them. A few seconds passed, the rays shut off and the basin retreated into the wall. Hoping the light rays had done their job, I turned my attention to getting dressed.

What Vianna referred to as a tunic was actually a two-piece affair comprised of a long-sleeved top that fell to mid-thigh, paired with matching leggings. Danaeus had worn a similar outfit when he brought me through the vortex. As I slipped on the heathery pastel blend of blue, yellow, and white, I considered Vianna's reluctance to tell me Green Eyes' name. Maybe if I tried a different tack.

"That man who healed me," I called into the main room. "Is he really a wizard?"

It wasn't Vianna who answered.

"The designation is not accurate, however, he might be deemed so on Earth."

I hurried from the ancillary. The Master Guardian stood in the open doorway to my room, his long white hair sharply contrasted against his aqua cloak. Vianna was nowhere in sight.

"I'm so glad to see you," I enthused, a little self-conscious about how thoroughly I meant it.

"And I, you. Your return to health is indeed miraculous."

"All due to the wizard. Can I visit him in the Healing Room? I'd like to thank him."

"You have thanked him by surviving." The Master Guardian studied me in that penetrating way of his. "I would like to spend the day together, just the two of us, while you become more acclimated to this environment. I am eager to show you the rest of our Sanctuary."

An entire day alone with the Master Guardian? My arm didn't need twisting. "Fine by me. Can we have breakfast first? I feel like I haven't eaten in a week."

He smiled. "Yet it has only been three days since your accident in the vortex."

"Three days?" A knot formed in my stomach thinking about home, John, and the kids. "How long can you stretch time?"

"Have no concern about that. Not even an hour has passed on Earth. Which means," his smile went solar, "you have many more days to visit with us. Now, you are hungry, yes?"

Interesting. That was the second direct question he'd dodged in less than a minute. I didn't know how long they could stretch time for or whether I could visit the wizard.

The Master Guardian pointed behind me. The table, which had been bare moments ago, was loaded with food. I didn't even ask how it got there, that's how hungry I was.

While we ate, the Master Guardian plied me with questions about my life on Earth. When I asked why he laughed at my description of Kiley's troubles at school, he said, "Your daughter reminds me of another girl I know. Please continue."

I did, to excess. Before I finished, he'd heard about my job, my house, my kids, my parents, even my Wretched Cousin Camryn. When I fell into complaining about John's job, the increased workload at Pierson & Todd, and the novel I wasn't writing, I finally put the brakes on. "Enough about me. This has got to be boring."

His expression gave nothing away, but his words were charged with a feeling I couldn't decipher. "I have long waited to have you beside me again, to hear about your life."

My eyes dropped to my empty plate as I struggled with how to respond. If I had "long waited" to be back with him, I wasn't aware of it. But I was with him now, and I didn't want to be anywhere *but* with him. And frankly, that scared me a little.

I looked up. He was smiling again. That smile of his could light up a stadium.

"Shall we walk?" he asked. I nodded. "Good. I know just the place to take you."

---

By the time we'd navigated the first few corridors, I lost all sense of direction—that is, whatever sense of direction you can have traveling passageways that all look the same. The Master Guardian said he wanted to surprise me, so he wouldn't divulge our destination. Along the way, he showed me various aspects of the Guardian Sanctuary, which was quite large and located entirely under the mountain. There were healing rooms, meeting rooms, recreation areas, rooms for eating in and special rooms for celebrations, galleries for art, a conservatory for music, even a school. Yet, with all those rooms, I hadn't seen a single person.

"Where is everyone?" I asked.

"Until I am certain you are up to it, I am limiting your contact with others. We need to protect your energy field from . . . interference."

We turned a corner. A doorway appeared on my right and a girl maybe a couple years older than Kiley stuck her head out of the opening. When she caught sight of me, she froze.

"Are you her?" she whispered, tossing a pile of her red hair behind her. Large hazel eyes grew even larger in her light brown face when she saw the Master Guardian standing behind me.

"What is your task now, Meilee?" he intoned, dropping his already deep voice even lower.

Meilee squared her shoulders and stared him down. "Do you mean the tedious exercise assigned by the teacher? Or the far more interesting one requested of me by my fellow students?"

He sighed. "I will not dignify that with an answer."

I gnawed on my fist to keep from laughing at Kiley's interdimensional twin sister as the Master Guardian escorted Meilee back into her classroom. She glanced over her shoulder at me and smiled. Devil that I am, I winked and grinned back at her.

His wayward student tucked safely inside, we continued on. "The school is my favorite part of our work here," he commented. "The faces of the children when they have learned some new idea, mastered another skill, brings me such joy."

I couldn't resist. "Even Meilee?"

He shook his head, but his eyes were alight. "Meilee must learn to channel her considerable talents and energy efficiently and with wisdom. She will be a Guardian someday—Master Guardian if my intuition is correct." His aqua eyes regarded me with a bold intensity. It wasn't the first time he'd done so after showing or telling me something, as if to gauge my reaction.

"Then, this is a training school for Guardians?"

I caught a flash of disappointment before he recovered his serene demeanor. I was certain he'd wanted me to remember something. I didn't like the hollow feeling that I'd let him down.

"Some of our Guardians have come from the school, but that is not its main purpose."

He steered me down a narrow passageway, while explaining that the students, who were self-selected, arrived from all over Amoran. I couldn't grasp the self-selection part, even after he explained it to me three different ways. Somehow, these kids just *knew* that they were meant to be students at the Guardian school. That they were willing to leave their parents, and their parents were okay with sending them away? I didn't think I'd ever be able to wrap my brain around that one. Especially when he told me how young they were when this great awakening occurred.

"Five?" I squeaked. I couldn't imagine letting go of Ryan or Kiley at that age.

"Yes. They know by the Earth-equivalent age of five that they are to serve in this way."

"Serve? You mean it's imposed on them?"

His eyes widened. "Dear Light, no. That would not be possible or right. They know because it is their choice. Indeed, it was their choice before they were born."

While I processed that tidbit, the Master Guardian further explained that these self-selected students were learning the ways of Guardian life so they could take their place among the larger Mountain community. Another awakening occurred in their teen years, when they would mysteriously—that's my word for it—learn what role they were to play. Some would become teachers, occasionally one would become a Guardian. But most would join the group of Assistants required to keep life under the Mountain running smoothly. Vianna was a healing Assistant who studied under the wizard. The man who led me to my room during my first visit was an Assistant who normally worked with food preparation.

"That doesn't seem fair," I said. "Some get to be teachers or Guardians while the rest have to be servants?"

"Have to be?" The Master Guardian shook his head emphatically. "If I understand what you mean by servant, they are no more or less a servant than I am. We must all serve in some way. The question is merely, which way?"

We'd stopped in front of—shock of shocks—another blank stone wall.

"So, Vianna's great awakening was that she wanted to be a healing Assistant?"

"That is her way to serve." His look pierced me, as if he could examine my consciousness with his eyes. "We all know, deep down, the way in which we are to serve. The way we have both chosen and been chosen to serve."

The more he talked, the more confusing it got. "How can you choose, yet be chosen?"

He shrugged. "It is one and the same to us."

Once again, he hadn't answered my question, but tired of trying to follow the threads of his logic, I pointed at the wall. "How do you know where the doorways are? In fact, how do you tell where you are to begin with?"

"Those of us who have been here for many years do not need help in that area. For newcomers, the patterns in the floor can be read much like a road map in your world. Have you noticed how the designs change from passageway to passageway?"

I hadn't noticed any color or shape at all, let alone ones that changed. I squinted at the gray-brown stone. I didn't see it at first, but on closer inspection, I caught faint lines impressed into the surface.

"Each unique pattern marks the corridor's resonating frequency," he added.

Whatever that meant. "And the doorways? I don't see any outlines for them. How do you tell where they are?"

He shrugged again. "We just know."

That wasn't going to help me if I ever expected to find my own way around.

With a flick of his wrist, a doorway appeared, and we entered a small, vacant room composed of the same stone as the passageways.

I hoped I wasn't going to disappoint him again.

"This is what you brought me to see?"

"No." The blue eyes shone. "This is."

With a flourish of his hands, all four walls vanished to reveal a lush forest.

# CHAPTER 6

Late morning sunshine filtered through the trees, dappling the ground with patches of light. A profusion of flowers scented the air with something like honeysuckle. I turned a full circle, only able to take in so much at one passing. Red bell-shaped blossoms sprouted from the sides of tree trunks. Bright orange cups bloomed atop slender stalks. Tiny lavender buttons carpeted mounds of low bushes. Golden vines with yellow and blue florets draped like feather boas over everything. I stepped beyond where the walls of the small room had been into a large patch of sunshine and tilted my face to catch the fullness of the balmy rays.

"Where are we? More to the point, how did we get here?"

"The Forest Portal transported us to the Guardian Forest. Would you like to go to the waterfall?"

Words pushed out of my mouth before I had time to think.

"I'd love to! I haven't seen it since—*oh!*" Hundreds of images crammed into my mind at the same time, squeezing my brain into a tiny, painful ball. Crying out again, I crumpled to the ground. The Master Guardian dropped down and yanked me to him so we were heart-to-heart. Waves of energy poured from his chest into mine, then found their way to my head where the chaotic collage faded as swiftly as it had come.

My new personal hero pulled in a deep breath, let it out in a long sigh, and released me. We regarded each other in silence for several seconds, his expression still laced with concern. I knew mine reflected sheer amazement. He searched my face again like he had on my previous visit. His lips parted, he sucked in another quick breath, and I wondered if we were feeling the same thing. Connection. History. *Affection.*

"Can you tell me what happened?" he asked.

"I'll try," I whispered, not wanting to break the spell we both seemed to be under. "It was so strange. And painful! My mind filled with pictures, way too many for me to grasp any one image separate from another. Even so, my brain tried to process each one individually, yet all at the same time." I shook my head. "That doesn't make sense, but it's the best I can do. I couldn't tell what they represented, but they felt like memories."

Was it even possible to know a memory purely by sensation?

The Master Guardian nodded thoughtfully, as if he understood. "And you are all right now?"

"I am," I replied, amazed at how good I felt.

"Shall we continue our walk?"

"I'd like that." Brain-busting slide show aside, it was great to be outdoors instead of the endless plain walls of the Guardian Sanctuary. He helped me to my feet and we set out at a leisurely pace. Along the way, I asked about the various plants we passed. My favorite was the *vallius* shrub, with its tiny red flower clusters and green, heart-shaped leaves. The Master Guardian explained that the refined juice of vallius leaves formed the base for most of the potions, drafts and elixirs used in the Healing Room, and aside from something called *nemestes*, it was the most important plant growing in Guardian Lands.

When we reached our destination, I smiled. "Waterfall" seemed a generous term for the stream that spurted over a small outcropping of rock. To be fair, it *was* water, and it *was* falling, if only from a height of five feet. Even though mention of it had triggered my brain-drain episode, I had no reaction to it now other than to think it kind of cute.

We sat on the mossy stream bank and were well into a discussion about fairybees and apple trees when footsteps announced someone's approach. I glanced behind me.

"Hey, there," I called to the wizard.

He fixed his eyes on the Master Guardian. "I need a moment with you. Now."

Huh. Let's try this again. "Hi. I really appreciate the healing you—"

"I require the Master Guardian," the wizard hissed, "not you." He shook his head. "How can we expect anything good from you when you cannot follow a simple direction?"

Having delivered that verbal slap-in-the-face, he stalked over to a rock wall that ran perpendicular to the stream. The rebuff stung, doubly so considering the intimacy we'd shared during my healing. But I wasn't the only person he'd caught off guard. The Master Guardian blinked several times, then joined the wizard at the wall where, through some trick of reflected sound, their hushed conversation reached me with crystal clarity. An old cell phone commercial came to mind and I snickered to myself. *Yep. I can definitely hear you now.*

"You are needed in the Healing Room," the wizard said. "At once."

"Dear Light! It would pose too great a risk to take Kerrin through the Forest Portal at present, and she cannot be left alone. There have been . . . complications. If I go, you must remain."

"Not possible," the wizard snapped. I could almost feel him clenching his teeth. "Call for someone else." He stalked further down the wall, followed by the Master Guardian. Whatever had provided my eavesdropping reception vanished. The bits and pieces I made out didn't add up to much until the wizard raised his voice. "I am not a child-watcher!"

I didn't need to be an interdimensional linguist to figure out what that meant. His earlier snub had hurt, but this just made me mad. Stupidly mad. I may have trouble thinking on my feet, but I have no problem leaping to them. Refusing to get stuck with an angry babysitter, I took off down the path. The two men were so busy arguing, they didn't notice my departure.

In light of the mental meltdown I'd suffered earlier, I probably should have been worried to be on my own. Instead, I was relieved to have a break from ever-watchful eyes and petulant healers. I have always been at home in woods. This forest, with its exotic beauty, was no exception. I itched to explore the side trails, but employing a modicum of common sense, I kept to the main path to ensure I didn't get lost.

About fifteen minutes into my solo journey, a diffuse edginess crept in. Something about this lovely forest seemed . . . off. I also wondered why the Master Guardian hadn't come looking for me when he seemed adamant that I shouldn't be left alone. I decided to abandon my impromptu hike and return to the waterfall, salvaging my wilderness pride by telling myself I'd been gone long enough to teach the whining wizard a lesson about who needed a babysitter.

I turned around and nearly slammed into two huge trees blocking the path; the same path I'd just traveled down. The trees were as wide as I am tall, yet barely a foot separated their massive trunks. I may be thin, but I am not that thin. I toyed with the idea of going around them, but mounds of thorny bushes stretched in a long line on either side, making quick passage around the leafy giants out of the question.

Curiouser and curiouser. *What Would Alice Do?*

I leaned forward to peek between the mammoth trunks, and *whoosh!* I was sucked through the narrow gap like I was no bigger than a teddy bear. I tumbled over, yelling at the top of my lungs until I came to rest on springy grass that smelled like roses and felt like velvet. With that bit of sensory encouragement, I sat up to discover what rabbit hole I'd fallen down this time.

Short, bushy trees, uniform in shape, formed a wall around a clearing about half the size of a Little League field. The trees were jammed so close together, it was difficult to tell where one ended and another began. Nestled below them, forming a second ring around the perimeter, were three precise rows of blue, yellow, and pink carnation-like flowers.

At the other end of the clearing stood a second pair of large trees, not as tall as the ones at the entrance, but spaced approximately twenty feet apart. Their lush, leafy branches grew espalier-like into the area between them, intertwining top and bottom to form a kind of aperture in the center. The opening was rimmed with a perfect circle of golden leaves.

*That can't be a random occurrence,* I thought, crossing the fragrant grass to get a better look. I was almost to the opening, when it suddenly filled with a swirling pink vapor that coalesced into the shape of a woman. She wafted through the air and floated in front of me, her misty form glowing with a soft radiance.

"We welcome you home for the fulfillment of your Promise and your service to the Light."

Her voice was gentle and sweet, yet full of authority. I instinctively liked her.

"I'm sorry. Truth be told, I don't remember you or a promise I made."

She smiled. "You are correct. Truth must be told. And you bring Truth with you, we see it in your heart. This is good. For your service to be complete, honesty must reign."

Gliding closer, she peered into my eyes.

"There is one who holds a key for you, as you hold a key for the others. Find the keys. Unlock the treasure."

Before I could ask what she meant, she kissed me in the center of my forehead and drifted back through the opening. My skin tingled where her ethereal lips had touched me. I rubbed my forehead, wondering who she was and what promise I had made. And someone had a key for me? If she was referring to the letter and its energy key, she was going to be disappointed.

Marveling at my close encounter of the mystical kind, I headed back across the clearing. The gap separating the two trees at the entrance had now magically become wide enough for me to pass through without the aid of a miracle. I slipped between the trunks and stopped dead. Once again, the landscape had completely changed. Rough terrain stretched before me, endless and unappealing. I turned around to reenter the clearing and ask the vaporous woman for assistance, but the two massive trees had also disappeared.

A sliver of fear shot through me. *Brilliant, Kerrin. Maybe you really did need a babysitter.*

I yelled for help, but the wind was my only answer as it rustled the leaves of nearby trees. That was a sound I normally loved. Now, it just made me feel lonely.

I hugged my arms to my chest as I mulled over my options. I could stay put and hope someone rescued me, or I could try and find my way to . . . God only knew where, at this point. Still, Door Number Two seemed the better choice, so I picked a direction and battled my way through the dense, prickly undergrowth. It felt like an eternity before I finally reached a path. It was overgrown and barely visible—hardly signs of recent use—but it was better than nothing.

I hadn't gone a hundred yards when I rounded a bend and let out a whoop of joy. As before, my way was blocked by two trees, their branches waving in a sudden breeze as if inviting me forward. Hopefully, the lady in pink would be able to help me.

There was barely enough room for me to squeeze between the trunks. I sucked in my stomach, pushed my way in, and groaned in disbelief. I was in a clearing, all right, but it wasn't anything like the one where I'd met the ethereal woman. Much smaller, it also lacked the well-groomed attention of its predecessor. Instead of neat, tidy rows of blooms, an explosion of wildflowers spread amoeba-like over grass that was badly in need of mowing. And the trees lining the circumference were each unique, as if someone had intentionally planted only one of every kind available. No vapor-filled opening here; just a tall table upon which rested a silver goblet. On the ground, several yards in front of the table, lay a wide stone slab. Two feet high, and about as big as a king-size bed, it was barely visible above the tall grass. Three large red flowers, like tulips, grew at its base.

Out of an abundance of caution, I kept to the edge of the clearing and made my way to the table. Close up, its long, narrow shape was more suggestive of an altar. I picked up the silver goblet and peered inside. It seemed dry, yet a potent aroma reached my nose, the smell spicy and enticing. I inhaled deeply.

Out of nowhere, an intense longing gripped me with such force, I almost burst into tears.

"How did you get here?" an angry voice demanded.

Startled, I whipped around and glared at the wizard. "Don't sneak up on me like that."

He quickly shifted his gaze. "I am seeking, not sneaking. You have been lost a long time."

I slammed the goblet down onto the altar-like table. "Just because you didn't know where I was, doesn't mean I was lost."

He curled his lip. "How can you not be lost when I have never seen this place?"

Leaving me to digest that comment, he turned in a circle, visually surveying the clearing until his eyes landed back on the silver goblet. He picked it up and gave it a healthy sniff, but the scent didn't seem to affect him the way it had me. As he inspected the goblet, I did the same to him. I figured him for a little older than my thirty-six years, and while he wasn't beautiful like the Master Guardian, he was handsome in his own right. His tan face was darker than my pale complexion, but our dark brown hair was nearly identical in hue, although his was straighter and not as thick. I'm not fond of beards, but his close-trimmed one seemed to suit him. And those green eyes. So like my own. I wanted another look at them, but except for that one time in the Main Chamber, he directed his gaze anywhere but straight at me. Was he avoiding eye contact for some reason?

He sniffed the cup again, then pressed his hand over his heart.

Maybe the scent got to him after all.

"I asked how you got here," he growled.

Then again, maybe not.

"I don't know. How did *you* get here?"

The anger drained from his voice, replaced by bewilderment. "I followed the path from the waterfall. Suddenly, there were large trees . . ." He trailed off, shook his head, then put the goblet back on the table. "This place has an unusual feel to it."

"Not a bad feel, though. It's kind of nice in a weird way."

"I insist that you tell me how you arrived here!"

Talk about mood swings. "I told you; I don't know. Like you, I followed a path in the woods and wound up here. The real question is, how do we get back?"

He frowned, then closed his eyes, pushed his hands out to the side, palms facing the sky, and chanted something under his breath.

*Oh, good grief.* I left him praying to the God of Map Apps and marched across the clearing.

"Are you coming, Zen master?" I yelled back at him. "It's this way." Honestly? I had no clue where I was going, but I figured I had as much chance of being right as Mr. Palms-Up did.

He must have agreed, because he stopped his silliness and trailed after me. He'd nearly caught up when he suddenly cried out, "Look!"

I turned around to see what all the fuss was about and did a double-take.

The clearing was gone, replaced by a dense grove of trees. We stood together, staring at the crowded gray-green trunks in silence. Then, as if following some unwritten choreography, we about-faced and stepped onto a well-traveled path that hadn't been there a moment ago.

No entry trees. No narrow gap to squeeze through.

"Does this happen a lot here?" I asked. "You know, things appearing and disappearing?"

He didn't answer. Irritated with his rudeness, I didn't press the issue.

In a matter of minutes, the Magic Path brought us to the waterfall where a disgruntled Master Guardian paced back and forth, stroking his beardless chin with small, anxious movements. My tight-lipped companion became quite chatty as he related the story of finding me in a "glen" no one knew about. I let the wizard do the talking as we made our way to the Forest Portal. I was going to mention the first clearing, but a gut feeling suggested otherwise, so I decided to keep my visit with the pink lady to myself. At least for now.

When we reached the general location of the Forest Portal, the Master Guardian made a small movement with his hand, and the walls of the portal room appeared around us.

He turned to me with an expression even sterner than the one he'd used on Meilee.

"Going off on your own was ill-advised. It worries me that I was not able to feel your presence once you went deeper into the forest. Of even greater concern, I could not sense either one of you for a time. Had you experienced another problem, I would have been unable to locate you. I do not like to imagine what might have happened to you then."

I gulped. Being scolded by the Master Guardian was no fun, especially when I knew how right he was. Before I could tell him I was sorry, he grasped my hands and fed me a nice, big dose of his lovely energy. Whatever he read in my expression made him smile. We stood like that for several moments, then he asked the wizard to take me to my quarters. When no response was forthcoming, he turned around to find out why.

Pretty hard to answer when you're not there. How had the wizard slipped away when I was pretty sure the Master Guardian and I blocked the only exit?

With no indication that anything was amiss, the Master Guardian walked me to my room.

"I will adjust the sleeping cloths for you," he said, once we were inside. He approached the raised stone slab, and the glowing curtains descended from the ceiling, stopping a few feet above the "bed."

"Sleeping cloths? Have we been gone that long?"

"You need to rest," was all he would say.

My body seemed to hear and obey his suggestion. I stifled a yawn and sat on the edge of the stone bed, barely registering that a thin pad and a blanket had been placed on the spongy surface.

"Did you ever make it to the Healing Room?" I asked, barely able to keep my eyes open.

"That need not concern you." He stroked the shimmering fabric above me with slow, precise movements. I had just enough time to lay down before my eyes closed.

# CHAPTER 7

**"I**t is time to arise," Vianna said, giving me a gentle shake. "The Master Guardian is on his way to have Morning Meal with you."

I rubbed my eyes. "It's morning already?"

"Yes. A fresh tunic is in the ancillary. You must change now." She hurried out the doorway.

*You must change now.* Wondering if her words were prophetic as well as practical, I considered my current predicament as I donned the heathery top and leggings. What was I doing here, anyway? When Danaeus dropped the bomb in my kitchen, he'd said that in a *few months* the vortex would implode, sucking Earth and Amoran inside. So, what was the rush? And how was I supposed to help? My affection for the Master Guardian seemed to be clouding my judgment. I'd rambled on to him yesterday about my life on Earth, yet I hadn't learned a thing about my role in all of this. Time to change it up. Today, I'd be the one plying him with questions.

The Master Guardian's timing was impeccable. I finished dressing and left the ancillary at the same moment he entered my room with a glowing smile and arms outstretched. Guessing what came next, I slipped my hands into his. I wasn't disappointed. That soothing sense of well-being permeated my entire body. It felt so good, I was afraid I'd stop caring about getting the answers I wanted. I frowned in spite of how wonderful I felt.

"Is this not restful for you?" the Master Guardian asked.

The wording of the question threw me. "No. Uh, yes, it's not . . . I mean it's not *not* restful. Oh heck. It's all good. You can hold my hands whenever you want."

"I am glad. But now, we must eat." He motioned behind me. Once again, the table, barren moments ago, held platters of food. I guess if an entire forest can rearrange itself on a whim, having breakfast appear out of nowhere isn't any more surprising.

When we were seated, the Master Guardian spooned something that looked like scrambled eggs onto my plate. The taste, far from eggs, was so indescribably fine, I let out a soft moan. I do love my food.

"On Earth," I said, getting back to my current mission, "breakfast is the first meal of the day, our bathroom is your ancillary, and the thing we sleep on is a bed. What do you call it?"

My plan was to begin small and work up to the big questions. He offered the Amoran names for objects without hesitation. The bed was a sleeping stone, or just "stone" for short. The light-weight blanket was a sleep cover, and the thin spongy pad on the stone was a resting mat. Resting mats were portable and could be used wherever a little extra cushioning was needed. Meals were referred to by time of day, i.e., Morning Meal, Evening Meal, etc., and were eaten in—where else?—the Meal Room. Simplicity was the watchword under the Mountain, the nickname for the Guardian Sanctuary. You ate in the Meal Room, you met in the Meeting Room, got healed in the Healing Room. In a place this unusual, I expected more exciting labels for things. On the other hand, his shimmering cloak was called a *pilea*, so it wasn't all boring.

Halfway through our meal, I skated into the danger zone.

"I'll have more of that yellow stuff, thank you, and by the way, what's your name?"

The three-tined fork he was holding stopped halfway to his mouth. I felt oddly satisfied that I had caught him by surprise—until he set the fork down and zeroed in on my eyes. I tried to match his penetrating gaze with one of my own, but he was a master and I wasn't even an apprentice. I winced as the space between my ears began to throb.

"Stop. That really hurts, El—" I choked off and gasped. Was that his name? *El?*

No. There was more to it, I was certain. My brain worked overtime to retrieve the rest. The stress set the room spinning in slow, jerking revolutions. *El . . . Ellie?*

Still more. *Ellie . . . what? Ellie . . . es . . . Ellie . . . es . . .*

In a blinding flash of insight, I knew who that magnificent face and those impossible eyes belonged to. It sounded like *Ellie-esser,* but my inner vision showed me the spelling of his name like the letters were lit from within.

I reached for the Master Guardian's hands. He didn't seem to be breathing; his expression fixed in neutral. An impulse encouraged me to savor this moment as his name bubbled up through my throat and past my lips. I had never realized how precious a gift it is to say a word. To make a sound. To experience the vibration in my body as I spoke the name of someone I cared for so profoundly, even if I didn't know why my feelings for him ran so deep.

Finally, I allowed myself the thrill of speaking. "Your name is . . . Eliasser."

The thrill was short-lived. I cried out as a fierce pain stabbed the base of my skull.

Eliasser bolted from his chair and knelt in front of me. "More images?"

"No," I squeezed out, and pointed at the back of my neck. Eliasser wrapped his hands around my throat. His fingers, warm as a microwave heat pack, pressed the spot where my hairline ended. Within seconds, I was fine. The guy was truly amazing.

I pulled away. "Wow. Can I take you home with me?"

"That is not possible." I smiled at his literal take on my question. "Are you all right?"

"Yes. Thank you!" I hugged him in gratitude.

People usually like my hugs. Not Eliasser. His body went rigid for several seconds, then he patted my shoulders twice with just the tips of his fingers.

"I'm sorry." I released him. "I didn't mean to make you uncomfortable. I'm guessing you don't hug much on Amoran."

Eliasser frowned. "Desire for that type of physical contact is not part of our design."

Design? Sheesh!

"I'll make sure to control myself." I laughed at his relieved expression. "Was it that bad?"

He gave the question ample consideration before replying. "I will admit, it was somewhat pleasant. Do you do this often on your world?"

"As often as I can. On Earth we are 'designed' that way."

"Does everyone hug?" He seemed interested now.

"More or less. With little kids, you give and get hugs a lot. Then there's hugging friends and family. That happens less, but it's still nice. Then there's . . ." I thought of John, and felt the heat rise to my mood ring face. "Let's just say there are different ways to hug."

Seeming satisfied with my answer, Eliasser returned to his seat.

"Now that I know your name, how about telling me the wizard's?"

"I cannot reveal that."

"You can't? Or you won't?" I felt my frustration growing.

"You must understand; it is for your safety that I—

"My safety? You can't tell me his name *for my safety?* That's crazy." Eliasser sucked in a breath as if he hadn't expected me to say that.

"It is not crazy. But it could make you so."

I was certain I'd heard wrong. "Telling me the wizard's real name could make me crazy?" Eliasser nodded. "No way. I've learned other people's names, and I'm still sane." *I think.*

"But they are not Guardians."

Now I had him. "Danaeus is a Guardian, yet he told me his name when he came to Earth, and look at me"—I waved my arms for emphasis—"I'm fine."

Patience is not one of my virtues. Eliasser seemed to have lots of it. His long, slender fingers traced the base of his goblet several times before he responded.

"Danaeus is indeed a Guardian. And yes, he did tell you his name." Eliasser's expression softened in a sad kind of way. "However, you are far from fine."

"What makes you think I'm not okay?" I asked wearily.

"You did not read the letter."

"I wasn't able to, remember?" Why was I being defensive about that?

"Without the transforming aspects of the letter, the vibrational in-congruence of Danaeus speaking his Amoran name on Earth should have produced discomfort in you."

"But it didn't."

Eliasser sighed. "No. We could only infer from that experience that the telling of our names here on Amoran, while you are in an Earth body, could be quite disastrous."

"Just telling me your names?" No longer hungry, I pushed my plate to the side.

"On Amoran, names are carefully selected to match the vibrational frequency at which a person's energy field resonates. As such, they are highly personal. Like memories, they will have the least potential to be damaging if they arise naturally within you. The pain you experienced just now when you recalled my name? You would have fared far worse if you had heard my name spoken aloud by someone else, particularly so if I had offered it to you myself."

"That makes no sense at all."

"Nevertheless, it is true. Each of our names is capable of triggering a perilous cascade of physical, emotional, and mental occurrences within you. The mental effects are most frightening, as they could render your mind—" He cut himself off.

"Render my mind what?" Unfinished sentences were rendering me exasperated.

He sighed again. "Let us save that for another day. For now, you must accept that all memories, not just names, need to surface as gently as possible. Paradoxically, we are speeding the process up as much as we can without damaging you. I may have mentioned this before."

"Something to that effect." I rubbed my temples, not just to ease out the increasing tension, but to make sure my head was still screwed on straight.

"Come," he said. "Today we will tour the Outer Grounds."

---

Eliasser and I stopped in the Main Chamber on our way to the Outer Grounds so he could explain the configuration and purpose of the tile mandala decorating the floor. Eight dark brown rays, like the spokes of a giant ships' wheel, crossed over a succession of nesting circles, stopping just beyond the outer rim of the "wheel." The circle of gold that lay directly beneath the portal was called, unsurprisingly, the Golden Circle. A few yards from the Golden Circle was the Inner Circle, a two-foot-wide band of tiny mosaic tiles in shades of blue, green, and magenta. Between the Golden and Inner Circles, the tiles were slightly larger and seemingly of every color imaginable. Much further out was the Outer Circle, another band of tiny mosaics, this one in purple, yellow and orange hues. As before, the tiles between the Inner and Outer circles were larger and of a greater color variety, although with a heavier reliance on red hues.

Eliasser had just begun an explanation of the energy significance of the layout when the Wicked Wizard of Amoran interrupted him.

"She needs you," the wizard called as he swiftly crossed the floor.

"Again?" Eliasser ran his hand through his silky white hair and sent an apologetic glance my way. "It seems after years of things running quite smoothly, my presence is now required at every turn. I fear we will have to postpone our walk. Unless—" His gaze moved to the wizard.

"I am too busy," the wizard huffed.

Eliasser narrowed his eyes. "Well, then. Now, you will be even busier." And he guided the unhappy healer to the edge of the chamber for a private chat.

I was tracing the tiled patterns on the floor with my shoe when the blond elf approached, shadowed by Danaeus.

Blond Guy took in the animated discussion across the chamber. "What's up with them?"

I hadn't done anything to deserve the persona non grata status the wizard had relegated me to, so I shrugged. "I guess his High Holiness doesn't want to be stuck doing daycare today."

"That is no way to talk about the Master Guardian," Danaeus fumed.

"I wasn't talking about the Master Guardian. I was referring to Mr. Stick-Up-His-Butt."

Danaeus spluttered something incoherent, but the elf laughed as Eliasser and the wizard made their way back to us.

"It seems you will be taking your tour after all," Eliasser said with a smile.

The stone-faced wizard stared straight ahead, resentment pouring off him like rain.

The elf regarded the wizard curiously. "I'd love to show Kerrin around if you don't want to."

"I suggest you make it a foursome," the Master Guardian said. "A day in the fresh air will do all of you some good." And he walked away before anyone could protest—not that it would have made a difference. I figured a "suggestion" from Eliasser was a fait accompli.

"I'll arrange for Midday Meal out," the elf said.

"Midday Meal?" Danaeus blustered. "I can't be gone that long! I have a lot of work to do, and it can't wait until—"

I raised my voice to drown him out. "You mean, like a picnic?" I asked the elf.

"I didn't, but that would be fun," he replied. "How about an Earth-style picnic?"

"I'd love it, Mr. Elf."

He chuckled. "Mr. Elf. That's cute."

"Not really. But I have to call you something, and it sounds better than Blond Guy."

"Blond Guy! I like that." He struck a model's pose and fluffed his short, wild hair.

"Forget it," I snorted in mock disgust. "I am not feeding that ego of yours. Which makes you Mr. Elf, and you"—I pointed a finger at the wizard—"Mr. Wizard." Fiendishly delighted when the wizard groaned, I upped the ante. "I could always call you Elf-boy and Wiz-kid."

"Just plain wizard will do fine," grumped my nanny.

The elf linked arms with me. "I like Elf-boy even better than Blond Guy, if it's all the same to you . . . Earth-girl."

"Done," I said, smiling.

Elf-boy talked nonstop as we traversed the tunnels leading to the Outer Grounds. His pale skin was the lightest of anyone I'd met on Amoran, and his slight build bordered on delicate. While he had no facial hair, his unruly mop-top looked like it had been styled in a wind tunnel. His tunic was different, too. Instead of the pastel heathery colors worn by Danaeus, the wizard and me, the elf sported a solid blue top that draped to his knees, and white leggings. I figured him for early thirties, and not handsome, but attractive in a way that was totally engaging.

At the end of a long corridor, the wizard opened a doorway and we moved outside into a large, natural courtyard. Curving stone walls grew directly out of the Mountain, then met about twenty yards ahead at a small, metal-slatted gate. Danaeus pompously informed me that it was called the Main Gate—a rather pretentious name, I thought, for the creaky contraption that barely came to my chest.

We traveled the red dirt path that led across the enclosure and exited through the gate, where the wizard pulled me aside.

"Memories may surface as you walk the Outer Grounds. Do not wander off," he said in a tone normally reserved for a three-year-old. "The Master Guardian has made me responsible for your safety, and has instructed me in what to do if things become difficult for you."

"Become? Thanks to you, we crossed that bridge a while ago."

I stepped away from him, then filled my lungs with the sweet-smelling air, silently agreeing with Eliasser that a day outside was exactly what was called for. The lemon sun beat down full and bright out of a cloudless turquoise sky. Clumps of flowers dotted Kelly green grass. To my right, a stream bubbled out from a channel in the Mountain and flowed parallel to the path for about forty feet or so. The path then veered sharply left, while the stream meandered off in the opposite direction. Just beyond where the path and stream split sat a grouping of large boulders in shades of gray and brown. Some were scooped out, providing chair-like seating, while others tilted at an angle perfect for leaning against to watch the water go by. When I shielded my eyes from the sun to see them better, the elf followed the direction of my gaze. "Resting Stones," he whispered in my ear.

"Ah. They wouldn't be for resting, would they?"

He rounded his eyes. "Was that sarcasm?"

"Who, me? Never." I pressed my fingers to my nose, then moved them straight out.

I didn't expect him to pick up on the Pinocchio reference, but he grinned and said, "Okay. But I *wooden* put it past you."

I laughed. "I like you, Elf-boy."

"The feeling's mutual, Earth-girl."

We followed the path as it wound between small hills sprinkled with low, bushy trees. Danaeus and the wizard remained silent while the elf and I gabbed away. He seemed to have a generous knowledge of Earth. So generous, he'd played a joke on Danaeus by dressing him like a cartoon dwarf for his trip to my kitchen. The mischievous elf, who had assumed I'd read the letter, thought I'd get the humor in the silly costume.

About a half-mile later, the path forked. Heading right, we traveled about twice that distance to reach a bloom-filled meadow surrounding a modest lake. The flowers grew straight to the water's edge, where the royal blue surface mirrored their stunning beauty. A craft resembling a large rowboat was secured to a pole on a tiny beach about ten yards wide. I thought the boat was made of wood, but when I ran my hand along its side, the material felt more like plastic resin.

"Can we take it out?" I asked the elf.

"We'll have to. The *glazzien* don't like being trod upon, so walking around the Mindsail Lake is not an option. They even complain if they're looked at too much."

"Wait. Are you saying these flowers are conscious?"

"Of course," Danaeus snapped. "Everything is conscious." He untied the thick, gold rope from the pole and tossed it into the boat.

I was sidetracked from sniping back at him when the elf snapped his heels together, bowed low, then extended his hand. "Madam," he intoned with courtly courtesy.

I stepped daintily into the boat and batted my eyes. "You know, Master Elf, if you lived on Earth, I'd say you watched too much television. Perchance, a certain show on PBS?"

He smiled as he climbed in after me. "In a sense, I have lived on Earth, and I love TV."

The wizard said nothing as he and Danaeus entered behind us, but Danaeus balked at the remark. "You are not supposed to divulge—"

"Oh, don't get your leggings in a bunch, Dwarf-boy," the elf broke in. "I wasn't talking about her past *here,* I was talking about my experience *there.*"

Danaeus grabbed a pole from the bottom of the boat and pushed us off with more force than was probably necessary. Since neither the elf nor I were seated, we fell into the center in a heap, succumbing to fits of laughter over our shared spectacle. Grumbling to himself, Danaeus stepped around us to get to the front of the boat, then sat down facing the water.

The wizard's voice was suddenly soft with concern. "Are you sure, Danaeus?"

"I can handle it," he grunted, all gruff and macho-like.

"Let him be, Wiz-kid," the elf said. "He's a big dwarf, relatively speaking. Now, while Danaeus drives the boat, I plan to regale our friend with my many tales of derring-do on Earth."

After the initial push to get the boat into the water, I couldn't see, hear, or feel any method of propulsion, yet we moved forward at a slow, even pace. The elf had a wonderful voice for storytelling, and by his own admission had made hundreds of trips to my world. I asked Danaeus if he'd ever accompanied the elf on his Earthly adventures. I figured his lack of response was more of his rudeness until the elf corrected that assumption. "It takes a great deal of concentration to propel the mindsail. He can't spare the energy to talk now."

The wizard hadn't spoken either since we'd gotten underway, even when I'd asked him a direct question. But he wasn't "propelling the mindsail," however one did that, and I was getting fed up with the silent treatment.

When we reached the opposite shore, the elf secured the boat, then hoisted Danaeus to his feet and helped him out of the mindsail.

"Just over that little hill"—the elf pointed—"we can have our picnic and allow Danaeus to recoup his strength." The two of them trudged on ahead.

The wizard stepped onto the beach, sighed loudly, then held out his hand. I accepted the reluctant offer of help and let him guide me out of the boat, but I refused to let go of him.

"Talk to me," I demanded. "Tell me what's wrong."

"Nothing is wrong," he said in a voice like ice. "Release my hand."

I tightened my grip. "Not until you talk to me. When you performed my healing—and I've been trying to thank you for that, by the way—I know you didn't harbor this ill will towards me. Now you act like I'm the worst thing that's dropped out of the vortex in a thousand years."

The color drained from his face, and he yanked his hand away with such force I nearly fell.

"I told you. There is nothing wrong."

"Right. That's why you treat me like shit. What is it? Sibling rivalry? We have the same eyes. Are you like . . . like my long-lost brother or something? And Mom and Dad like me best?"

He curled his lip, just like in the forest. "We are not blood-related."

"I'm as glad about that as you are, champ. But I must have done something to piss you off."

"I have no idea what you are talking about."

"Cut the crap. I know what I felt when I looked into your eyes after I crash-landed in the Main Chamber. We know each other. I don't know how, I don't know why, but we go back a long way. A really long—"

A sudden, visceral sense of our connection rocked me to my core. The feeling-memory hit me so physically, I lost my balance. And this time, I did fall. Flat on my face.

# CHAPTER 8

"**B**lech." I spit out a mouthful of sand and sat up to brush the rest from my face.

The wizard crouched down and jammed his hand between my breasts.

"Hey!" I slapped his arm away. "What's with you? Back off, pervert."

"You are being ridiculous. I must assess your energy."

"Yeah? Assess this." I pointed a specific finger in the air. "I'll make you a deal. Tell me what's wrong with you and I'll let you fool around with my energy."

"There is nothing—"

"Oh, screw you."

I catapulted to my feet and climbed the hill as fast as my wobbly legs would take me. My babysitter scurried after me, his face now lined with worry as he called to me to stop.

*As if.* I didn't give a flying fig how much trouble he caught from Eliasser if I came to some harm. But I was in no shape to outrun him. I reached the top of the "little hill" ready to pass out.

"Kerrin . . . wait," the wizard panted behind me.

"Why?" I called back. "Do you plan on treating me differently? If not, then go to hell."

I tried to clomp away again, but my legs rebelled.

"Please . . . wait." He wheezed out the request so nicely, I complied. That, and I could barely breathe. He caught up with me and we gulped for air, daggering each other with our eyes. Then, in one of those weird emotional flip-flops, we started to laugh. A few giggles at first, but soon we were gasping hysterically. It was a full minute before we calmed down enough to talk.

"We're pathetic," I said, collapsing onto the soft grass.

He plopped down next to me. "Why would you not stop when I asked?"

"You're pretty clueless, aren't you? Because you wanted me to, of course."

I don't know why that was funny, but like a couple of six-year-olds telling knock-knock jokes, we had to get through another round of giggles. His laughter, silvery and light, made me want to laugh even more. Eventually we quieted and lay back on the grass, observing the sky. A single white puffball drifted by, reminding me that I hadn't seen a cloud until now.

He was first to break the silence. "I am sorry. Everything you said is correct, yet I have no explanation for my actions." He sighed. "I cannot even offer you a reasonable guess."

I rolled over to face him. "Thank you. I appreciate the honesty. I'm actually very easy to please." He smiled, but kept looking at the ocean of turquoise above us. "I don't know about you," I added, "but I'm hungry. We should get down there before Grumpy eats all the food."

We descended the hill and rejoined the others in another grassy meadow, this one with only a few sparse flowers—the nonbiting variety.

"How far are we from the Mountain?" I asked.

"An interesting question," the elf said. He shrugged off a little brown backpack. A backpack I hadn't seen until now. "But not so easy to answer."

I rolled my eyes. "Why am I not surprised."

He withdrew a red-checked tablecloth from the backpack. "Like our unique relationship with time, space on Amoran is also subject to variations you won't find on Earth. For example, that forest is only a half-mile away."

I transferred my astonished gaze from the bulky items he continued to pull from the small pack to the tree line that seemed many miles distant. "How is that possible?"

He didn't answer as he snapped the tablecloth out with a flourish, then let it go. Flat as a board, it floated to the ground. A wave of his delicate elf hand, and presto!—a picnic basket showed up at his feet. Another wave and plates and utensils appeared on the tablecloth in table-set order. A third wave and food materialized on serving dishes. The coup de grâce? An uncorked bottle of champagne chilling in an ice bucket.

"Outstanding," I said. "Do you have any orange juice? I love mimosas."

The elf grinned. "I know. I thought you could use a dose of Earth right now."

"You are so right. Thank you, Ari."

*Ari?* The name had popped out of my mouth without any forethought. Like a sleeper wave, vertigo surged out of nowhere. I sank to the ground, moaning as I dug my fingers into the grass in a futile attempt to steady the gyrating universe.

A flask touched my lips. The contents smelled worse than a garbage dump.

"No!" I jerked my head away, which only made the rocking and spinning worse.

"Yes," the wizard insisted. "It is the only thing that will help."

The flask returned to my mouth. The odor made me want to throw up.

"I said *no.*" I hit the container and heard liquid slosh onto the grass. There must have been only one flask of the disgusting brew, because Ari cried out in dismay and Danaeus yelled for someone to *do something!*

The wizard grabbed me, I guess to inject me with heart-to-heart healing like the Master Guardian had done in the forest. But I fended him off with the same baffling frantic drive that impels a drowning person to fight a rescuer. I simply couldn't let go of the patch of ground I'd anchored myself to, even though it heaved me around like a carnival ride. My mind had turned into a bizarre parody of whack-a-mole, only my version starred memories that snapped out of sight before I could tell what they were. The harder I tried to grasp onto them, the faster they vanished and the dizzier I became. I had no choice but to let them go and wait out the storm.

The spinning finally slowed and my mind calmed. I looked up, touched by the worry on Danaeus's face as he tugged at his scruffy whiskers. "Does this happen often?" he asked.

"It comes and goes. Each time, it's a little different."

"I didn't realize . . ." His voice trailed off.

Meanwhile, Ari was positively buoyant. "I am so glad you remembered my name. I was sure I'd slip up soon. The only other names I'm struggling to keep secret are for this guy," he pointed at the wizard, "and the Master Guardian."

"Then you're in luck. I got Eliasser's name earlier."

The wizard's eyebrows poked straight up. "You did? When?"

"This morning at breakfast. I guess you call it Morning Meal."

"I wonder why he did not mention it to me." The wizard stroked his beard. "We assumed it would take weeks for the memory of names to surface. This changes everything."

"Again? What does it change this time?" He didn't reply, but gazed thoughtfully out at the forest. One thing hadn't changed. My healer-wizard still wouldn't look directly at me.

Ari, deep in celebration mode, began a childlike chant. "You remember my na-ame, you remember my na-ame." He switched to a victory cheer, then tried to moonwalk across the grass. Giving up on that, he broke into an improvisational dance. "Happy feet! I've got happy feet!"

"Is he always like this?" I asked Danaeus.

"Insufferably so," Danaeus grumbled. But I detected the hint of a smile. It seemed my name-game vertigo had pried open the door between us.

Ari stopped hopping and joined us on the cloth, which had magically grown to blanket-sized proportions. "Eat up, Dorothy. You are definitely not in Kansas. Then again, you never have been. I have, though, and there was this one time when—"

Danaeus groaned, but I settled in to enjoy the company, which was finally companionable.

---

I squinted into the distance as we picked at leftovers. "Is that the forest I visited yesterday?"

"Yep," Ari said, squeezing the cork back into the champagne bottle.

"And it's really only a half-mile away?"

Ari answered me while keeping an eye on Danaeus, who had just served himself a hefty portion of a cake-like delicacy. "The mechanics of it are complex. Simply put, the exaggerated distance we perceive is an illusion caused by a distortion of the Transition Space."

If that was putting it simply, I was in big trouble. I thought back to my first trip through the vortex and the picturesque valley I'd encountered.

"The Transition Space seemed odd. Beautiful, but odd. Like it isn't really . . . real."

The wizard regarded me appraisingly. "You are correct. It is also an illusion, one that functions as a holding area for anyone who might enter the vortex by accident."

Danaeus crammed his mouth so full of the golden cake, he couldn't close his lips.

"But that's not likely to happen, is it?" I asked. "It's not as if my family room gets a lot of foot traffic from the outside world, and opening the portal is a fairly intricate process."

"It didn't used to be," Ari said. "And the portal wasn't always inside your house."

"And," the wizard added, "long ago, the portal could open on its own. That possibility had to be provided for, for everyone's protection."

With all the magic they seemed to possess, I didn't see why they were concerned about keeping safe from strays. "Why didn't I make it to the Transition Space this time?"

"That was done on purpose," Ari said. "You need to travel directly through the vortex now."

"Minus the energy inversion, I hope." The experience of nearly being torn apart was still fresh in my mind.

The three men eyed each other; they'd done a lot of that during our picnic.

"Okay, enough with the meaningful looks," I exclaimed. "What aren't you telling me?"

"We can't promise it won't happen again," Ari confessed. "But it's unlikely to. The inversion you suffered was caused by an unforeseen fluctuation in vortex energy."

"Unforeseen? Does that mean you usually foresee them?"

The wizard shrugged. "We are able to predict inversions with great accuracy."

"Except this last time," I pointed out.

"Except this last time," he echoed, and like an echo, his voice sounded hollow.

We nibbled in silence for a while. I felt drowsy, although I didn't think it was the champagne's fault. I had a sneaking suspicion it was nonalcoholic. I usually can't have more than one mimosa without falling all over myself in a giggling mess. So far, I'd consumed three. But they tasted better than any I'd ever had, so I wasn't complaining.

"What exactly is this big problem in the vortex?" I asked.

The wizard stretched out on his side and propped his head on one arm. "It is an imbalance caused by an enormous shift in dimensional energy. Unlike prior shifts, this one started inside the vortex and is generating fluctuations in vibrational levels that are beyond comprehension. And the rift it has produced!"

Uh-oh. "Can you back up? I'm already lost. What's a dimensional shift?"

He reached forward to pick at some *visinnima*, a vegetable mixture with a taste and texture like tempura. When he leaned back again, his eyes traveled slowly up the length of my body, stopping just above my chin. "A dimensional shift is a normal part of cosmic evolution. During a shift, all matter and energy within a specific area of space accelerates in velocity sub-atomically until it arrives at a new level of vibrational expression."

Oh, boy. I was two-for-two in the "I don't get it" category, but this time I kept mum.

"Vortex energy reacts to these escalating frequencies," the wizard continued, "by fluctuating to stay in balance. Because this dimensional shift originated inside the vortex, the fluctuations are more dramatic, causing a kind of vibrational backwash. That is where the problem lies. The backwash has created an enormous rift in the vortex that widens daily. It must be repaired or else—"

"Earth and Amoran get sucked inside. I remember this part."

All three of them looked at me with hopeful expressions. I hated to disillusion them.

"I'm sorry. I only remember that because Danaeus mentioned it when he came to Earth."

I sorted through what I'd learned so far, determined to understand at least some of it.

"So, the rift caused unforeseen fluctuations in vortex energy, and that's why I got trapped in the energy inversion?"

"Indirectly," Ari said. He slapped Danaeus's hand when the dwarf tried to snag a second helping of cake. "Although, we're no longer certain that it *was* an energy inversion. It's more like all hell broke loose inside the vortex, as though space-time momentarily turned in on itself. In all honesty, it's a miracle you made it through in one piece instead of ending up as scattered random molecules on the other side of the universe."

*Scattered random molecules?* The center of my chest felt like I'd chugged a glass of ice water. There were several beats of charged silence as Ari picked at the grass, Danaeus folded and unfolded his napkin, and the wizard stared at the not-so-distant forest.

"Here." Ari pushed the plate containing the last two pieces of cake at the wizard and me. "You better eat these now or Danaeus and I will fight you for them."

I was grateful for a diversion from bleak thoughts, but Battle of the Bundt?

"As much as I love dessert, Ari, I don't think I'll come to blows over it. Besides, can't you make more in your traveling kitchen?" I pointed at the backpack.

Ari just smiled. The wizard and I reached for the cake plate, but he got there first and snatched the larger portion, leaving me little more than a mouth-sized piece.

"How considerate of you," I snapped. I figured the scathing look I sent his way would be lost on him; his gaze never went higher than my nose or lower than my forehead. But this time he stared straight into my eyes. Electricity buzzed through my body like I'd been zapped by a mild electric shock. Yet it wasn't painful or unpleasant. In fact, the way my insides vibrated and my eyes tingled felt good. I wondered if he experienced the same thing, but he gave nothing away as he took a tiny bite of his cake, closed his eyes, and sighed like a man in love.

I snorted. "Oh, puh-leeze. Nothing tastes that good."

I shoved the small square of cake into my mouth. Then I chewed. Then I swallowed. I'm pretty sure I made some seriously obscene sounds along the way.

"Oh my God," I whispered, when my mouth was finally free. "This is way better than chocolate. Can you please make more?"

"Sorry," Ari said. "The instructions say to use sparingly."

"This slice of heaven comes with instructions?"

He laughed. "I'm kidding. Still, best not to overdo it. It's a very rich elven treat that I only make on special occasions. Your return to Amoran definitely falls into that category."

My face, already warm from the sun, grew warmer from the compliment. "Thanks. I think you just made my day."

"How can a person make a day?" Danaeus asked, as he combed food out of his whiskers.

I yawned. "You explain it to him, Ari. I'm pooped."

"And I'm your pillow." Ari patted his outstretched leg.

I hesitated. It seemed too intimate a thing to do with a man who wasn't my husband.

"Think of me as a brother," Ari said, as if he read my thoughts.

"Okay, that works. I really am exhausted."

I rested my head on his thigh, and in a rush of recognition, I somehow knew I'd used my elf friend as a pillow in the distant past, after many walks and numerous picnics. The knowledge filled me with a sense of security I hadn't experienced since I'd arrived on Amoran, and I drifted off contentedly to sleep.

———————

My first hint of consciousness was hearing Ari and the wizard discussing something.

"Well, that *is* strange," Ari whispered. "Any idea why it's happening?"

"No. She is different than I expected. I need to think through what to do about it, so please do not tell anyone yet."

I was different than he'd expected? Different from what?

"I won't." Ari made the promise readily enough, but he sounded unsure. "It will affect the Reparention if you can't—"

"I know," the wizard cut him off. "I am painfully aware of that."

The long pause that followed allowed me to pretend I was just waking up. Wondering what the "Reparention" was, I fluttered my eyes open in a way I hoped was convincing.

Ari smiled down at me. "We should head back now. Danaeus is already at the lake."

I eyed the detritus of our feast. "What about cleanup? Can you fit this into your little bag?"

Ari kept smiling, crooked an index finger at the mess, and everything vanished.

I sighed. "Can you teach me that trick?"

Ari laughed, which apparently was my answer. Too bad.

When we arrived at the lake, I was so caught up imagining all the things I could accomplish with time-stretching and Ari's Finger-Snap-Insta-Clean, that I climbed into the front of the boat and sat down like Danaeus had when he piloted the mindsail. Realizing the mistake I'd make, I decided to save face and turn it into a joke.

"My turn," I chirped. As if I could make a boat run on thought!

"Hey. Give it whirl," Ari said. "You were one of the best at willful focusing. The only person who could do you better was this guy." He pointed at the wizard, who waved his hands frantically in what must be the interdimensional sign for *Stop! Cease! Desist! Shut up!*

Ari, on a verbal roll, missed the cue. "Danaeus, do you remember the races they used to have? I thought they'd sink both mindsails that day when they—" He broke off at the dwarf's stormy expression. Ari's pale face went even whiter as he turned to me. "I'm such an idiot. Not to mention terrible at keeping secrets. Are you all right? Please say you're all right."

Poor Ari. I could've kissed the gabby elf for the juicy tidbit he'd let slip about my supposed past, even if it might make me go temporarily insane. Erring on the side of caution, I waited several moments before responding. "I seem to be fine. And if I was so good once, then this should be a breeze."

I thought I was still joking, but my tone came out serious. I must have shocked the others into silence with my preposterous claim, because no one said a word as Ari and Danaeus climbed aboard. The wizard unhooked the rope, pushed us off and hopped in.

The boat jumped forward, then came to a halt. It was my moment of truth.

*Oh, crap. Just tell them you were kidding.*

I didn't. I couldn't. Because I really did want to pilot the mindsail.

I closed my eyes and tried to focus willfully. However a person actually does that. A tortuous lifetime of seconds ticked by as the boat sat motionless on calm, clear water. Danaeus grunted every so often, but the wizard and Ari kept quiet until Ari finally cleared his throat and asked if I would like help. "No," I barked, then felt like a jerk. How did I expect to accomplish this feat when I didn't know what to do?

"We cannot wait," the wizard said. "I will take over."

Well, that just made me more determined. *I so want to do this.*

As if I'd pressed a button, an image of the boat coasting across the lake sailed through my brain. Then I felt motion inside me, like a warm breeze blowing through my solar plexus.

Motion? *Inside me?* That couldn't be right. Had the wind picked up?

I opened my eyes. There wasn't any wind, yet the boat was inching forward. Had I made it do that? I glanced over my shoulder to find the wizard blinking as if he didn't quite believe what he was seeing. Now I *really* wanted to make the mindsail . . . sail.

I closed my eyes and got a mental replay of the boat gliding across the lake, followed by that puzzling sense of internal motion. I peeked at the water. We were still moving, but not by much. I squeezed my eyelids together and chanted inwardly, *come on, dinghy, do it!*

Once again, I glimpsed mental footage of the boat slicing through the water. And here, I made an intuitive leap. As soon as I experienced the breeze wafting through the center of me, I brought the image of the boat and the feeling of movement together.

We shot ahead so fast, I fell backwards into the wizard.

Righting myself, I knelt for better stability and thought about how much I wanted the boat to go. When the mental picture reappeared, I merged it more slowly with that feeling of internal motion. The boat moved forward at a swift, steady pace. Like a little kid, I wanted to shout, "I did it!" But Ari was right; it took tremendous concentration to pilot the mindsail, which made me doubly surprised when we reached the opposite shore in half the time of our previous trip.

"You've still got it," Ari said as he helped me out of the boat.

"That was amazing," I exclaimed. "And fun. It's weird, though. Instead of it draining me, I feel like I can take on the world. I can't believe I did it. I'm not dreaming, am I?"

I was so excited it took me a minute to realize that Danaeus was stalking up the path, shoulders bent over. "Oh boy. Is he mad because I made the boat go faster than he did?"

"No," Ari said. "He's always been extremely proud of your abilities."

It sounded like a compliment, but Ari folded his arms across his chest, his expression pensive. The wizard stared at the lake with a tight-lipped frown.

"Then what's wrong?" I asked, bewildered by the sudden change in all three of them.

Ari looked away. "This is all my fault. I've already said too much. Let's get going."

That was the sum total of our conversation until we reached the Main Chamber. Danaeus headed toward one of the tunnels, but when Ari turned to follow, I pulled him back.

"What did I do wrong? Why is everyone upset?"

He wouldn't look me in the eye. "It would be easier if you didn't physically resemble your old self. Especially for those among us whose hearts broke when you left Amoran."

"That is enough!" the wizard exploded. He grabbed Ari by the arm and dragged him out of the Main Chamber, leaving me alone and confused in the Golden Circle.

# CHAPTER 9

I wasn't alone for long. Vianna slipped out of one of the tunnels and motioned for me to follow her. We walked the passageways in silence, which was fine with me. I was too annoyed to talk anyway. The Guardians claimed they wanted my memories to return, but when one did, they shut me out. I refused to think about the hearts I'd supposedly broken. By my reckoning, I hadn't done anything to anybody. And what had Ari meant about "my old self?"

Inside my room, Vianna headed for the ancillary, saying she would be ready for me soon. Ready for what, she didn't bother to tell me.

I picked up my fuzzy wool sweater from the back counter and hugged it to me like a stuffed animal. A present from John, the touch of something so loved and familiar made me homesick for my family.

"The shower is ready," Vianna called to me.

My spirits lifted at the thought of hot water cascading over my body. I joined her in the ancillary where she stood beside a wide opaque cylinder that reached to the ceiling. I was no longer surprised that the monolith had appeared out of nowhere.

"It is best to remove your tunic," she said, "although you may leave it on if you prefer."

"Won't it get wet?"

Her finely shaped brows drew together. "Why would it get wet?"

What a question! "Because it's water. Or doesn't water make you wet on Amoran?"

Her eyes rounded in disbelief. "What would water be doing in an energy shower?"

"Energy shower?" I stared in dismay at the cylinder. "No hot water?"

"How could water possibly get you clean? And who would desire such an experience?" She shuddered as if to dislodge a particularly unpleasant association.

Thrown by her bizarre questions, I just said, "I'll leave the tunic on."

"As you wish. Close your eyes once you are inside."

I entered the cylinder through its slender opening and did as instructed. The backs of my eyelids glowed for a few seconds, then it was over. I stepped out of the cylinder and looked down. All traces of dirt from when I'd fallen earlier were gone. I had to concede the energy shower worked, but it sure didn't satisfy like my shower back home.

We left the ancillary together, but Vianna kept going out the doorway to the corridor. The wall reappeared, leaving me alone once more.

With a surge of stubbornness, I shed my tunic and pulled on my Earth clothes just in time for the doorway to open again. A smiling Eliasser came several steps inside. He took in the rumpled tunic on the floor, then me in my jeans and sweater, and his smile wavered.

"I'm going back to Earth," I said with as much conviction as I could muster. But I had miscalculated the growing effect the Master Guardian had on me. I made the mistake of letting our eyes meet, and that mystifying affection I felt for him rose up stronger than ever.

"Do you not wish to take Evening Meal with me?" he asked.

I hardened myself as best I could. "What I wish is that Danaeus had never shown up in my kitchen."

Eliasser quickly crossed the floor. "If that were true, you would never have returned to us." His eyes and his voice softened. "To me."

Was the Master Guardian of the Seventh Vortex guilt-tripping me? If so, it backfired.

"You have no idea what this is like for me, do you? A few days ago, I was a normal person. Now I drive boats using my mind. *My mind!* Not only are Danaeus, Ari and the wizard mad at me because of it, I'm not completely sure how I managed to do it in the first place."

Faced with that intense blue-eyed scrutiny, I swallowed hard.

"I want to go home. I miss my family."

Eliasser kept up his unblinking stare as he sat on the edge of the sleeping stone and reached for my hands. I knew any hope of holding my ground would vanish the minute he touched me. I meant to clasp my hands behind my back to prevent that, but like they belonged to someone else, those same disobedient hands pushed forward and slipped inside his.

Warm and comforting, his energy moved through me.

"Do you understand what is happening when I do this?" he asked.

My last drop of resistance evaporated. I sat next to him on the stone.

"You mean, besides making me feel wonderful?"

He smiled. "Yes, besides that. You are experiencing a connection with who you really are. A great store of knowledge resides deep within your mind and your heart. Part of that knowledge is who you are and what you are here to do. And the part that you must play in repairing the vortex. The part, I might add, that only you can play."

"Then you're out of luck. I'm a small-town working mom who has to have dinner on the table at six o'clock every night no matter what state of disrepair the universe is in." I steeled my gaze, trying to convince him. "I'm an average woman doing average things in an average life."

His voice dropped so low, it was almost hypnotic. "That is your conscious mind speaking; it only accepts the role that you are accustomed to. I am trying to awaken you to your true identity. But I cannot force your memories to return, or else—" He stopped, tightened his grip, and sent me a double dose of whatever poured out of his amazing hands.

"Rest," Eliasser said. "When you arise, we will share Evening Meal."

I lay back on the stone, as sleep was already overtaking me.

———

"*You* were the ogler at the Tea Leaf Café?"

Ari laughed as we swung down another corridor. While we waited for Evening Meal to begin, he was teaching me the route from my room to the Main Chamber, and from there to the Outer Grounds.

"Yep. I make a pretty cute old codger, don't I?"

"Cute? Hah! More like rude and obnoxious."

"Hold on there, Earth-girl. I'll admit to being obnoxious, but I'm never rude."

"If you say so. But why leave me a book in the library? Especially after the letter fiasco."

We'd arrived at the end of the corridor leading to the Outer Grounds. Ari's only response was to point at the wall. I moved my hands up and outward while thinking "open" just like he'd shown me, but I still couldn't make the doorway appear. Aggravated, I turned on him.

"What if I hadn't gone to the Tea Leaf that day? Or the library? How could you be certain I'd find the book—and take it home? And what if I didn't bother to read it once I got it there?"

He eyed the stark span of wall sympathetically, linked his arm through mine, and patted my hand. "There, there. No need to take it out on me. You'll open it eventually."

"I'm not mad about the doorway!"

I felt my nose to make sure it wasn't elongating as Ari chanted, "Liar, liar, pants on fire."

"Come on, Ari. Answer me."

"I will. On the way to the Guardian Meal Room. It's time to eat and I'm starved. All this walking . . ." He held the back of his hand to his forehead and batted his eyes.

"You're as bad a drama queen as Danaeus," I grumbled.

"Oh, I'm much better at it than the dwarf. And I knew you'd find the book—and take it home—and read it—because I followed you everywhere to make sure." He tsked. "Off-brand tissues at the discount store. Really, now. Don't you know how much lint those things produce?"

I made a face at him. "Really, now. What business is it of yours if I—" My eyes popped open so wide I must have looked like a Muppet. "You followed me *everywhere?*"

"Hey. Nothing like that. I'm not a peeping elf."

"You are if you're watching me that closely. Exactly how does this surveillance work? I only saw you at the library and the café."

We crossed the Main Chamber and took the corridor next to the blank section of wall where my penchant for symmetry insisted an eighth tunnel should be. He still hadn't answered, so I pulled on his arm to make him stop. "How do you watch me?"

Ari shifted his feet. "Let's just say I can see you when you can't see me."

Gee, how helpful. "That means you're either really good at hiding or you can make yourself invisible. Why couldn't you just hand the book to me?"

He bit his lip and looked away. "I'm not supposed to have direct contact with you on Earth. Not now, anyway." Leaning against the corridor wall, he shoved his hands into pockets I hadn't known existed in our tunics. After my nap, I'd changed from my Earth clothes into the Guardian Sanctuary two-piece outfit. Momentarily distracted now, I checked my top. The seamless garment had no side openings, at least none that I could find. Of course, the way things kept appearing and disappearing here, there was probably some way to—

*Plink.* A piece of my Amoran puzzle fell into place.

"Were you in my family room when I found the letter?"

Ari gave a discouraged nod. "You stared at it for so long, I was sure you had read it."

"I may have been staring at the paper, but I couldn't read it. I nearly blacked out, and by the time my vision cleared, the phone rang again, and I had to leave."

"I didn't realize that at the time." His head dropped forward. "I returned to Amoran as soon as you left the house. It's what I was supposed to do, but I can't help feeling like it's my fault we're in this mess."

And there went another puzzle piece.

"I went back into the house that day because I couldn't shake the feeling I'd forgotten to do something." I sighed. "I guess that part is true. When I opened the front door, I heard the sound of running water and thought I'd left a faucet on. But it must have been the portal opening. Seconds earlier and I would have discovered you."

"I wish you had. Maybe I could have prevented this situation. Because of me, the Reparention might fail."

During our walk, Ari had clued me in that the Reparention was, quite simply, the repair job for the vortex. But he wouldn't tell me why fixing the vortex had to wait until after New Year's on Earth, or why the Guardians had to bring me to Amoran now instead of, say, after Christmas.

Ari's drooping shoulders got to me. I knew instinctively that he didn't spend a lot of time feeling sad, and I didn't think he should start now on my account. At a loss for words, something unusual for me, I fell back on one of my Grandma Eloisa's favorite sayings.

"It's okay. Things usually happen for a reason."

Ari jerked his head up and looked at me as if I'd said something important. Then, for reasons known only to the goofy elf, he broke into a loud rendition of an old Beach Boys tune.

I laughed. "I guess you do 'get around.' Maybe I should call you Earth-boy instead."

I sang along with him as we traveled the rest of the way to dinner. Ari had told me that all eighty Mountain inhabitants usually ate together in the Main Meal Room. But with the Reparention coming closer, the Guardians would be taking their meals in the smaller, more intimate Guardian Meal Room to shield their energy, both to and from others.

At the doorway to the Guardian Meal Room, I stopped to study the surroundings while Ari went inside. The sparsely appointed room contained a wooden table shaped like the letter C, the open end of which faced the doorway. Eight straight-backed chairs, placed at even intervals around the outer curve, reflected back from the highly polished dark brown surface. Five stools occupied an alcove to my left; to my right, a small group of people talked quietly. Aside from Ari, I only recognized Danaeus, the wizard, and Eliasser, who broke free to greet me.

"Did you sleep well?"

"Yes. And I've worked up an appetite with Ari's help."

Eliasser smiled. "Then let us begin our meal without delay."

We sat together at the midpoint of the "C." That seemed to be the signal for the rest of the attendees to take their places as well. I waved to Ari and pointed at the seat to my left, but a man with long, medium brown hair, graying at his temples, got there first. Like the wizard, he had tan skin and a full, close-cropped beard. A boy, perhaps a little older than Ryan, dropped onto the chair next to him. The man smiled warmly, but the boy frowned as he boldly inspected my face.

A woman with short, silver hair placed herself next to Eliasser. I tried not to gape, but aside from Eliasser's small spray of crow's-feet, everyone I had encountered so far had baby-smooth skin. However, the creasing on this woman's olive-toned face clearly showed the passing of time. And yet, like Eliasser's white hair and delicate lines, her wrinkles seemed out of sync with whatever her true age might be. She fixed her gaze ahead, her expression neutral. For some reason, her lack of acknowledgment of me cut deeper than the rudeness of Danaeus, the wizard and the boy combined.

Eliasser covered my hands—they were folded into a tight ball on my lap—with one of his own as he addressed the group.

"Many years have passed since the eight of us shared Evening Meal. I, for one, feel such lightness in my heart." He shook his head, seeming bemused. "But where are my manners? There are introductions to be made. We will use titles," he said to me, "for those of us whose names you have not yet recalled." Eliasser gestured with his free hand. "To your left are the Master Technician and his son."

"What are you Master Technician of?" I asked.

"The Seventh Vortex," the man answered. "Although, it is a somewhat grandiose title, as my son and I are the only vortex technicians at the current time."

"Does that make you the Assistant Master Technician?" I said to the boy. He just scowled.

Eliasser indicated the woman to his right. "And this is our Master Healer."

With one swift movement, she turned and stared. Her dark gray eyes seemed to bore into me. I mumbled "hello" and looked away, nearly undone by the strongest feeling of recognition yet.

"Now that introductions are complete," Eliasser said, "I would like to say a special blessing in gratitude for the presence of our dear companion, who completes our Guardian circle. Please help Kerrin feel at home, especially as the circumstances of her return are far more challenging than we had ever imagined they would be."

I missed the blessing as I pondered Eliasser's statement. If I completed the Guardian circle, did that mean I was a Guardian, too? Which begged the question, when during my life on Earth had I had time to be a Guardian on Amoran? I barely had time to get the laundry done!

Contrary to the request to "help Kerrin feel at home," no one talked to me besides Eliasser and the Master Technician, who patiently explained the name and origin of each item I scooped onto my plate. Ari and the wizard were thoroughly engrossed discussing some game. Danaeus managed to throw the occasional glare my way—guess he was still mad at me—while the Master Healer continued to ignore me. Then there was the Master Technician's son, who studied every move I made until I frowned at him and he finally let me alone.

After dinner, Eliasser announced there would be music and dancing to celebrate my return. Worn out by the emotional undercurrents during the meal, all I wanted to do was go back to my room and sleep some more. But I figured even on Amoran it wouldn't be polite to eat and run.

"I hope you like our way of dancing," Eliasser whispered. "It is quite different from what you are accustomed to on Earth."

A group of men and women entered the room carrying instruments that resembled guitars, a flute, and a string bass, and settled onto the stools in the alcove.

Eliasser and the Master Healer went to the front of the room and stood opposite each other.

"The First Dance of Life, please," Eliasser called out.

A single note reverberated throughout the room.

Eliasser and the Master Healer closed their eyes and lifted their arms out to the side.

Another long note sounded.

They bent their arms up at the elbows.

A third note rang out. This one, held the longest, seemed to resonate inside my head. When it died away, the musicians began to play a haunting, yet beautiful, melody. The music actually vibrated inside of me, as if each note originated there instead of coming from the instruments. Blood pulsed in my temples. Needing a distraction from the intense feelings, I focused on the dancers' intricate movements and beatific expressions. That's when I noticed that Eliasser and the Master Healer still had their eyes closed! What's more, they remained closed throughout the short dance. Yet the two Guardians mirrored each other perfectly without ever colliding.

The dance ended, leaving me as breathless as if I had been the one exerting myself. I didn't think I could sit through another one, but before I could catch Eliasser's attention, the next dance began—this time, with the wizard as his partner.

The Master Healer returned to the table, sat next to me, and proceeded to stare at the side of my head. I refused to look at her, but it didn't matter. Her relentless scrutiny was undoing what little self-control I had left. Enough, already.

I thrust up out of my chair, but with astounding strength, she yanked me back down. I landed hard, gasping in surprise as she clamped her hand on my chin like a vise, holding me rigid so her cold, gray eyes could pierce through me. Eliasser's ocular probing was intense, but it was kindergarten compared to the way she forced her way into my psyche. It felt like parts of my brain were tearing loose and repositioning themselves. And God, did it hurt.

"Let me go," I hissed.

She held tight and kept drilling, and drilling, and—

"Stop it," I shouted, and slapped her arm away with a resounding crack.

Except I missed and got her face instead.

Like I'd pressed "pause" on a remote control, the music stopped and everyone froze.

Licking my suddenly dry lips, I darted a glance around the room, taking in the shocked expressions. Then, I did the only thing I could think of in the spur of the moment. I ran.

---

The muffled sounds of night were a soothing balm for my frayed nerves. I'd finally managed to open the doorway to the Outer Grounds. Supported by a Resting Stone, I tilted my head to view the sky. Thousands of tiny lights winked at me. It was a breathtaking sight on a beautiful world. But they weren't my stars. And this wasn't my world.

The Main Gate creaked open and I tensed. I didn't know what level of transgression I'd committed by shouting at, then slapping the Master Healer. In my opinion, she got what she deserved. But I also knew that my behavior was probably way over the top as far as the Guardians were concerned. Heck, it was over the top for me as well.

I fixed my eyes on the stream, barely visible in the rising moon's light, hoping to prolong the time before I would have to face an angry Eliasser. Or worse, the Master Healer.

Then, a strange thing happened. Without looking, I knew with astonishing clarity who was approaching. Stranger still, I relaxed.

The wizard sat down and crossed his legs. Like quiet tendrils, some essence of him—some energy, for lack of a better word—seemed to work its way through my bruised emotions. The effect was both soothing and familiar. I tried not to think about how intimate it felt.

"Thank you," I said.

"For what?"

I wasn't sure I could put it into words. "I guess . . . for being with me right now. And for not battering me with your eyes the way certain people do."

His only response was a deep sigh.

"On the other hand, you won't look at me at all. Why not?"

He studied the ground, then gently separated fronds of grass. "Do you see the little bug there? It carries its dwelling on its back. When it scurries from blade to blade with—"

"Wait. Does this have anything to do with what I asked you?"

I thought the interruption might put him off, testy as he sometimes was. But he surprised me with a sheepish grin. "No. I was just trying to avoid your question."

Well, well. Did a sense of humor lurk beneath all that solemnity? "I'm not letting you off the hook. Answer my question. Simply, please."

"All right." He threw his hands up. "I *simply* cannot tell you."

"Of course you can't." I laughed at the sheer ridiculousness of my situation. "It's one of those secrets that would make me go crazy, right?"

His brows furrowed as if he'd missed something crucial. "Why is that amusing?"

"It isn't." Then I chuckled some more at the way he scrunched up his face.

"But that is not reasonable," he said. "For every effect there is always a cause."

"Oh yeah? We had quite the giggle-fest on the hill yesterday. I don't recall any particular cause for that."

He was right, though. Something about that handsome face, all puckered and serious, "caused" me to laugh again. And like I'd found the emotional release I needed, I kept laughing. Meanwhile, the man who needed a cause for every effect jammed his lips together, probably to prevent contamination from my groundless hilarity. But in the end he succumbed to the contact-high of contagious laughter. We were winding down when the Master Guardian found us.

"Will you share what is so humorous?" Eliasser asked.

"I'm not sure why we're laughing," I said, "but it feels better than being angry." *Or lonely. Or scared.* My dwindling laughter came to an abrupt halt.

Eliasser pursed his lips. "How curious. Now you are sad."

I sighed. "As I told you before, I need to go home. Your ability to stretch time doesn't make me miss my family any less." At Eliasser's disappointed look, I quickly said, "I'll come back soon. How about the end of next week?"

The wizard slid a glance at Eliasser. "You have not told her?"

I felt my breath catch. "Told me what?"

Eliasser's expression shifted into neutral. "Please ready the portal for Kerrin's return."

The wizard frowned, but left without comment.

"Told me *what?*" I repeated.

Eliasser held my hands. As if the warmth enveloping me wasn't enough, he polished me off with a wonderful smile. Then he lowered the boom. "We need you here every day."

"No! You can't be serious." The lines around his eyes tightened, indicating he was, in fact, quite serious. Well, so was I. "Once a week is all I can manage."

Eliasser shook his head. "That will be insufficient. It is not only your memories which the letter would have imparted to you, but the return of abilities you once possessed. Without them, the Reparention is doomed to failure. We hope to bring you back to your former self, however in order to do so, we will need you here on Amoran for days and weeks at a stretch."

"*Weeks?*" I felt sick just thinking about it. "I can't be gone that long. My kids . . . my family."

"With time-stretching, your absence each day will be a few hours at most. Now," he said, as if it was a done deal, "when can you leave Earth each day so we can anticipate your arrival?"

I intended to argue how impossible it was for me to come that often. Instead, my mouth went on autopilot, babbling my full schedule. "Weekends are out. It would be way too hard to access the portal unnoticed, and even if I could, I'd have to invent a story about where I'd gone. I can get away on Monday, Tuesday, and Wednesday during my lunch hour. I don't work on Thursday or Friday, so I can give you both those days—five hours, maybe six. Would that make up for weekends off?"

I wanted to slap myself silly. I'd just offered him most of my free time.

His eyes lit up. "When can you come next?"

"Monday at noon," I replied, unsure how I would actually pull it off.

Eliasser walked me to the Main Chamber. With a wave of his hand, my Earth clothes materialized in my arms. I was startled at first, but then I wound up laughing. If he could make them travel from my room to the Main Chamber, why not just pop them onto me?

Eliasser tipped his head to one side. "Have I done something funny?"

"No, it's just—" I broke off as the glow in the center of my chest reserved only for him grew so pronounced I couldn't speak. Ambushed by a kind of reverse homesickness, I hugged a surprised Master Guardian, then hurried beneath the portal, where the wizard pressed a necklace into my hand.

"Take the amulet," he whispered, as if I knew what he was referring to. I glanced at the brushed silver pendant with a raised tree of life design, then back at him. Our eyes met, and my body buzzed with that strangely pleasing electricity until the blue misty light lifted me from the Golden Circle.

# Chapter 10

I pushed myself up from the family room floor and staggered into the kitchen. I sorely needed confirmation that the clock in the media player wasn't lying to me, so I checked my cell phone. Wow. It really was only one thirty. I'd spent five days on Amoran when little more than an hour had passed on Earth.

I changed back into my Earth clothes and stashed the tunic, amulet, and wizard's book in my bottom dresser drawer, trying to ignore a queasy sense of duplicity over hiding Amoran from my family. To take my mind off that, I attempted to write. But after ten minutes of staring at a blinking cursor on a field of white, I gave up.

John called when the movie let out. He was stopping at the mall to get Ryan some new pants to replace the ones he'd suddenly outgrown. When John suggested I meet them at the salad bar place for dinner, an invisible band around my rib cage eased. I hadn't realized how anxious I was about facing them. This gave me more time to get a grip.

And that's exactly what I did. I gripped the vacuum cleaner and danced around the house to my favorite cleaning music; coincidently, a Beach Boys CD I'd borrowed from my mother. Nothing like physical activity and off-key singing—mine, not the Beach Boys—to put things in perspective. I continued my housekeeping binge right up until I had to leave. *Perfect,* I thought, as I folded the last of the laundry. I was in a much better frame of mind, the house was as spotless as my house ever gets, and I was definitely ready to let someone else do the cooking.

But when I got to the restaurant, my spirits took a nose-dive. At a booth in the corner, squeezed in next to John, was Wretched Cousin Camryn.

Camryn's campaign to make my life miserable began when we were toddlers and escalated yearly until we were in junior high, when she set her sights on the new boy in town. She'd never forgiven me for "getting to him first," as she wrongly put it, and had spent the last two-plus decades doing her best to undermine our relationship. John and I usually laughed at her silly attempts at flirtation, but I was in no mood for putting up with her crap after all I'd been through the past few days.

I slapped a selection of salads, pasta, and bread onto my plate and sat down across from her.

"Hey 'Cuz," Camryn gushed. "How fortunate I ran into John. He invited me to join you." John's eyebrows poked up and he gave a surreptitious shake of head. "How's that *little* job of yours?" she added in a fake-sweet voice.

"Fine," I said, spearing a chunk of broccoli with unnecessary force. I refused to let her drag me into one of her "my job's better than your job" competitions. She'd referred to my income once as nothing more than "pin money." It was just like Camryn to employ some old-fashioned saying to impress John and his love of clichés and odd turns of speech. I'd looked it up once, although I couldn't recall the exact meaning at the moment. Same with "amulet." I'd have to research that one when I got home. Why had the wizard given it to me? He'd acted like I should know what it was. It must have some purpose, but—

"Kerrin?" John's voice was light with amusement. "Are you on the planet with us?"

"Oh, God," I choked out. "How did you know?"

John's smile faded.

*Okay. That was stupid. Commence damage control.*

I forced a laugh. "I meant to say that I got back a few hours ago."

Ryan snorted. "From Planet of the Ditzoids."

I smiled. "I'm not ditzy, just tired."

"*You're* tired." Camryn's hand flew to her forehead, but unlike Ari, she wasn't doing it to be funny. "Think how tired you'd be if you worked full-time saving lives like I do at the hosp—"

"Ryan!" I cut in. "Tell me about your new pants."

Saving lives, what a joke. Camryn worked in outpatient admissions.

"I didn't get any," Ryan said.

"Why?" I looked at John. "Didn't they have anything in his size?"

"I don't know. When we finished with Kiley, it was time to meet you."

"Kiley! I bought her enough clothes last month for two girls her age." I turned a withering glare on the youngest Scott. "You've got some explaining to do, missy."

She blinked and gave me a helpless shrug. "Dad asked if I needed anything."

I tried to tell Kiley what I thought of her innocent child act, but Camryn talked over me.

"Oh John," she oozed, twirling strands of bottle-blond hair around painstakingly manicured fingers. "It's so wonderful that with all the hours you work, you spend the day with your kids so your wife can write her *little* book. You are *so* lucky, Kerrin." She turned her brittle smile on me, nearly blinding me with her blizzard-white teeth. I was imagining how much damage my fork would do to those perfect veneers as I shoved the tined metal into her mouth, when Eliasser popped into my thoughts. He'd had an unusual reaction to my Camryn stories.

"How terribly sad," he'd said, "that your cousin believes she must take the Love that is meant for others. As if she is not already filled with Love just by being alive. As though the Light would somehow pass her by." And he shook his head like the thought greatly distressed him.

I set my fork down and stared at my plate. I hated to admit that Camryn was right about anything, but I truly was fortunate that John was so supportive of my creative pursuits. But the fact that he worked so many hours? That was all on him. I hadn't wanted him to take this ridiculous job and I'd told him so at the time. As for Camryn? Shoot. I wouldn't really jam my fork into her mouth. I just thought about doing things like that. Which is probably why I like writing so much. Because I can pretend to do things like that. That is, when I manage to sit down and write at all. Which I hadn't done today even though that's what John *thought* I'd been doing. And that made me feel guilty, and—

"Kerrin?" I looked up and met John's eyes. "You were a million miles away. You didn't even notice when Camryn left." John tapped his spoon on the side of his plate. "Are you okay? You've seemed out of it the last couple of days."

*You mean, ever since a certain dwarf dropped in for a visit?*

"Like I said, I'm just tired." Then I hurried to the dessert area to stuff my fibbing face with a Mt. Everest-sized bowl of chocolate pudding topped with lots of snowy whipped cream.

———————

That evening, I coaxed the knots out of my hair while ruminating about the long day I'd had. Long *days*, actually, considering the time I'd spent on Amoran. I mentally ticked off the highlights: I'd almost died, annoyed a dwarf and a wizard for no apparent reason, eaten a magical picnic lunch, sailed a boat using my mind, and slapped the Master Healer.

I am usually a nice person, but I wound up snickering at that memory.

"What are you giggling about?" John slipped his arms around my waist and looked at my reflection in the mirror.

I froze for a second, then continued combing my hair. "The book I'm writing," I lied.

"Great. Sounds like you made good use of the time."

Ulp. "I guess you could say that."

He studied my mirror image. "Did you do something different with your hair?"

The question surprised me. I rarely did anything different with my hair.

"Nope. Same old me."

"Huh. Oh well." John nuzzled my shoulder, then peeked up with a sly grin. His work schedule had been so crazy, we'd not had any significant time alone for several weeks.

I smiled into the mirror and raised my eyebrows up and down.

Instead of the ardent response I expected, John scrunched up his nose.

"What's that look for?" I asked.

"I can't put my finger on it," he said thoughtfully, "but something about you is changed."

I threw the comb down and kissed him as passionately as I could without knocking him over—partly because it had been weeks, and partly because I needed to shut him up. If Amoran had already changed me in some discernable way, I was in big trouble.

More so than I knew. A few seconds into the kiss, my lips began vibrating like I'd stuck them on my electric toothbrush.

"Oh," I groaned, the buzzing sensation nearly intolerable.

John mistook my exclamation for a moan; a sign he should keep going.

He slipped his hand under my shirt.

Beneath his fingers, my skin prickled like pins and needles.

I gasped, unsure what to do, what to think.

John misread that reaction, too. With a seductive chuckle, he kept working his way up. It was all I could do to keep from recoiling as my stunned brain tried to process what was happening.

I never thought the expression "saved by the bell" would mean so much to me, but I was nearing panic mode when his cell phone rang. It was his boss, Steven, with another work crisis.

John clicked off, swore in frustration, gave me a quick kiss, and left. He didn't return home until long after I'd gone to bed.

---

Monday morning, I hunched over my desk at Pierson & Todd, struggling to stay focused on the mini-skyscraper of files rising out of my inbox. It was a lost cause. Anticipation over my lunch hour jaunt to Amoran kept hijacking my mental process. The bit of work I did complete had to be redone, thanks to all the mistakes I made.

"Kerrin?" Dave's voice cut through the fog that used to be my mind.

My eyes drifted to the clock. How had that happened? It was already noon. Forget anticipation, I was going to be late.

"Whatever you need, Dave, can it wait? I've got plans." I fumbled my purse out of the drawer, slung the strap over my shoulder, and rushed toward the door.

"You'll need to cancel them, I'm afraid. Something's come up with the mini-mall developers. Tom's ordering takeout; we'll be working through lunch."

I followed Dave to the meeting room, wishing I had some way to let the Guardians know I wasn't coming.

---

At ten past noon the next day, I stood beneath the portal in my family room. Since I was running late again, I decided to wait till I got to Amoran to change out of my Earth clothes. I tied the tunic pieces around my waist, slipped the amulet over my neck, and tucked it beneath my shirt. According to my folklore book, an amulet was a charm worn to, among other things, ward off evil. I couldn't imagine why the wizard had given it to me. The Guardians didn't strike me as a superstitious bunch, but I figured it wouldn't hurt to wear it for now.

Ready at last, I emptied my mind and inhaled deeply as I reached my hands above my head. Holding my breath, I focused on the portal for several seconds. Then I thought, *Open,* visualizing the result as I exhaled forcefully and brought my arms down with a slight twisting motion.

Ari had said my first few attempts to call the vortex might take me a full minute or two. But as I drew in a breath and lifted my hands a third time, the ceiling vanished, the misty blue light spiraled down, and I was drawn up into the brilliant rainbow tunnel.

My trip through the vortex was without incident. No fierce winds or putrid green energy, just the equivalent of gentle breezes and gorgeous colors. When I landed in the Main Chamber, the wizard was there to greet me. More accurately, to *not* greet me. Without so much as a "hello," he pivoted and stalked off. I lagged behind to put some distance between us as I debated how to handle this recent mood swing of his, especially considering how well we'd gotten along right before I left Amoran last time.

After traipsing down several corridors, he called irritably over his shoulder, "Hurry up. We need to get to the Meeting Room. You are already a day late."

"And a dollar short?" I quipped. Debate over. Sarcasm, it was. "It's great to see you, too! Mostly because of your warm, fuzzy attitude. I feel so welcome! So cared for, so well-liked."

With an impatient flick of his wrist, he opened a doorway, then spun around, green eyes flashing. "You are hard to like right now."

"Yeah, well, you're not exactly my idea of a good time, either."

I brushed past him into a small room with a round table. The wizard took a seat with the other Guardians as Eliasser leapt up, face awash with relief. "Thank the Light. When you did not arrive yesterday, I grew concerned that something had happened to you."

"I'm sorry if I worried you. We had an emergency at work and I couldn't leave."

Danaeus growled out, "The vortex imbalance is bigger than any problem you might have on that insignificant speck of a planet."

What. A. Jerk. "That's my home, you twerp. Show a little respect."

The Master Healer's gray eyes darkened. "Earth is not your home."

"What are you talking about? Of course it is."

She stared me down. "Are you sure?"

And just like that, I wasn't. My knees went so weak, I had to lean on the table for support.

Eliasser gave the Master Healer a hard look, which didn't seem to faze her in the least, as he helped me into a chair. Taking the seat next to me, he reached out, but I waved him off.

"Whatever you have to say, do it without priming me first. I want to hear it straight."

Eliasser hesitated, then withdrew his hands. "I question the wisdom of telling you this now, but the damage has already been done. The Master Healer is correct. Earth is not your original home. You are from Amoran."

His aqua eyes burned with a bright intensity. I wondered if he was waiting for my mental meltdown to begin. In its thankful absence, I developed an advanced case of motor mouth.

"That can't be right. I've spent my whole life on Earth. And I'm pretty sure that up until now, my life hasn't included Amoran. Although," I held a finger up, "there was that vision you showed me, the one with the fairybees and the apple tree, so I guess I must have visited here at some point. I just don't remember visiting, is that right?" Before Eliasser could get a word in, I rambled on. "Unless it's like those people who think they've been abducted by aliens and have blocks of missing time. Except I don't have any missing time, so how could I have memories of being here if I don't remember visiting and I don't have any—"

"Kerrin," Eliasser interrupted. I looked expectantly at him. "The vision I showed you was from your Amoran life. Not a visit you made as an Earth dweller."

Chills rolled through me in waves. "That can't be true. It isn't possible."

"It is possible. And it is true." He sighed. "Long ago, you were forced to leave our world and live on Earth. It was only supposed to be temporary, but then . . ." His voice went thick with emotion. "Then, you had to . . . to remain there for . . ." he faltered to a stop.

I was prepared for how Eliasser pulled my heartstrings, but not for the words that tumbled out of my mouth as a result. "I'm so sorry."

His brows furrowed. "For what are you sorry?"

I wasn't really sure. Somehow, an apology just felt right. "I guess for whatever made you send me away."

"Dear Light! You were not—" He broke off, frowning. "If the Foreseers would allow it, I would tell you the whole truth. Rest assured; you have nothing to be sorry for."

Another round of chills danced up my spine. I *had* been sent away, I could feel it in my bones. I just didn't know why. And as far as having nothing to be sorry for? The way some Guardians treated me put the lie to that statement.

Eliasser worked his way back to a semblance of a smile, then he lifted his hands and wiggled his fingers. I smiled back, but declined the invitation. I was finally getting some honest communication from these people and I wanted to make the most of it. One dose of his lovely, calming energy and I might be less inclined to press for answers.

"Why couldn't I come back?"

Eliasser let his hands drop to his lap. "You had to remain entirely on Earth until the Reparention was close at hand, something we did not know when you departed."

I shook my head. "I have an album full of baby pictures from Earth, and I don't remember living here. Yet you said I left Amoran long ago. *How* long ago?"

"I cannot—"

"A thousand years," the Master Healer exclaimed. "Ten lifetimes."

Eliasser glared at her. "Not another word from you," he thundered.

A thousand years? If that was true, it meant that the vision of the apple tree and the fairybees Eliasser showed me during my first visit happened *more* than a thousand years ago. I glanced around the table at Ari, Danaeus, the wizard, the Master Technician, and his son. I'd supposedly broken one, or more, of their hearts. When I left Amoran. Ten centuries ago.

I leaned forward in my chair and did another visual sweep of the table.

"Exactly how old are all of you?"

What a strange experience it is to be in a room full of people simultaneously holding their breath. A little like wading through the bloated air of an approaching storm. But the arrival of Assistants bearing trays of food allowed the storm, temporarily, to bypass us.

Eliasser's taut face rearranged itself as a young woman set a platter in front of him.

"Thank you for bringing Midday Meal to us, Clarisanna," he said warmly.

"You are most welcome, Master Guardian," she replied with equal warmth. She was strikingly pretty, with teak-colored skin and hair to match that descended from a knot at the top of her head in a cascade of tiny ringlets. I returned the smile she gave me, relieved to discover that not all Assistants were silent or somber, and that someone other than Ari and Eliasser seemed glad to have me around.

The atmosphere in the room transformed as everyone dug into the food. The wizard and the Master Technician conferred about the vortex. The technician's son debated the merits of his new school schedule with Eliasser. Ari and Danaeus argued about who had taken the most turns at "rotation" recently, a concept I found interesting. Mountain residents—including the Guardians—were required to serve in as many capacities as they were capable of during a given period. This included setting up and clearing away the Main Meal Room, restocking supplies in the Healing Room, herb-gathering, and a host of other jobs.

The Master Healer didn't join in the chatter as she picked at her food. Following her lead, I ate my second group meal in Amoran as quietly as I had my first, the conversational hum like soft background music. When I spoke again, I asked a question I assumed was innocuous.

"I need to get the time conversion down so I can come and go from my home without being detected. For instance, I can only be gone for one Earth hour today. How long does that net me on Amoran with time-stretching?"

"That requires an explanation," the Master Technician replied. "Regaining your abilities will take some doing, so we are pushing time-stretching to the limit. This places a great strain on the normal time continuum—indeed, even to time-stretching itself—but we have no other choice." He smiled. "To answer your question, you have five days to spend here during this visit."

"Five days? That's pretty impressive." I shook my head in amazement, thinking of all the mothers I knew who would love access to that kind of magic. "And you're certain I can count on this? I won't leave Amoran one day, thinking I'm still on my lunch hour, only to have it be two Earth days later when I arrive?"

The eyes of the Master Healer riveted on me.

"You'd never get back that late," Ari said.

I didn't miss the qualifier. "What aren't you telling me, Elf-boy?"

Eliasser adopted the most adorable, confused expression. "Elf-boy?"

Ari smiled and shrugged it off. "It's extremely rare, but time, as expressed through the vortex, can jump forward a little more than expected."

I was slogging through a qualifier quagmire. "Care to be a *little more* specific?"

The Master Healer kept staring at me. On impulse, I met her scrutiny head-on.

"No more than an hour late," Ari said. "An un-stretched Earth hour, that is."

"An hour! That could be a problem if I land in my family room at the wrong time." The Master Healer's expression went stony. I sensed I'd touched a nerve and decided to follow a hunch. "Are you sure time has never skipped forward more than that? Like weeks? Or months?"

A flicker of fear disturbed her composure before she broke eye contact.

Eliasser assured me that time rarely moved forward, and never so drastically. But I knew differently, and so did the Master Healer. While the specific memory eluded me, I felt certain that time had leapt wildly out of bounds once, and with disastrous consequences.

I didn't need to dig deep to trust my instincts. She avoided my eyes for the rest of the meal.

# Chapter 11

When the remnants of Midday Meal were carted away, the discussion turned to other matters. It was time to gather *nemestes*, the Master Healer informed everyone. This clearly wasn't something they looked forward to, as the proclamation was met with varying degrees of moans and groans. Even Eliasser grimaced.

The Master Technician announced that the vortex was stable, enabling him to make some long overdue adjustments to the energy signatures—whatever they were.

Tomorrow's practice—what kind of practice was never disclosed to me—would be delayed an hour as the adjustments needed to "set."

The meeting dragged on covering more topics I knew nothing about. After it ended, I stood in the corridor with Ari, Danaeus, the Master Technician and his son as they discussed a game they loved. This group was full of surprises. I would never have pegged them for sports nuts.

"Come join us," Ari said. "Garrammon is loads of fun. We can teach you in no time."

I eyed him with disbelief. "You haven't spied on me that much in my Earth life, or you'd know I'm not athletically inclined."

"I wish the wizard would play with us again," the son of the technician said.

"I do as well," his father agreed. "It is not like him to turn down Garrammon without good reason. He is changed of late, and not for the better, I fear."

"He's different now?" I asked.

"Oh, yes," the boy answered. He seemed to have reconciled his initial dislike of me. "He is usually much happier, and he is the best Garrammon player there ever was. But he keeps to himself now, ever since—" The boy broke off, red blotches dotting his face.

I didn't need to be a mind reader to complete his sentence. *Ever since you came.*

The wizard entered the passageway and tapped Ari on the forearm. "They need you."

Ari rolled his eyes and went back into the room.

"There goes our game," Danaeus grumbled. "Unless you are available." He looked hopefully at the wizard.

"Please?" the boy said. "We need a fourth."

"Why not ask our *visitor* to play," the wizard said, coating the word with disdain.

I laughed. "Ooh. Ouchie. Was that supposed to hurt my feelings, Wiz-brat? According to Eliasser, I'm no more a visitor than you are."

"Then Garrammon should appeal to you." His even tone was full of challenge.

"And if it doesn't?"

His silent smirking said it all. I didn't know why he had a problem with me, but I wasn't going to waste my energy trying to figure it out.

"Just to set the record straight, I have no interest in playing Garrammon. Draw from that whatever conclusion you like." I spun on my heel to leave, but my hair-flip and exaggerated saunter were upstaged by Ari, who ran out of the room yelling about energy disruptions. Like racehorses at the starting gun, the Guardians in the hallway bolted down the corridor.

"Hey! What about me?" I called after them.

They disappeared around the bend without a backwards glance.

I peeked in the room. Eliasser and the Master Healer were nowhere in sight.

That was odd. I hadn't seen them leave.

I leaned against the corridor wall and considered my options. I should probably wait for the Guardians to return, but I was bored from the meeting, irritated by the wizard's attitude, and restless to be doing something other than sitting idle. One small problem. I didn't know where in the Mountain complex I was. Haphazard wandering could get me hopelessly lost. I'd already gone that route in the forest.

The forest! There was an idea. I'd love to visit the pink lady again, maybe ask her a few questions about the promise I'd made, and what she meant by keys and treasure. But in this maze of look-alike tunnels, how was I going to find the Forest Portal?

As if it heard and obeyed, the floor emitted a faint glow in swirling shades of orange. I stared at the amorphous shapes formed by the moving colors. Had I somehow triggered the "road map" Eliasser told me about? But the patterns seemed so random.

I bent down and ran my hand over a section of stone. Nothing changed.

I thought about my experience piloting the mindsail and opening doorways. The common thread seemed to be intention. Or motivation. Maybe both. Either way, it was worth a try.

I pictured the grassy clearing and wished with all my being to be in the forest. To my delight, the orange shapes billowed forward, pulsing in sequence, moving in the opposite direction from the one taken by the Guardians. Kind of like arrows pointing the way.

Excited by my progress, I followed the "arrows" from one corridor to the next until the pulsing ceased halfway down a narrow passageway. Assuming I'd been led to the Forest Portal, I used the same technique Ari taught me for opening doorways. Success!

Once inside the bland, small room, I conceded the greater difficulty lay in activating the portal itself. As best I could recall, I reproduced the hand movements Eliasser employed on our previous visit to the forest. Nothing happened. Then I tried the method for opening the vortex portals. The room stayed just as it was. Frustrated to be so close, and yet so far, I waved my hands around like an idiot, shouting, "Open! Open!"

I got nowhere. I was about to give up, when I thought once more about piloting the mindsail, opening the vortex portals, and how and when the "road map" appeared. In every instance, I'd used a quiet determination to achieve a positive result. In my impatience now to get going, was I trying too hard? Striving? Struggling?

I took a deep breath, stilled my body, calmed my emotions, and filled my mind and heart with how much I wanted to be in the forest. Then, making a small S-shaped wave of my hand, I exhaled while thinking *open*. The room disappeared and I was standing in the forest.

I did a little victory dance, then set out to find the pink lady's home. About a hundred yards past the waterfall, I stopped and looked around. The trees, the side trails, even the color of the sky seemed different than when I was here last. Maybe this wasn't such a good idea after all. On the other hand, everything had worked out okay before. And even if I didn't find the clearing, being in the forest was a treat in itself.

Having convinced myself to stay, I continued on. Every so often, I turned around, hoping to find my way blocked by a pair of massive trees. But I was disappointed in that regard, and as time went on, I became concerned about Eliasser's reaction when he realized I was missing. Figuring I'd already worried him enough for one day, I about-faced and headed back.

That's when I spied the towering trees I'd been looking for. Instead of straddling the path, as they had on my first visit to the forest, they now grew alongside it. And I'd passed this way moments ago, but with no leafy giants in attendance. The gap between the trees was wider today and I passed through the opening with ease. Sighing with contentment, I strolled to the center and sat down on grass as soft as bunny fur.

The next thing I knew, I was being gently "willed" awake. I pushed myself up and gazed into eyes that beheld me with amusement.

"We are not often visited by those whose greatest need is sleep," the misty pink woman said.

"I'm sorry. I must have been more tired than I realized. I didn't mean to take a nap."

"Your body must acclimate to much now. Rest is necessary."

Another ethereal woman, this one in shimmering yellow, wafted through the leaf-rimmed opening and joined her pink counterpart. They floated before me, a few inches off the ground.

"We offer assistance, Daughter," they said in unison. "You have questions?"

At last, some answers. "I do. For starters, why did you just call me Daughter?"

"You will know that in time," the yellow one said.

Uh-oh. More frustrating ambiguity.

I tried again. "Who are you?"

"We are the Foreseers."

Now I was getting somewhere. If I understood Eliasser correctly, the Foreseers were the ones who decided how much I could be told.

I glanced around the clearing. "Where am I?"

It was the pink one's turn to respond. "You are in the Glen of the Foreseers."

They hovered, watching me. All the pressing things I'd wanted to know were pushed aside by something I hadn't intended to say. "I haven't told anyone I've been here."

"No, you have not," the yellow Foreseer agreed.

That made me smile. I liked the way they phrased things. Simple and to the point.

"I want to keep visiting you, yet I don't know if it's okay, or why I feel compelled to keep it a secret."

They studied me, but with such kindness, I didn't mind the prolonged eye contact. Contrary to the painful probing of certain Guardians, it felt great.

"Search your heart," the pink Foreseer commanded, and she rose several feet into the air.

It was my turn to study them, as I contemplated their request.

The yellow Foreseer asked, "Why, when asked to search your heart, do you look to us?"

"Because," I whispered, awed by the gentle power they exuded, "I think you know my heart better than I do and I'd like to know why."

She smiled. "Dear one, you need only to remember who you are; then, you will provide your own answers." They glided backwards. "Come as often as you wish, Daughter. You will know when to share this Truth." And they disappeared through the opening.

I left the Glen, retraced my steps along the path, and activated the Forest Portal. Back at the Mountain, I exited the portal room and touched the corridor floor. Picturing my quarters, I again wished with all my being to be there. Like a magical GPS, the "arrows" appeared and led me to my room.

Pleased with myself, I opened my doorway—and walked straight into Vianna. *Busted.* I wanted to keep my visit to the Foreseers' Glen a secret until I knew "when to share this truth," as they put it. Never good at lying, I was struggling to invent a story to explain where I'd been, when Vianna took the problem out of my hands.

"I am relieved that you have finally returned from your meeting with the Guardians. You are overdue for your midday potion."

Was it possible she didn't know about the energy issue that caused the Guardians to leave me on my own after the meeting? That could work in my favor.

"Be advised," she continued. "These stabilizing drafts must be consumed throughout the day while you are on Amoran." She thrust the goblet at me. "They will keep you from . . . from . . ."

"Freaking out?" Her brows knit together, and I couldn't help smiling. "Never mind. I get it."

I accepted the cup of sour, smelly stuff, held my nose, and gulped the entire contents. *Ack!*

Vianna claimed the empty goblet and left my room, still under the impression I'd been with the Guardians for the past several hours. At Evening Meal, I learned that Eliasser assumed I'd been under Vianna's care during the same period.

I hadn't corrected either of them.

---

The disruption in the vortex was benign, but time-consuming, which was good news for me. For the next two days, it kept the Guardians busy, allowing me to sneak away and visit the Foreseers every morning and afternoon. I loved my time with them. With great patience, they answered what questions they could, and offered me a level of acceptance I'd found nowhere else beneath the Mountain. I did wonder if they were stuffing information directly into my mind while I slept, as I felt compelled to take a nap the minute I arrived in the Glen. When I woke up, I felt stronger, more alert, and more receptive. I asked them about it, but they just smiled.

The Guardians wouldn't tell me what my part in helping save the vortex was or why we had to wait two months to do it. I didn't understand the long lead time, but even the Foreseers wouldn't touch the subject of my role or the due date.

I discovered another bonus to the freedom provided by the Guardians' preoccupation with the vortex. In my Earth life, time to myself was a rare and precious commodity. I had all I could do to take care of my family, my job, and the many volunteer assignments that went along with kids and their activities. But on Amoran? I was three days into my lunch hour trip, and I had two more time-stretched days to go. Back on Earth, where no one knew I was gone, they had no reason to miss me during those sixty minutes. Meanwhile, I got to take a vacation on an amazing planet for *five days!* I was beginning to see an upside to this scenario.

The downsides? My family might not miss me, but I missed them, the ache only partly mitigated by the novelty of Amoran. Then there were the potions. They were godawful, and made me feel sick and dizzy. Last, but definitely not least—my mental health. What was happening to me was so unbelievable, I couldn't rule out that I'd simply lost my mind.

Right as the vortex issue was resolving, I had another one of those painful brain episodes that would have turned Eliasser's hair white if it wasn't already the color of fresh snow. I dissuaded him from assigning Vianna to watch over me that night by swallowing my potions and promising to go right to bed. He finally agreed, but only because these potions contained a soporific that would ensure I slept until late morning.

But I didn't sleep in the next day. In fact, I woke earlier than usual. I'm not sure how I knew that; there were no clocks beneath the Mountain. Yet I felt certain enough to risk a quick trip to the Forest. It would probably be my last time with the Foreseers for a while, since the Guardians would no longer be tied up all day with the vortex.

I was halfway to the Forest Portal when I heard a group of Assistants approaching from a side corridor. To avoid being seen, I made a U-turn and blundered down several passageways. By the time I stopped, I'd lost track of where I was. I looked to the magical GPS in the floor, but the patterns were barely visible and there were no pulsing arrows to get me back on course. As I wandered aimlessly, debating what to do, a doorway opened up ahead. The wizard moved into the hall followed by a line of children. A little boy said something and the wizard responded with that silvery laugh of his. I marveled at how happy and carefree he seemed—until he saw me, and his expression froze so fast I thought his face would crack.

"What are you doing here, Kerrin?" he demanded.

Meilee, the red-haired girl I'd met the other day, looked confused.

"But I thought her name was—"

"Silence!" the wizard barked.

"—different," she finished, looking from her teacher's angry face to my smirking one.

I was working up a suitable retort for him, when the Master Healer spoke from behind me.

"Meilee. You have been told this Guardian's name?" She inflected the sentence as a question, but her tone made it a statement of indisputable fact.

"Yes," the girl grudgingly acknowledged.

"And what is it?"

She sighed. "Kerrin."

"Then, 'Kerrin' is what you will call her."

Maybe it was witnessing the wizard go from mirth to misery at the sight of me that pushed me over the edge, but I couldn't resist stepping in. What had Meilee done wrong? For that matter, what terrible transgression had I committed?

"Do you know me by another name?" I asked the girl.

"No," she admitted, "but I—"

"Do not interfere with my students," the wizard exploded.

I had fun pretending he didn't exist. "Meilee, is there a name you wish to call me instead?"

"Oh yes," Meilee exclaimed. "I have dreamt about you since you last came by. You were shining like a fountain of light, and the vortex grew arms and folded those arms around you, and you blended with the colors inside and became a rainbow."

The wizard and the Master Healer traded an alarmed look.

*Nyah, nyah,* I thought.

"And what has that to do with my name, Meilee?"

"There is a word in the ancient language of the elves that means 'ribbon of light.' That is what you reminded me of in my dream. If you will allow it, I would like to call you Marrahnae."

It had a familiar ring to it, but I wasn't sure why. "Well, Meilee, I have it on good authority from the Master Guardian that names are highly personal. Therefore, *I* will decide what people call me. And you have my permission to call me Marrahnae."

The Master Healer had moved to my side during this exchange. She was hard to read, yet I had the impression she secretly enjoyed my boldness. Good. I wasn't through. It was Mr. Wizard's payback moment for being such a snot.

"One more thing, Meilee. Never be afraid to challenge an old idea with a new one. A good teacher will always welcome questions, no matter how many you need to ask."

I strolled past the wizard, whose face had so many emotions battling for time that I laughed out loud at him. I'd almost escaped around the corner when the Master Healer called my name—my Earth name, of course. I turned and stared defiantly at the short, squat woman, who observed me through eyes that were little slits.

"Where are you going?" she asked.

"The forest," I said, before I could censor myself.

The narrowed eyes appraised me. "On your own? Interesting. Why?"

"That should be obvious. It gets me away from you."

A sea of open mouths, including the wizard's, followed my barb.

But the Master Healer smiled. Weaving around the children, she made her way to me.

"We will walk together now, but not to the forest. I have something else in mind."

She clamped a hand on my elbow and didn't let go until we were in the Main Chamber, in front of the blank wall where it seemed to me an eighth passageway should be.

"Open it," she said, pointing at the wall.

"Excuse me?"

"Was the request unclear?"

"No, but the requester is. How do you expect me to open it, whatever it is?"

"You propelled the mindsail. You have accessed the forest on your own. You should have no trouble with this. Open it. Now."

I wasn't surprised that she would test me, but by how badly I wanted to pass. I looked from her storm-gray eyes back to the wall, wondering if this was another portal. I'd refined my technique with the Forest Portal, perhaps this one was similar. With an S-shaped wave of my right hand, I simultaneously imagined an open door and the feeling of "open."

When the wall before me vanished, I forgot that I'd been trying to impress her. Through a rounded archway was the most beautiful garden I had ever seen.

# CHAPTER 12

I followed the central pathway to a three-tiered fountain, stepped up onto the wide stone ledge that surrounded it, and walked the circumference, dazedly drinking in the splendor. Like my initial reaction to the forest, there was so much to see I couldn't take it all in at once. Cranberry-colored vines crawled up latticework trellises, then wound their way through ivory bushes as tall as me. Shrubs that looked like topiary creations sprouted pink flowers on alternating rings of burnt orange and rich cream. Light purple blossoms spilled over each level of the fountain. I pulled off a sprig and sniffed; a scent resembling gardenia perfumed my sinuses.

Tucking the sprig behind my ear, I hopped down and took the path to the right. The topography was basically flat, although the path looped back on itself several times, much like a switchback on a mountain trail. I'd assumed the portal had beamed me somewhere far-flung, like the forest. But one of the switchbacks traveled close to a wall before the path turned sharply away again. The wall curved upward, its sandy-yellow color transitioning to eggshell, and then to blue. Craning my neck, it seemed it was the sky I was looking at, but it grew so naturally out of the wall that I wasn't sure if it was an illusion or if I was really outside.

I made a quick circle of the garden, then set out again at a more leisurely pace. A little way past the fountain, I stopped to study a narrow flowerbed of what looked like roses, although the few blooms in evidence were tiny and without fragrance.

When I turned around, the Master Guardian was sitting on a bench behind me.

"Where did you come from?" I asked. "That seat was empty a moment ago."

He patted the space beside him and smiled. "How do you like the garden?"

I refrained from taking issue with the unanswered question and sat down. "It's lovely. The flowers are . . . well, I don't have words right now. Heavenly comes to mind. And is someone experimenting with different kinds of grass?"

"That would be a project of our Master Technician and his son. Did you see the patch with alternating blocks of color?"

I glanced down the path to our right. "Yes. The one like a chessboard. But I don't think I would have chosen purple and pink for the squares."

"Should I change the colors?" a third voice asked.

I turned back, surprised to see the Master Technician. Where had *he* come from so fast?

"I am open to suggestions," he added, eyes twinkling. His irises were a unique shade of silvery-gray.

I laughed. "You won't want my opinion on anything to do with gardening or aesthetics. But like a lot of critics, I know what I don't like."

"That would be a place to start. My son and I—"

"Andreissen!" The name burst out of me. My head throbbed and my throat began to close. "But . . . but . . . we call him Anders. And you are . . . you are . . ."

I sucked at the air like a fish out of water as the garden went black.

---

I came to with the Master Healer leaning over me. Her eyes immediately locked on mine. Searching. Probing.

I winced. "Must you?"

"Yes." The Master Healer pulled back, then addressed Eliasser. "She is fine."

"Says you," I snapped.

Eliasser helped me to sit up. It was just the three of us now; the Master Technician was gone. I was so irritated with the Master Healer, that when Eliasser handed me a goblet of brown, foul-smelling gunk, I shook my head.

"I won't drink that, even if it's a miracle migraine cure. On Earth, we try to keep our kids off drugs. Then I come to Amoran where I'm forced to down unrecognizable substances with no better explanation than a nebulous promise that it's for my good."

Eliasser searched my eyes, albeit more gently than the Master Healer had. "You do not trust me," he said, shoulders sagging as if weighed down by the realization.

"Don't take it personally. I'm not sure I trust myself anymore."

His mouth tightened into a thin line. I was trying to come to terms with how profoundly he affected me, especially the part of me that wanted to chug the gelatinous gunk for his sake alone. Yet it was that desire to give myself over to him that scared me more than anything else. It was so unlike me, it was no wonder I didn't trust myself.

"I'm sorry," I said with quiet determination. "But I won't drink that without a good reason."

Eliasser glanced sideways at the Master Healer. She had her back to us as she bent over to pinch off a few spent flowers from one of the rose bushes. "You know how I feel about this matter," she said, as though he had voiced a question aloud.

Eliasser's drooping shoulders lifted with a deep sigh. "I will give you a reason, but only if you promise to consume this when I am through."

"Fair enough."

"All right. Imagine that your unrecalled memories are confined behind a gate, one that is stuck shut. When something forces the gate to open, a memory is freed. The gate then swings back and is once again stuck. However, since the gate has opened once, it will open more easily the next time. And so, with every memory released, the gate loosens a little more."

"In my case, that's a good thing, right?"

"True, except that this gate can also swing inward, allowing the ambient energy of Amoran to flood your consciousness. Your body and mind, designed for the vibrational field of Earth, can become overwhelmed. This will help prevent that."

He held the cup out again, but I shook my head. I wasn't about to accept his incomplete answer as payment in full for my question. I sensed there was more.

"The whole truth, Eliasser."

I didn't know if the Master Healer's grunt was one of approval or disapproval. I kept my gaze fixed on the Master Guardian. With the exception of his face paling slightly, nothing happened for a few moments. Then, he placed the goblet on the ground, clasped his hands together and stared down into the murky liquid.

"The rapid influx of Amoran energy can create an accumulation of concentrated power deep within the psyche. The potency of this is so intense that a person's brain will struggle to regain its equilibrium, damaging itself in the process. These potions provide the most reliable protection against this. They are designed to rapidly infiltrate your cells with the least disruption to your Earth body."

He picked up the goblet and swirled the contents.

"But the remedies themselves are not without danger. Some will enhance your ability to receive more Amoran energy while suppressing that same energy so you do not receive too much, too soon. Others will keep you from remembering too quickly even as they widen the pathways for more memories to surface—all with the goal of keeping your energy balanced."

I couldn't believe what I was hearing. "That's your idea of balance? Potions that send me in opposite directions at the same time? That's insane."

"No," he said, his bleak expression testament to the severity of what he was saying. "Insane is what you will become without them. We call it *pentuma.* Your brain essentially tears itself apart in an attempt to achieve balance. There is little, if any, warning. Caught quickly—meaning within minutes—there is some hope of recovery. If not, death occurs so fast that at least you would not suffer too long."

I could barely draw breath from the tightness in my chest. What had I gotten myself into? Was I already pentuma? What if I really *had* lost my mind? Is that where this world came from? What if . . . instead of sitting on a bench on another world, I was actually confined to a padded room, pumped full of antipsychotics, unaware that—

"Kerrin?" Eliasser's voice brought me back to reality. At least I think it was reality. "Are you all right?"

"God help me, no," I exhaled. "I need to know I'm not already insane. I need some control over what's happening to me. Damn it, I didn't choose any of this!"

"You are always in control," the Master Healer said in her dispassionate way. "And you always have a choice."

"Do I?" Her flat assurance grated. "What if I leave Amoran and never return? Does my ability to choose reach that far?"

There was a sharp intake of air behind me. I swung around to find the wizard gaping in disbelief. Where the hell had *he* come from?

"Yes," the Master Healer said. "Your ability to choose includes choosing not to, although I caution you to think carefully before making your decision. Search your heart with great diligence. Be certain of your reasons or you will live with regret—not the most desirable teacher." And with that, she disappeared down the path.

How could I know for certain what the right choice was? Who could I trust, especially if I no longer trusted myself?

"I need time to think," I said to Eliasser. "Can I stay in the garden for a while? Alone?"

He offered me the goblet. "Provided you drink this."

I could only choke down half of the gloppy, salty potion in one sitting. Eliasser agreed to leave as long as I promised to finish the rest. Once he was gone, I breathed a sigh of relief.

Until the wizard plunked down next to me.

"Get lost," I grumbled. "I don't need a child-watcher."

"I know. I just want to sit here with you."

"Why? You don't seem to like me, and I can't say I'm thrilled with you either."

I got up and headed down the path to put some distance between us, stopping occasionally to study an unusual flower. The wizard shadowed me, but so discreetly, I easily ignored him.

Halfway around the garden, a blue and yellow bird about the size of a crow swooped down and perched on a bush in front of me.

"Hey, bird," I whispered. "Got any advice for someone who's trying her best not to go pentuma?" As if in answer, the bird trilled the most beautiful song.

*Well. If I have made this world up, at least I'm a positive sort of lunatic.*

"I have not heard a *papayen* sing in many years," the wizard said, his voice soft with wonder as he came to stand beside me.

"Is it a good omen?" I asked, surprised that his presence no longer bothered me.

"We are not much for omens, here. It is a good thing, certainly. They only sing when they have something important to say."

"You're joking."

"I never joke."

That *didn't* surprise me. "Hmm. I asked it if it had any advice for me."

"Then you should pay attention to what it tells you."

And I worried that *I* was a nutcase.

When the song finished, I, who joke as often as I can, bowed and addressed the warbler.

"Thank you for sharing your wisdom with me. I will take it under advisement."

The bird flew to my shoulder and trilled a few more notes.

"Oh . . . my," the wizard said. "That is quite unusual." He reached out tentatively, and the bird hopped onto his hand. "Amazing. I have never seen a bird do such a thing."

The papayen deposited the end result of its lunch on the wizard's sleeve and took off.

"Hah! I've definitely seen a bird do that," I said, and we both laughed.

With the ice wall between us melted, we completed the circuit of the garden. The wizard explained various plants along the way, but preoccupied by my own thoughts, I was only half-listening until he said, ". . . and there are many more varieties of rainbow plant, although not in this garden. I am not much of an expert on them; it is Balthasarre—*Oh no!*"

The poor guy looked like he'd stuck his finger in a socket as he scanned my face for signs of mental collapse. But I was thrilled to learn the Master Technician's real name, even if I was headed for another blackout—or worse, pentuma.

"Balthasarre. Thank you. I almost had his name earlier before my brain fried."

The wizard squeezed his eyes shut. Guessing him to be something of a perfectionist, I figured this slip must be hard on him.

"I won't tell anyone," I said. "It can be our little secret."

"That will not be possible. She will know the minute she sees us that I have erred."

He had to be talking about the Master Healer. "What'll she do, ground you?" He seemed baffled, so I explained. "It's an Earth expression that means—wait a minute." I grabbed his arm. "Nothing happened when I heard Balthasarre's name. I feel fine. In fact, I feel great. No dizziness, no mind-splitting headache. That good news should soften the blow."

He frowned. "There is always the possibility of a delayed reaction."

"Geez. Are you always this upbeat?" Judging by his wrinkled brow, I'd confused him again. "Never mind. Trust me, I'm fine." I clicked my heels in the air to prove my point, after which he insisted I show him how to do it. He had trouble coordinating the part where you lift off on one foot, but when we reached the fountain, he had it down. We exited the garden, chatting about plants and potions, which should have jogged my memory about the unfinished goblet of goo I'd left behind.

The Master Healer stood at attention just outside the Garden Portal. She glanced at the wizard, shook her head in disgust, then pointed at one of the corridors. He trudged off.

As soon as he disappeared from view, the Master Healer pulled me toward to the Golden Circle and handed me my Earth clothes.

"Wait. This is a lunchtime visit. I should have another day or two day left."

Her face was inscrutable. "If I understood you correctly, you wish to exercise your *control* and go back to Earth, to *choose* whether you will ever return."

Was that really what I'd meant to do? Funny, I didn't feel like I was the one in control.

"Where is Eliasser?" I asked, suppressing a sudden tremble in my voice.

Her mask didn't budge. "He could not bear to watch you leave us—again."

She might as well have ripped out my heart and crushed it with her foot.

I turned my back on her to call the vortex. I knew the Master Healer had chosen her words to provoke a reaction from me. I wasn't about to let her see my face and give her the satisfaction of knowing how well she'd succeeded.

# CHAPTER 13

I recovered from the Master Healer's blatant attempt to upset me by the time I reached my family room. I collapsed onto the couch and stared out the picture window, absorbing the sights and sounds familiar to me. I heard my neighbor mowing her lawn. Thanks to our bizarre weather lately, it hadn't been consistently cold enough to stop the grass from growing. The whistle of a freight train punctuated the mower's buzzing. A bird lighted on the oak tree in my backyard and began to sing. It was such a fairy-tale cliché that I smiled. Regardless of the Master Healer's contention, Earth *was* my home. I would return to work and spend the next few days pretending Amoran didn't exist, and was, in fact, a figment of my imagination. How I felt after that would determine for me whether I ever returned.

I didn't realize what a challenge I'd set for myself until I got back to the office and tried to concentrate on my files. That other world—the one that wasn't real—kept intruding into my thoughts. It was a miracle I made it through the afternoon without royally screwing up.

But I didn't fare any better at home. As I folded towels, warm and fluffy from the dryer, I caught myself wondering how they did the laundry beneath the Mountain before reminding myself that Amoran was a delusion.

I wondered about something else when I found one of my favorite snack dishes in the trash. Was I really that distracted that it wound up there instead of the dishwasher? The color of the aqua plate reminded me of Eliasser's eyes. I tried to imagine where he was right now. Was it nighttime in the Guardian Sanctuary?

*Where, Kerrin? The place that doesn't exist? The person who isn't real?*

Swallowing the lump in my throat, I dumped the salad I'd just made down the garbage disposal before catching my mistake.

Ryan walked by and congratulated me.

"Way to go, Mom. That's the only good place for vegetables."

———————

I woke up shivering in the middle of the night and snuggled closer to John.

"You're ice cold," he said sleepily. "Are you all right?"

"I don't know. I can't seem to warm up."

He wrapped himself around me and stroked my hair, murmuring that everything was okay. The chills left me, but John didn't abandon his warming effort. He walked his fingers up to the open neck of my nightshirt, pausing along the way at a few choice areas.

I was definitely warmer now. Downright toasty in places that had not seen a lot of action lately. "Mmmm," I said, making the same sound I do when presented with chocolate chip cookies straight from the oven.

John chuckled, then started what promised to be a long, lingering kiss.

My lips buzzed with a sharp, discordant energy, far worse than what I'd experienced on Saturday night. I tried not to flinch, but when John reached inside my nightshirt, the touch of his fingers on my bare skin was like sandpaper. Then came that odd pins and needles sensation. I cringed and pulled away, muttering that I must be coming down with something. John said he understood, but there was an uncertainty in his voice I'd never heard before.

———————

I slept late the next morning. John was already gone, and the kids were downstairs arguing as they made their breakfast. Groggy, I stared into the bathroom mirror at my pale reflection and the dark circles beneath my eyes. *Guess I really am coming down with something.*

I was so exhausted by the time the kids left for school that I called in sick to work. I stumbled to the kitchen and tried to make a cup of tea, but I couldn't lift the teakettle after filling it with water. It wasn't until my legs began to shake and my breathing came in ragged gulps that I finally remembered the potion I'd neglected to finish back in the garden on Amoran.

*Oh, God. What have I done?*

With what little strength I had left, I dragged myself to the family room, then collapsed on the floor. I lay there, convulsing with chills, unable to call the vortex, certain I was dying.

I thought I was hallucinating when Ari's face appeared, floating in a cloud of blue mist.

"Hang on, Kerrin. I'll have you home soon."

*Home.* I closed my eyes and sank into frigid darkness.

---

I roused a bit, and recognized the Healing Room by its pinkish-gray walls. Eliasser sat in a chair beside my healing stone, his gaze directed behind me. "Warm the covers. Make the *firenosse* elixir a double batch. We will need it before the night is through."

He lowered his eyes, and seemed surprised that mine were open. "Kerrin?" But winter tightened its grip and stole me away from him.

My next window of consciousness arrived. Eliasser was still at my side, staring vacantly at the floor. I wanted to get his attention, but I couldn't move. All I could do was watch him. Not that that was a chore. I'd followed the Master Healer's advice as I lay on the floor of my family room, believing I was about to perish. It had not taken long for me to search my heart and make the appropriate choice. If I lived, I would help the Guardians fix their vortex. But not for any heroic reason.

Eliasser lifted his head, and the smile that lit up his face when he saw that I was awake filled me with a giddy happiness.

"Can you speak yet?" he asked.

I could only manage a slight shake of my head.

"Then do not try. Are you warm enough?"

My body felt like it was wrapped in ice. I shook my head again.

Eliasser held my hands, and I grew slowly warmer as his energy worked its magic.

"We nearly lost you again." He shook his head as if he couldn't quite believe it had almost happened a second time. "Ari found the half-filled goblet you left behind in the garden. He rushed to Earth without consulting the rest of us. And thank the Light he did. You needed the full amount of that potion to stabilize your energy. Without it, your Life Force was slowly being cut off and could not sustain your Earth body." Eliasser sighed. "Ari barely got to you in time. But at least it was not pentuma, in which case, he would have been too late."

I vowed then and there to never again reject my potions.

Eliasser regarded me for a moment. "I understand from Ashara that you had a certain intention when you last left for Earth. If you need more time to decide whether you will join us in the Reparention, we can return you to Earth as soon as you are well."

I struggled to open my mouth, but he held a finger to my lips. "You must rest now."

---

As soon as I could talk, I told Eliasser I didn't need any more time to decide. Whatever it involved, I would do my part in the Reparention.

Giving me one of his incredible smiles, he asked what had convinced me to stay.

"Not what, who," I whispered, my eyes suddenly moist. "I don't understand why, but my heart is so filled with love for you, it's like you are a part of me."

As true as that last part was, I hadn't meant to voice it out loud. And I probably shouldn't have, considering the way Eliasser's cheeks tinged with red. But he didn't say anything. Afraid I'd embarrassed him, and uncomfortable myself, I pretended to find the ceiling extra fascinating.

---

It took several days before I was well enough to be released from the Healing Room. Since I'd called in sick to work, no one would be expecting me until mid-afternoon on Earth. With time-stretching, this gave me three and a half weeks to spend on Amoran. Eliasser said it would take nearly that long for me to recuperate fully from my ordeal. Then, he added with obvious pleasure, I could attend the Guardians' daily meetings. If I was up to it, I would even be allowed to participate in "practice."

I still didn't know what they practiced, but I was in no hurry to learn or attend more of their meetings. Especially now. Maybe it was a side effect of my most recent brush with death, but my thinking was as fuzzy as when I'd pulled all-nighters in college. And the memories that were supposed to keep surfacing seemed even more repressed. Yet, one thing had ramped up. My emotional radar was working double-time. As if I could read their feelings, I sensed a growing discontent among the Guardians, but I couldn't pin down what it was about.

Discontent was nothing new where the wizard was concerned. He'd gone back to treating me as a nonentity—on good days. The rest of the time he gave snide a whole new meaning.

One morning, as I approached a meeting room, I overheard two male Assistants discussing me. I flattened myself against the corridor wall outside the open doorway to eavesdrop.

". . . And that is not all," one of them was saying. "I heard they are no longer certain her body will withstand the vortex energy at the crucial moment."

"I thought the transforming of an Earth body was impossible any-way."

*Transforming? Into what?*

"That is true. But there is no other choice, because of who she is," the first Assistant said.

"But is it really her? She looks the same, yet she has none of the required skills or abilities. Even he seems to think—"

"Shh! Here he comes."

I didn't have to guess who *he* was. The next voice I heard was the wizard's.

———————

My growing friendship with Ari and my secret meetings with the Foreseers helped me to deal with the troubling undercurrents. Eliasser was being quite protective of me now. In order to secure his permission for my daily visit to the woods, I borrowed one of my daughter's "grind 'em down" techniques. Waiting until he was thoroughly distracted with a problem, I squeaky-wheeled the poor man until he gave in, admitting there was a way he could ensure my well-being while I was in the forest. When I asked him how, he said he couldn't tell me, then hurried from the room.

*Gee, there's a new wrinkle,* I thought. *Something I can't be told.*

The Foreseers had quite an agenda for our time together. Among other things, they were teaching me a series of meditations to open up what they referred to as the seven main energy centers in the body. Then I would learn the final meditation to combine the centers into one "energetic whole." According to the Foreseers, this was important to the task I would need to perform during the Reparention. When I asked what that task was, they said the Guardians would have to tell me. When I asked the Guardians, they refused to talk about it. I was getting the distinct impression I wasn't going to like this job, whatever it entailed.

The schedule for the Reparention was not set in stone, a little detail I learned when Eliasser called an emergency meeting ten days after Ari rescued me from the floor of my family room. Since I was still on the mend, I figured I wasn't included. I was happily heading for the Forest Portal when Ari stopped me.

"No frolicking in the forest today, Earth-girl. Your attendance is required." With an odd sense of foreboding, I followed him to the Meeting Room and took my place next to Eliasser.

"I canceled Reparention practice and called this meeting because of recent changes in the vortex," Eliasser said. "In the event the Reparention needs to move up, we must begin Kerrin's instruction immediately."

So that's what practice was. "I didn't realize you have to rehearse for the Reparention," I said. "Besides, once my memories return, won't I automatically know everything I need to?"

Danaeus snorted and shook his head.

Eliasser frowned at him before setting me straight. "We have developed procedures in the past thousand years that you would not know about. And it appears," he added heavily, "that to wait upon full recall would not be wise."

"Okay," I said. "Can we start with the vortex? I'm not really sure what it is or how it works."

The wizard muttered to himself, but it was still loud enough for everyone to hear. "Her ignorance will be the end of us."

"Dear Light," Eliasser exclaimed. "What is going on, here?" He stared hard at the wizard, then turned back to me. "It seems your fellow Guardian has poorly phrased his desire for your memories to return."

"It seems my *fellow Guardian* doesn't believe I am one," I snapped.

Eliasser's bewildered gaze traveled to the Master Healer.

"This surprises you?" she said.

Eliasser sighed, then faced me again. "Ask us anything you like, no matter how simple your query may seem. We will *all* welcome your questions and help you in any way we can." He glared at the wizard and Danaeus until they each mumbled their agreement.

"Good. Balthasarre, as our Master Technician, please explain the vortex to Kerrin."

"I would be delighted," Balthasarre effused. The light shining from his eyes rivaled Eliasser at his sunniest. "The vortex is a conflux of energy created billions of years ago that can spiral in two different directions at the same time."

I may not know anything about vortexes, but I was pretty sure spirals only went one way.

"That sounds . . . impossible," I ventured.

"It is." Balthasarre held his hands up as a kind of helpless laughter rolled out of him. His easygoing manner was infectious, and I smiled. "The most important thing I can impart to you is that you must *feel* the vortex in order to understand it. I can *tell* you that it does the impossible by spiraling from both ends. I can *describe* how the portals open out of those spirals, and how they have changed location over time. I can even *explain* how the vortex connects and stabilizes Earth and Amoran. However, to truly know what the vortex is, you must experience it fully. Not here." He pointed to my head. "But here." He indicated my heart.

A physical sensation, like waves of warm water, rose up within me. The effect it had on me was like the Foreseers' meditation on Love. Now I understood why Balthasarre's eyes sparkled even at the mention of the vortex.

"This . . . this *feeling*," I whispered, tapping my chest. "Is it the vortex?"

"Yes." He beamed at me. "It is a part of you."

"You mean, like, physically part of me?"

The wizard gave a dismissive flick of his hand. "That can no longer be true, considering the inferior shell she is housed in."

The disparaging allusion to my Earth body was too much for Balthasarre. "That was cruel and heartless, Makashannar!"

Cries of alarm filled the room. Eliasser pulled me to his chest, probably to give me the heart-to-heart resuscitation he thought I'd need after hearing what must be the wizard's real name.

"Wait." I pushed him away. "Let's see what happens."

The Master Healer leaned forward to watch me. Sixty seconds ticking by can feel like forever. When the minute passed, I smiled at her. "Nothing. I feel absolutely nothing."

The wizard—Makashannar—stood up so fast, his chair fell over backwards. "I trust you will find that reason enough for me to reject our *fellow* Guardian." And he stormed out.

Eliasser and the Master Healer held each other's gaze for so long I thought they'd both have massive headaches. "I will go," she said at length, as if they'd had a conversation. "You are needed here."

After she left, Eliasser stroked his chin as he eyed me with concern. "Are you certain you are all right?"

"Positive."

"Very well, then. Balthasarre? Please continue."

Balthasarre gave me the *Vortex for Dummies* version of vortex mechanics, but it was still a stretch for my nonscientific mind. However, through his patient and much-repeated instruction, I was able to get down a few of the basics.

There were vortexes all throughout the universe, each with its own set of Guardians, and all with the same purpose—to connect and stabilize different "dimensional realities." A vortex could compensate for minor fluctuations in its energy field by balancing light energy with dark energy. I didn't know if it was the same kind of dark energy that scientists on Earth had discovered, but decided not to ask, as I was already having trouble keeping up.

When larger energy fluctuations occurred, the Guardians had to intervene or the altered energy could damage the worlds on either end. These larger fluctuations weren't necessarily deadly, but did require diligent, exhausting, and sometimes hair-raising efforts to rectify.

The problem in the Seventh Vortex went beyond either scenario. The dimensional shift that had originated inside the vortex was wreaking havoc with its ability to maintain balance. Every so often, the vortex slowed, causing the swirling energy to churn erratically. Then, the self-correcting nature of the vortex kicked in with something unexpected. Using short, counter-spiral energy bursts, the vortex essentially shocked itself—almost like jump-starting a car—into rapid forward movement again. The downside? The vortex now spun at an even faster pace than before, which raised the vibrational rate of its energy field, eventually throwing it even further out of balance. This cycle had been repeating itself for quite some time, creating an enormous rift between the light and dark energy. The Guardians had to repair the rift and restore balance to the vortex before it collapsed in on itself in a massive implosion.

Except for a few clarifying questions, I managed to keep my busy mouth quiet while Balthasarre explained all of this. But when he said that this particular dimensional shift had been detected over a thousand years ago, I wondered aloud why they had waited so long to fix the problem when it only seemed to get worse with each cycle.

Balthasarre opened and closed his mouth several times, but it was Anders who answered me, his young voice small and sad. "We learned the hard way what *not* to do."

At that moment, the energy in the room underwent its own shift, kicking my emotional radar into overdrive and heightening my intuition. And I was sorry it did. The discontent I'd been picking up for days? It had to do with me. For some reason, the Guardians were unhappy with me. Even Eliasser. The hurt I experienced over that insight prompted me to demand more from them. I'd agreed to stay on Amoran without knowing what was expected of me. My affection for Eliasser aside, I should have held out for that much.

"I need to know what's involved in the Reparention," I stated as firmly as I could.

Balthasarre leaned forward in his chair. "We must infuse the vortex with a unique form of energy when implosion is only a few hours away. Right now, we believe that timeframe will occur around late December on Earth. To introduce the energy any sooner would have fatal consequences. That is why we must wait."

"And how do we infuse the vortex?"

Balthasarre looked a question at Eliasser, who nodded his assent.

"In a sense, we Guardians are the infusion. We have to enter the vortex and deliver this unique energy to the critical area. The vortex will be so volatile by that point that our bodies could not survive inside for long. And so, we must transform them into pure energy."

I listened with a mixture of fascination and disbelief as Balthasarre described that through rigorous practice, it was possible to increase the rate at which the cells in a person's body vibrated. When the cells vibrated fast enough, the body converted into a ball of white energy, termed a light-body. The Reparention plan called for us to enter the vortex, link our energy fields together, and transform into our light-bodies as a group. Next, we'd channel our group energy through this linked energy field to increase its potency. When the energy was strong enough, it would be released into the center of the vortex, creating a small explosion that would shock the spiraling mass back into balance once and for all.

Forget the vortex, my mind was imploding. But recalling Makashannar's smug dismissal of me, I resolved to not give up, even if it meant stretching the truth a Texas mile.

"I think I get it. Good thing I watched Star Trek, or this would make no sense at all."

Ari's laughter cut through the mounting tension. "Well, there's an accolade for TV. I can see the news teaser now. *Television Helps Save Known Universe—Details at 11:00.*"

The rest of the Guardians laughed along with Ari and me, although I couldn't imagine them understanding the reference. Eliasser, chuckling longer than the level of humor warranted even if he did understand it, rose up saying something about Midday Meal.

My evasion-detector shifted into high gear. "It's too early for Midday Meal, Eliasser. You're avoiding something. What is it? I want the truth."

Wrapping his pilea tightly around himself, he said nothing.

I made my voice as hard as the Master Healer's. "I demand that you tell me. *Now.*"

Eliasser thrust his jaw forward. "You were not so intractable before."

Did he mean before I left Amoran a thousand years ago? That was a no-brainer.

"I'm not who I was before," I snapped, suddenly angry with him. "Deal with it."

Eliasser's eyes never left my face, but they lost their aliveness. It was like witnessing a death. I couldn't believe I'd been that harsh. But when I tried to apologize, he waved me off.

"All right," he said stiffly, retaking his seat. "Here is the rest that you are so eager to hear. During the Reparention, you and Makashannar will have to merge your light-bodies and become a single light-entity. The two of you, acting as one, must absorb the entire amount of energy our group has generated. The energy will continue to grow within you, making it even stronger. At the crucial moment, you will expel that energy as a single charge directed to the most volatile part of the vortex. You two are the only ones who can do this. Without both of you, acting together, the Reparention will fail. Do you comprehend what I am saying?"

"Yes," I said, feeling scolded rather than merely informed.

"The two of you will be alone at this point," Eliasser hammered away. "The rest of us will have left the vortex because even in our light-bodies, the energy would destroy us."

"Wait. Are you saying it won't destroy Makashannar and me?"

His shoulders sagged like they had that day in the garden, when he had to explain pentuma to me. I was reminded of Atlas holding up the world.

"We cannot be certain how you will fare. It is possible you will not make it out of the vortex alive, or survive even if you do."

I had to swallow hard before I could talk. "I don't understand. What will happen to us?"

Eliasser's iron mask slid into place. "That is enough for now."

"No, it is not," Balthasarre rasped out. "Kerrin is asking for the truth. We should not deny her that." His silver-gray eyes regarded me sorrowfully. "I will not deny her that."

"Do as you wish," Eliasser barked. He clamped his jaw shut and stalked out.

A strained silence followed his departure. Anders looked everywhere but at me. Danaeus shifted in his seat and stared at the wall. Ari leaned forward, cradling his head.

*Uh-oh.* "How bad is it?" I asked Balthasarre.

He took a deep breath, then held my hands. They didn't impart energy like Eliasser's did, but his touch was warm and comforting, nonetheless.

"You and Makashannar will possess tremendous power in your joined light-body. This power should shield you from harm while you deliver the energy burst. Afterward, you will have a few minutes until the balancing explosion occurs. In that short time, you must get to the Amoran portal, remanifest your separate physical bodies, and immediately leave the vortex. Your physical bodies will be somewhat protected by the intense energy fields the two of you will continue to project, even after you separate. Whatever injuries you do sustain we can hopefully treat in the Healing Room, although recovery will be lengthy. In any event, until the vortex settles down, returning to Earth will not be possible for weeks, months, or even—"

"I get it," I broke in, scarcely able to hear the words that came out of my mouth. If anyone was going to tell me this, I was glad it was Balthasarre, who had a son, who might understand what this meant for me and the family I might essentially be leaving behind.

"Should I go on?" he asked, his eyes rimmed with regret.

"There's more?"

His expression turned grim. "There are several possible outcomes if you are still inside the vortex when the explosion happens. They are less appealing."

A hollow place inside me began to ache. What was coming if he'd already given me the best-case scenario?

"If you are still in the vortex, but far enough away from the explosion when it occurs, the shock wave will force your physical body to rematerialize at once. In the unlikely event that you live long enough to make it out of the vortex, we will place you in restorative stasis until you are stable enough to be worked on by our healers. After that," he gave a helpless shrug, "recovery is uncertain."

"On the other hand, if you are too close to the explosion, it will vaporize your light-bodies and drive the energy particles that you are made of clear across the cosmos. Since you would no longer possess a discrete consciousness, at least you would not suffer past—" He broke off and cleared his throat.

I could barely breathe. He must have saved the worst for last.

"The third possibility has to do with the Darkness, what we call dark energy, within the vortex. I must impress upon you that the Darkness is neither good nor bad. It simply is what it is—an accumulation of extremely dense energy with an immense gravitational pull. This dark energy will continue to expand in scope and power right up until we perform the Reparention. Its gravitational pull could drag you deep inside it at any moment, before or after the explosion. Once inside the Darkness, its density would basically imprison you forever."

"Wouldn't it just kill me?" My hopeful tone amazed me. Perspective is a remarkable thing.

Balthasarre shook his head with an air of desolation. "You would be condemned to an agonizing existence as a disembodied consciousness. And it numbs what consciousness you do have, making it difficult to find your way back, if ever you could."

"It sounds like hell," I whispered.

"That would fit my definition of it," Ari said.

# CHAPTER 14

Midday Meal was a somber affair that Eliasser, the Master Healer, and Makashannar did not attend. Lost in some pretty desperate thoughts, I stared at my untouched plate of food. I wasn't sure what was going through the minds of my fellow Guardians, but I knew what was ricocheting around in mine. I was a plain, ordinary person from Earth, who had to somehow transform into a ball of light, then merge with a man who detested me so we could shoot a bolt of energy out of us, after which we'd probably die . . . or worse. To top that off, no matter what scenario played out, I'd be separated from my family for weeks, months, or perhaps eternity. No wonder the Guardians had avoided telling me my true role in the Reparention. I'd already moved through shock and terror to a kind of numbness. At least that was less painful.

I reached for the pitcher of green liquid that tasted like a banana smoothie and filled my goblet, hoping that a fluid diet would be easier to get down. I sipped at my cup, thinking about Makashannar. I no longer blamed him for rejecting me. Even if I had read the letter with its energy key, I was still in an Earth body, something seen as a drawback, and not just by him. My abilities, or lack of them, would directly impact the success of the Reparention. And by extension, everyone's life. Everyone. Everywhere.

"You need to eat," Ari said. "It's important to keep up your strength."

I replied with manufactured buoyancy. "No worries, fair elven lad. I'll just borrow some energy from the wicked old wizard—my new best friend and power buddy. I may have to wait until he stops hating me, though."

Ari grinned. The Earth-savvy elf understood my fallback defense mechanism.

"Just a little *dark* humor?" he said, and we snickered.

"How can you?" Balthasarre's alarmed face swung from Ari to me. "That Makashannar cannot accept you, and what the two of you will face, is no reason for laughter."

The reprimand from my defender of only a few hours ago set my cheeks burning.

"You've just finished telling me I may not live to see my kids grow up. If I can't stop what's coming, then maybe I *should* laugh. Maybe all of us should spend the next—however long we have left—laughing our asses off."

"There was a time," he squeezed through his teeth, "when you would not have spoken so."

*Et tu, Brute?* "Well, Balthasarre. Maybe when my memories return I'll be better equipped to hold my tongue like I used to. That is, If I'm not dead by then."

Intense physical exhaustion, like I'd gone on a ten-mile hike, descended out of nowhere. I retreated to my room and slept through till morning. When I woke up, I went straight to the Forest Portal. I really needed a visit with the Foreseers.

Eliasser came around the bend as I lifted my arm to open the portal room.

"Did Ari find you?" he asked in a flat tone.

"Was he looking for me?"

Eliasser nodded. "He felt you should join us for morning practice."

Ari felt I should join them. Not Eliasser.

"When?" I asked, working to keep my tone as unemotional as his. It was hard, though. The man who recently couldn't bear to watch me leave, now regarded me with an expression so neutral it bordered on cold.

"As soon as Morning Meal is finished," he said.

And we made our way, silently, to the Guardian Meal Room.

Practice began with a group meditation to raise our energy levels. Thanks to my lessons with the Foreseers, I kept up admirably. So far, so good.

Next came training exercises on transforming our bodies into energy. I'd pretended to understand it yesterday, but I really didn't. When I asked Eliasser to explain it to me again, he shut his eyes and frowned.

Ari came to my rescue. "Think of it this way, Kerrin. Your true Self is really a big ball of vibrating energy. That great body of yours is only a costume you put on to live your current physical life." He wiggled his eyebrows.

I laughed. "Thanks for the compliment."

"Anytime." He smiled. "So, the real you already existed as the soul who would become Kerrin once your Earth parents provided you with the means to do so as their little baby. And such a cute baby you were, too," he added with a wink.

Danaeus grumbled. "Oh, for the Love of the Light. Can we get on with this?"

Ari shot Danaeus a dark look before continuing. "Your body and soul are both comprised of energy. The only difference is that your body's energy vibrates at a much slower rate, which is why it appears physical. In order to transform it into light energy, we have to increase the vibrational rate of that dense, physical energy until it no longer appears, or is, physical."

Ari talked like this was an everyday thing. Easy peasy.

"Not to worry, though," he went on. "While Earth's density makes it nearly impossible to convert a physical body into light, it won't be as hard on Amoran, where we have the elevated energy signature of the entire planet to support us."

Unaccountably, I began to shake. "I don't care what planet you live on. People can't just turn themselves into balls of light!" The rest of the Guardians stared at me as if I'd proclaimed that water wasn't wet. "And even if it is possible, I don't have an Amoran body. What if you've pinned your hopes on me and I can't do it?"

"You will do it," Eliasser stated in that same neutral/cold voice, "because the cells in your body will respond to the potions, practices, meditations, and vibrational adjustments, just as the cells in our bodies will. Being from Earth, the experience will be more difficult for you. However, we will all achieve the same result. We *must* all achieve the same result."

The Master Healer whispered something to Eliasser. He nodded, and without so much as a glance my way, said to the other Guardians, "Kerrin is welcome to take her walk in the forest. The rest of us will continue with practice."

————————

Eliasser's curt dismissal of me cut deep, but when I reached the Glen, I'd managed to calm myself enough to pass through the twin trees without looking like I'd been crying. As compassionate as the Foreseers were, it didn't seem fitting to arrive with a tear-stained face.

There were seven Foreseers in all, although only two showed up at any given time. Each Foreseer "presided," as they put it, over a specific energy center—on Earth we called them chakras—hence the different colors. In addition to the pink and yellow Foreseers, I'd now met the blue, red, green, and orange ones. I didn't know what color the seventh Foreseer was. Referred to as the Elder, she seldom visited the Glen anymore.

I sat in the middle of the clearing with my back to the opening and closed my eyes. I liked to see if I could sense when the Foreseers appeared, and what colors they were as they hovered behind me.

I felt the first one enter and head my way. But today she played a trick.

"You're in front of me," I said. I kept my eyes closed until I could guess her color.

"Good. However, we never trick. You shall certainly be tested, but never tricked."

I hadn't voiced the part about her tricking me out loud. "Can you read my mind?"

"We know your thoughts, Daughter."

I liked the way she said that, as though Daughter was my name.

"We know your heart, also, and it is filled with sadness. Why?"

If she knew what was in my heart, then she also knew why I was sad. Apparently, she wanted me to tell her anyway.

"I'm not what the Guardians expected." In another flash of heightened perception, I knew which Foreseer she was. I decided to try something new. Instead of talking, I *thought* to her.

*"You're the red Foreseer."*

*"Well done,"* she spoke into my mind. "Now, what is it the Guardians expected?"

I opened my eyes. "At the very least, a faster return of my memories, along with whatever skills and abilities I used to possess."

"And who is the correct judge of how skilled you are and what abilities you possess?"

"Eliasser? The Master Healer?"

"Neither. You have placed power into the hands of other Guardians which rightfully belongs to you. Reclaim it." She searched my eyes, producing, as it always did with the Foreseers, a sense of well-being rather than intrusion. "There is more. Speak."

I shrugged. "I think they want something from me. Something I can't quite figure out." I sighed. "Something I fear I won't be able to give them."

She smiled as if pleased. "Your intuition grows stronger."

Apparently so. I sensed another Foreseer float into the clearing and approach from behind.

*"Blue,"* I thought.

*"Excellent,"* the red Foreseer replied. *"Communicating this way is crucial to fulfilling your promise."* She returned to audible speech as the blue Foreseer came front and center. "Today we explore another energy center. When blended in harmony, what do red and blue create?"

I was free to take my time thinking through my answer, as the Foreseers never rushed me. No dismal dwarf tapped his foot impatiently at my slowness; no waspish wizard sighed in exasperation over my ignorance. I sent the Foreseers a mental hug of thanks, then turned my attention back to the question. I assumed the request had nothing to do with color per se. Red symbolized the emotions and power, and blue represented what they called Pure Thought.

"Knowing?" I posited. The Foreseers used the word as a noun, and as best I could ascertain, it was not the same as having knowledge, but rather, meant the kind of intuition that reached deep into the heart of things. "Or . . . Truth?"

They answered by blending themselves into the loveliest shade of purple I'd ever seen.

"Both, for they are one and the same."

Their united voices sounded now in my mind.

*"There are truths hidden in the hearts of some of the Guardians. Honesty must reign for the Reparention to succeed. You bring with you many skills and abilities; you possess many gifts. One is honesty and a bridge for Truth. Be that for them. Now, we begin."*

I didn't try to decipher what that meant, as they often spoke enigmatically. They led me through a meditation that opened the energy center within my mind, as well as connecting the ones we'd already explored—heart, emotions, and creative force.

When it was time to leave, I asked the Foreseers for one last bit of help.

"It bothers me when the Guardians withhold information from me, yet here I am doing the same thing to them. When should I let the others know about my visits to you?"

"First you must discover what they want from you and share that knowledge with them. You will know the moment. Trust yourself." And they disappeared through the opening.

----

Things came to a head the next day at Morning Meal when conversation turned to the Reparention. As Balthasarre went over some technical details with our group, my thoughts wandered off to work on the problem of the Guardians' expectations of me.

"Did you understand that, Kerrin?" Eliasser asked at length, employing that same flat tone he'd used with me since the vortex meeting.

I guess one of his expectations involved my paying attention.

"Sorry, Eliasser. I—"

"Never mind," he snapped, no longer neutral. "It was useless to ask you."

"—I didn't hear what you said," I finished.

The room went silent. Everyone stared at the usually kind and loving Master Guardian, who squeezed his eyes shut and whispered, "Dear Light. What is wrong with me?"

Ari recovered first, rising to my defense. And as he did, I finally understood what the Guardians wanted from me. How could I have been that dense? It was so obvious, I was surprised I'd missed it. I was right, though. It was something I'd never be able to give them.

"Stop it," Ari cried out, with a sharp glance at Makashannar and Danaeus. "You should be helping Kerrin, not criticizing her every move. You *know* I'm the reason she's in this position." The look he turned on me was full of apology. "I'm so sorry I screwed things up. But try to see the last thousand years from their point of view. They missed you terribly, waiting for you to return, waiting for you to be—"

"Her again," I cut in, unable to keep the bite out of my voice. "Not me. Not Kerrin. *Her.*"

I addressed all of the Guardians now. "You say you want my memories to resurface so I can do my part in the Reparention; but that's not the real issue, is it? You don't want *me* with her memories; you want *her*—exactly how she was when she left. No wonder some of you can't stand me. It's *her* that you miss." I couldn't look at Eliasser. "It's *her* that you love."

No one offered a rebuttal. That unspoken confirmation was like a fist in my gut. I pressed on, trying to ignore the way my heart was shattering into little pieces.

"Even if I had been able to absorb the letter's energy key, I'm not sure your missing friend would have come back the way you expected her to. Considering that she would have had to share my body, my personality, and my emotions, you still would have been stuck with an idiot from Earth who doesn't know a vortex from a hole in space."

Eliasser flinched. "That is not at all how we see you."

"Yes. It is. I sense it from almost everyone here; even you, my sweet king."

Every drop of color drained from Eliasser's face. I don't know why I called him that, but I couldn't dwell on it now. I had to finish while I had the emotional stamina.

I got up and stood in front of Makashannar, who boldly met my eyes without blinking. The electrical buzz was so pronounced I could barely speak. "I can't believe I'm saying this, but I actually feel sorry for you. You grieve the loss of her so deeply, yet you won't admit how much, even to yourself. Instead, you make me pay daily because I'm here and she isn't."

Makashannar lowered his head, but not before I caught the intense suffering reflected in his eyes. Worse, for an instant I felt his suffering as if it were my own. Reeling from the impact of his pain, I had to put some distance between us.

My footsteps on the stone floor were the only sound that dented the morgue-like quiet. When I reached the doorway, I turned around, as one last thought came to me. The Master Healer's face was as ashen as Eliasser's. Not one of the Guardians would meet my eyes.

"I misspoke before. You don't all want me to be her. Ari accepts me for who I am. And, come to think of it, so do they." I waved my hand in what I hoped was the general direction of the forest. "But not as if I'm some sort of booby prize they have to tolerate because they can't get the real deal. They actually like me as Kerrin. As if who I am is exactly who they expected. And who they wanted."

Eliasser spoke so softly, I barely heard him. "Of whom do you speak?"

I blew out a sigh of relief. The moment had come. "The Foreseers."

The room exploded with cries of shock, amazement, and doubt.

"Silence," Eliasser bellowed. "Calm yourselves, right now." When order was restored, he turned to me. "You have seen the Foreseers?" he asked with thinly veiled skepticism.

"Yes, I have seen the Foreseers," I parroted, unsure what the attitude was for. It's not like I'd gotten an audience with the Pope.

Eliasser didn't appear convinced. "When did this . . . event . . . happen?"

"The first day you took me to the forest and I went off on my own."

That surprised him. "And you said nothing to me? Why?"

"I'm not sure why I didn't tell you that day, other than a gut feeling. After that, the Foreseers said I would know when the right time had arrived. This must be it."

"You saw them again?" Eliasser didn't mask his astonishment. "When did *that* occur?"

"It would be easier to say when I have not seen them," I replied, puzzled by all seven Guardians' dumbfounded expressions. "On my second visit, they told me to come as often as I wished. And I do. Every day. Twice if I can manage it."

When the room erupted again, I took that as my exit cue.

# CHAPTER 15

I felt as if a huge weight had been lifted from my shoulders and I knew just who to share it with. I decided to pass on the Forest Portal and try an alternate route to the Glen of the Foreseers via the Mindsail Lake. This would keep me away for most of the day, which was fine by me. I needed a long break from the Guardians.

I stopped by my room to gather a few supplies. Ari had given me the backpack from our picnic lunch as a souvenir, "minus the magic," he'd said with a smile. I stuffed my resting mat and sleep cover into the backpack, then added some fruit and monzennez from the ever-present bowl on my table, an accommodation the Guardians made to my snacking needs.

I reached the exit for the Outer Grounds, took a deep breath, and opened the doorway. The Mountain had felt oppressive to me recently. Now, freed from its constraints, I fairly skipped across the courtyard and out the Main Gate into another glorious Amoran morning.

I followed the route that Ari, Danaeus, Makashannar, and I had taken the day of our picnic. When I reached the fork in the trail, I opted to do a little exploring and went left instead of taking the right-hand path to the Mindsail Lake.

The trail meandered around low rolling hills. Small, mushroom-shaped trees, looking more like overgrown bushes, nestled in the crooks between rises. I'd gone about a mile when I came across a flat, grassy area roughly the size of a tennis court. It was bordered on three sides by steep, tiered hills that resembled a natural stadium. Bold white lines defined a square that took up three-quarters of the flat area. A thinner line divided that square into two equal sides. I was pretty sure I'd found the Garrammon field.

I climbed to the top of the far hill. A gradual slope eased down the other side to a small, glistening body of water that barely qualified as a pond. A tiny beach, with sand so white it sparkled like sugar, lay directly below. Willowy trees, like in the Transition Space, lined the opposite shore. Beyond them, the land rose up sharply, then stretched out in a grassy plateau.

Choosing to save the pond for another day, I doubled back to the fork and continued on to the Mindsail Lake. Much to my delight, I piloted the mindsail with the same ease as before. On the opposite shore, I secured the boat and walked to where we'd had our picnic. I rolled out the resting mat, ate my lunch, then lay back to watch the sparse clouds drift by. A full stomach and the warm sun made me drowsy. When my eyelids insisted on closing, I didn't fight them.

———

My nap ended mid-afternoon, judging by the position of the sun. Surprised I'd slept that long, I set out across the meadow at a good clip. I reached the woods quickly enough, but it took some hunting before I found a narrow trail leading inside.

I'd fallen in love with this lush, canopied forest, even with its unpredictable nature. I made my way along cool, shaded paths, stopping now and then to study the plants and flowers I came across. I bent down at one point to examine an unusual purple, blue, and pink variegated flower with a cinnamon scent. When I stood up, two giant trees were directly in front of me. Once again, the Foreseers had plunked their glen down right where I would find it. Smiling, I squeezed between the trunks.

During my longest session ever, the green and yellow Foreseers congratulated me on my honesty with the Guardians, then led me through a lengthy process to complete my energy center instruction. Afterward, they conferred with each other privately and congratulated me once more. I had achieved enough "internal harmony" for them to teach me how to unite all seven centers. That single meditation seemed to take forever to get through, and I almost had to stop from sheer restlessness. But they encouraged me to persevere, and when I succeeded, it was like turning on internal heat lamps from my tailbone to the top of my head. The energy flowing up and down my spine was like nothing I'd ever experienced. I felt incredibly grounded, yet more open emotionally. That part had me concerned. I was by nature far more emotional than the rest of the Guardians, who already had trouble dealing with my Earth . . . expressiveness.

By the time I left the forest, the sun had just set and a full moon hung directly above the horizon. I hiked across the meadow, then up the incline above the Mindsail Lake. When I crested the rise, I froze. On the beach below, a lone figure rested in what should have been an empty mindsail. I didn't have to work at guessing the identity of the occupant. Moonlight reflected off his dark hair and bathed his forest green pilea in a ghostly shimmer.

I had hoped to avoid contact with all of the Guardians until tomorrow. Especially him. Unsure what to make of this development, I took my time descending the hill.

Makashannar didn't acknowledge my presence until I stepped onto the sand.

"May I accompany you back?" he asked quietly, without meeting my eyes.

"How did you get here when I had the mindsail tied up on this side of the lake?" The Guardians weren't the only ones who could use the nonanswer ploy.

He hesitated, seeming to choose his words with care. "I did not require the mindsail."

There was only one other route that I knew of. "You went through the Forest Portal and walked all the way here just to ride back with me?" I had to admit, I was impressed.

He didn't acknowledge that, just reached for my hand, and I let him guide me into the boat.

"Would you care to propel the mindsail?" he asked.

Since I was the one who'd brought the boat here in the first place, his offer seemed presumptuous. If he hadn't shown up, that's exactly what

I would have done anyway. However, as long as he was here, I had a better idea.

"I'll take a raincheck."

He glanced at the sky, seeming perplexed.

I smiled. Was he actually checking for rain?

"What I mean is, I'd like you to drive. But can we go slowly? It's such a beautiful night, I'd like to enjoy it." I didn't confess the real reason—prolonging my arrival back at the Mountain. Whatever fallout there would be from my little speech, I was in no hurry to find out.

With a brief nod, he pushed us off and stepped gracefully to the front of the wobbling boat. A full minute ticked by. If I hadn't seen the back of his pilea shift ever so slightly now and again, I would have sworn he stopped breathing. When he turned around at last, the boat inched forward at a slow, even pace. I guess willful focusing was a piece of cake for him.

The moon's silvery light darted across the surface of the water as we rode in silence. Too much silence. Some unnamed thing hung like a funereal drape between us. I needed him to talk about it. My emotional radar was particularly sensitive where Makashannar was concerned. In the same way I had experienced his pain earlier, whatever was bothering him now was tying my stomach in knots.

"I think I understand how you feel," I ventured.

He stared at the bottom of the boat. "Do not take offense, but you cannot possibly understand."

The discomfort inside me grew. I had to try again. "Was she . . . I mean, were you two . . . ?" I hesitated, unclear why the question I wanted to ask seemed wrong. "Were you, you know, together? A couple?"

"We were not designed that way."

"Not designed that way? Meaning you weren't designed to be a couple?"

He sighed. "Not in the manner of being a couple that you are familiar with."

That cleared up . . . nothing. "Eliasser said that Amorans aren't big on physical contact. But . . . you have babies, right? So you must . . . you know."

"All I can say is, things are not the same here as they are on Earth."

Sensing he wouldn't offer any more on the subject, I gave up. I didn't think we'd accomplished much, but at least the pain in my midriff eased.

White fog curled over the lake as the mindsail proceeded at a slow, even pace. I relaxed and allowed my thoughts to drift along with the current. But one idea presented itself with such persistence, I decided to break the quiet.

"So far, I've only had problems when I remembered names on my own, which is the opposite of what Eliasser said would happen. And the strength of the response has had little to do with the depth of the relationship. You'd think Eliasser's name would have produced a monumental brain freeze for me, but his was the least intense reaction of all. What's more," I touched Makashannar's arm as if to drive my point home, "I've had no reaction when someone's name has been accidentally divulged."

"That has been a surprise to us all. When Eliasser went to the Glen to consult—" Makashannar snapped his jaw shut.

"The Foreseers," I finished for him. It was my turn to sigh. "What is the big deal?"

Makashannar shook his head. "You do not understand the nature of the Foreseers."

"Maybe it's lucky for me that I don't."

His eyes widened. "I had not considered that. Perhaps you are right."

"Wow. Can I get that in writing?" By his expression, I half expected him to dig in the pockets of his pilea for pen and paper. "Never mind. What did the Foreseers tell Eliasser?"

Ripples lapped at the sides of the mindsail as I waited for Makashannar's answer. Fog now obscured the shoreline in all directions and muted the light of the moon, but he didn't seem concerned. I imagined his willful focusing had programmed our entire trip back.

He cleared his throat and looked at me—or as close to "at me" as I guess he felt he could.

"The Foreseers said your recall of names is different because of your Earth body, but that all is well. And most important, that we should release our judgments of you."

Hoping I could keep Makashannar talking, I carefully formulated another question.

"Aside from my own Amoran name, there is one other person whose name I don't remember yet. Well, maybe two. Wouldn't it make sense, based on all that's happened, to tell me the Master Healer's name instead of waiting for me to guess it?"

"What makes you think there are two names for you to remember?"

I shrugged. "Just a feeling."

Suddenly, it was like a part of my psyche slipped to the side, allowing an aspect of myself to surface that was both familiar and yet unfamiliar. "Wait! It's what I used to call you. A kind of . . . nickname, I guess."

Makashannar wet his lips. "If a nickname is like a fond-name," he whispered, "then perhaps you are sensing my fond-name."

"I'm sure that's it. I have a fond-name, too, don't I? And you gave it to me."

Dismay etched his face.

"I'm sorry," I said quickly. "I don't mean to hurt you. I have to remember I'm not *her.*"

"But you are. And you are correct. With the exception of Ari, we did not trust that the soul of our absent companion could be who now dwells within you."

Put that way, it sounded a little creepy.

Makashannar smiled, but it was the bittersweet kind, edged with sadness. "Even though your physical appearance is remarkably like hers, you are different in so many ways. But it was clear how badly mistaken we were when you told us about the Foreseers. They would never have permitted you to access the Glen, or to go there so often, if you were not her. And yet, it is what you called Eliasser that had the greatest impact on us. When you and I were younger, you insisted that there could be no greater fond-name than to say 'Eliasser' and let it resonate within the center of your Being. However, one day, after hearing stories a traveler brought from another world, you called Eliasser your 'sweet king.' He has been thus in both your hearts ever since."

Tears pricked my eyes as a vivid memory of that lovely day unveiled within my mind. I was about to thank Makashannar, when the mindsail scraped hard against sand. I stood up, but my end of the boat was still in the water. It tipped to the side and I lost my balance. Makashannar saved me from a tumble overboard by grabbing my tunic and yanking me down—right on top of him. He was decent enough to muffle his cry of pain.

Thoroughly embarrassed on several counts, I rolled off of him. "Sorry about that. My parents were going to name me Grace, but my mother figured I'd never live up to it."

"I did not know that about you," Makashannar wheezed out.

I laughed. "That was a joke. Boy, you do take things seriously."

"I guess I do at that," he admitted with a grin.

We were lying side by side in the bottom of the boat, when out of the blue, a warm and wonderful energy field engulfed us. I glanced at Makashannar. His smiled widened and he closed his eyes. Since he didn't seem worried—quite the opposite judging by the slow, deep breaths he was taking—I closed my eyes and matched him, breath for breath. Soon my body felt like it did after an hour-long massage. I would happily have stayed in that boat all night long, but a few moments later, the energy field dissipated.

Makashannar stirred. "We should go."

I sat up, resisting the urge to ask him what had just transpired, as though talking about it might spoil what we'd shared. As I looked around, I had a more pressing question.

"Tell me, Mr. Wizard. How did we wind up back where we started?"

He studied the shoreline, then groaned. "And without my noticing. The fog was not that thick. But you must stop referring to me as a wizard. That was a complete invention of Ari's."

"I wondered about that. So, no Wizard of Amoran?" I was kind of disappointed.

He shook his head. "When it became clear that we needed names other than our own, Ari insisted I be referred to as a wizard."

"Why? Don't you have some other title?"

"I do. Ari thought my role translated to 'wizard' and would be easier to say than Assistant Master Healer. He is quite taken with all things 'Earth,' and wanted me to pick from a list of famous Earth wizards. I argued against it, but by that time, the Master Healer's patience with us was spent. She decreed, 'You are "the wizard," he is "the elf," and we are now done.'"

Makashannar had replicated her flat tone and imperious manner perfectly.

"Hey. You're pretty good at imitations."

"But not so good at operating a mindsail without full concentration." He looked at the sky. "We will have to hurry. The nighttime showers will be coming soon."

"So that's when it rains." In all my trips to the forest, the weather had been sunny and pleasant. I didn't relish the idea of getting caught in a storm. "Could we drive the boat together? Combine forces to make it go faster?"

"I have never considered such a thing," he said, his tone implying, what would be the point? "I suppose we could try, though. How do you propose we proceed?"

"Well. You're more skilled at this, so you should probably get behind me."

"Why would that matter?"

"I don't know. Maybe your greater force will move forward to combine with my lesser force? I'm just guessing. The worst that will happen is we'll be dead in the water. Oops—sorry," I added, at his disturbed look. "It's just an expression."

He seemed relieved. Did he really think I meant we'd die? It's no wonder he didn't joke.

We held up our hands and began the imaging necessary for locomotion.

Wrong move. The boat pitched violently and almost tossed us into the lake.

I reached behind me and pulled him closer so that our bodies touched. It was an impulsive thing to do, but it worked. The rocking ceased.

"Okay," I called over my shoulder. "Let's try the imaging again."

"More slowly this time." He clasped my hands. "And one of us should take the lead."

"Tag, you're it."

I swore I felt him smile at that. I snuck a peek behind me. His eyes were already closed, but he *was* smiling. Then, I felt something else that nearly stopped my heart. Makashannar might not be "designed that way," but I sure was. I turned forward, trying to convince myself I'd only imagined experiencing a flash of attraction.

"We should take some deep breaths to center ourselves," he advised, raising his voice to compete with the increasing wind.

"Centered. Yes. Good idea." I most definitely needed centering.

To help me focus, I concentrated on the meditation the Foreseers had just taught me instead of the way Makashannar's chest pressed into my back with each inhalation.

"That should do it," he said after a minute or so. "Now, begin."

I was right about combining our effort; it sent us flying across the lake. We reached the opposite shore, tied the mindsail to the pole, and set off down the path toward the Mountain with the wind whipping at our clothes. The air grew so chilly that I stopped to pull the sleep cover out of my pack. In answer to Makashannar's questioning look, I confessed I was freezing.

With swift, practiced movements, he removed his pilea and wrapped it around me.

"But now you'll be cold," I protested.

"I am rarely cold." He hadn't let go of the pilea. "What I am is sorry. You *are* her, and I deeply regret the part I played in letting you think you were not her. I mean, were not *you*. Oh, this is impossible!" He grasped my hands and held them to his chest. "You came back to us in an Earth body with numerous lifetimes of experience stored in your soul. There is no way that you could be the same as when you left. But that is what we wanted and our expectation punished you. It was unrealistic and cruel. Please. Forgive me."

"I do forgive you," I said, surprised that it was true. "Now you have to forgive me."

"Why? You did nothing wrong."

"That isn't what matters. Each one of you has to forgive me for leaving, and for coming back to you changed. Trust me on this. It's just the way it works."

"But it was not your—*Oh!*"

A pulsing energy field cut him off, rolling through us in waves. My heart beat faster with each swell. With an overwhelming urgency, I needed to plumb the depths of his downturned green eyes, to push past the electrical buzzing and crawl inside his very soul. I needed to see *him*. I think he struggled with the same longing, because the sigh he expelled was more a moan of frustration. Then, as if resigning himself to something he couldn't fight, he lifted his face. My heart banged against my rib cage, partly from the escalating energy, partly in anticipation of what might happen when we met each other's gaze at such close range. "We should not do this," he breathed. But he didn't stop moving.

Our eyes were nearly level when my body shook with such force, I collapsed against him.

"Potions," I gasped. "I haven't . . . all day . . ."

He threw his arms around me and squeezed so hard I couldn't breathe. My heart rate went through the roof, followed by rapid, intense movement, like being on a roller coaster. Dizzy and disoriented, I wondered if he was carrying me all the way back to the Mountain.

But a moment later, I was in my room. The Master Healer ripped me from his arms.

"You should not have risked it," she said to Makashannar. "What if you had—" Noticing my open eyes, she cut herself off and her expression softened . . . a first! It didn't prevent her from forcing me to drink the most vile-tasting substance I'd been subjected to so far. When I finished gagging it down, she helped me onto the sleeping stone.

"Now," she whispered, brushing the hair off my forehead. "Sleep, little one."

---

*A robed figure bent over a large, black cauldron, the gnarled hands stirring, stirring.*

*"Who are you?" I asked.*

*"You know very well who I am," a woman's voice snapped.*

*"Why would I ask if I already knew?"*

*"Why indeed?" she huffed. Stir. Stir.*

*"I'm not playing twenty questions. Are you going to tell me your name, or not?"*

*"Such impatience. But our time grows short. I am Ashara."*

*And it was the Master Healer who raised her face to me.*

---

"Did you sleep well?" Ashara asked, eyeing Makashannar's pilea with amusement. I'd refused to relinquish it last night, treating it like a security blanket.

"I slept very well, thank you." I snuggled into the green folds as we regarded each other like two cats, tails twitching. Who would pounce first?

"I added a little something to your stabilizing draft," she said at length.

"Did you, now." *Twitch. Twitch.* "I bet you'd like to know if it worked."

"Well?"

"What's the matter? Can't read my mind today?"

That earned me a rare smile. "You should try Garrammon. You will enjoy the volleys."

I was spared the need to lob the ball back when the doorway opened. The Master Guardian waited on the threshold, hands folded in front of him, head bowed.

Ashara helped me to sit up—I was a little unsteady—then left us.

I'd thought this moment would be difficult, but the sight of Eliasser looking so remorseful pushed away any reticence I might have had. Rubbing my eyes, still heavy with sleep, I eased off the stone . . . and my legs gave out. I'm not sure what was in their Morning Meal mush, but the Guardians were extremely fast at times. Eliasser caught me before I hit the ground.

I took advantage of the situation to wrap my arms around him and bury my face in his chest.

"I'm sorry," I whispered.

His body went rigid. I should have realized that such a level of physical affection would be too much. I was about to let go of him, when his breath released and he sank into my embrace.

"You are full of surprises," he said, pulling me closer. "I come to ask you for forgiveness and you apologize to me. Is this not backwards?"

"Not in my book." I tipped my head to look at him. Once again, it felt as if part of me slipped into the background, allowing another aspect to surface. "I didn't say all that I could have yesterday. Makashannar suffers greatly the loss of his absent friend. But you miss her even more. You may not understand this, but she needs you to forgive her. For leaving you. And because the only way she can return to you is like this. As me. As this different—" My voice cracked.

Eliasser sighed. "Can you forgive me for the pain I have caused you?"

"I already have."

He tightened his arms around me. When he finally let go, his smile turned self-conscious. "I find that some of your differences are actually quite . . . pleasurable."

I laughed. "I'll turn you into a hug-junkie yet."

---

The next several days were like a rebirth for me. My relationship and status with the Guardians underwent a dramatic shift, thanks in large part to the Foreseers endorsement of me. I now attended practice on a regular basis, and if the Guardians harbored any misgivings about my capabilities, they kept it to themselves. On the downside, information about my past was still under wraps, a condition that continued to frustrate me.

Makashannar retreated into himself once more. It saddened, but didn't surprise me. While Eliasser was growing to accept me for who I was—metaphorical Earth warts and all—I don't think Makashannar could make the leap.

Oddly enough, the Guardians' need for me to be like *her* might have kept her in the background. Now that the pressure was off, little things edged into my awareness—an insight, an unusual turn of phrase—things I knew instinctively belonged to my Amoran self. I didn't tell the others; it seemed counterintuitive now that most of them accepted me as just plain Kerrin. But secretly, I'd begun to embrace the growing identity as if it were truly mine, thinking it would help me during the Reparention. That's what I told myself, at any rate.

Ari finally dragged me onto the Garrammon playing field. Halfway through my first game, I was hooked, which is pretty remarkable considering I feel about sports the way Ryan feels about vegetables. Then again, Garrammon wasn't your usual game. It was similar to some of the games played on Earth, but with one major difference. None of those games featured a ball that popped in and out of dimensional reality on a whim.

When visible, the ball was volleyed back and forth with the aid of handpieces. These glove-like contraptions strapped around a player's wrists and fanned out from their fingers like the webbed foot of a duck. If the ball disappeared for a third time during a round, the handpieces had to be quickly removed and the ball fielded with bare hands. At other times, one player from each team had to move to the sidelines, leaving the other two to battle it out. When both of these conditions happened simultaneously, you were—as Ari so Earthily put it—screwed.

Ari, Balthasarre, and Anders were accomplished Garrammon players. Danaeus had never quite mastered the game, but loved it with a passion. I think he was grateful for my company now, as I made him look good. I knew from casual conversation that Makashannar was virtually unbeatable. But although he accompanied us to the field every day, he never joined in. Instead, he sat under a tree at the top of the far stadium hill, the one with the pond on the other side. It didn't make sense that he would come with us and not play, and I could think of only one reason he was there. Eliasser had sent him along to child-watch me.

Back on Earth, it was still Wednesday, the day I'd called in sick to work. On Amoran, nearly three weeks had passed. I was so busy now that the days sped by. Even so, the longing for my family became a crushing weight in my chest. A few days before I was scheduled to return to Earth, I asked if I could go home early. Ashara declined, citing a lack of time, of all things.

"The Reparention will arrive sooner than we think," she warned.

But Eliasser relented. "I think we can spare a few days on our end. Kerrin will be back tomorrow, after all."

I gulped and said nothing other than thank you. I didn't want to think about tomorrow.

After morning Reparention practice, I made my fourth trip back through the vortex. I touched down in my family room with plenty of time to perform a reintegration meditation Ashara had taught me. It was supposed to adjust my energy levels so that I could still function on Earth without losing what I'd gained on Amoran.

I opened my eyes after completing the meditation and sat quietly, savoring the view through my picture window. I'd done the same thing twenty-four Earth hours ago, yet so much had happened to me on Amoran during that time. While I still found it hard to believe that I was crucial to saving two worlds, I now knew, deep in my heart, that it was true. And I would do whatever it took to preserve them both.

# CHAPTER 16

I drove to Glenwood Falls Elementary School with the windows rolled down, enjoying the warmth of another atypical balmy day. Ashara's meditation left me feeling as if I didn't have a care in the world. So much so that I questioned why I'd been in such a hurry to leave Amoran early. *This bi-dimensional life isn't so bad,* I thought with smug satisfaction as I leaned against the split rail fence to wait for school to let out.

I should learn not to be smug. Ever.

When the end-of-school bell rang, it was like an emotional alarm clock went off, waking me to how much I'd missed my family. I paced in front of the play structure, more annoyed than usual at Kiley's predictable lateness. When she finally burst through the double doors with a swarm of her friends, I crushed her to me, murmuring how much I loved her.

"Moooom," she hissed. "Are you out of your mind?"

I wished I could tell her the good news. I now knew I wasn't out of my mind!

We drove to the junior high to pick up Ryan and my nephew, Robert. I thought I had myself emotionally in hand, but when Ryan climbed into the front seat—it was his turn to ride shotgun—I told him what a great kid he was and how much I had missed him, and then (shudder) I hugged him in front of his sister and cousin.

He disentangled himself from my clutching arms. "Mom, you are such a freak. I've only been gone for six hours."

There was no way I could tell the truth; for me it had been several weeks. Nor could I think of a clever way to get around this motherly transgression, mostly because I was on the verge of tears.

It only got harder the next morning when I had to blame my red eyes on an allergy attack as I saw the kids off to school. It was my first official marathon day on the other side of the vortex. The five and a half hours I'd be gone from Earth would equal nearly a month on Amoran. By the time I landed in the Main Chamber, I was a complete wreck. Eliasser became so distressed at the sight of me that he sent for Ashara.

She was not the least bit affected by my tears.

"I will not minimize your life on Earth, but your role as a Guardian must come first. That is where your focus should be when you are here."

"Tell that to my heart," I grumbled, wanting sympathy instead of a lecture. Her eyes flickered for a moment, then her expression became impassive once more.

"Your heart will have far more to miss if the Reparention fails."

The reminder didn't stop me from being mad at her, but I knew she was right. No matter how homesick I became, it would be a lot worse if there were no Earth to go home to.

---

Over the next ten Earth days, I settled into my new schedule. But the "focus" required to fulfill my role as a Guardian exacted its payment from my Earth life. First to go was the writing contest, but it provided such a great cover for my absentmindedness, I let everyone believe I was charging ahead to produce the next Great American Novel. I blamed my screw-ups—and there were many—on the distraction caused by my "creative process."

It might have been easier if John had been home more to pick up the slack. But John's boss, Steven, kept dumping more responsibility on my husband, whose disposition was rapidly deteriorating. One morning, John went on a tirade, bitching about everything from his favorite work shirt not being washed to the razor blades I hadn't bought. "I'm working double-time, Kerrin," he shouted. "What do you do all day that you can't do a little laundry?"

I wanted to shout back, "I'm saving the goddamned planet!" Since I couldn't do that, I threw the question back at John and his insane job. "Why don't you stand up to Steven and just say 'no' for a change?" I stormed out the back door, slamming it with enough force to rattle the windows, then hiked up the mountain trail behind my house to take time to cool down. This kind of fight wasn't like us. We weren't the type to yell at each other, but that was getting harder to avoid. What was going on with my usually calm, easygoing spouse?

To make matters worse, on the rare occasion John was home long enough to initiate making love, I turned him down with a feeble excuse. The bizarre symptoms I'd experienced previously had worsened. There was no way I could tell him that the minute he touched my bare skin, it felt as if every nerve ending in my body vibrated like fingernails scraped on a blackboard. I ran it by Ashara once, although I didn't confess what John and I were doing when it happened. She muttered that the reaction was not harmful and walked away before I could say another word.

But that was not the end of my Earth-bound woes. Among the new employees hired to help with our increased workload was a young man named Michael Asher. Mike was a great worker, and he went above and beyond the call of duty to assist me. At first, I appreciated the special attention, as I desperately needed the help. But Mike was also a major hugger. Since we were all huggers in my office, I couldn't really fault him for that. However, he found reasons to hug me so often, it became annoying. When I complained about it to Megan, she smiled.

"I think Mikey has a crush on you."

"Good lord!" I snapped. Some days, my moods weren't any better than John's. "What is he thinking? Not only am I married, I'm ten years older than him."

"Ever hear of a cougar? Besides, he might not realize you're married." She pointed at my bare ring finger. My wedding band was being repaired after a mishap with the garbage disposal. Our local jeweler promised he could make the damaged filigree center good as new. It had been a month already, and I was still waiting.

"Shoot. Never thought of that." And until recently at Pierson & Todd, it hadn't been necessary. We'd been a small, tight-knit group that had worked together for years. Still, Mike should have realized that his behavior was inappropriate. I certainly didn't encourage him.

I started mentioning John at every opportunity, hoping Mike would get the hint. But when he showed up at an outdoor event for Kiley's Girl Scout troop, I knew I was in trouble. The papers he'd brought for my signature could have waited a day. When he went to hug me, I took him aside and made it clear where we stood. He seemed to take it okay, but I called Dave to make sure he had a talk with Mike just in case I hadn't gotten the point across clearly enough.

In the midst of all this physical and emotional mayhem, my parents came home early from one of their retirement trips. I learned this the hard way when Mom knocked on my door at ten past noon on a Wednesday. I was behind schedule for a lunchtime trip to Amoran, a delay which had already cost me a day with the Guardians.

"I wanted to surprise you," Mom said. Her eyes narrowed as I planted myself in the doorway and refused to let her in.

"You succeeded," I mumbled, then blew her off with a weak excuse and practically shut the door in her face. When I finally touched down in the Main Chamber, Ashara scolded me for missing a crucial practice session.

Back on Earth that evening, I tried to make up for being so rude to my mother by treating my parents to dinner at the salad bar restaurant. Normally my favorite dinner haunt, I barely touched what little food I'd put on my plate. My dad didn't seem to notice as he entertained the kids with stories about their trip to Egypt and Greece. But when I passed on the chocolate pudding, my mother raised her eyebrows until they disappeared under her salt and pepper bangs. Unlike her typically blunt self, she didn't say anything until we got back to my house.

"What's wrong?" she demanded, as we sat at the kitchen table. My dad, Kiley, and Ryan were in the family room watching one of their favorite sitcoms. John, of course, was at work.

"Nothing," I replied.

"Is it John's job?" she persisted.

"Everything's fine."

I got the parental version of The Look. "Don't bullshit me, Kerrin. What the hell is it?"

Mom's bluntness included what my strait-laced dad referred to as lively euphemisms.

"Do I have to apply thumbscrews? I'm going grayer as we sit here, daughter dearest."

Maybe it was calling me daughter that did it, bringing to mind the Foreseers and my other life. I'd split myself in two in order to be Kerrin the Mom and Kerrin the Guardian. Now, one of them needed a chance to vent. I unloaded on my mother for twenty minutes, until I said without thinking, "I couldn't even keep my doctor's appointment because of my trip to—"

"You went on a trip?" she cut in.

Like I'd been dipped in quick-drying cement, I sat motionless while my mind spiraled like the vortex. And then, my spiraling mind suddenly snapped.

"Oh, Mom. The most incredible thing is happening to me." I knew I shouldn't tell her, but my heart lightened at the thought of confessing my secret life!

I dove into my story, but I didn't get far.

Mom cut me off with a laugh. "This is a joke, right?"

"No. I told you, this is real. These people, this world, it's all real."

"Oh, come off it."

I gave her a "whatever" shrug, heaved a sigh and folded my hands in my lap.

She leaned forward. "You really believe you've been sucked up by some magical force in the family room and whisked away to a fairy-tale world with dwarves, elves and wizards?"

"He's not a real wizard, but the other two are the genuine article."

Her eyes widened. "Have you told anyone else about this?" She took my blank stare as an invitation to lecture, babbling on about lonely women whose husbands work incessantly, and how modern life makes people crack from the stress of juggling too much, and how—

I tuned her out. I shouldn't have been surprised that she didn't believe me. I still had trouble believing it myself, and I was living it. When I tuned back in, she was scrolling through her phone, looking for the contact info for a psychiatrist they'd met on a photo safari last year.

A safari shrink? I think not.

"Mom?"

"He might not be covered by your insurance, but I'm sure Dr. Bouchard can—"

"Mom!" She stopped scrolling. "You're right. I was just kidding. I needed to get an honest reaction for the book I'm writing."

She looked at me long and hard, then grinned. "You really had me going there. I never figured you for an actor." She chuckled, shook her head, and spooned more sugar into her coffee. "I guess we know where Kiley gets it from."

*Not hardly,* I thought. But I forced a laugh and agreed with her.

---

On the Amoran side of the vortex, the Guardians were still under orders not to reveal anything about my past for fear of "vibrational repercussions." It was frustrating for all of us when someone had to stop mid-sentence with the realization that to go on might endanger me in some ill-defined way. I confronted Eliasser with how silly this was, pointing out that whenever a name or memory had been accidentally divulged to me, I'd had no negative reaction at all.

"That may be," he said, "but we must protect you from energetic overload. Pentuma is a constant concern. The Foreseers deem this path to be wise, and it is to their wisdom I defer."

My visits to the Foreseers became less frequent, as they declared it was time for me to rely on my own "knowingness." When I repeated this to Ashara, she pressed her lips together so tightly they turned white. It was her typical response to anything the Foreseers said, and it made me curious. But it wasn't the only thing that had me scratching my head.

For example, what was up with Amorans and water? It wasn't even served as a beverage. When I shared a story at Evening Meal about a swim trip my family had taken, I had to explain to the Guardians what I meant. I thought Balthasarre and Eliasser were going to choke on their dinner.

"You get *into* the water?" Balthasarre had asked.

"Yes," I'd replied.

"And you enjoy it?" This from Eliasser.

Mystified, I'd nodded. They'd grimaced and shook their heads as if I'd said I like to stick nemestes thorns under my fingernails for fun. But they never explained why, as though it would be impossible to do so if I didn't already understand.

And then there was the conundrum known as Makashannar. As our Reparention practice schedule slowly increased, we had to fit Garrammon in whenever we could. Makashannar continued to tag along with the five of us—Balthasarre, Anders, Ari, Danaeus, and me—but he would only watch from the top of the hill, never play. It made no sense considering how much he supposedly loved the game. Even if Eliasser had sent him to child-watch me, couldn't he join us for a few matches? I just couldn't figure the guy out. He rarely spoke to me, and avoided physical contact with me of any sort. Once during Reparention practice, I tapped his arm to get his attention and he recoiled as if I'd hit him. I kept my distance after that.

Practice. What a hoot. To the Guardians, the idea of turning into a ball of light was an accepted, somewhat reverential occurrence. I kept hoping they were pulling my leg, and would soon 'fess up to what I *really* had to do. But they were serious, as Eliasser assured me one day.

"The process is quite simple. After we achieve the deepest meditative state we are capable of, we then instruct our cells to lighten up."

I burst out laughing. "Lighten up? Seriously? Do you have a bridge to sell me, too?"

Poor Eliasser looked confused. "I do not understand. Why do you need a bridge?"

Ari and I shared a smile, then he said, "Lighten up is a quick-phrase, which means we've packed a few words with a lot of energy and intent. 'Lighten' means we are commanding the cells in our bodies to shine with light. 'Up' refers to our vibrational rate, which must increase substantially in order for our cells to complete the transformation into light energy."

"I will demonstrate for you," Eliasser said. He backed away and closed his eyes. And just stood there. For five full minutes. I was getting bored silly when I noticed a faint glow emanating from the edges of his body.

Was that it? Maybe it wasn't so hard to do after all.

And then, in a blinding flash, Eliasser the person was gone, replaced by a dazzling sphere of light. I shielded my eyes from his brilliance and burst into tears.

Eliasser reverted to his physical form and grasped my hands to feed me energy. "I am sorry. I did not mean to upset you."

"I'm not upset," I sniffled. "I'm not sure why I'm crying, I just . . ." I trailed off. Words couldn't describe what I felt, save for this; Eliasser was even more beautiful as a ball of light.

I glanced around the circle. "Can all of you do that?"

Ari shook his head. "Like the timing of the Reparention, we have had to wait until recently to practice turning to light. Makashannar is nearly there, while Ashara is even more adept than our Master Guardian. But don't worry, Earth-girl. You're not alone."

Anders shyly touched my arm. "Danaeus and I can barely make our bodies glow."

"And I," Balthasarre said, "have only been able to transform the upper half of me. Quite embarrassing, considering all the practice I have had."

"What about you?" I asked Ari. He smiled and shook his head. I took that to mean that, like me, he couldn't do it either. "Okay then. So I'm not in bad company."

In a rare moment of emotional disclosure, Makashannar groaned. "You misunderstand. Ari does not even have to try." His eyes glinted with what looked like envy. "Go ahead. Show her."

Ari shifted and stared at his feet. "I think we should just get on with practice."

"I agree," Eliasser said. He sent me one last dose of energy, then let go of my hands and we began our meditation.

I did eventually get to see Ari's version of turning to light. We'd been out sailing together on the Mindsail Lake, taking turns at the "helm." As we walked back to the Mountain, I asked him what Makashannar meant when he said Ari didn't have to try to turn to light.

Instead of answering me with words, Ari showed me.

I couldn't blame Makashannar for being envious. Without any warm-up meditation, Ari transformed into a blue-white sparkling orb. Then *poof*—he was physical again. And *poof*—back to a brilliant ball of light. He blinked in and out of light form about a dozen times before I told him I'd seen enough. I didn't have the same emotional response as when Eliasser turned to light, but Ari's light-body was still a gorgeous sight and I was afraid he might break something with all that flipping back and forth.

The strength and depth of my growing affection—love, really—for Eliasser was another thing that puzzled me about my Amoran life. Whenever I asked him about the intense connection we seemed to share, he smiled and changed the subject to something he was always willing to talk about. The One Light.

I thought the vortex was the be-all and end-all of the Guardians' existence, but the driving force behind everything they did was something called the One Light. Eliasser's first attempt to teach me about it occurred after Midday Meal. Big mistake. Happily sated and ready for a nap, I kept losing that all-important focus.

What he described was a basic creation story. First, there was Nothing. Then there was Something. How this Something managed to arise out of Nothing wasn't clear, except that it miraculously "thought" itself into existence! Then the Something thought again and was spontaneously transformed into a brilliant, blazing energy. Voilà! The One Light was born. The One Light did its own thinking, and before long the universe was teeming with all sorts of interesting stuff made out of Something that was originally Nothing.

Right. I never could do lectures well, a trait that seemed to hold true on Amoran as well as on Earth. The third time Eliasser tried to make it all the way through the story, I closed my eyes, just for a moment. The next thing I knew, he was prodding me awake. "Some things have not changed in a thousand years," he proclaimed with a laugh.

Eliasser and Ari were the two bright spots in my Amoran life. Fortunately for me, Ari was also the only Guardian who found it difficult to dodge my questions, a weakness I shamelessly took advantage of. With a little strategic arm-twisting, I could get Ari to talk about off-limits topics. Like the day I pointed out that it didn't take a geriatric specialist to know something was very different about the aging process of Amorans. We had just finished several rounds of Garrammon when

I "persuaded" him to spill the beans by threatening to never sing old Beatles songs with him—something he had a particular fondness for.

"All right, all right. You drive a hard bargain, Earth-girl. But I'm not telling you everything, or I'll catch hell from Ashara and Eliasser."

The others had already returned to the Mountain, while Ari and I stayed behind for a postgame snack. We settled beneath our favorite tree at the top of the hill, the same one Makashannar usually staked out for himself. As Ari talked, he stripped away the soft outer bark of a stick of *solsatta,* an unusual vegetable that grew on trees.

"Basically, the elevated energy of this planet affects everything—how food grows, how long people live, even how they live. But inside the boundary of Guardian Lands, the energy concentration is considerably greater. Because of that, Amorans who live beneath the Mountain have a much longer lifespan than their counterparts on Amoran proper."

He finished peeling the solsatta, bit off one end and chewed slowly.

"And that would be . . ." I prompted.

Ari looked sideways at me. "The average Amoran lifespan is about three hundred years, but beneath the Mountain, it's anywhere from five to ten times longer."

I quickly did the math. "But that's as much as three thousand years!"

He passed the solsatta to me and I took a bite, enjoying the pungent sweetness of the crunchy vegetable. "This concentrated energy, is that why Amorans avoid touching each other?"

Ari shook his head. "They don't avoid it, they just don't have the same need for it. And it isn't all of Amoran. Once again, things are different under the Mountain." His brows furrowed. "I've never really understood it, though. Regardless of ambient energy, elves revel in physical contact of all kinds." To my surprise, the unabashedly open and gregarious elf turned slightly pink. "Um, I wasn't just referring to—"

"Yeah, yeah. Judging by what a big flirt you are, I'm betting elves have a healthy appetite in that area." He laughed at that. "Let me get this straight," I went on. "Are you saying . . . I mean . . . doesn't anyone under the Mountain ever . . ." Now I was reddening, to his obvious amusement. "Stop grinning at me like that! How come Eliasser didn't know what to do the first time I hugged him, yet there's a school full of children. Did they arrive by magic?"

Ari snorted. "They'd have to if it was up to Mountain dwellers to produce them. Amorans are fully equipped to do what is necessary to have children. However, the same intense drive to 'connect' that way"—he used air quotes for the word—"doesn't exist on this planet. And beneath the Mountain, they don't 'connect' at all."

My mouth dropped open. "Never?"

"Never. It's not as far-fetched as it might seem. The same elevated energy that increases their lifespan suppresses those desires, so they never feel the need."

"How do you account for Balthasarre and Anders?"

"They came here from a distant part of Amoran when Anders was a small child."

Something about this wasn't adding up, but I wasn't sure what it was. "So the Mountain completely takes away the urge to merge? Physically that is?"

"Yup. Well, for most of them, anyway." With a guilty look, Ari bent over to re-tie the wraps on his shoes, which clearly did not need fixing.

"Most of them? Explain please."

He groaned, and kept fiddling with the wraps.

"Ari? Don't make me hurt you."

"I shouldn't say anything else, although there probably isn't any harm in—Ow!" He sat up. "Stop twisting my arm. Have you seen a shrink about these violent tendencies?"

"That Lonely Hearts Club Band is going to contain just you in a minute."

"Oh, fine! A few of the Guardians will never need the natural suppression of the Mountain's energy because they can't feel desires like that. It isn't part of their makeup."

Eliasser and Makashannar had both made references to "not being designed that way," but I hadn't imagined it went this far.

"Do they have all the right parts?"

Ari rolled his eyes. "Yes, they have all the rights parts, as you so delicately put it."

"But they can't do anything with them?"

"Geez, Kerrin, this is getting awkward. No, they can't do anything with them, but the only reason for that is because they are incapable of feeling those urges. Does that make sense?"

"Not really." I squinted out at the lake. It looked cool and inviting, and I wished I could take a swim. "You said a few. Who are they?" When he didn't answer, I whined, "Oh come on. I've already guessed Makashannar and Eliasser. What harm can it do to tell me who the others are?"

He bit his lip. I tried a different form of manipulation, complete with puppy dog eyes. "Please? Please, please, please, please . . ."

He broke down and laughed. "I am such a soft touch. There were originally four of them. You're right about Eliasser and Makashannar. Just add to that Ashara and . . ." he looked pointedly at me.

The idea was so far out my range of experience that it took a moment for what he was implying to sink in.

"Oh, God. Me, too? I was like that before I went to live on Earth?"

"Hard to believe, right?" He grinned and poked me in the side.

"I'm not sure you meant that as a compliment, but between you and me, I could use some of that suppression when I'm here for weeks on end." I sighed. "Unfortunately, the energy doesn't seem to affect me that way at all. In fact, if anything, I'm even more . . . you know."

He snickered again, which only added to my embarrassment. Recalling his earlier comment that elves revel in touch of all kinds, I said, "What about you? I'm guessing you're a lot more like me, so how do you live with—"

I broke off as Ari clenched his jaw and his face creased with pain.

"I'm sorry," I mumbled. "Your sex life is really none of my business."

He didn't say anything, and in the silence that ensued, I mulled over all that I had learned, coming at length to an important conclusion.

"Ari?"

"Hmm?"

I smiled. "I'm glad I got the chance to live on Earth, because I do like to 'connect.'"

"So do I," he said. But he didn't smile in return.

———

The two Earth weeks I'd been traveling between dimensions netted me over five months on Amoran. The disproportionate amount of time I spent there was warping my perception of my Earth life. When I touched down in my family room, it was now like entering a foreign land, while the world at the other end of the vortex felt more and more like home to me. I still couldn't recall specific memories from my previous Amoran life, but the woman I had once been kept impressing herself into my thoughts, my personality, and occasionally into my speech patterns.

Increasingly, I felt her presence within me. And we both wanted to stay on Amoran.

# CHAPTER 17

Ten Earth days before Thanksgiving, I stood in the Main Chamber with the rest of the Guardians after a highly successful morning practice. The closer we got to the Reparention, the faster our bodies responded to our meditations and potions. Danaeus had finally managed to convert his vibrationally heavy body to light; molecule for molecule, it was even denser than my Earth one. Balthasarre and Anders had achieved full light-form a few Earth days before that. That left me as the only Guardian who couldn't shine like a small star.

I consoled myself with the knowledge that I had something to be proud of, too. Our vortex repair plan required each of us to raise our vibrations and connect our individual energies to the rest of the group while still remaining in physical form. During the Reparention, we would have to accomplish this with great speed and no margin for error. We'd then enter the vortex where Ashara would "cement" this connection in place by joining our consciousnesses together through something called the Mind Link. My months of training and meditating, during which I commanded all the cells of my body to "lighten up," had paid off. I could raise my vibrations nearly as well as my teammates. However, without the ability to morph my cells into light energy, the raised vibrations were not going to do me much good in a volatile vortex. But at least I'd moved forward.

I stuffed down my own disappointment and congratulated Danaeus as he pumped his fist in the air while yelling, "Yes! YES!"

I'd taught him that.

Eliasser and Ashara were so pleased with our progress, they granted us the afternoon off. Balthasarre proposed that our hard work be rewarded with a picnic in the Outer Grounds, but Ari suggested a celebration dinner instead.

"That is an excellent suggestion," Eliasser said. "I am unavailable this evening. Would tomorrow night be acceptable?" We agreed enthusiastically, even Makashannar. Encouraged by his openness, I smiled across the circle at him. He just looked away.

Ashara whispered something to Balthasarre, who frowned, then gave a resigned nod.

Ari rubbed his hands together. "Let's bring out the scentflames."

"What are scentflames?" I asked.

Danaeus looked thoughtful. "It's a fragrant bit of fire that makes you feel . . ." his voice petered out as a dopey smile worked its way across his face.

"Get a grip, Danaeus!" Ari said. He turned to me. "Think aromatherapy, only much better."

Ashara reacted like she'd been stuck with a pin. Her body went ramrod straight and she searched our faces, one by one. When her eyes found mine, they went hollow with what looked like a mixture of grief and fear. The hairs on my arms shot straight up.

"Ashara . . . ?" Eliasser said tentatively. She turned away and hurried from the Main Chamber. Eliasser pursed his lips and followed after her.

Anders's young face was lined with worry. "Is it the vortex?" he asked his father. "Ashara is always the first to feel a shift in its energy field."

"She would have told us so," Balthasarre replied. "I think we are safe in that regard."

The rest of us breathed a collective sigh of relief, and the knot that had formed in my stomach at Anders's question eased a little. The schedule for the Reparention kept moving up, with the latest prediction placing it close to Christmas Day on Earth.

"*Excuse me,*" Danaeus whined, "but aren't we supposed to be celebrating?"

I smiled. "You're right. And I can't think of a better way to celebrate than by playing Garrammon. Are you game?" I asked Balthasarre.

Ari groaned, but the Master Technician was impervious to my puns.

"Not today. Ashara wants Anders and me to hull the last batch of nemestes pods."

"She certainly hijacked your afternoon off," I grumbled. Sometimes the Master Healer was a Major Horror.

Balthasarre shrugged. "Since we are celebrating tomorrow night, she decided that we should not mind giving up this free time now." With that, father and son left for the Healing Room.

"Darn. That leaves only three of us," I said.

Ari elbowed me. "You've become quite the glutton for punishment."

He had to be referring to my mediocre Garrammon skills. "I guess I am. I've never been one for sports, but I'm becoming as addicted to Garrammon as my father is to golf."

"Oh, well, that *is* serious." Ari grinned and linked his arm through mine. "Did I ever tell you about my first game of golf on Earth?"

"Save me," I stage-whispered to Danaeus.

"Now Kerrin," Ari protested, "you know you love my Earth stories."

"Not when I'd rather be playing Garrammon."

I'm not sure what impulse got my feet moving, but I stormed across the Golden Circle as if I were invading enemy territory and planted myself in front of Makashannar.

"Your arms aren't broken. Why not join us?"

"Yes, come with us," Danaeus begged. "You love this game. You used to play it all the time with . . . um . . ." He snapped his mouth closed and stared at the ground.

Oh, brother. There was only one reason for Danaeus to shut himself up like that.

"Let me take a wild guess." I narrowed my eyes at Makashannar. "I'm the one you used to play Garrammon with, right? And, from what everyone says about your playing ability, I bet you beat the pants off me."

Danaeus gasped. "I don't remember your pants coming off."

Ari laughed. "It's just an Earth saying. A strange one, I'll admit."

"Yeah, well, that's not all that's strange," I continued, directing my comments to Makashannar. "If you want to play Garrammon, fine. If not, don't tag along after us, whatever we decide to do. I don't need a babysitter, and I can't take your cold, silent watchfulness any longer. It makes my stomach hurt."

Even though I'd tried to stay calm, the last sentence came out sounding more like a shout. I stalked back across the circle, wishing I didn't always feel like the odd one out in the Guardians' emotionally tidy world.

But Makashannar surprised me. "I will play Garrammon with you," he said quietly.

I turned around, too shocked to respond. It didn't matter. He was already halfway across the Main Chamber, heading for the corridor to the Outer Grounds.

"Well, that went swimmingly," Ari said, crossing his eyes.

"I'm sorry I yelled at him, but he treats me like a nonperson. I couldn't take it anymore. Thanks, you guys, for putting up with me." I smiled at Ari and gave Danaeus an impulsive hug.

Danaeus, cheeks in full rosy bloom from my quick embrace, said gruffly, "Let's get going."

"What about Midday Meal?" I asked. "I'm starving."

Clarisanna, my favorite meal Assistant, entered the chamber toting a large basket.

"The Master Healer asked me to bring this to you. I hope it is to your liking."

I peeked under the cloth cover. It was Midday Meal to-go, all of my favorites. How had Ashara known we would need it, and then timed its arrival so perfectly? I sighed, almost feeling guilty about how much I didn't like her sometimes.

"It's wonderful, Clarisanna. Thank you."

Danaeus, Ari, and I made our way to the Main Gate where Makashannar was waiting for us. As he had done on my first trip to the Outer Grounds, he held the gate open for us to pass through, then motioned me to remain behind while Ari and Danaeus went on ahead.

"I would like to apologize," he said. "I do not mean to cause you discomfort."

"Then don't treat me like a pariah." It was clear by his expression that he didn't know what a pariah was. "Forget it. Thanks for the apology."

On the hill above the Garrammon field, we ate a light meal of fruit, monzennez, and visinnima. Then Ari set up our beginning teams—Ari and me versus Makashannar and Danaeus.

The initial match lasted a dozen or so rounds, each one more intense. Makashannar played stiffly for the first few rounds, as if holding himself in check. But when Ari returned a series of volleys in quick succession, Makashannar's eyes lit up and he threw himself into the game. Face flushed, smile widening with each pass, he was truly a master player. During one aggressive volley, when only two players could remain on the field, Danaeus and I backed out of the way of the rapid-fire exchanges. Ari missed the ball, ending the round.

It was time to switch partners. Makashannar and I were now paired against Ari and Danaeus. As we played, Makashannar shouted commands at me, guiding me to better moves. "Pass now. Hold it, I have this one. You need to . . . oh, almost."

The playing tips he gave me were useful, but they weren't the reason for my sudden improvement. The sound of his voice talking about Garrammon reached deep inside me, triggering recollections of past plays—and I mean *long* past. Memories surfaced and integrated quickly, not only in my mind, but my body as well. As though my muscles were recreating themselves, my game was improving, literally by leaps and bounds. When we took a break before switching partners again, I told Makashannar, "You'll be sorry you helped me. Prepare to eat dirt."

Danaeus, confused as ever by my Earth-isms, asked why Makashannar would need to consume soil. Before I could explain the reference, Makashannar flashed me a mocking grin.

"Are all Earth people infected with such ridiculous optimism?"

Ari coughed out his laughter. "Oh, good hit. Ball's in your court, Earth-girl. What's your response to that bit of Amoran arrogance?"

"That it wouldn't hurt Serious Sam"—I jabbed my thumb at Makashannar—"to be a little ridiculous once in a while. As for optimism? My glass is always half full; in fact, I'm hoping to see it all the way full right now. Danaeus? Pass me that carafe."

We quenched our thirst with *nivinnis* juice while Ari and I described golf to the other two. Makashannar, who simply could not comprehend why someone would bend over a stick, then use it to strike a ball that was *always* visible, was happier and more relaxed than he'd ever been in my presence.

When our break was over, I decided to tap into that ridiculous optimism of mine.

"How about Danaeus and I pair up against you and Ari?" I asked Makashannar.

Makashannar's smile was pure provocation. "If you think you are up to it."

"Oh, I'm up to it. But are you? How about a little wager? Loser has to take the other's turn helping Ashara gather nemestes."

He tossed his head back and laughed. "How kind of you. I will enjoy the rest."

"We'll see who gets to rest." I beamed him a confident smile, then turned around and grimaced. What was I thinking? I'd recently learned firsthand what nemestes gathering was like. The sticky, prickly plant had to be extricated from clay-like soil without damaging the roots. Roots that seemed to stretch to the very center of the planet. Worse, this had to be done in the heat of a stretch of land called the Endless Plain, all while trying to avoid the glazzien flowers, which were known to bite if disturbed. Even Eliasser balked at gathering nemestes.

And yet, it wasn't a given that I'd be saddled with Makashannar's nemestes duties. I now had a card tucked up my sleeve. When Ari first taught me the essentials of Garrammon, he let me in on one of the strategies for dealing with the disappearing ball. Ari had said that if I concentrated hard enough and closed my eyes right after the ball vanished, I'd "see" where it was headed. It was an incredibly hard skill to master, especially in the middle of a fast-moving game. While the rest of the Garrammon-playing Guardians could do it on occasion, Makashannar's success rate was the highest. But even he couldn't pull it off with any regularity. Ari had admitted, flat out, that I wasn't expected to be able to do it at all.

However, during the last round before our break today, I'd shut my eyes for a moment to blot out the bright sun. To my complete astonishment, an image of the ball skated across the backs of my eyelids. When I opened my eyes, the real-life ball popped into view right where

I'd "seen" it. I was so stunned I couldn't react. I figured it had to be a fluke. A short while later, though, it happened again. All I did was blink, and I still saw the invisible ball. If I could get control of that ability, I might have a chance at giving Makashannar a run for his money. And the element of surprise was on my side, as I hadn't mentioned this to the others. I figured I was entitled to a few secrets of my own.

With the gauntlet thrown down, the four of us returned to the field. The intense rounds we'd played earlier were barely a warm-up compared to what happened next. The serves were coming so fast and hard now that it was a challenge to see the ball even when it was visible.

We were well into the first round when the ball vanished. I tipped my head down so Makashannar couldn't see what I was doing, and quickly closed then reopened my eyes. Smiling to myself, I faked running in one direction, but leapt to where I knew the ball was headed. When it reappeared, I spiked it just beyond Makashannar's outstretched arm, ending the round. The incredulity on his face nearly did me in with pride, but it was followed by a look of such forceful determination that I gulped.

"Watch out," Ari exclaimed. "You've done it now."

"Good," I said, unwilling to give ground. "He probably needs a little real competition."

Ari and Danaeus guffawed, and I joined in, laughing at my pigheaded presumption. That lapse in concentration cost me the next play. It was my turn to shoot Makashannar a warning glance. "I won't make that mistake again," I said.

Makashannar and I began playing so fiercely, that at first I didn't notice Ari and Danaeus moving over to the sidelines to wait out the volley in progress. The ball was a blur as we slammed it back and forth until it vanished. Makashannar blinked, then gave it a resounding smack with his handpiece. Now visible, the ball sailed my way, presumably out of reach.

"Game over, as you say on Earth," he called, a little too gleefully for my taste.

I was already sprinting backwards. "Not yet, it isn't!" I jumped up, nicking the ball with just enough force to send it across the line and in bounds by a hair's breadth.

A stunned Makashannar quickly rallied, fell to the ground, and rolled toward where the ball was about to touch the grass. His handpiece slipped under the ball and he sent it skyward.

"I don't believe it," Ari shouted.

I dashed back to field the high pitch, giggling at the sheer impossibility of what Makashannar had done, as well as how silly he'd looked doing it. Meanwhile, he scrambled to his feet, then hunched over, hands on his knees, laughing. He was still doubled over when I pounded the ball back his way—nice and high. "I've got you now," I gloated, fully expecting the ball to soar over him before he could rise up and get it.

Wrong again. Makashannar uncurled himself and leapt into the air like he was wearing moon shoes. He tapped the ball so gently, I didn't think it would make it over the center line. But I couldn't risk it. I galloped forward right as the ball vanished for a third time, signaling we had to play open-handed. Makashannar and I flung off our handpieces, closed and opened our eyes, and ran straight toward each other. The ball popped back into view between us, then vanished again. We threw out our hands to keep from crashing into each other, but were too late. We collided, lost our balance, and thudded to the ground in a giggling heap, clutching each other's tunics. And then, Makashannar was gone.

Not physically gone. He didn't disappear like the Garrammon ball. I just couldn't feel his body any longer. Or mine. It was like we'd transformed into an energy field, one that pulsed with exquisite sensitivity. And, oh my God, I wanted more of it. Lots more.

That lovely pulsing stopped, but I had no chance to register disappointment. A low humming vibration took its place, building in strength, second by second. I could feel our bodies again, our fingers still clutching each other's tunic. Unable to stop myself, I pulled Makashannar closer. Closer . . .

The humming increased. We breathed in tandem now, a jagged rhythm, like gulps of air after a crying spell.

His arms slid around me and tightened. My heart rate soared. We were as physically close as we could be and still be wearing clothes. But I needed to be even closer. I needed to be completely inside his energy field with him.

Suddenly, Makashannar shoved me away, bolted up and hurried off.

I lay where I was, gasping for breath, unwilling to move, uncertain that I could.

A hand touched my shoulder. "Are you okay?" Danaeus asked.

"I think so," I croaked. I let Danaeus help me to my feet. It was an effort not to look or sound as devastated as I felt.

"We'd better head back," Ari said, frowning in the direction Makashannar had retreated.

It was a quiet post-Garrammon walk to the Mountain. As we passed through the Main Gate and crossed the grassy courtyard, I broke the pensive silence.

"Did either of you notice anything strange after Makashannar and I ran into each other?"

"No," Ari said. "Unless you mean the hug-fest you were having."

Danaeus blushed. "Must you be so indiscreet?"

I had the impression he was defending my honor, which struck me as sweet but unnecessary in the Mountain's sexless society.

Ari laughed and pretended to twirl a mustache. "Indiscreet is my middle name."

His joking cut through the tension that had prevailed since we left the Garrammon field, and our conversation moved on to other things.

We were almost to the Main Chamber when my muscles offered up a sudden, vigorous protest to the workout I'd put them through. I held onto Ari for support as my legs began to shake. "I shouldn't have played that hard."

Ari gave my arm a squeeze. "But it was worth it, wasn't it?"

"Oh, hell yeah. Except for the part where I can't walk right now."

Danaeus, using his gruff "nothing affects ME" voice, offered his shoulder and said, "Lean on me." Ari began singing the Earth song with the same name and I joined in. We taught Danaeus the chorus, and by the time the three of us made it to the Main Chamber, we finished at the top of our lungs.

Danaeus gave me a quick hug—the first one he'd ever initiated—then left to do his rotation at setup duty in the Main Meal Room. Ari waited until Danaeus disappeared down a corridor, then faced me with an expression much too serious for the fun-loving elf I'd come to know.

"I'm not sure how to handle this yet," he said, "so please don't let Eliasser or Ashara know what happened with you and Makashannar."

So Ari *had* noticed something strange. Worry lodged in the pit of my stomach. "Is something wrong with Makashannar?"

Ari looked grim. "I don't know. But I plan on finding out."

# CHAPTER 18

I rolled off my sleeping stone the next morning and hobbled to the ancillary to take my "shower," cursing the lack of hot water beneath the Mountain. I'd been so exhausted after yesterday's Garrammon match that I skipped Evening Meal, downed my nightly brews, and went straight to bed. I was far less stiff and sore this morning, and I had Ashara to thank for that. Along with my usual slew of potions, she'd added one to ease pain and relax my muscles.

When I got to the Guardian Meal Room, Eliasser, Ashara, and Makashannar were absent.

"Where is everybody?" I asked.

Ari looked pointedly at Danaeus, Anders, and Balthasarre, then raised an eyebrow at me.

"Where is *everybody?* Passed math class, did you?"

"You know what I mean," I retorted. "And yes, I did. I'm very good with numbers."

Anders grinned. He enjoyed our good-natured bickering.

"Makashannar is ill," Balthasarre said. "Ashara and Eliasser are with him now."

He offered me the vegetable mixture that looked like scrambled eggs but tasted so much better. I scooped a generous helping onto my plate, reflecting that in all the time I'd spent on Amoran, I had not consumed a single meat dish. And I hadn't missed it either. Now, if they could only manage a bowl of chocolate pudding.

"What happened to him?" I asked, as the cold knot of fear from yesterday returned.

Ari's jaw tightened. "I went to his room last night to check on him and found him barely conscious. I brought him to the Healing Room and told Ashara what I saw when Makashannar pushed you away yesterday. It looked like he was in a lot of pain, and it wasn't from the impact of the two of you running into each other."

Balthasarre laid a hand on my arm. "Do not worry. He is much improved already, and Ashara thinks he will be fully recovered by tonight's celebration dinner."

I nodded to Balthasarre, but kept thinking about what Ari had said. If his observation about Makashannar being in pain was correct, what had caused it? I agreed that the physical impact itself hadn't been enough to do it. Besides, when we clung together on the ground, I'm pretty sure we were feeling the same thing, and it wasn't pain. In a weird way, it was a little like—

*Oh, God. Cancel, cancel, cancel.*

I tried to obliterate the rest of the thought, but ideas aren't as easily cut off as the spoken word. The sentence completed itself, despite my attempt to suppress it.

*It was a little like making love, without physically making love.*

"Are you okay?" Ari asked. "Now you're the one looking awfully pale."

"I'm fine," I squeaked, and ate the rest of my meal in silence.

---

With Ashara, Eliasser, and Makashannar unavailable, Reparention practice was called off for the day. I wasn't up to Garrammon just yet, so I asked the others if they'd like to join me for a walk. Anders and Balthasarre couldn't—they had to attend to some new anomaly in the vortex. It wasn't related to the Reparention, but still posed a risk for my trips back and forth. Danaeus also declined; he wasn't much of a walker. Ari accepted, and the two of us strolled to the Garrammon Lake, the name for the petite body of water just beyond the Garrammon field.

We completed a circuit around the tiny lake, which was barely large enough to even qualify as a small pond on Earth. I was sweating now, more from the weather than the exertion. For the first time, the Amoran air felt uncomfortably warm and humid. In contrast, the light blue water sparkled with a tantalizing coolness.

"I'd really like to go swimming," I said, pushing a damp lock of hair off my forehead. "What's the big deal with Amorans and water?"

"It's complicated. The short explanation is that it would be no more reasonable for an Amoran to hop into a pool of water than for you to dive into a pile of concrete."

"Oh, come on. It's not as if a person could actually do that."

Ari shrugged. "Depends on your vibrational frequency."

"You're serious? Wait—" I held my hand up. "Don't answer that. How about a Rule of the Day. No more talk of vibrational frequencies and energy signatures. Let's just have fun."

"You want fun?" Ari stared at the glistening blue water and smiled. "Ready?"

"Ready for what?"

"Swimming."

"You're kidding."

"Nope. Elves love to swim."

"Great! What about bathing suits?" I looked down at my tunic. "Can we swim in these?"

Ari's smile turned provocative. "We could take them off."

"In your dreams."

He laughed. "Don't worry. I'm not trying to . . . oh, what's the Earth term for—"

"Hit on me? You're not trying to hit on me?"

"No, I'm not. And rest assured I won't." He shook his head as if the notion was absurd.

"Thanks loads," I said. "Ever hear of female pride?"

My attempt at mock indignation turned out to be the real McCoy. Aside from being married, I wasn't attracted to Ari that way. But it was a blow to my ego to have him laugh at the idea. Which was silly, because one of the things I cherished about our friendship was the way we could be physical without sexual tension. Sometimes, we curled up beneath the tree above the Garrammon field and took a nap together after a long, hard match. In fact, our relationship was a lot like my friendship with Tom and Dave, which meant I'd wondered more than once about

Ari's sexual orientation. I'd never asked Ari about it, though, as if the topic was off-limits for some reason. My injured pride pushed me past that line.

"Ari? Please tell me you're gay, or I won't know whether to be relieved or insulted."

He frowned. "Just be glad," he said, his voice tight.

Glad about what? That he wouldn't hit on me? There was more to this, I could feel it. But witnessing the grim set to his mouth, I realized suddenly that I was tired of trying to pry information out of people. And I *had* just said we needed to have fun.

"Well?" I whined. "Can we swim with our tunics on or not?"

The impish smile made a comeback. He ran into the lake, dove underneath, and resurfaced several yards out. "What are you waiting for, pokey?"

"You are such a brat," I yelled, and I dove in after him.

We spent the next half hour swimming and splashing around like a couple of kids. When our fingers shriveled and our teeth chattered, we dragged ourselves out of the lake and stood shivering on the sand. "Care to conjure up a couple of towels, Elf-boy?"

"Who needs towels?" Ari closed his eyes, held his hands up and turned in a circle. "With each revolution, ask the sun to move the water from your body back to the lake."

A few Earth weeks ago, I would have signed his commitment papers. Now, I did as instructed. The temperature grew warmer and water wicked away from my skin. In no time we were dry, tunics and all. "I am duly impressed," I said. "That is one handy piece of magic."

"Thanks. I came up with it on my own and I'm rather proud of it. Hungry?"

"Yes, now that you mention it. Are you going to make it arrive out of thin air?"

"Nah. I have something else in mind." He led me to a row of low-lying bushes that hugged one edge of the beach. Lifting a large, broom-like branch, he reached in, picked two golden-yellow spheres, and handed one to me. "*Granommus* fruit. Just ripening. Very tasty, and packed with enough food energy to last us until dinner."

Just ripening? I hadn't even known the fruit was there.

We climbed the hill and sat with our backs to the tree. We polished off the granommus—it tasted vaguely like mango . . . *yum!*—then fell into one of our companionable quiet times. Ari closed his eyes, and I was growing drowsy. Knowing sleep would descend upon me soon, I allowed my thoughts to drift aimlessly, until a random fly-by caught my attention.

"Ari?" I whispered. "Are you awake?"

"I wasn't," he said, keeping his eyelids closed.

"Right. That's why you answered so fast."

"I'm trying to take a nap, here."

"I can see that, Sleeping Beauty. So tell me what I want to know and I promise I'll shut up. Where do you come from?"

He remained as motionless as a Resting Stone.

"Stop pretending you didn't hear me. A few days ago, Danaeus told me about the Dwarf-world—how he slipped through a dimensional variance, whatever that is, and became trapped on Amoran. He said you're not from this world either, but he wouldn't say anything more."

Ari's warm brown eyes finally opened, but there was nothing warm in his tone.

"Danaeus should learn to hold his tongue," he snapped.

Surprised by the strong reaction, I defended my fellow Guardian.

"Don't be mad at him. It would have come up eventually. Even you have referred to 'elves,' plural. Is there an Elf-world out there?" I waved my hand at the sky.

Ari fixed his attention on the lake, his face oddly revealing in its complete lack of expression. I didn't know what the issue was, but finding out wasn't important enough to spoil our afternoon. "Hey, forget it. If you don't want to talk about it, it's okay by me."

He sighed. "It's not that I don't want to."

"If you're referring to the gag order around my past, telling me where you come from shouldn't be a problem, right?"

A shiver rose up my spine in response to Ari's silence, a sure indication that my past and Ari's homeworld were linked in some way.

"I so hate this," I grumbled.

"Me too, Earth-girl." Then, as if the thought had only just occurred to him, he added, "Except, you weren't always an Earth-girl, were you?"

"I assume you mean my stint on Amoran, unless you're hinting I'm really an elf."

He gave my nose an affectionate tweak. "No, you've never been an elf. Pointy ears would not become you." Ari studied me for several moments. "But you helped save this elf's life once, which is why I'm going to tell you as much as I can without risking your life in return."

"I saved your life? Me?" That was difficult to believe. I am hardly the courageous type.

"Yes. You." Ari watched me with that expression that was no expression. "About fifteen hundred years ago, the Elven High Council learned that the Fifth Vortex—the vortex for my homeworld, Elvener—would become unstable and possibly implode. For several centuries, we monitored the energy patterns, adjusting them as necessary. Things seemed to settle down and we thought we'd succeeded." He sighed and stared out at the lake again. "But our early manipulation of vortex energy ultimately made things worse, something we discovered several hundred years later. And several hundred years too late. Implosion was now a certainty."

"Oh, Ari." A sudden, intense sadness pierced me.

"There was good news, though. Not long after Elvener received its death sentence, a Mirror Vortex appeared."

"That's a new one on me."

Ari looked thoughtful. "Without getting too technical, it's as if the original vortex clones itself. You wind up with two vortexes that are energetically linked, but not identical." He frowned. "That's not it exactly, it's more like they are—"

"Stop right there. I'm good with 'two vortexes for the price of one.'"

He nodded. "One of the Mirror Vortex portals opened onto Elvener, but instead of the opposite portal linking Elvener to her sister world, it connected us with Amoran. That's how we first made contact with the Guardians of the Seventh Vortex. When they learned of our predicament, they insisted we bring our people to Amoran to live."

"What about your sister world?"

Ari shook his head. "It was uninhabitable. No one had ever lived there."

I nodded, although I hadn't realized that not all worlds anchoring a vortex were populated.

"On the day we were to begin the transfer," Ari continued, "I was in the Mirror Vortex for a final energy check when it unexpectedly convulsed and nearly killed me." He squeezed his eyes shut and shuddered. "The dark energy was monstrous in size. If it hadn't been for Makashannar—"

"Makashannar was there?"

The corners of Ari's mouth tightened. I knew the signs all too well.

"Please, Ari. Don't stop now."

He gave a frustrated shake of his head. "As far as I'm concerned, the restriction on talking about your past is unnecessary, if not outright ridiculous."

"Then screw the gag order. Listen instead to those amazing elven instincts of yours."

He looked at me then as if he were seeing me—really seeing me—for the first time.

"You're right." He shifted so that we faced each other. "Makashannar entered the Mirror Vortex from Amoran at the same time I went in from Elvener. When the Mirror Vortex convulsed, he threw himself into the chaos to rescue me before implosion occurred. He got us back to the Amoran side, but our Life Forces had been so drained by dark energy that we were paralyzed. With minutes left before implosion, you raced in and brought us the rest of the way to the Amoran portal. You pushed me out, then turned to help Makashannar. But the vortex winds had already dragged him back the other way—straight toward the Darkness.

"The Amoran portal was nearly closed by then. You were still trying to get to Makashannar when Eliasser fought his way in and found you. It's a miracle he got you out when he did because the Mirror Vortex abruptly folded in on itself and vanished. I didn't need to be on Elvener to know what happened to the Fifth Vortex. I lost everything. My family, friends, my Eternal Companion . . . everyone . . . gone in an instant."

Raw emotion set my body trembling. "Eternal Companion?"

"On Earth, she would be called my soul mate."

"Oh, Ari." My throat ached and tears stung my eyes. But Ari went on as if he were merely reciting the history of Garrammon.

"We thought we'd lost Makashannar, too. A few days went by, and then we found him, lying unconscious in the meadow near the Garrammon Lake, right where the Mirror Vortex portal had been. No one knows how he got there. He spent four months in the Healing Room before he woke up. He refused to talk about what happened, but I think that experience, and his brush with the Darkness, haunts him to this day."

My brain spared me the visuals, but the extra energy went into the feeling-memory of an event that occurred over a thousand years ago, yet felt as if it were happening now. Waves of grief crashed over me as I re-experienced the loss of Ari's world. Of Makashannar, presumed dead until his miraculous reappearance. And the months of anxiety spent waiting for his mind to return. That was when Ari and I had bonded so deeply.

I waited until I could talk with only a modicum of shaking in my voice. "You seem so calm. I know this event is ancient history, but I can barely keep my tears at bay."

"Why should you? As for me, well, elves can't cry. Our emotions don't work that way."

"You can't *cry?*" That was harder for me to believe than people who don't feel the need for sex. "What do you do with your sadness?"

"We have our ways of dealing with it." He smiled ruefully, and I wondered if we were thinking the same thing. That once upon a time I'd known that elves don't cry. And that, like the rest of the Guardians, for whom tears seemed anathema, I probably hadn't cried much either.

Ari's smile disappeared. "After we found Makashannar, we learned the Seventh Vortex was going to face an even greater challenge. From that moment forward, all our attention focused on healing Makashannar and figuring out what to do to keep Amoran from suffering the same fate as my homeworld. Other than to process what went wrong, we never mentioned Elvener again. I don't know why, except . . . maybe the grief was too overwhelming."

That did it. I was trying to hold myself together, to act more like a Guardian. But I am blessed with strong emotions and the equipment to express them readily.

My wavering voice went husky. "My emotions do work that way, and I can't seem to stop them. So, I hope you don't mind if I cry for the two of us."

# CHAPTER 19

"Feel better?" Ari asked, once the remembered grief had worked its way through my system.

"Yes. I usually do after a good cry. How are you doing?"

"I'm all right, thanks." He noted the position of the sun. "We have time for a quick swim. I'll race you to lake." He bolted up and dashed down the hill.

"Cheater! Nothing like giving yourself a head start." I ran as fast as I could without tumbling head over heels, caught up with him at the water's edge, and yanked him back.

"Oh, and I suppose you consider that fair." He pushed me sideways and tried to scoot ahead, but I latched onto his tunic.

We hit the water together.

As we were struggling to dunk each other, I caught movement out of the corner of my eye. Eliasser, Danaeus, and Makashannar stood near the shoreline, gaping in disbelief. Ari and I high-fived over Makashannar's return to health, but then Ari took advantage of our ceasefire to push me under. When I sputtered to the surface, a panic-stricken Danaeus was inching toward the water, hands outstretched as if to save me.

"Don't worry, Danaeus. I'm okay. I even like this."

"Forget about him," Ari muttered. "Playtime's over. Dad's mad."

"Dad?" I laughed. Then I rammed Ari backwards so I could beat him out of the lake. But he got me with a flying tackle and we went down with a whale-sized splash. After some more wrestling, we exited three-legged race style so that neither of us could claim we were first.

Eliasser shook his head as if what he had just witnessed was incomprehensible to him. "I do not understand this . . . this . . . flailing about in the water. How do you propose to dry yourselves?"

"No problem," I said, proud to show off the magic I'd learned. I closed my eyes and moved in a circle with my hands held high. Warm air currents circled around me, drying my tunic. But there was a difference now. A gentle rolling pressure accompanied the warmth that felt simply marvelous. I welcomed another Amoran energy treat, and kept circling, and circling, and—

"Uh, Kerrin?" Ari said.

I opened my eyes. A gorgeous glowing pink mist spiraled around me.

Eliasser's jaw dropped open. "How in the name of the Light—" He choked off and stared at Makashannar, who was now encircled by an identical spiral of pink mist. With a strangled cry, Eliasser moved inside my spiral. Grasping my hands, he planted them on his chest and slammed his eyes shut. A vibrating energy moved between us. When it stopped, the misty spirals were gone.

Eliasser opened his eyes again and sighed as if he'd just averted a disaster.

"What's wrong?" I asked.

"Ashara is waiting for you back at the Mountain," was his inadequate reply. He turned away from me and grabbed Makashannar by the arm. As they hurried across the sand, Eliasser said in a low voice I think I wasn't supposed to hear, "You must tell her soon."

"Tell me what?" I shouted after them. But they walked on, heads bent together, followed by Ari and Danaeus.

I set off at a slower pace, allowing the others to pull farther ahead. The arrival of the pink mist and Eliasser's strange reaction to it, along with Ari's story of the destruction of Elvener, had given me a lot to think about, the kind of thinking I wanted to do alone.

The four of them stopped at the fork in the trail and waited.

"I'm going to take my time," I called out. "You can go on without me."

Eliasser waved, and they moved around the bend and out of sight.

Lost in thought, I ambled along, enjoying the solitude. As I approached the Resting Stones, a group of fairybees passed me on their way home from the orchard west of the Mountain. I held out my hand, and one landed on my palm and danced intricate circular patterns. Overwhelmed with affection for this beautiful world—*my* beautiful world—I turned away from the Resting Stones, looked out across the rolling hills, then back to the little bee in my hand. She danced one more circle and lifted into the air. I tracked her flight against the turquoise sky, but now it was Earth that occupied my thoughts. I didn't know how much longer I could keep up the charade, could continue living on two worlds without losing my mind.

My eyes followed the tiny bee to a Resting Stone and my breath drew in sharply. I was no longer alone. Makashannar leaned against a stone, watching me. He let a few moments go by, then uncrossed his arms and approached with slow, even steps. When the electrical buzz began, his gaze drifted to the side.

"I am not able to explain why I had to leave you yesterday," he said. "It is . . . complicated."

"Can you at least tell me why my touch causes you pain?"

"You know about that?"

I rolled my eyes, even though he couldn't see me do it. "You flinch whenever we have contact. Except for yesterday."

He grew thoughtful. "I guess that is true. I am sorry if that has proved difficult for you. I know how much you need to embrace people."

And here we'd been having a moment. Too bad he had to go and ruin it.

"I don't *need* to embrace people, I *like* to. And there are plenty of people who like to hug me back, so you're off the hook. Besides, I wouldn't hug you now even if—"

His hands went up in a gesture of surrender. "I am sorry. My choice of words was . . . I did not mean to offend you. I am sure that hugging must be . . ." He grimaced. "Nice."

"Oh, my God." I started to laugh now. "You are so full of it. Tell the truth. You'd rather harvest nemestes than have someone wrap their arms around you and give you a big squeeze."

He smiled. "In that you are wrong. A hug would be preferable."

His eyes brushed by mine briefly. The electrical charge at such close range set every nerve in my body tingling. *Good lord,* I groaned to myself. *I think I'm becoming an energy slut.*

And then he did it again. "Brush" went his eyes and "tingle" went my nerves, and I had to fight the urge to ask him to do it over and over and . . .

"I am not supposed to do that," he confessed, his voice low and conspiratorial.

"I won't tell," I said, thinking I'd be a fool if I did.

He nodded, then his expression became so serious, I worried what was coming next. With one last fleeting look at my eyes, he whispered, "That is my way of hugging you. It is the only way that I can."

I flushed clear to my toes, and not just from the eye-buzz. The regret in his voice didn't match with a person who detested the idea of hugging. Quite the opposite, in fact.

I finally unfroze my mouth. "Thanks. That's the nicest thing you've ever said to me."

"For that, too, I must apologize. I have been—"

"Uh . . . I need to go. Ashara is waiting for me."

I couldn't care less about Ashara. I was afraid of what I might do if Makashannar became any nicer—like pin him down and make him look at me for hours.

------

When we got to the Main Chamber, Eliasser intercepted us. "Ashara is busy," he said, sounding pleased. "However, I could use help with preparations for the evening's festivities."

"I'm all yours," I said, equally happy to trade Ashara for Eliasser.

He gave me a heart-warming smile, then said to Makashannar, "The potion to help with your problem should be ready soon. Go to the Healing Room and—"

"No need," Ashara called out. She emerged from a corridor with a magnum-sized carafe.

Makashannar gasped. "You expect me to drink all of that?"

Ashara sent him a look that dared him to speak another word. "Eliasser, you will need to child-watch our very brave Guardian to make sure he takes his potion." She handed Eliasser the carafe, then crooked a finger in my direction. "You are with me."

I caught the flash of disappointment on Eliasser's face before his expression slipped into neutral. We hadn't spent much time alone lately and I think we were both feeling the lack.

"I'll come find you after Ashara is through torturing me," I promised him.

"That will not be possible," she said. "You will be with me until the dinner begins."

I bristled. "No, I won't. I need to get ready."

Her eyes became little slits. "I will help you get ready." She stared at Eliasser and Makashannar. "Well? What are you two waiting for?"

I've never punched anyone, although I've wanted to. Now was one of those moments. But Eliasser didn't seem annoyed. Instead, he studied Ashara until her face softened. Then he nodded as if she'd said something. She grabbed one of his hands and held it briefly before letting it go. They each touched their heart, smiled, and then Eliasser left with Makashannar.

I gaped at Ashara as she watched them depart, feeling as if I'd witnessed an intimate exchange I had no business seeing.

She turned slowly to face me. "What are you gawking at?"

"Well, genius. I'm looking your way, so it must be you."

She ignored the barb. "Why?"

I folded my arms across my chest. "Dig it out of my brain if you want it so badly."

I mentally cringed, bracing myself for the pain I knew would follow when she did.

But she burst out with a belly laugh. "What is the saying you have on Earth? A block of wood from . . . ? No, that is wrong. A chip of something? From a piece of wood?" She shook her head, but the frustration was good-natured, not caustic as it usually was.

The words had a familiar ring to them. "Oh. Do you mean, 'a chip off the old block'?"

"Yes, that is it." She laughed again. "And you certainly are."

"How would you know? Oh, right," I said, sparing her the need to answer. "You had me under surveillance on Earth. And I am nothing like my mother."

Her laughter trailed off, replaced by a lopsided grin I found disturbing. "It is not your mother I was speaking of." She glanced around the Main Chamber, then narrowed her eyes. "No one needs to know how I am going to transport you to my quarters. Understood?"

"We're going to your room?" Never mind the baffling travel reference, or how she blatantly made clear it should be kept secret. Ashara was a very private person. Not only had I never been to her room; I didn't even know where it was.

"Yes, and to get there," she said, "we will have to either move . . ."

When she didn't finish the sentence, I asked, "Either move, or what?"

"No, no. It is one word. Ethermove. Close your eyes." I obeyed, and she wrapped her arms tightly around my waist. Suddenly it was as if my body had been shot through with adrenaline, followed by intense pressure and a feeling of rapid movement. I'd experienced the same sensation when Makashannar brought me to my room after our moonlit ride on the Mindsail Lake.

Within seconds, the movement ceased, replaced by a tingling sensation. When Ashara said I could open my eyes, I felt like Silly Putty that had been left by a heater too long. My legs buckled and I dropped straight down onto a plush, maroon carpet that covered most of the floor. My fingers stroked the fluffy pile as I looked around in complete astonishment. From what I knew of the Master Healer, I would have guessed her quarters to be austere. But they were just the opposite.

Mismatched furniture in a hodgepodge of colors filled the room. Dead center sat a low, Japanese-style table surrounded by four short, red velvet hassocks. An overstuffed couch faced a tall, shallow alcove in the opposite wall. A dozen or so large oval stones lay on the alcove floor. An old rusty shovel was propped next to the opening.

Banners covered every wall surface except where the doorways were. Billowing fabric, resembling upside-down sails, draped from the ceiling. The tops of the "sails" had been drawn back up and secured to gold hooks. The sleeping stone—I had to look hard to find it—was pushed against a wall, an unusual configuration under the Mountain.

An assortment of seemingly random objects—pottery, knitted swatches in something like sheep's wool, ornamental sculptures of wood and wire—rested on shelves, end tables, and the floor. Most intriguing was a collection of small fertility statues grouped on a narrow stone slab near the sleeping area.

My eyes met Ashara's. "You surprise me."

"Do I?" she said evenly.

"I thought you disliked Earth. This suggests otherwise."

Without commenting, she helped me onto a hassock, then busied herself at the counter. The anomalous sound of running water reached my ears. After some clinking and sloshing, she came back to the table with two china cups and an honest-to-God ceramic teapot. Steam drifted out of the spout, releasing a heavenly aroma into the air.

"Is this real tea?" I asked. Ashara smiled and nodded. I poured a cup for each of us, took a tentative sip, and sighed. "It's perfect."

"Yes. Strong black tea is one of my favorite things from Earth."

"When were you there?"

Sidestepping my question, she asked, "Have you thought about what you will wear tonight?"

I looked down at my tunic and shrugged. "I'll get a fresh one."

Ashara smiled again. She'd smiled more in the last half hour than in all the months I'd been coming to Amoran. It made me distinctly nervous.

"I have just the thing," she said, her voice tight with emotion. She reached into a covered basket at her feet, removed a pile of aqua fabric and handed it to me.

I relieved her of the cloth and let it fall open. It was a gorgeous tunic, luminescent like Eliasser's pilea, although a shade lighter. A wide ribbon of tiny white pearls decorated the front, from the Nehru-style collar to the mid-calf hemline. Considering the length, the matching leggings seemed superfluous.

"Oh, Ashara. It's beautiful."

"It is your dress-tunic. I kept it for you, just as you asked me to do a thousand years ago."

I felt the blood drain from my face as Ashara fixed me with a stare that had my head aching.

"The time has come for you to know more and I must help that along. I can no longer wait for memories which may never surface."

"Never? I could remain ignorant of my past forever?"

She seemed bent on replying in non sequiturs. "You now know about Elvener?"

"How did you find out?" I blurted, before realizing I'd inadvertently tattled on Ari.

Ashara gave a dismissive wave of her hand. "Surely you have surmised by now that very little escapes my notice. Ari was right to share the story of that tragedy with you. As painful as the truth may be, secret-keeping must end."

Painful? I'd wanted to know the truth ever since I first arrived on Amoran, but when she put it that way, I wasn't so sure. My head felt heavy all of a sudden, as though weighed down by the burden of too many thoughts. I folded the dress-tunic onto my lap, drew my knees up and rested my head on them as I waited for the Master Healer to continue.

Ashara gazed off at the fertility statues. "It was the Foreseers who determined that you and Makashannar were crucial to rebalancing the vortex. In order for you to succeed, your Life Forces required periodic augmenting until the Reparention. Increasing a physical being's Life Force is unpredictable and can be highly dangerous. Neither of you refused, though. You saw it as a privilege to serve the One Light in that way, even though doing so could claim your lives."

I must have been a different person back then. Privilege is not how I'd define what Makashannar and I had ahead of us.

"We augmented your Life Forces for over a hundred years before a peculiar and wholly unexpected phenomenon occurred. Your bodies were involuntarily trying to turn to light and merge. If you merged too soon, the destruction of the Seventh Vortex would be assured. Since merging would have to wait for another thousand years, we had a dilemma."

I coaxed my head upright. "You had to separate us."

She nodded. "We tried sending you to different parts of Amoran, but the pull between you breached even that distance. Your energies worked furiously to seek each other out, exhausting you both in the process. It became clear that regardless of where on Amoran you were, you might eventually succeed in transforming into light and merging."

"From opposite sides of a planet?"

"Yes." She faced me. "The only solution we could devise was to send you to Earth."

"Not Makashannar?"

"He is not a Vibrational. You are. That quality allows you to exist in other dimensions. Even so, we did not intend on moving you permanently to Earth. We would need to bring you back to Amoran for brief periods of respite and Life Force augmentation. While you were here, Makashannar would be given a potion to make him sleep until you left once more. But most of your time would be spent on Earth."

*Abandoned*, was the word that came to mind.

"It was terribly painful for all of us, but especially for you and Makashannar. You had grown that much closer, that much more connected through Life Force augmentation."

She continued, her sentences clipped, as if by shortening them they became easier to say.

"We held a farewell party. It lasted for days. Dancing, feasting, storytelling. You wore that tunic. Makashannar wore an identical one." She sighed. "You were both so beautiful. Glowing with light. When the end drew near, you danced. You and Makashannar. One last time."

She stopped and swallowed some tea before pressing on. I hugged my knees as tightly as I could, grateful that I'd cried out all my tears a few hours ago. I did not want to show that weakness to Ashara ever again.

"I wanted you to wear the dress-tunic to Earth. You declined and asked me to save it for you. 'I will be back soon enough,' you said, with such trust, such innocent surety in our plans.

"In the Main Chamber, you removed the amulet you had worn since your Amoran life began. You placed it around Makashannar's neck and asked him to keep it safe for you. He refused, but you insisted, almost as if you knew you would not return." She cleared her throat and swallowed again. "And then, in a swirl of blue light, you were gone."

Small, shallow breaths were all I could manage when Ashara finished her story. I showed her the amulet Makashannar had given me when I first returned to Amoran. "Do you mean this?"

She peered intently at it. "How curious. That is his. He must still be wearing yours. He put it on the day you left for Earth, and as far as I know, he has never removed it."

Ashara then regarded me in a way that suggested I was about to be shoved off a cliff.

"Makashannar will wear his dress-tunic tonight. And you must wear yours."

I was over the edge in a free fall.

"That's cold, Ashara, even for you. What possible motive could you have for inflicting that kind of pain, not just on Makashannar and me, but the rest of the Guardians. Are you really that heartless?"

She blanched. "It is not heartlessness that prompts this action, but the need to heal a very old, very deep wound. For the others to see you in this tunic will be the first step." Her face pinched in. "You are correct, though. Like all such healings, there will initially be more pain."

"If you're trying to convince me . . ."

"Trust me. Wear it. Please."

The pleading in her voice broke through my defenses. Never had Ashara *asked* me to do anything—she'd only given me orders. Against my better judgment, I nodded my agreement.

She reached across the table for my hand. "Allow me to help you get ready."

# Chapter 20

Ashara and I stood in the corridor outside the Guardian Meal Room. Soft music and snatches of conversation drifted through the open doorway. I peeked inside. All Guardians were present except Makashannar. Ashara had let everyone know that we would be wearing our dress-tunics, and my stomach was doing flip-flops.

"I'm having second thoughts about this."

She nudged me forward. "Take the first step toward healing."

I moved self-consciously into the room. All sound ceased, even the musicians stopped playing. I didn't need a mirror to know how much color had risen to my face. In a way, I was glad I couldn't remember the painful parting that my dress-tunic symbolized.

Eliasser closed his mouth, crossed the room, and held my hands, his eyes soft with unspoken feeling. Flustered by the uncomfortable silence, I muttered, "Can I go now?"

It was a pet phrase of mine, one I used when I wanted to avoid things like nemestes gathering or lectures about the One Light. Using it now had the effect I'd hoped for.

"I will not keep you here against your wishes," Eliasser said with a small smile. "However, I imagine you must be quite hungry by now."

My ample appetite was well known among the Guardians, who joked I ate enough for two of them, something that wasn't true for my Amoran self. Along with my pet phrase, that small reminder of the difference between who I was then, and who I am now, seemed to break the somber spell the dress had created. Ari made a juvenile comment about my eating habits, and with the nervous twittering that followed, the tension in the room began to ease.

Ashara signaled the musicians to resume playing. With a pointed look at Ari, Danaeus, Balthasarre, and Anders, she waved them toward a side table set with a tantalizing selection of appetizers. Obeying her nonverbal command, they gravitated to the food. Then she turned to me and nodded. I smiled my thanks, guessing she'd orchestrated that to give me a few moments alone with Eliasser. His hands, still wrapped around mine, began to feed me energy. I gratefully accepted the nourishment he offered. It was a different way of being fed; much more satisfying than snacking on monzennez.

When I could no longer take in his energy without melting into a puddle on the floor, I withdrew my hands and placed them over his chest. "Why is it that of all the people I have ever known, on both worlds, it is you that I love the most?" I hadn't known, until that moment, how true it was. Or that it was possible to love another person this much and not be *in love* with them. I looked into Eliasser's eyes—eyes that were shining—and patted the area over his heart. I felt a thrill of excitement as the unique cadence belonging to my former self found its way into my speech. "Here, my sweet king. It feels like I belong inside your heart. Not outside in the world, but inside of you, as if it is where I have always belonged."

I'd done an admirable job of turning Eliasser into a hug-junkie. His arms encircled me before I could move mine to reciprocate. I stayed there, squashed to him, loving every second.

"Why?" I asked again. "What connects us in this manner?"

He sighed. "Some questions cannot ever be adequately answered with words. And for the rest? You will have to wait, longer than you would like, I fear."

Saturated with his peaceful energy, I couldn't be mad at him for the deflection.

I pulled back, grinning. "You are a master of many things, including obfuscation. Although, to be consistent you should have said"—I lowered my voice as deeply as I could in imitation of him—"'I cannot tell you,' or 'that is a story for another day.'"

"Dear Light. Am I that predictable? Ah, well. There is merit to be found in consistency."

I surveyed the room, admiring the festive decorations. Normally, both meal rooms were fairly bland, as the Guardians believed food should be consumed with little distraction. But tonight, bright banners adorned the walls, and something that looked like crepe paper streamers hung from the ceiling. Luminescent orbs the size of softballs floated in the air at one end of the room. They glowed in an assortment of rainbow colors, adding to the party atmosphere.

"They're lovely. Are they some kind of balloon?"

"I do not know what balloons are. What you see are Ether Lights. They exist in the unseen substance of the universe. I am able to bring them into physicality, but only for brief visits."

He looked beyond me and sadness clouded those brilliant aqua eyes. I didn't have to intuit the reason when silence descended once more.

My throat tightened. "I can't do this to him."

Eliasser sighed again. "It is too late. You already have." And he turned me around.

Makashannar stood in the doorway, his aqua tunic—a perfect match to mine—rising and falling with his rapid breathing. He was staring, not at me, but at his fists, clenched at his sides. As if it cost him great effort, he straightened his fingers and slowly lifted his head. His gaze traveled up my pearl-encrusted tunic until he was looking directly into my eyes. Then he pressed his eyelids shut as if the sight of me was too much to bear.

Eliasser's voice shook as he called to the musicians, "Play something! The rest of you, take your seats!" He lowered his voice again. "Go to him, Kerrin. He needs you now."

I could think of only one thing Makashannar might need as I stood in front of him.

"I should never have let Ashara talk me into this," I said, barely keeping my anger in check. "I'll change into something else, and if it will make it easier for you, I'll skip the celebration dinner, too. I don't want to hurt you anymore than I already have."

"I beg you, do not go," Makashannar breathed out. He brought my hands to his heart and curled his fingers around mine. "At times, the pain of your first departure from Amoran is as fresh as if it were yesterday. But it will be even more painful if you leave now." He raised my hands to his lips and kissed my palms. "Please. Stay with me."

The room suddenly grew way too warm.

"I . . . uh . . . I thought you couldn't touch me."

He smiled. "Ashara devised a shielding draft that lets me have contact with you. As long as the shielding lasts, I can also look at you, provided I do not come nearer than this." He moved in closer and locked eyes with me. The buzzing was absent, but my heart rate sped up instead. Unsure what was happening, I took a wobbly step back.

"That's . . . great," I said with effort. "Um . . . it's been a long day, and I'm—"

"Hungry?" Makashannar interjected. "What a surprise."

It took me a moment to realize what he was doing.

"Sarcasm? You've been hanging around Ari too much."

The green eyes sparkled with mirth. "I learned this from you, not that I am complaining."

Shoot. Why couldn't he have grown this sense of humor months ago? I extricated myself from his grasp, only to have Ashara clamp onto my wrist.

"You and I are switching seats tonight." She led me to the space between Eliasser and Makashannar, then took my regular seat on Eliasser's other side. I could think of only one reason for the musical chairs. Most likely it duplicated where we'd sat the day I left Amoran for Earth.

We joined hands and Eliasser offered a blessing for our food, our friendship, and the Reparention. Makashannar kept a tight grip on my hand long after the blessing ended. When he finally released me, the way he slid his fingers off mine bordered on a caress.

---

Celebration hummed in the air as platters of scrumptious food circled the table. My fellow Guardians were in high spirits—joking, laughing, gently teasing one another. It made perfect sense. Aside from our successful practice, the shock of Makashannar and I wearing our dress-tunics was behind us. But in my case, I felt like I'd vaulted over a hurdle only to hit a brick wall. For the past five months, I'd wanted Makashannar to treat me like everyone else. Now that Ashara's potion freed him to do that, he seemed to be making up for lost time. He was a regular chatterbox tonight, and as he talked, he touched my arm, my hand, my shoulder, even the back of my head once. Whenever he made contact, my face went hot and my heart beat faster. I didn't want to offend him, especially after his reaction to seeing me in the tunic. But when Anders requested he sing a particular song, Makashannar practically massaged my back as he answered, "I am happy to." In self-defense, I pulled away from him.

He stood up, then leaned over to whisper in my ear. His warm breath on my neck made me break out in goose bumps. "Are you all right?"

Was I? All of a sudden, I couldn't think straight.

"I'm . . . a bit tense," was the best I could come up with.

He gave my shoulder a squeeze. "The scentflames will be ignited soon. That will relax you."

He joined the musicians, picked up the guitar-like *camballa,* and strummed the opening chords. I hunched forward in my chair, silently thanking God, the Light, and anyone else who might be listening that Makashannar was away from me, if only for the duration of a song. I needed breathing space from his presence. I needed to figure out what was going on. Maybe his new shielding draft made him radiate some kind of energy that affected me strangely.

Alas, my window of respite slammed shut when Makashannar began to sing. With each note that crooned out of that full-lipped mouth, tiny feathers stroked my heart. Before long, I felt as light and free as those imaginary feathers.

The song finally ended, but Makashannar wasn't through undoing me. His emerald eyes sought me out, then showered me with uncensored affection. Body, mind, heart, and soul—every aspect of me reacted to that look of Makashannar's with the kind of love I'd only experienced with one other person in my life. And I'd married him.

I wrenched my eyes away and stared at the table, gripped by disbelief. Then dismay. Then guilt, as my personal universe turned inside out.

*This can't be. I'm married. I love my husband. Well, usually. What do I do now?*

"You must eat," Eliasser said.

"What!?"

He pointed at my plate. "You have barely touched your meal."

"Oh. Sorry. I'm . . . distracted."

Eliasser took my vague but honest words at face value. He insisted again that I eat something, then went to help Balthasarre bring in the scentflames.

Thankfully, Makashannar remained where he was, waiting for Ari to join him. Meanwhile, Anders and Danaeus sang across the table to each other in some kind of chant that sounded like a limerick set to music. I nibbled at my food. I knew it should taste good, but in my current emotional state, it had all the flavor and texture of a communion wafer.

Eliasser and Balthasarre returned with three metal containers shaped intriguingly like Aladdin's lamp and placed them on the floor in front of table. I leaned closer to watch as Ashara lit the thick, yellow wicks protruding from each lid. Smoke, like tiny yellow cotton balls, puffed out of the spouts, then disappeared.

The tightness in my neck and shoulders instantly eased. Could it really work that fast?

I breathed in the jasmine-like scent and the rest of my tension faded away.

Oh . . . *boy!* I sprawled across the table, hung my head over the edge, and filled my lungs with as much air as I could.

"That will be quite enough," Ashara said, yanking me back into my seat. "Scentflames are sufficiently potent. You do not need to throw yourself at them."

"You are no damn fun."

"My job is not to provide you with fun, but to ready you for what is to come."

"Hey. That sort of rhymed." My speech slurred as the Master Healer wavered in and out of focus. "You're a poet and you don't even . . ."

"Turn them down," Ashara commanded Eliasser. "Or she will not last the hour."

When the turning-down was accomplished, my emotions stabilized and the room came back into focus. I wasn't tipsy any longer; now I just felt like I didn't have a care in the world. As a bonus, my appetite returned, and I cleared my plate while Ari and Makashannar took turns relating an adventure they'd had in a village outside Guardian Lands. More stories followed, each one funnier than the last. I had a pain in my side from laughing when Makashannar left the floor and plunked down next to me, his face flushed from performing.

"Your presence is requested," he said, adding a smile that nearly beat out Eliasser's.

"My presence?"

Makashannar pointed at Ari.

"Your turn," the wily elf called from the front of the room. "Well, our turn."

Ari wanted me to perform something? What did he have in mind? A little skit about driving my kids to school?

"Come on, girlfriend," Ari wheedled. "Let's *rock* this Palace of Stone."

Now I knew what he wanted me to do, but singing old Sixties tunes when we were alone was one thing. Getting up in front of the Guardians and making a fool of myself? Quite another matter. But my furious head shaking did nothing to deter him. When the scentflames emitted another puff of yellow smoke, I caved.

"Oh hell, why not?" I made my way to the "stage" and winked at Ari. "Hey, Elf-boy. Do you want to know a secret? I'll tell you while I hold your hand."

He laughed. "But first, let's show these squares how well you and I *get around.*"

I waved my hand at the camballa, and Ari picked out the beginning of our favorite Beach Boys tune. Halfway through the song, the Guardians were tapping their feet and singing along with the chorus—even Ashara. Ari and I added dance moves to our singing, and the high mood continued as we bumped hips and shimmied our way through our full repertoire of pop singles. I would never have guessed that the Guardians of the Seventh Vortex would enjoy good old-fashioned rock 'n' roll.

My voice finally gave out, ending the Kerrin and Ari Show. Ari returned the camballa to the musicians as I said, "Who's next? The night is still young, as the saying goes. Balthasarre? Anders?" They just laughed at me. "Danaeus? Oh, I know!" I aimed a devious grin at Ashara. "How about you, secret Earth-lover?"

Her face went chalk-white. Was it possible no one else knew about the fertility statues, teapot, and velvet hassocks? Any chance I might have had to salvage the moment was lost when Eliasser rose slowly from his chair.

"I am next, my Light."

*My Light?* I couldn't speak, couldn't move, couldn't really even think. My heart felt certain it was an endearment, the kind that makes speaking the words, "I love you," seem meaningless by comparison.

"I warned you earlier not to do this," Ashara said. "Remember that when this night is over."

"I will only dance, nothing else. Extinguish the scentflames. I want this to occur without any external assistance." Eliasser held up three fingers to the musicians, then walked to me and bowed. "Will you perform the Third Dance of Life with me?"

"Dance? You mean . . . like you do here?"

He nodded soberly.

"Oh, Eliasser. I don't even dance much on Earth, and when I do; well you've just seen what that looks like. I doubt I could manage what you do here for dancing."

He held my hands. "Would you be willing to try? For me?" He telegraphed such longing, my insides twisted. Suddenly, I wanted to perform the Third Dance of Life with Eliasser as if I had lived my whole life waiting for this moment.

"Yes, my sweet king," I whispered to him. "For you, I will try."

He smiled his gratitude and walked me further out onto the floor. We faced each other while the musicians played the introduction—three notes in sequence, with a substantial interval between them. Each note seemed to drop down inside me where it vibrated nonstop, layering on top of the previous note. Then, the sounds combined into a single vibration that resonated up my spine and out the top of my head. I glanced at Eliasser and saw confirmation in his expression that I was about to experience something extraordinary. I closed my eyes and let go of his hands—and the last of my inhibitions.

My body came alive when the melody began, every cell singing with joy as I swam within a sea of sound. In the same way that blood flows through veins, or a heart beats, my arms and legs moved without thought or consideration on my part, creating a kind of euphoria that emanated from the core of my being. Like the dances I'd witnessed at my first Amoran dinner, my eyes remained closed and there was no physical contact. But the energy that passed back and forth between Eliasser and I was phenomenal. What's more, I *knew* the dance. Eliasser and I had often performed it together, starting when I was a few years older than Meilee. It was an ecstatic celebration of Life and the Love that drives all living things.

When it ended, I felt like I had inhaled the aroma from twenty scentflames.

I opened my eyes. Eliasser was in front of me, mirroring my pose. His blissful smile as he held me in his gaze increased my own joy. It seemed there was no end to the love I had for this man, nor any indication that it would ever stop growing stronger.

"There is another with whom you should dance tonight," he said, moving aside.

Makashannar stepped forward and grasped my hands. Some part of me wanted to decline, as if by dancing with him, I was crossing a line that would forever change my life. But immersed as I was in the rapturous aftermath of the Third Dance of Life, I couldn't refuse.

"What is the name of this dance?" I asked.

"This dance has no name," Eliasser replied.

"What if I don't remember it?"

"It does not need to be remembered," Makashannar said. He brought my hands to his chest. "Trust me. Trust *us*. You will see."

Eliasser smiled at Makashannar, as if pleased by what he heard. Then to me, he said, "There are twelve introductory notes. Allow yourself the gift of experiencing all that they provide you with." After that cryptic comment, he went back to his seat.

Makashannar's eyes were already closing as he released my hands and backed up. I kept my eyes open for as long as I could, studying every nuance of his face, committing it to memory like this was the last time I would ever see him. The thought made me so sad, that when the first two introductory notes reached in and touched my heart, I wanted to cry.

The third and fourth notes burrowed into me, filling me with Love. I still wanted to cry, but now it was from sheer joy.

When the fifth note played, my eyes finally closed. Seven separate bars of light appeared in my mind, each one a different color of the rainbow. They tumbled aimlessly, end-over-end.

The sixth, seventh, and eighth notes sounded. The seven bars of colored light stacked themselves, one on top of the other, until they formed a column of rainbow-striped light.

Notes nine and ten rang out. In a burst of energy, the rainbow column split lengthwise into two equal parts, then each part transformed into a pulsing white light.

At the eleventh note, the two pulsing lights began to spin, slowly at first, then with increasing speed, dancing jubilantly around each other.

The twelfth note reverberated until the two pulsing lights merged to form a single brilliant light that radiated intense Love energy. That's when the dance began.

Once again, my body moved across the floor of its own accord, although with a difference. This dance didn't need to be remembered because we improvised a new version each time we performed it. The two pulsing lights that merged into a single brilliant one represented Makashannar and me. Our individual lights were incredibly bright, but when joined together, our light increased a thousand-fold. I began to grasp what he and I were expected to do during the Reparention, and for the first time, I felt awed and humbled by it, instead of just afraid.

When the dance ended, I opened my eyes. Makashannar and I were facing each other, our bodies almost touching.

And then, they were touching. He'd pulled me into his arms. With all the Love coursing through me, I didn't think twice. I accepted his embrace the same way I would have accepted one from Eliasser, but with drastically different results. If I'd had any doubt about my attraction to Makashannar, that ended it. My Earth body simply wanted more from him.

Except . . . I hadn't always been in an Earth body. Before I'd left Amoran that first time, I had been an asexual being like Makashannar.

Where would we be now if I hadn't been forced to live a series of lifetimes on Earth? With Earth feelings. And those insistent Earth needs. The original plan was for me to return periodically for respite. Why had that changed?

A series of images flipped through my mind, answering my question.

I stumbled back, nauseated.

The images slowly repeated.

I gasped. "No . . ."

When the montage played out a third time, I finally stared at Ashara, whose eyes were sunken into the ghostly whiteness of her skin. "Don't," I squeezed out. "Please . . ."

The rest of the Guardians seemed bewildered by what was unfolding. But not the Master Healer. My body trembled with such force, I didn't know if I could walk unassisted.

"Send the musicians away and bring me to Ashara," I whispered to Makashannar.

He seemed uncertain, but asked them to leave. Then, with his support, I made it to the table and knelt down between Eliasser and Ashara.

"It wasn't your fault," I said to the Master Healer. "Why do you blame yourself?"

"Because, little one, I delivered you to your death," she said, her tone drenched with bitterness. "I never doubted the Foreseers' assertion that you could live successfully on Earth. I should have made them define their idea of success. Since that day, I have hated them."

Her words hit me like a physical blow. "But their counsel is always wise and always right."

"Is it?" Her cheeks flamed. "Did you not wonder why an old shovel rests against the wall in my room? I keep it as a reminder to never again compromise my vigilance for the Truth; to never again trust without questioning."

New pictures flipped through my brain, even more horrific. "I am begging you to stop," I said, barely able to speak. "It will only hurt them."

"For that, I am truly sorry. But I have carried this secret far too long, and in so doing, I have lived a lie." She stared at her clasped hands, where no color remained in the knuckles. "I left you on Earth in the care of

Naomi, an old healer. Her village was poor, the peasants ignorant. Still, I trusted her. Naomi was a good woman, well-skilled in the healing arts. And the Foreseers had given their blessing on the arrangement. So of course, I thought I had nothing to fear."

A muffled sob escaped her, sounding more like a full-blown wail in the graveyard quiet of the room. Makashannar's grip on my arms tightened. My heart thumped in my throat as Ashara collected herself and went on in a monotone.

"I returned in a week to bring you back for a short visit. But when I reached Earth, time had shifted. I landed in that wretched village months beyond my intended arrival. Naomi had just been dragged to prison for practicing "magic." But not you . . . so young . . . so beautiful . . . so innocent. Instead, you had been beaten after they . . . after . . ." A single tear slid down her cheek.

"Enough," Eliasser thundered. "I will not listen to anymore."

"You will have to," Ashara said, her voice laced with regret. "This story must be fully told."

Every pair of eyes were riveted on Ashara. Anders and Balthasarre seemed confused as to exactly what had happened to me, but Danaeus and Ari apparently understood. The dwarf covered his face and tears squeezed out between his fingers. Ari's eyes were hollow with pain. But it was Eliasser's tortured look that concerned me the most. I wanted to spare him what was coming, but I couldn't. I now believed Ashara was right. She had to finish.

I nodded as if she'd asked my permission to go on. And with each word she uttered, more images rolled through my mind, stronger and clearer than ever. My head began to throb.

"I found your broken body on the dirt floor of that hovel you lived in. Barely alive, you still managed to smile at me through your tears and asked if you could come home. I did not answer; I could not bear to accept the truth. 'Where is the Light?' you asked me. 'Earth is so dark, and it keeps getting darker.' Then I saw the recognition in your sweet, green eyes that you would not be coming home. With your last breath, you asked me to give Makashannar a message. But 'Tell him . . .' was all you could say before the Light left your eyes for good."

Another sob caught Ashara by surprise. She swallowed several times before she could go on. "I could not bring your body back here, not in the state it was in. I had to dig a hole—"

"Please," Makashannar said in an anguished whisper. "Say no more."

Ashara didn't look at him, but her expression softened. "I took care of things, then I came back to Amoran to—"

"You told me," Eliasser cut in, his voice like ice, "that she was unable to return to us *yet*. And then, when she still did not come home, that the Foreseers said she must now live on Earth."

"And so they did. *After* her Amoran body died and she was pulled into Earth's cycle of incarnations. I did not lie to you, Eliasser, although I omitted so much of the truth that it amounts to the same thing. I could not bring myself to tell you how she died—you, who love her more than anything in the universe except the Light." Ashara flinched as she turned away from Eliasser's angry face, now transformed by unimaginable grief.

Her eyes met mine again. "I went to the Foreseers to ask them what went wrong. They claimed nothing was amiss. You were destined to take this path. Living in the Earth dimension would strengthen you for the tasks you had to perform when you eventually returned to Amoran.

"I was furious. I demanded to know how they could have deceived us. They reminded me that deception is not possible for them. And then they said things happen as they should. That is when I told them I hated them. I have not spoken to them since."

The ache in my heart now matched the throbbing in my head. I was grateful to Ashara for leaving out the details. The memory of what I'd experienced was bad enough for me, but for the Guardians? They knew nothing of the kind of fear, hatred, and violence I'd met on Earth. And Ashara's concealment of the truth, even though she had done it to protect them, only made it worse. If they couldn't get past this, if they held onto their hurt and anger, we would not be able to function as a group and there would be no Reparention.

The pain in my head continued to grow as I took Eliasser's hand, then Ashara's, hoping to serve as a bridge between them.

"Ashara, I do not believe there is anything to forgive you for. Not even for withholding the truth about my death. You did that out of love, and the burden you have carried all these years, I cannot imagine. But I will forgive you anyway. And I forgive the Foreseers for what you see as their deception. We must . . . all . . . forgive—" I screamed as swords of fire seared my brain. If I could have ripped off my own head, I would have gladly done so.

---

A goblet touched my lips. The contents smelled like a sewer. I gagged and twisted away.

"Drink it," Makashannar cried, his voice an octave higher than usual. He held me steady and poured the vile stuff down my throat as Eliasser fed me enough energy to light a small city.

I choked, bent over the side of the healing stone, and vomited. I had no idea how I got to the Healing Room.

When I was a child, my father warned me never to linger under the eaves of our house during winter. An icicle—some were as long as two feet—could loosen and fall, driving its point into my head. I think I now knew what that might feel like. If this was pentuma, Eliasser was right. A quick death would be merciful.

A cool rag washed my face. Another goblet pressed to my mouth. "No more," I pleaded.

"Yes, more," Makashannar exclaimed. He force-fed me another round of hell, which I managed to keep down as Eliasser continued to recharge my batteries. I lay on the stone, whimpering; screaming made it hurt more.

Makashannar rubbed his hands together, then placed one over my heart, the other on the crown of my head. Energy poured from his palms. His energy was different than Eliasser's—sweeter, but less intense. Between them, the pain slowly lessened and I sighed with relief.

Makashannar searched my face, then squeezed his eyes shut. "Thank the Light. It is over."

Eliasser brought my fingers to his lips and kissed them repeatedly, all the while continuing to feed me energy.

"Was that pentuma?" I asked.

Eliasser nodded. "We got to you in time."

"I can see why you worry about it." I sighed again. "Where is Ashara?"

Makashannar's mouth tightened. I looked at Eliasser, at the angry lines now contorting the Master Guardian's face.

"Tell me where she is," I demanded. Ashara needed to heal from this night just like the rest of us. As strong as she was, I knew she couldn't do it alone.

When neither of them answered me, I pulled away from Eliasser and made motions like I was getting up. "If you won't tell me, I'll go find her."

"Stay put," Eliasser said. "She is in the healing area behind us. She is . . . not feeling well."

"No. I don't imagine she would be. I know you're upset with her, and you have every right to be. But she needs you, Eliasser."

"Her pain is of no consequence," he snapped. "She reaps what she has sown."

This cold fury was so unlike him. I wanted to help him somehow, but I couldn't think what to do. So I held his hands and tried to send him energy. Other than a slight warming, I wasn't successful, but the gesture moved him. The area around his eyes softened first, followed by the rest of his facial muscles. Using the moment to my best advantage, I held one of his palms to my cheek. "I am begging you, my sweet king. You, whom I love more than life itself; forgive her. If not for her sake, or for yours, then do it for me."

"I will consider your request," he said at length. He kissed my forehead and left.

My tears, oddly absent till now, threatened to break through. I pressed my palms against my eyelids to forestall them.

"One more potion and you may sleep," Makashannar said.

The sweet contents of the cup reminded me of the drink we'd shared after my accident in the vortex, when Makashannar healed me with the Integration Link. And it had a similar effect. With my vision already blurring, I said, "The message I wanted Ashara to give you was this: 'Tell Makashannar we can never truly be parted. Tell him I will always love him . . . tell him . . .'"

That was as far as I got before the potion pulled me into its somnolent embrace.

———————

*The hands on a grandfather clock spun wildly forward as Kiley flew over the playground at her school. She fell and broke off one of her wings, screaming as daggers of purple light rained down out of the portal.*

*"Kiley," I yelled. "KILEY . . ."*

"What is it?" Ashara asked as she sat on the edge of the healing stone.

"A nightmare." I rubbed my eyes. "How long have you been here?"

"Several hours."

"Where is Makashannar?"

"Resting."

"Did Eliasser—?"

"We have an understanding. Tell me your dream."

I did as requested. "Do you think it's a premonition?"

"Possibly. I am sensing unusual energy emanating from the vortex, unlike anything I have ever encountered." She frowned. "What do you make of the clock hands?"

She didn't try to probe my mind, but something about staring into her cool, gray eyes made my thoughts come together more easily. Then I wished they hadn't.

"A time-shift?"

She nodded. "I am afraid so."

"Oh, no! I need to get back to Earth."

"Impossible," Eliasser cried, storming through the doorway. "How can you even consider it?" He looked at Ashara as if she were the one who suggested I leave. "All that Kerrin experienced at the celebration dinner must be integrated here, in this dimension. It will be too much for her to be removed from us now. The dancing alone has initiated vibrational changes that—" He broke off, perhaps recalling that Ashara had warned him not to dance with me.

Makashannar ran in from the adjacent healing area.

"What is going on? Kerrin should be sleeping."

I looked from Makashannar to Eliasser, afraid to give them the news. "I think . . ." I paused, feeling the surety of it in my bones. "I am certain there has been a time-shift."

Eliasser paled. "No."

Ashara seemed to be waiting for me to make a particular move. In a flash of insight, I knew what it was. I borrowed her flat, imperious tone to deliver my edict.

"My daughter is in some kind of trouble and I need to leave. Now."

Eliasser and Makashannar protested in tandem, but Ashara smiled as if I'd passed an important test. "You have made your decision, Guardian?"

"Yes. I have."

"I moved your Earth clothes to the healing ancillary earlier. You know what to do."

Marveling at her foresight, I changed as fast as I could and hurried to the Main Chamber, accompanied by all three of them.

Eliasser's fingers dug into my arms as we stood beneath the portal.

"I do not want to send you back to that . . . that place."

I touched my hand to his cheek. "You and Ashara have taught me all too well these past few months. Guardians go where they are needed, when they are needed. Right now, I am needed on Earth. I'll be fine, and I promise you; I will return this time."

The man who patted my shoulder tentatively the first time I hugged him now embraced me with such strength that my ribs ached. I let that be, accepting his immense gift of Love, which reached me even through the distress he felt. I waited for him to lessen his grip before letting Ashara pry me away.

"Be careful," she cautioned. "We do not know how far ahead time has moved, or what you will encounter when you arrive."

"I understand. Ashara . . . I may not be able to come back to Amoran for a while."

"I am aware of that," she replied, her tone once more matter-of-fact. Instead of annoying me, as it usually did, I found it comforting.

Makashannar held his hands out to me, then sucked in a breath and withdrew them.

"Is the shielding draft wearing off?" I asked.

He sighed, nodded, then retreated a few steps and looked straight into my eyes. The usual shock of electricity turned into a lightning bolt that almost knocked me over.

"I will be back," I vowed, hoping it didn't turn out to be a lie.

# CHAPTER 21

I dropped out of the portal and hit the ground running. The digital readout on the media player confirmed that time had shifted. It was two o'clock in the afternoon. I prayed it was still Monday. I prayed even harder that it was still November.

I pressed the blinking button on my old-fashioned answering machine, relieved to hear the date stamp. Time had only jumped forward by an hour, not days or weeks.

Relief vanished as I listened to the first message. Kiley had fallen off the play structure during lunch recess. The nurse thought her arm might be broken.

The second message was the nurse again. When she couldn't reach me at any of my emergency numbers, she called John, who was next on the list.

The final messages were from John, telling me he was on his way to school, then Megan from work, wanting to know where I was and if Kiley was okay.

The front door slammed open as I hit the erase button. In two seconds flat, John was in the doorway to the family room. "What are you doing here?" he yelled.

My brain short-circuited at the sight of him. "Uh . . . listening to the messages."

"You're listening to them *now?* Where have you been for the past two hours?"

He'd caught me so off guard, I said the first thing that came to mind, which happened to be the truth. "I was sleeping."

"Sleeping?!"

"Yes, John. Sleeping!" I had been. Just not on this planet. "What about you? Weren't you on your way to the school?"

"That's where I was headed when I saw your car in the driveway." His eyes narrowed. "Where were you sleeping that you couldn't hear the phone ring?"

His suspicious tone raised my hackles. "I was on the couch. I'll explain why in the car. Let's go. Kiley needs us," I said self-righteously, as if John were somehow at fault.

I was so busy thinking up a story to tell him, that we made it to the front porch before I remembered my purse was still on the kitchen table. John went to start the car while I retrieved my bag. As I hoisted it over my shoulder, an idea came to me. I turned off my cell phone, then high-tailed through the house, silencing the ringers on the two landline phones. That accomplished, I locked up and left.

As we drove to the school, I told John that I'd come home from work so exhausted, I skipped lunch to take a quick nap. "I really needed to sleep, so I turned off the house phones and set the alarm on my cell for thirty minutes. I can't believe I slept through it." I took out my phone and studied the display. "Oh, crap! I meant to set the ringtone to high, but I must have shut the phone off by mistake." I tossed it back in my purse, hoping the weak excuse would do.

John didn't respond. He said nothing, in fact, for the rest of the drive.

When we got to the school, he turned off the motor, stared out the windshield and frowned. I hoped he wasn't going to quiz me further about those two hours, but after an uncomfortable silence, he merely said, "Come on. We shouldn't make her wait any longer."

---

Kiley was in fairly good spirits for a kid who just broke her arm. A trip to the emergency room confirmed that the break was a simple one—a few weeks in a cast should take care of it. But she'd bruised a couple of ribs in the fall and would need to stay home for the next several days. The ER doc instructed us to give her the pain pills he was prescribing around the clock for twenty-four hours, then taper off over the next two days. She could return to school on Friday.

We stopped at the pharmacy on the way home. John went in to fill the prescription while I waited in the car with Kiley, my mind still racing with thoughts of Amoran and the celebration dinner. Fifteen minutes later, John still hadn't come out. I turned on my cell phone to call him, but Megan rang through first.

"Thank God I reached you. I've been worried sick, and not just about Kiley. Where have you been? What's going on?"

I babbled like an idiot as I filled Megan in on Kiley's injury, then used the same "sleeping" excuse I'd given John for why I hadn't been reachable.

"Kerrin?" she said, when I came to a breathless halt. "Are you all right?"

"I think so." I forced out a laugh that was not very convincing. "I'm blaming Tom for my napping needs. He's overworking all of us."

"That's not what I meant. Are you all right . . . emotionally? Lately, you've seemed, I don't know . . . kind of *off*."

"I can't really talk about it," I said truthfully. "I'll call you later. John and I need to figure out who'll be staying home for the next few days."

"Okay. I'll let Tom know what's up."

John finally made his appearance. He flung the car door open, thumped down in his seat, jammed the key into the ignition, and gunned the motor.

"That must have been some line," I said, pocketing my phone.

Silence.

"Is everything all right?"

"I don't know, Kerrin. You tell me." He slammed the car into reverse.

"What are you talking about?"

I didn't get an answer, and with Kiley in the car, I let it go. John drove us home, hands clenched on the steering wheel, jaw on lockdown.

John's sister pulled into the driveway right after we did and parked next to us. Nancy had picked up Ryan and her son, Robert, from karate. She took one look at Kiley's bandaged arm and gasped. "What happened?"

John's eyes blazed. "You didn't tell Nancy about Kiley?"

Crap. I should have called her in case we were late getting home, but I'd completely forgotten what day it was. It felt like half my brain was still on Amoran. "I'm really sorry," I said to Nancy. "When Megan called, I—"

"Priceless!" John spat out. "Your job is more important than our family?"

Nancy gaped at her brother. John had always been one of those genuinely nice guys. He could get angry, but he had never been mean-spirited.

I sent Nancy a warning look, and she herded Ryan, Kiley, and Robert toward the front door.

"You have a cell phone," I shot back at John. "Why didn't *you* call Nancy? Why is it my responsibility to process every detail of our lives?"

"Your daughter is a detail?" he snapped.

"That's not what I meant and you damn well know it!"

Despite Nancy's attempt to get the kids out of earshot, Kiley overheard our exchange. She stared at us, blue eyes widening.

John turned sanctimonious. "This is not the place for an argument."

"Then keep that in mind the next time you start one," I hissed, and stomped up the front steps. My hands shook so badly, it took me three tries to fit the key in the lock. I hurried to the kitchen, not sure who I was angrier with—John for being such a jerk, or myself for losing it so fast.

I nuked some tea and slapped a sandwich together for Kiley.

John entered the kitchen and zeroed in on the plate. "You're eating *now?*"

"This is for Kiley," I forced through gritted teeth, "who can't take painkillers without food. But you probably forgot that, because I'm the one who's expected to remember those details."

"What the hell is wrong with you?" John seethed. Nancy took a step into the kitchen, then paused, looking uncertain. John's back was to her, and he didn't seem aware of her presence. "Your daughter is lying in the family room, in pain, and all you can think about is how much work poor little Kerrin has to do? How selfish can you be?"

"You think I'm selfish? Do you have any idea how much work I've missed over the years to take care of a sick child? But you ride to the rescue once—just *once*—and suddenly you're Saint John the Blameless? Answer me this, John; answer selfish little me. How much work time will you lose to take care of Kiley?"

John's cell phone tinkled the theme to *The Prisoner.* "Yeah," he barked into the mouthpiece. His eyes drifted to the wall clock. "I can be there in an hour."

I snorted as I picked up Kiley's tea and sandwich. "Case in point," I said as I passed him.

John turned around and saw his sister in the doorway. "Why didn't you tell me she was there?" He grabbed my arm, and the mug spilled over. Tea poured down the front of my shirt.

"Stop it," Nancy cried. "John! For God's sake, what is your problem?"

John stormed by us and banged out the front door.

I set the dishes down and ran upstairs. When I returned, Nancy made no comment about my red eyes or the twenty minutes it had taken me to change my clothes. She was sitting on the couch with Kiley, who already looked drowsy from the medication. I flashed back to the broken arm I'd had when I was a little younger than my daughter. The first night had been the worst.

"Hey, sweet pea," I said. "How about you and I camp out in the den tonight?" Kiley nodded. "All right. I'll make up the sofa bed, then come and get you."

With Nancy's help, we had the pullout couch ready in record time. But Kiley was already in dreamland. Nancy and I carried her to the den, tucked her in, then tiptoed out.

"Are you up for Chinese?" my sister-in-law asked. "My treat."

I smiled. "You're a lifesaver."

"Are you kidding? After that lovely display by my charming brother, I need to do something to repair the family name."

Nancy left to get our dinner. With Kiley asleep in the den, and the cousins upstairs in Ryan's room, I had a little time to myself. Thoroughly exhausted by the demands of both worlds, all I wanted to do was eat, fall into bed, and sleep for a week. But I knew it was important to balance my energy when I returned to Earth, so I sat on the couch in the family room to do Ashara's reintegration meditation.

It took several tries for me to clear my mind. Before I could move on to the next step, my body began to feel the same kind of vibrating pressure it did when I was inside the vortex.

No. That wasn't quite right. As crazy as it seemed, it felt like the vortex was inside of me, not pressing in on me from the outside. I wasn't even sure what I meant by that. How could the vortex be inside of me? Yet the description felt accurate, the sensation familiar.

Then, the familiarity got up close and personal. Waves of pulsing energy rolled through me. I opened my eyes, half-expecting to see Makashannar in my family room. He wasn't—at least not physically. But his presence permeated the air, seeping into my pores until it seemed like we were the same person. The sweet intimacy of it was like our connection during the Integration Link, and my heart spontaneously filled with joy.

As abruptly as it began, the pulsing energy stopped and the connection to Makashannar was gone. Exhaustion crept back in and I slumped against the sofa, confused and curious. The Guardians had never warned me something like this could happen, especially not on Earth. I leaned my head back and closed my eyes to think it through.

I must have been more tired than I realized. I woke with a start when Nancy returned, talking a mile-a-minute as she made her way down the hall.

"You'll never guess who I ran into. Hey," she called from the kitchen. "Where are you?"

"I'm coming." I hauled myself off the couch and joined her at the kitchen table.

"When I got to the *Golden Dragon,* your demonic cousin was just leaving with that complete moron she's dating. You know, the one who looks like he could be John's twin? Except, her guy has no brains." I smiled as I opened the plastic bags of takeout. "Anyway, Camryn gave me one of those shit-eating grins of hers and asked me how you and John were doing. Standard drill for Camzilla. I usually lampoon her with things like, 'They're as in love as ever,' or 'happily humping their way through marital bliss.'"

I laughed. "You said that?"

"Wish I had this time. But I blew it. All I could picture was John treating you like dirt, then freaking out and dumping tea all over you. Instead, I mumbled some inane comment like, 'as well as can be expected, considering Kiley's accident.' That fake smile of Camryn's got even bigger—I mean, does she keep Crest Whitestrips in business, or what?—and she said, 'I know all about Kiley's arm. John told me himself.'"

When had he done that? I couldn't imagine him leaving the house and ringing Camryn up for a quick chat about Kiley. If he had, our marriage was in bigger trouble than I thought.

I hunted down the few large spoons that were clean and stabbed one into each container, pretending the spoons were knives and the food was Camryn's heart.

Nancy called the boys to the kitchen, and we feasted on the generous assortment of Chinese gastronomic delights. When our gorge-fest was over, the boys returned to Ryan's room.

"So," Nancy said, "are you going to tell me what's going on?"

My friendship with Nancy dated back to junior high, before John and I became a couple. Attempting to pass off the fight she'd witnessed as normal wasn't a viable option. I began with John's job, the logical place to start. Then, it was as if a dam broke. All my Earth-bound woes poured out—the demands of my job, lack of sex, keeping up the house, lack of sex, taking care of the kids (I didn't add, while saving the universe), and of course, no sex.

When the river reduced to a trickle, Nancy said, "This is too weird. Bob and I just went through something similar."

"I had no clue. Why didn't you say something?"

She gave a helpless shrug. "I was afraid of what you would think. I know," she added, at my look of disbelief. "It seems stupid to me now. But at the time, I didn't want to admit to myself how bad things were, let alone admit it to anyone else. I was too scared and ashamed to tell you that my marriage wasn't working."

Nancy was a very private person, but with all we'd shared over the years, I was hurt she'd kept me in the dark. And surprised I hadn't picked up on it. Unlike John and me, Nancy and Bob had kept their troubles well hidden.

"Is everything okay now?" I asked.

"Mostly. It took six months and the help of a good marriage counselor."

"Six months? I still can't believe you didn't say anything."

She shook her head. "We're on you right now. I can't believe you and John aren't having sex anymore. You guys are like rabbits. How long has it been?"

I grimaced.

"That bad? Wait." She jumped up. "Hold that thought. I'm about to float out the door."

She ran upstairs to the bathroom, giving me a chance to ponder just how long it had been. Factoring Amoran into the equation, I hadn't had sex for over five months. I couldn't tell her that, of course. But what about on Earth?

I thought back to early October. Ryan and Kiley had both been invited to sleepovers on the same day. John and I could make some pretty sweet music together, but that night had been spectacular. The kids came home the next day, bragging they hadn't gone to sleep at all. John and I just smiled. We hadn't slept much either.

John was so busy at work, we didn't try again until after my second trip to Amoran. That's when I first experienced a weird physical sensation when he kissed me. And ever since then, John hadn't been able to touch or kiss me without causing me discomfort or outright pain.

*My second trip to Amoran.* That's when Makashannar performed the Integration Link. Vianna had worried about his health, but he'd said his health wouldn't matter if I died. I understood that now, knowing how crucial the two of us were to saving the vortex. But what if the Integration Link affected *my* health, or changed me somehow? I wasn't able to touch Makashannar without inflicting pain, and John couldn't touch me for the same reason. How ironic would that be—if the man who couldn't make love had made it so I couldn't either?

Nancy breezed back into the kitchen. "Well? How long has it been?"

There was no way I could tell her the truth. I just said I couldn't stand to be physically close to John and that it had been going on for over a month.

"Huh. Not wanting him to touch you at all is pretty extreme. It's probably caused by the anger you've built up over the past year because of his job. I don't mean this as a guilt trip, but can you see where John might be angry too? It's as if you've completely rejected him."

As if? That's precisely what I'd done. I couldn't divulge the real reason, so I steered the conversation away from me. "Is that what happened to you and Bob?"

It was the right move. Nancy launched into her saga, and we spent the next hour discussing relationships, sex, and marriage counseling until she checked her watch.

"Cripes. Gotta run." She called up to Robert to get his butt downstairs, then glanced into the family room and pointed at the flashing red dot on my phone machine. "You've got messages. Maybe my rotten brother called to say he's sorry."

"Not likely." I made a mental note to turn the ringers back on, but not till tomorrow.

"Why not give my marriage counselor a try?" Nancy dug in her purse, then thrust a business card into my hand. I stared at the pastel pink card with swirling magenta vines and a double heart insignia ringed by a profuse spray of roses. Red, of course. And the name? Joy Parks, PhD. I refrained from making the obvious joke. *Joy Parks? With whom?*

"The card's a bit much," I said.

"Kitsch on steroids. Bob almost refused to go because of it. But she knows her stuff."

"Yeah, well, I can't see John agreeing to something like this."

"Remember his amateur magician days? Give him an ultimatum. Tell him this is the only way to get you between the sheets for a little physical magic. There's an incentive to prioritize."

Robert bounded down the stairs and straight out the door.

"Hey," Nancy called after him. "Say goodbye to Aunt Kerrin." She sighed. "Kids."

Nancy reminded me to lock up, something she had only begun doing since a recent spate of robberies in town. I secured the door after she left, then listened to my messages. Megan had called again to check up on us, and John's terse voice announced that he'd be working late—so late that he'd spend the night at Steven's business condo in the city.

Relieved by that bit of news, I phoned Megan.

"How's Kiley doing?" she asked, after I apologized for not calling her sooner.

I filled her in, then said, "She's sleeping now and I'm hoping to join her in a minute. I have to stay home until Friday, but I can do some work here. Can you bring me the urgent stuff tomorrow during lunch?"

"I'll do better than that. I'm heading to the office early—really early—to try and make a dent in the pile on my desk. I'd already planned on taking a break at around eight o'clock. How about I bring your work to you, along with some breakfast?"

Kiley's cry of pain startled me. I looked at the clock, surprised to see how many hours had gone by. "Thanks a million. See you tomorrow."

I brought Kiley a glass of milk, hoping it was enough to buffer her sensitive stomach. She swallowed the pill, finished the milk, and handed me the empty cup, her eyes no more than slits. Wrapping her good arm around my neck, she pulled me down onto the sofa bed with her. My head had barely touched the pillow when I fell into a deep, dreamless sleep.

# CHAPTER 22

K iley whimpered again at four in the morning. I fed her another round of painkillers and milk, Set the alarm on my cell phone for seven o'clock, and we both fell back to sleep.

I woke in time to hear the shower turn off upstairs. I shuffled to the kitchen, grateful that I had the rare teenager who didn't need to be bulldozed out of bed in the morning.

I opened the refrigerator to get the eggs for Ryan's breakfast. Next to the milk bottle was a large, empty space where the leftover Chinese food should be. That was odd. The takeout cartons had been there at four o'clock when I got Kiley her milk and meds.

I loaded the toaster with bread, scrambled the eggs, and poured them into a fry pan.

"Hey Mom," Ryan shouted down the stairs. "Who's the guy in our backyard?"

"What guy?"

"Uh . . . take a look. He just came out of the woods. He's heading toward the road now."

Our property abutted a forest at the base of a mountain. People did not typically wander into our backyard. I parted the curtains on the windowed back door, but didn't see anyone. I turned the doorknob expecting it to hold firm, but it pulled open with ease. Huh. I was sure I'd locked it before I left for work yesterday, and as far as I knew, no one had gone out that way since then. I slid the deadbolt in place, trying to recall if I had checked it after Nancy left last night.

Ryan's voice sounded behind me. "He's one fast dude. He's already gone."

I gave Ryan his breakfast and a glass of orange juice, then sat across from him. "Did you unlock the back door after I went to bed last night?"

He looked at me like I was nuts to even ask. "Get real, Mom. Why would I do that?"

"Never mind. What did this guy look like?

"Older dude. Maybe like thirty? Jeans. T-shirt, baseball cap."

If thirty was old, I was afraid to know what Ryan thought of his parents' ages.

I changed the subject. "About yesterday . . ."

My son made rare eye contact. "You mean the fight?"

I sighed. "Yeah, the fight."

"Why don't you guys go to a shrink?"

"A shrink?"

"It worked for Uncle Bob and Aunt Nancy. Robert says they're a lot happier now."

Nancy thought she and Bob had kept their marital discord a secret. But Robert had figured it out anyway, which made me curious as to what was going through my kids' heads.

"Ryan, have I seemed different to you lately? You can be honest with me. It's usually better if we tell the truth." I winced at the qualifier I'd put on truth-telling.

He looked straight at me, hazel eyes unblinking. "You've been a total space-case, Mom. I never know if I'm going to find my socks in the freezer or my lunch in the dryer."

"I'm so sorry, honey. I've been preoccupied." That was the under-statement of the year.

Ryan grinned. "No worries. I get to tell my friends these funny stories about you."

In spite of things, I laughed. "Glad I could be of use."

He stuffed a wad of eggs into his mouth and swallowed without chewing. "You'll be fine."

The unsolicited vote of confidence moved me. "What makes you say that?"

He shrugged. "I don't know. I just know you'll be okay." Then he grimaced, and I wondered if these precious moments of openness between a mother and her teenage son were about to end. I took care of the rising lump in my throat by washing it down with some tea.

"Thanks," I said gruffly. "Finish up. I think I hear Nancy's car."

I opened the front door before Nancy had the chance to knock.

"How are you doing?" she asked, stepping into the entryway.

"I'm okay. Kiley's still asleep. I guess that's good," I said uncertainly. "I didn't think the pain pills would knock her out like this, though."

Ryan trudged down the hall toting a backpack that weighed more than a bowling ball. He was gnawing on a granola bar and stuffing two extras, plus an apple, into his jacket pocket.

Nancy smiled. "How can kids eat so much?"

"That reminds me. Ryan, did you finish the Chinese food during the night?"

Ryan was back to being a full-fledged member of the Parents-Are-All-Nuts Club. He treated me to an eye-roll that must have strained his optic muscles. "No. And I didn't unlock the door either. What do you think? I went out and had a midnight picnic with the squirrels?"

"Of course not, I just—" He was already out the door. "Oh well. Guess I'll have to come up with something else for lunch. Kiley will be disappointed she missed out."

"Did John come home last night?" Nancy asked.

I shook my head. "It was just the three of us. Par for the course, these days."

She frowned. "Then who ate the leftovers?"

As if her question tripped a switch, three disparate events fell together—the missing food, the unlocked door, and the man Ryan had seen in our backyard. My skin crawled to think one of the homeless men who sometimes camped down by the river might have entered my house while I was sleeping and helped himself to a meal. As far-fetched as that seemed, it was the only explanation I could think of.

I shared my theory with Nancy, who did not seem at all relieved by my rationale.

"John shouldn't leave you alone like this. Have you told him what happened?"

"No. And I don't plan to. I'm perfectly capable of taking care of myself," I said defensively.

"Right. Is that before or after some guy wanders in for a bedtime snack? John needs to know. If you won't call him, I will."

"Feel free," I said, with a "whatever" shrug. "He'll hear it better coming from you anyway."

Nancy shook her head and left. She backed out of the driveway, and Megan pulled in.

I helped Megan hoist a file box out of her van. "You weren't kidding, were you?" I said.

Megan sighed. "Thanks to the wonder of electronic communications, we received ten design change requests overnight. I officially hate all technology. Used to be we could call it a day at five o'clock."

"You mean, back when dinosaurs roamed the Earth?"

She laughed. "I do feel that old sometimes. Old. Dated. I remember when there were no cell phones, GPS, social media, or internet madness."

"Well, come on in, old geezer. We can sit in our rockers and hash over the good old days before Kiley wakes up."

Intrepid modern workers that we were, we did nothing of the sort. Megan set up her laptop, and we ate our scones and slurped our tea as we plowed through half the box.

Megan transferred the computer files to a flash drive and handed it to me. "And that's just scratching the surface."

"Crap."

"Yeah. Tell me about it." Megan studied me for a long moment. "I meant that two ways. Tell me about it. What's going on with you?"

I gave her a condensed version of the story I'd told Nancy, focusing mainly on the growing tension between John and me, culminating in the argument we had yesterday. I left out the part about not having sex. I just couldn't go there this morning.

We cut our conversation short when Kiley wandered out of the den.

"Hey, sport. How're you doing?" Megan asked.

Kiley held her arm up and mumbled something unintelligible.

"Time for me to be a mom," I said to Megan.

"I should get back anyway. If you need anything, anything at all, call me. Day or night."

"Thanks. And believe it or not, thanks for the work."

She made a wry face. "There's plenty more where that came from."

---

Kiley was hungry enough for a full breakfast. As she ate her pancakes and eggs, we talked—about school, her friends, the boy who had a crush on her that she didn't really like. But whenever she mentioned his name, her cheeks reddened and she wouldn't meet my eyes.

Eventually the conversation turned to the fight John and I had the previous day. Kiley's take on things was a bit different than her brother's.

"You are not getting a divorce," she proclaimed, jabbing a finger at me.

"Oh, honey. Of course we're not. Lots of couples argue."

"You and Dad don't. Not like yesterday."

She was right about that. Vitriolic clashes had never been our style. "Everything will work out," I assured her, hoping it was true. I wouldn't even think about the possibility that I only had a month or two left on Earth, making my assertion even more problematic. Ever since I'd learned of the multiple-choice fates Makashannar and I would face during the Reparention, I'd been in denial about all of them. It was the only way I could make it through each day.

We popped a movie into the media player. Halfway through the film, Kiley began to make little moaning noises. I checked the clock; she was overdue for her pain pill. I fed her some toast and the medication and settled her on the sofa bed in the den. Within twenty minutes she was sound asleep. That still didn't seem right to me, so I called the pharmacy to double-check the dosage. The technician insisted the prescription had been filled correctly, although the dosage was higher, but not unheard of, for Kiley's age.

I went to the kitchen to get one of the remaining scones Megan had brought, but the Tea Leaf bag was not on the counter where I'd left it. I checked the front and back doors again. They were definitely locked, so I must have forgotten where I put the bag. I was on my way back to the kitchen when I heard the unmistakable whoosh of the portal opening. I hadn't called the vortex, which meant someone from Amoran was about to pay me a house call.

I ran into the family room, where Ari shoved me onto the couch and threw himself on top of me. I tried to push him off, but he pinned my arms down.

"Don't move," he hissed.

Slivers of purple light, like flaming raindrops, shot out of the portal and landed on my throw rug. The smell of charred cotton reached my nose.

"What the hell was that?" I cried.

"I wish I knew," Ari said.

We sat up. I now had a bird's-eye view of my carpet. It looked like it had charcoal measles.

"Holy crap. Did those flaming lights almost hit us?"

Ari smiled. "And I bet you thought I was just trying to hit on you."

It was so like Ari to make a joke when I had purple fire running loose in my family room. I returned the humor, immensely glad to have my elven BFF sitting next to me on my couch.

"No. Remember? You told me you would never hit on me and that I should be glad."

He chuckled. "I did at that. Sorry. I'm a little rattled. I've been dodging purple bullets since yesterday."

"You've been here since yesterday?" I pouted. "Why didn't you let me know?"

"Believe me, I wanted to. But during this lifetime of yours, I'm not supposed to contact you directly on Earth. I'm not even supposed to get too near you in a disguise."

"I don't see what difference it makes now that I know about Amoran."

Ari was wearing faded jeans and a sage green T-shirt, the same outfit he'd had on the day Danaeus came to tell me my entire life was about to change. I smiled at the memory of the two of them pinching the last two Thin Mints.

"This isn't a complaint, Ari, but why are you here?"

"Makashannar asked me to make sure you were all right. Neither of us could bear the thought of you coming back to Earth alone after what we learned at the dinner." Ari stared out the window. "That was the only lifetime I didn't watch over you. If I had, I might have been able to prevent what happened. I've looked after you ever since. Every lifetime, start to finish. Up until this one, you weren't able to recognize me for who I really was. That's just how it had to be." The thought seemed to depress him.

I gave him a quick hug. "I'm sure you took good care of me. I wish I could remember it. But now I do know who you are, and you have no idea how much your friendship means to me."

His eyes scoured my face. "Oh, I have a pretty good idea. Anyway, I'm afraid there'll be hell to pay when Ashara and Eliasser discover I 'snuck out of the house.' I told Makashannar to let me take the blame, but he's too honest for that. Me? I've been on Earth enough to appreciate the value of little white lies."

I sighed. "Is there such a thing? It seems to me that lies have a way of catching up with you, even the ones you tell to keep from hurting someone."

"Or to save your own skin? That's all I wanted Makashannar to do. No, they won't be at all happy with him, or with me. Especially since the vortex is suffering purple seizures at the moment. I've tried to return to Amoran on three separate occasions, and each time it's the same story. I'm met by a bunch of mini lightning bolts."

"Speaking of which," I checked out the rug again, "how do I deal with this? The burn marks will be hard enough to explain, but what excuse can I use to keep my family out of the family room so they don't get nailed?"

"You're safe on that count. The purple light-spikes only come when I call the vortex. I don't know about the state of the rug. Maybe you've taken up smoking?"

"Not very believable." We stared wordlessly at the carpet. Ari's purple "light-spikes" nagged at me. I felt certain I'd seen them somewhere before.

"I'll help you come up with something, but I think better on a full stomach. Hint. Hint."

I smiled. "Hint taken. I'll rustle up some good old-fashioned Earth grub. Guaranteed to give you good old-fashioned Earth-style indigestion. I had plenty of that last night."

He patted his stomach. "Me too. It was the Szechuan shrimp."

It took me a few beats to catch on. "You're the leftovers thief?"

"In the flesh. I did a pretty good job of slinking around unnoticed until Ryan saw me."

"Which makes you my backyard prowler, too. What possessed you to go outside so early?"

Ari rolled his eyes. "Use that vivid imagination of yours."

I thought about it and grinned. "Ryan beat you to the bathroom this morning."

"My, how quick you are." Ari gave me a sly smile. "You could say that when nature called, I was forced to call upon nature."

"Oh, please. You can do better than that."

"I will. After you feed me. I ate the scones, too, but I'm still ravenous. Earth's energy field increases my appetite something fierce, but it messes with my manifesting magic on occasion. I've had to rely on whatever I could scrounge."

"Well, I won't have a famished elf on my conscience. Come with me."

In the kitchen, I offered Ari my current menu.

"Tuna salad? Soup? I could make you an omelet and some pancakes. This restaurant serves breakfast all day."

Ari went with breakfast, and as a special treat, I fried up some bacon for him. He packed away seven pancakes before deciding he'd had enough.

"I do love Earth food," he said, sopping up the remaining syrup with the last bite of pancake. Leaning back in the chair, he closed his eyes and smiled. He looked so cute, blond hair poking out in all directions, hands laced behind his head.

I placed my lips an inch from his ear. "You didn't think this meal was free, did you?"

The brown eyes shot open. "Cut that out. I was almost asleep."

"That fast? I don't think so. Now, help me with the dishes."

"I'll do you one better." He got up. "You rest while I load."

I raised my eyebrows. "You know how to run a dishwasher?"

"I'm multi-talented," he replied smugly.

My snappy comeback died an early death at the sound of the front door opening. Ari and I locked eyes. "I've got to get you out of here," I whispered.

I scrambled to the back door, fumbled the deadbolt open, and turned around.

The room was empty. A heartbeat later, John came into the kitchen. Ari's plate visually blared at me like a guilt alarm. I carried it to the sink with shaking hands, reminding myself that John couldn't possibly know whose dish it was.

"Would you like something to eat?" I asked, suppressing the tremble in my voice.

"I ate before I left the office."

"Tea?"

"Yeah."

Yeah? I left the rude answer alone and updated him on Kiley while I fixed the tea. He listened without responding, and I eventually abandoned the one-way conversation. When I handed him the mug, he said, "Let's take this outside."

An inauspicious choice of words, I thought. Did he only mean take the tea outside? Or the fight we were probably headed for?

Out on the deck, we sat on opposite sides of the picnic table in a silence-standoff. When I couldn't take the strain any longer, I asked him what was wrong.

"For starters?" he spit out. "Who's your blond lothario?"

My heart began to pound. Had John seen Ari? "What are you talking about?" I mumbled.

It was a pathetic attempt to stall for time, which didn't fool John. "You know damn well what—excuse me—*who* I'm talking about."

Too flustered to come up with a better answer, I blurted out the only thing I could think of.

"Do you mean the prowler?"

"Prowler?" John seemed taken aback. "What prowler?"

"The one Nancy called you about this morning. Or did she forget?"

John took out his cell. He didn't look at the display, just cradled the phone in his hand like he was weighing it. "No," he said. "She didn't forget. She left me a voicemail, several in fact." He shrugged. "I didn't get around to listening to them."

Right. He didn't want to hear Nancy yell at him. Continuing with the prowler angle, I told John about the man Ryan had seen in the backyard. When I finished, John tapped one of the speed dial buttons on his phone.

"Who are you calling?"

"Dan, of course," he said, referring to our friend Rebecca's detective husband. "We should report this guy. He could be related to the break-ins on the other side of town."

"Don't," I exclaimed. Even though the call might not complete, thanks to our inconsistent cell reception, I couldn't risk it. "It was probably some poor homeless man."

John's jaw slid out of joint as he aborted the call. "I didn't think you'd want me to go through with it. I want the truth, Kerrin! Who's the jerk from the park?"

I was totally confused now. "What jerk from the park?"

"Do you really want to play this game? I saw Camryn at the pharmacy yesterday. She said a hot, blond guy was hanging all over you last week when you were at the park with our daughter's Girl Scout troop, for Christ's sake."

Camryn. I should have known. I pictured dragging my worthless cousin through the portal and heaving her into the Darkness. How I would revel at the sight of her over-painted mouth widening in horror as blackness filled the hole where her soul should be.

"First off," I said, trying to control my temper. "The 'hot blond guy' is a coworker, one of the new guys at work. Second, he's hardly what I would call hot, not that I was looking at him that way. And he only came to the park to bring me some papers to sign."

"Camryn said you hugged him."

And I'm going to *slug* her. "I didn't hug him, he hugged me; there's a difference. Although, to be fair, he deserved a hug. He'd helped me with a huge chunk of my work."

"And that explains why he was all over you?"

Oh, how I hated Camryn. "He wasn't all over me. He tried to hug me once."

I didn't understand why, after all these years, John would believe anything Camryn said, but I decided a little honesty would work wonders to smooth things over.

"Look. Mike Asher had a crush on me. But I took care of it."

John's nostrils flared as he banged his fist on the table. "Then why did you say his name in your sleep two nights ago?"

"What? That's impossible, unless I was having a nightmare."

"You said, and I quote, 'Tell Mike Asher, now we can never truly be parted. Tell him I will always love him.' That doesn't sound like any damned nightmare to me!"

I'd said that? "This is ridiculous, John. I do not love Mike Asher, now or ever."

I paused uncertainly. Something about that last part rang a bell.

*I do not love Mike Asher,* I repeated to myself. *Now or ever.*

That wasn't it. *I do not love Mike Asher, now or . . .*

I froze. *Mike Asher now . . . Mike Asher now . . .*

Makashannar. John had translated what he heard into something that made sense to his ears. However, I hadn't uttered words of love for Mike Asher, but the message I'd wanted Ashara to give to Makashannar a thousand years ago. The weird thing is, I'd said those words in my sleep Sunday night, a full Earth day before the celebration dinner on Amoran.

*Tell Makashannar we can never truly be parted. Tell him I will always love him.*

"Look at me," John demanded.

It took every ounce of my strength to meet his gaze without flinching.

"Are you involved with Mike Asher?"

"Absolutely not!"

John's jaw tightened again. I knew he didn't believe me. I had to come up with a story convincing enough to explain what he'd heard me say.

A story! "I think I know what happened," I exclaimed. "Wait here."

I'd been keeping a handwritten journal of my visits to Amoran. I retrieved it from the den and brought it to John. Thank God for my scrawl! He squinted at the barely legible printing. I pointed to Makashannar's name on one of the pages.

"I must have been dreaming about the book I'm writing. That's one of the characters. See how close his name is to Mike Asher's?"

John frowned. "Why did you say you loved him?"

This I was prepared for. "Sometimes writers fall in love with their characters."

"You're joking."

"No, it's true. It's supposed to be a good thing. It means you're really into the story."

John shook his head. "Sounds mentally unhealthy to me."

Since I'd be hard-pressed to defend my psychological well-being at the moment, I closed the journal, hoping this latest fight was over.

"Kerrin. It's been six weeks since we made love."

Nope. Not over.

"When I try to get you interested, you pull away like you can't stand me touching you."

I let out a shaky breath. My emotional tank was now running on empty, and I didn't have it in me to invent another story. I'd have to tell him some version of the truth.

"You're right," I admitted. "Something in me has changed, and it makes that kind of closeness physically painful. I don't mean to hurt you, John, but I need time to sort it out."

John was quiet for a moment. When he spoke, his voice was laced with sorrow. "That feels like the first genuine thing you've said to me in a while. I'm scared, Kerrin. Day by day, I feel like you're moving further away from me, going somewhere I can't go."

The accuracy of his insight stunned me. "I'm sorry. I don't know what to do."

"Could a doctor help?"

The last thing I wanted to do was discuss this with a medical person on Earth. But the Reparention had to remain my top priority, and these constant fights were taking a toll on me.

"That's a good suggestion. I'll schedule a visit with Dr. Bouchard."

John brightened. "Maybe we could go together."

Ulp. "With your unpredictable work schedule, it might be better for you to call him right before my appointment. You could give him your perspective on things over the phone. Besides, his office is so busy right now, I probably won't get in to see him until at least next week."

I had no idea how busy Dr. Bouchard's office was, but John didn't question it.

"As long as I know it's happening." John smiled with genuine warmth, then glanced at his watch. "I'd better get going. Duty calls."

Duty calls? Tell me about it.

I waited until I heard his car pull out of the driveway, then went inside. I tried to close the back door, but it opened again as if blown by a gust of wind. I reached out to give it a good shove, and Ari materialized in front of me. He jammed his hand over my mouth, stifling my cry of surprise.

I peeled his fingers away. "I won't scream for the cops, even if you are my prowler."

Ari didn't smile. "Why haven't you told us?"

"Told you what?"

"What you have to deal with when you come back to Earth."

That's when the full extent of Ari's magic sank in. The invasion of privacy stung and embarrassed me. "I see. Must be convenient to make yourself invisible. But did you have to follow John and me to the backyard?"

Ari folded his arms across his chest, but said nothing.

"And as for what I have to deal with here, what would you have me do? Complain at Morning Meal that my marriage is falling apart when the Guardians' job is to keep the vortex from doing the same thing? Should I have confessed that I can't concentrate at work anymore? Or that I still have to do all the things for my family that I did before with even less help from my husband? The same man I can't bear to have touch me anymore?"

"We needed to know," he said, frowning.

"Why? I didn't think my Earthly troubles were part of the 'honesty must reign' decree."

"But they are. The emotions you experience on Earth can affect the integrity of our group energy. We're so close to the Reparention now, and so connected, that what happens to any one Guardian, in essence, happens to all."

"That's a depressing thought." Something in his expression worried me. "You're not going to say anything to the rest of them, are you?"

He sighed. "I'm sorry. I have to."

Oh, just ducky. My forced celibacy with John was going to be an agenda item at our next Guardian meeting. I could hardly wait.

"What about the problems I experience on Amoran?" I grumbled.

Ari looked curiously at me. "If you're keeping them a secret, then the same thing applies. Secrets eat up an incredible amount of energy. In order to be open channels for the Light, we have to be free of blockages—emotional, physical, mental, and spiritual."

I didn't relish what keeping my "channel" open would mean for me and a certain dark-haired, green-eyed Guardian when I admitted my true feelings for him.

Ari grimaced. "We'll all have to bare our souls before too long." He didn't sound any happier than I was at the prospect. "Anyway, it's time for me to brave the portal once more. Pray a purple light-spike doesn't attack me."

"Let the Guardians know that I can't return until Monday. Kylie goes back to school on Friday, but I'll have to work that day to make up for lost time. Ashara won't be happy, but there's nothing I can do."

Ari gave me a quick hug. "I'm not happy about it either, Earth-girl. I miss you."

I followed him to the family room and kept out of range as he called the vortex. His back was to me, so he didn't notice when a glowing fog appeared between us. A woman's silhouette took form within the rippling silver light. At first, I thought she might be a Foreseer, but the shape was all wrong and she didn't feel like a Foreseer. Whoever she was, she appeared to be speaking. I couldn't hear her, but I experienced an unusual vibration in my head as if her words were somehow imprinting into my mind. When the sensation stopped, she faded away, and a sudden, cold fear drove me forward. I slammed into Ari, knocking us both to the floor. Behind us, a glowing purple mini-dagger pierced the rug.

"Thanks," Ari exhaled. He stared desolately at the portal. "How am I going to get back?"

I had a strange feeling that I knew the answer, courtesy of the lady in the mist.

"Sit on the couch and don't get up until I tell you to."

Ari protested, but at my insistence, he reluctantly obeyed. Running on sheer impulse, I raised my arm above my head, rotated my hand, closed it into a fist, and pulled downward.

Out of the portal came a small blob of purple.

Ari cried out and sprang to his feet.

"No. Stay there. Trust me," I said.

The purple light's pace was unhurried now. Instead of a mini-dagger, it looked more like a glowing raindrop. I continued the pulling motion with my right hand as I stretched my other arm out in front of me. With delicate precision, the purple light landed on my left palm and swirled in a circle, reminding me of the fairybee that had danced in my hand.

*"How pretty you are,"* I thought to it. *"Will you allow my friend safe passage?"*

The little blob of light transformed itself into a beacon of white luminescence that shone straight up through the portal.

"Hurry," I said to Ari. "This won't last long."

"How in the name of the Light did you do that?"

"I can't explain it. But if you leave right now, you'll be safe."

Ari stepped into the light and was gone.

That's when I remembered where I'd seen the purple spikes before. In the premonition dream I'd had of Kiley's accident and the time-shift, they had rained down out of the portal.

But what were they? And why were they suddenly here?

# CHAPTER 23

Over the next few days, I tended to Kiley and worked on the files Megan brought to me each morning. I solved the problem of the burn marks on the rug by moving it in front of the fireplace and claiming to have left the fire screen open during a roaring blaze. My current forgetfulness would make that plausible. Dangerous, but plausible.

I had a few more episodes of that vortex-is-within-me vibration. Also, once or twice a day I'd feel Makashannar's presence, then the connection would abruptly sever. I planned on running all of it by the Guardians when I got back to Amoran. Aside from being unexpected, the weird vibrational impulses messed up my sleep patterns. I hadn't had a good night's rest all week.

Being forced to stay home gave me a chance to spend some quality time with Kiley. I even convinced Ryan to hang out with us one afternoon instead of retreating to his room or gluing himself to the computer. We sat at the kitchen table with a bowl of popcorn while I shared stories about their childhood, the kind of family tales that sound funnier with each retelling. I watched my kids' faces, treasuring every smile, every laugh, every teasing comment. I missed them so much when I was on Amoran. The opportunity to be just a mom, and not a Guardian, was a priceless gift. If I lived through the Reparention, I vowed to never again take the simple pleasures in my Earth life for granted.

Kiley was cleared to return to school on Friday and I went back to work, dreading the first glimpse of my inbox. Thanks to Megan bringing me files, I had kept up fairly well. The tower rising from the tray on my desk was only one-third as high as I'd expected. Even so, sneaking off to Amoran at noon for an hour was out of the question. It would be poor form for me to do anything other than work through lunch after having missed so much time this week.

Around ten fifteen, Megan stopped by. "It's great to have you back. I've been going nuts here without you. Not to mention, Mikey has been pining away."

I groaned. "I thought I'd taken care of that."

"Not well enough, apparently. I helped you out, though. I told him, gently but firmly, that he needed to get a life, preferably with someone his own age who wasn't already married."

"I hope he got the message." I shook my head. "Why did he pick me to fall in love with?"

Megan's expression suggested I wasn't from Venus—or Mars, for that matter.

"That question wasn't serious, was it?" she asked.

"Um . . . sort of."

"Jesus, Kerrin. I know you and John have been together since you were barely out of the playpen, but you can't have forgotten the Golden Rule of love. You don't choose who you fall in love with, you only get to decide what to do about it."

She dumped more files on top of my stack. At my look of dismay, she smiled. "Don't worry. I won't abandon you in your hour"—she eyed the inbox—"make that hours of need." She dropped onto the chair beside my desk. "I'm all yours today."

I thanked her profusely and we went to work. We had finished straightening out one mess in the accounts, and were about to start on another, when Dave's assistant burst through the door.

"We've been ordered to take the afternoon off," she exclaimed. "Dave wants the building cleared out by noon. He says we've been working too hard and we need to remember how to have fun—especially Tom, who's losing his sense of humor. The two of them are heading out to the lake now, but anyone who's up for it can meet them later on for happy hour at the Gnarly Bough—drinks are on the bosses." She skipped out of my office.

Megan stared at the fat folder in front of her. "If we dig into this now, we won't be able to stop by lunchtime."

I eyed the Pile-o'-Files waiting to be worked on. "Dave did say we have to leave by noon."

Megan laughed. "God forbid we should disappoint the signer of our paychecks!" She slapped the folder shut and tossed it back onto the heap. By eleven o'clock, we were driving out of the parking lot. I waved goodbye as Megan headed north and I turned south toward my house.

Five minutes later, I stood in the family room and called the vortex, ready to step out of the way of the purple light. But the portal was clear and I made it through to the Main Chamber without a problem.

Grateful to be back, I closed my eyes, lifted my hands into the air and turned in a circle. It was Ari's drying dance, as I'd come to think of it. Warm air currents moved around me, the feeling as marvelous as when the pink mist surrounded Makashannar and me at the Garrammon Lake. I wasn't in need of drying, so I decided to request something else. I thought of each individual Guardian, then the group as whole, and asked for our safe return from the Reparention.

When I felt complete, I opened my eyes, then blinked to make sure I was seeing clearly. Eliasser stood facing me, the beautiful mist surrounding us both. He moved his hands out to the side, palms up, and nodded at me. I matched his movements, and the pink mist transformed into a brilliant white luminescence as Eliasser began to chant:

*"Born inside the spiral of Light, within the vortex spinning.*
*Born of energy, born of Light, as in the beginning.*
*To return is to go forward; to leave is to come home.*
*To love is to remember you are never here alone."*

I recalled this recitation! My body tingled as we repeated the verse together. The next part was Eliasser's alone.

*"Light of my Light, come into your Knowing.*
*Light of my Light, to keep the Love growing.*
*Light of my Light, the Dream you are sowing,*
*Light gives to Light, our Gift overflowing."*

We aimed our palms at one another. Energy poured from our hands, cycling between us. It was my turn now, and my voice rang out with a surety that felt fantastic.

*"The gift of your Light, which gave me my start,*
*The gift of your Life, of which I am part,*
*The gift of your Love, which flows through my heart,*
*In Light and with Love, we are never apart."*

Eliasser pressed his hands to mine. The energy seemed to quadruple! I almost backed away from the intensity, like the heat of flames at close range. It was time for us to speak together again, and our voices blended in a kind of vibrational harmony.

*"To Light, I will lead you.*
*In Light, I become you.*
*As Light, I release you.*
*For All are One."*

The brilliance faded and the energy dissipated. My body still trembled in the aftermath, yet I felt wonderful.

"Thank you," I whispered. "What a terrific way to be greeted."

"You are most welcome. Is this where I say, 'it was good for me, too'?"

I burst out laughing. "Did Ari tell you to say that?"

Eliasser just smiled. "You remembered the words perfectly. Do you know what they mean?"

"It's a prayer, right?"

"True. But what kind of prayer?"

I thought about his question as we left the Main Chamber. The words triggered something in my memory, but I couldn't grasp what it was until we arrived at my room and the nebulous feeling assumed a more definite shape.

"It has something to do with the connection we have."

He nodded approvingly, then dropped the subject as he studied my face with concern. "Do you need to rest?"

I'd caught my reflection in the hall mirror before leaving Earth—pale and drawn, with dark circles under my eyes. But I was too thrilled to be back on Amoran to care about that.

"Rest? God, no." I went into the ancillary to change and called through the opening as I tossed on a tunic. "How soon is practice? I never thought I'd look forward to it like this. I haven't eaten anything, though. Should I—uh-oh. Did you start time-stretching? You didn't know I'd be back today, so . . . come to think of it, how *did* you know I'd be here?"

I emerged from the ancillary to find Eliasser laughing. In response to my "what gives" look, he said, "I have not seen you this excited since—" And then, he clamped his lips together.

*Ah. Home, sweet home. Land of the unfinished sentence.*

He tilted his head to the side and answered one question from the barrage I'd thrown at him.

"The Guardians are gathering in the Meeting Room to discuss current changes in the vortex. Do you feel up to joining us?"

"Of course I do." I flew out of my room and down the corridors, wishing I could ethermove. When I reached the Meeting Room, I burst through the open doorway and sing-songed in my very worst Ricky Ricardo imitation, "Luuucy! I'm hooome."

The room was completely empty—of people and furnishings.

I backed out to get my bearings, and that's where Eliasser caught up with me. When I explained what I'd seen, he shook his head. "How curious."

We went in together. Eliasser glanced around. "You are correct. This room is indeed vacant." Then, with a smile I can only describe as sly, he said, "I shall have to remedy that."

Eliasser waved his hand with a grand flourish and most of the back wall disappeared. He let out a low, throaty chuckle as I gawked in amazement. On the other side of the wall-that-was-no-more was a second room. Ether Lights floated in the air like little glowing balloons. The Guardians were grouped behind a buffet table filled with every kind of treat imaginable. And smack dab in the center was—

"No scentflames!" I cried out. The association with the celebration dinner, and what happened at the end of it, was too strong.

But no one heard me, because they shouted "Surprise!" then started singing, *For She's a Jolly Good Fellow*. I was laughing so hard by the final off-key note that Eliasser had to help me into a chair. Before leaving my side, he said the scentflame was the only way Ari could get them to sing the preposterous song.

Ari pinched out the wick, but not without taking a deep inhale first. "I do love a good scentflame!" he said, commandeering the seat next to me.

"We have twelve-step programs on Earth for that kind of problem," I said, still laughing. "Whatever possessed you to pick that little ditty?"

"I don't know. Maybe I just wanted to see if they'd do it."

"My—how Ari of you, Ari. Was the party also your idea?"

He nodded. "I tossed the ball out, but they all ran with it." He snatched two goblets of fairybee wine from the table behind us and handed one to me while inspecting my face.

"When was the last time you had a good night's sleep? I've seen corpses with more color."

I nearly choked on my first sip. "You're a great tonic for self-esteem."

He smiled, then said, "Seriously. How are you doing?"

"As well as can be expected." I grimaced into my cup. "Ugh. What a trite thing to say. But it's true. John worked late every night, so that helped." Bringing up John reminded me. "How much did you tell the Guardians about my Earth issues?"

I glanced across the room at Makashannar, who was refilling his goblet. My palms went sweaty and my heart fluttered just at the sight of him. I was in big trouble.

"All of it. That's partly the reason for this party." Ari took in my frown. "There's no way around it. I'm truly sorry about that, but I meant what I said about keeping our channels open."

Ashara advanced on us. She was a tad more discreet than Ari in commenting on my appearance. "Rest. You need plenty of it. Now drink this before you eat anything."

She whisked the fairybee wine out of my hand, replacing it with a large cup of something brown and slimy looking. I decided not to argue with the boss, downed the glop, then got up to make the rounds. Chicken that I am, I saved Makashannar for last, waiting until he was talking with Balthasarre so I wouldn't have to be alone with him. I needn't have worried. As I approached them, Makashannar quickly excused himself to refill his plate. It was just as well. I hadn't figured out when or how to tell him about my attraction to him.

Balthasarre and I chatted about his new gardening project, then I returned to my seat and began to drift off. Ashara saw me nodding and insisted on bringing me to my room so that I could get that much-needed rest. On our way out, she remembered that she had to tell Anders and Danaeus something, so I propped myself against what remained of the wall between the two rooms to wait for her. On the other side of the partial wall, out of sight, but within earshot, Eliasser and Makashannar were arguing. I edged closer to eavesdrop as Eliasser exclaimed, "You still have not told her?"

"I have not had time," Makashannar snapped.

"You could have taken her aside this evening."

"She only just returned! And she is not ready."

"Not ready?" Eliasser sounded incredulous. "The vortex appears to be unstable again. What if she is needed sooner than we previously thought?"

"Did you look at her? She is exhausted. Think of all she has had to process in just a few days. What she recalled at the celebration dinner alone is reason to hold off. It caused her to go pentuma! And now, the torment she must deal with on Earth."

Torment? I wouldn't have put it quite so strongly.

Makashannar continued. "I do not know if she is strong enough yet to . . . accept . . . to—"

"Nonsense!" Eliasser cut in. "How can you think she is not strong enough to know her true identity? Her strength will now come from learning who she is, not by keeping it from her. Even the Foreseers believe it is time."

There ensued a silence so charged I could feel the electricity of it through the wall. Several moments ticked by with no response from Makashannar.

"I am sorry if this is difficult for you," Eliasser said at length. "But I insist that you tell her as soon as possible. You need to begin practice-merging with her, and when you do, she must have full knowledge of what she is doing and what is at risk." Eliasser's tone finally softened. "However, she is not the only one at risk. I am growing more concerned about you. Are you all right?"

"Yes. I . . . I am only tired."

"Then come with me to the Healing Room. I would like you to try something."

Their voices faded away.

"Heard enough?"

I turned with a start. Ashara was inches from my shoulder.

"Guess not," I said, keeping my cool. "I still don't know my big, secret identity."

---

Ashara fed me another potion before I went to sleep. It was supposed to produce copious dreaming, which she believed would help me in some way. But her plan backfired. I didn't recall a single dream; worse, I lay awake for hours thinking about Makashannar. I had secretly hoped that when I returned to Amoran, my feelings for him would have magically disappeared, like so many things did on this world. But my reaction to him last night had ruined that possibility. I was in love with him, pure and simple. And I would have to tell him soon. Probably before practice. Which meant right after Morning Meal. *Ulp.*

With that weighing on me, I trudged to the Meal Room like a condemned prisoner heading for the gallows. Clarisanna, the food Assistant in charge for the day, seemed surprised to see me.

"Morning Meal will be delayed an hour. The rest of the Guardians are not awake." She smiled. "I understand they were up quite late."

Thank the Light! A stay of execution. "Please tell them I've gone for a walk. They should start without me if I'm not back in time."

---

Glittering reflections of sunlight on water were beginning their early morning dance across the Garrammon Lake. The bright sparkles drew me in, and I submerged with a gentle dive. I swam until I grew short of breath, then dried myself off with Ari's drying dance, sans pink mist. It had only appeared two times. Once with Makashannar and once with Eliasser.

I sat on the little white beach and worked my toes through the silky sand as I thought about the conversation I'd overheard between Makashannar and Eliasser. What other identity could I possibly have? As much as I'd missed the Guardians during the past week on Earth, I was becoming increasingly frustrated with the way they kept things from me, even when they didn't have to for my "safety." I had a right to know the whole truth.

I took a few deep, cleansing breaths and tried to focus on the beautiful Amoran morning. But my thoughts went right back to Makashannar. Megan believed that we don't choose who we fall in love with, but I wasn't so sure. Couldn't I have done something to prevent this mess? If only I'd seen it coming.

*Didn't you?* my inner voice accused. *What about the intimacy the two of you shared during the Integration Link? Or the way you felt when his body pressed into yours on the ride across the Mindsail Lake? How about when you clung to him on the ground during the Garrammon match?*

My inner voice could be a real pain in the ass sometimes.

*That's just this energy thing we share,* I argued back. *It's not the same as being in love.*

The next thought in my head did not come from me.

"*The energy you share with Makashannar is the One Light in expression. And what is the One Light, if not Love?*"

"Who are you?" I demanded, shaken to find someone other than a Foreseer in my mind.

My question went unanswered.

Judging by the way the sparkling reflections on the lake had shifted, Morning Meal had already begun. I hurried to the Mountain, where the Guardians were halfway through their breakfast. The swimming had perked me up, but the walk back left me feeling shaky again. I heaped my plate and dug in, hoping something to eat would restore me. If a good meal didn't help, I might have to ask Ashara for a sleeping potion and go back bed for the day. I was no good to anyone in my current condition.

The eight of us remained at the table after the dishes were cleared so that Ashara, Eliasser, and Makashannar—who hadn't so much as glanced at me during the meal—could work out a new practice schedule. As we waited for them to finish, Anders, Danaeus, and Ari argued over who had been assigned the most nemestes duties recently; this seemed to be an ongoing debate among them. Meanwhile, Balthasarre and I discussed an atypical energy signature emanating from the vortex, most likely caused by the purple spikes of light. That reminded me to tell him about how I had experienced the vortex when I was on Earth.

"This connection with the vortex," Balthasarre said, "did it feel intimate in a way?"

"Yes, strange as that seems." I pursed my lips. "And yet, it was more than that."

Balthasarre held my hands with the kind of gentle strength I'd come to expect from him.

"Say whatever comes to mind now, Kerrin. Even if you deem it silly or impossible."

The encouragement helped. "Okay. This may sound crazy, but for those few moments, it seemed like the vortex was inside me. Not that it *felt* like it was inside me but that it actually *was* inside me. Do you understand what I'm getting at?"

"Yes," he breathed out. I thought I heard a catch in his voice. "Go on. What else?"

In the periphery of my awareness, I registered that all other talk had ceased.

"There isn't anything else," I said, confused by the sudden undercurrents rippling through the room. This type of thing had not boded well for me in the past.

"I believe there is," Balthasarre said. "How often did you feel this sensation?"

"I didn't keep track. I had a lot on my mind." I heard my defensive tone and cringed. My self-control was slipping as sleep deprivation chipped away at my physical and emotional stamina. Eating had helped, but the effect was wearing off, and I was shaky again.

"Maybe once or twice a day," I finally said.

"Once or twice *daily?*" Balthasarre squeezed my fingers. "Reach inside you. Some part of you knows what this is."

His silver-gray eyes took on a hypnotic quality. And then, in a flash of intuition, I understood the full measure of what had transpired in my family room.

"You're right," I whispered. "When it happens, it's as though, for an instant, the vortex and I are one and the same. I can't believe I'm about to say this, but it's as though I *am* the vortex."

"Dear Light," Eliasser cried out, eyes wide with shock. "You should have told me this the moment you arrived!"

"I'm sorry," I said, surprised at what sounded to me like a scolding. "I didn't mean to—"

I choked off as the final straw fell onto this camel's back forcing my shaky self-control into a complete collapse. The downside to my love for Eliasser was that he could hurt me more than anyone in the universe. I'd worked so hard to bear the title of Guardian, to be able to do my part to save the vortex. But I still couldn't turn to Light, which made the shambles my Earth life had become all the more painful. And now, to my sorry surprise, the apology I'd intended to offer Eliasser was bashed out by a flood of uncontrollable fury.

"Why didn't I mention it? Good question, Tight Lips. Maybe if you think hard enough, you can provide your own answer. You certainly don't provide me with any."

Seven shocked faces stared at me. I knew I should stop the unfolding tantrum, but there was no dam powerful enough to hold back my river of rage.

"Do you expect me to read your mind, Eliasser? To magically figure out what you want to know so you don't have to bother asking me? I didn't think you were that cruel."

Eliasser's face turned stony. I don't know why, but that pissed me off even more. I was suddenly sick to death of the Guardians and their tightly wound emotions. I shoved up out of my seat and paced back and forth. And kept right on ranting.

"Didn't you understand anything Ari told you about my Earth life? I can't function there anymore. And, let's be honest, I can barely function here. I may as well die during the Reparention, because I won't be fit to live on any world when it's finished."

The death wish put me over the top. Eliasser leapt from his chair and rushed toward me like he thought I was going pentuma again.

I stumbled backward. "Don't you dare come any closer, or I swear to you on your precious One Light, I'll jump into the vortex and never return."

Eliasser must have believed me, because he stopped mid-stride. But then he nodded at Makashannar, who began to inch out of his seat.

"Oh, no you don't!" I jabbed my finger at Makashannar. "That goes for you, too, you secretive son of a bitch. Freeze."

He took me literally, remaining in a half-crouch as I hurled my pent-up anger at him.

"You're the worst one of all. I'm a freaking yo-yo on a string around you. You're nice, then you're not. You're open, then you're closed. You talk, then you don't. You won't come near me, then you touch me and—" I choked off. Now wasn't the time. "Who the hell am I, Makashannar? More to the point, who are *we?* And don't hand me any of your 'she's not ready for it' crap. I feel our connection. I feel *you.* Even on Earth."

Eliasser's face paled to alabaster. "What do you mean when you say you feel him?"

"Oh, for Christ's sake. I meant exactly what I said. No subterfuge. No hidden agenda. No carefully chosen words. I feel him, Eliasser. And here's another thing I probably should have mentioned the minute I landed back in Amoran instead of *praying* with you. It's a little like me and the vortex. Not only do I feel Makashannar's presence, I feel whatever he's feeling, almost as if we're the same person."

"Kerrin," Eliasser whispered. "Please. I need to know something."

"No! You don't need to know anything nearly as much as I do. And you can stop calling me Kerrin, because I'm not her anymore. I can't even pretend to be her; just ask my husband who would like his wife back." I squeezed back tears, unwilling to let the Guardians see the Volatile Earth-girl cry once more. "But how can I be anyone else when you won't tell me who I really am?"

I bolted from the room and ran toward the Main Chamber. I didn't really want to go back to Earth. I just couldn't think of any other way to escape the Guardians. But when I emerged from the last corridor, I didn't know whether to laugh, cry or scream. Eliasser stood in the Golden Circle, arms folded across his chest. Why hadn't it occurred to me that he could ethermove, too? Probably everyone could do it, but me. Which only made me angrier.

I charged across the colorful tiles. "Out of my way."

"Listen to me," Eliasser pleaded.

"I'm done listening. Back off."

He was infuriatingly calm. "I will not. There is something I must tell you."

"You're too late. Now, move it."

He tightened his arms. "If you want me to move, you will have to knock me down."

So I did.

"Move," I screamed. Seized by the same fear I'd felt in my family room when Ari was trying to get back to Amoran, I body-slammed Eliasser, pushing him out of harm's way. We hit the floor together, there was a flash of purple, and the center of my forehead exploded in pain.

———————

An ocean of soft, white fog surrounded me; the silence, oppressive. I tried walking, but the pervasive whiteness made it feel like I was marching in place. Disoriented, I covered my ears against the incredible noise of soundlessness and begged the unbending quiet to release me. Just when I thought I would lose my mind, the air came alive with a golden-white luminosity.

I'd never seen her before, but I knew it was the Elder Foreseer as soon as her vaporous body floated into view. She watched me without speaking.

I couldn't tolerate more silence. "Am I in the forest?"

She shook her head. "You are now in our domain. Out of space, out of time."

"Am I . . ." I swallowed. "Am I dead?"

"The physical form your Life Force inhabited has ceased to function. Your Life Force has departed it."

"But I can't die now! What will happen to the Reparention?"

"Were you not desiring to walk away from your Promise?"

Her tone held no judgment, yet I felt terrible anyway.

"Not really. I was just so angry with the Guardians for keeping things from me."

Suddenly, all I could think about was Eliasser. How I would never again experience the tremendous love emanating from his hands, or gaze into those limitless aqua eyes while he laughed at some silly thing I'd done.

And then I remembered the way I'd treated him.

"Oh, Eliasser," I whispered, my heart twisting in pain. "I'm so sorry."

"Do you apologize for saving his life?" the Elder asked.

"I saved his life?"

"Indeed. Had you not placed yourself in the path of the purple light, it would have pierced Eliasser's heart. He would have been irreparably damaged. We could not have helped him."

"So, I died in his place?"

She nodded. I felt better until I recalled why Eliasser had been beneath the portal at that moment.

"It's still my fault, Foreseer. He wouldn't have been there if I hadn't provoked him."

"That is true. Had Eliasser not been provoked, this incident would never have occurred."

"Yes. That's exactly my point."

"Instead, a shower of purple flames would have torn Anders's physical body in half tomorrow. He, too, would have been irreparably damaged."

I broke out in chills. Who knew dead people could feel cold?

"Then, I guess it was meant to be. Right?"

"All things happen as they should. We know you understand this, Beloved Daughter." She hovered in front of me. "Are you ready to fulfill your Promise?"

I looked down at my hazy shape. "I don't see how. What good can I do without a body?"

Her smile of ethereal warmth was tinged with amusement. "I have no body, yet I do tremendous good. Is not your idea somewhat limiting?"

"I never thought about it like that."

"No, you did not."

I marveled again at the way the Foreseers spoke the truth without any rancor or judgment. They just called it as they saw it.

"Beloved Daughter, we have always known that you will fulfill your Promise. We have never doubted; it is only you who doubt. We see in your heart that you judge the events which brought about the demise of your physical expression. Know you now, with all your Beingness, that nothing—No Thing—happens without reason." A glowing hand lifted my chin so that I was forced to look at her in spite of a sudden rush of timidity. "Dearest Light, what you judge so harshly in yourself is the very gift you bring to the other Guardians; it is what they need most from you; it is the key. And the one who holds the key for you has the greatest need of your gift. Indeed, of all your gifts."

I didn't know what she meant, and I said so. She surprised me by laughing.

"Oh, but you do, and you have just spoken it. Do you not see that?" I shook my head, and her expression deepened into one of great compassion. "You will in time. Remember; for the Reparention to succeed, all truths must be shared. *All Truths.* Let honesty continue to reign in your heart, as it does in this very moment. And now, you must fulfill your Promise."

"But . . . I'm dead."

She must have found me quite entertaining, because she laughed again. "*You* are not dead, my beloved Light. It is only the physical shell that housed your Divine Essence which lies lifeless beyond the veil."

"Okay, then how—"

"Physicality is a wondrous creation, is it not? Treasure it!"

She touched the top of my skull and the inside of my head began to buzz.

"We offer you a gift of knowledge, Daughter. You were born within the vortex—formed from Light, as Light. On the glorious day you entered physicality, we named you Meirashannar—Light-bearer of Truth."

There was a tremendous rush of air around me as I slid into something cool and confining. The buzzing escalated nearly beyond my ability to endure it, then ended with a loud crack. It seemed like an eternity passed before I could coax my eyes open.

I was still in the Main Chamber. Makashannar was at my side, his back to me.

"Ashi?" I whispered. It was the fond-name I'd bestowed on him when we were younger. He'd given me one on the same day. Learning my original name must have triggered memories.

Makashannar—Ashi—looked up like he expected to find me floating above the circle.

I tried again to get his attention, but my vocal cords felt as though they hadn't been used in years. "Ashi . . . here."

His gaze traveled down, then his eyes grew wide as he stared at me in bewilderment.

"Kerrin?"

"No," I wheezed out. "Meiri."

His eyes filled up at the mention of the fond-name he'd chosen for me; because, he'd said, I was always so merry.

The physical effort of speaking took its toll. Being dead must be pretty draining, because that's the last thing I remembered until I woke up in the Healing Room.

# Chapter 24

I wrestled my eyelids apart. Ari was snoozing in the chair next to my healing stone. I fought a tickle in my nose, but lost the battle and sneezed. So much for Ari's nap.

"You're awake," he said, his voice gravelly from sleep.

"I might say the same for you, Elf-boy."

He grinned. "I'm so glad you aren't dead."

"That makes two of us. How long have I been out?"

"A week."

"A week? How am I going to make up for all that missed practice? It's not like I can afford the time off." I tried to get up, but Ari pushed me back down.

"You're lucky to be alive. Now shut up and rest."

I laughed. "Have I told you lately how much I love you?"

"Pre or post mortem?" I made a face at him, which brought back his smile. "As far as practice goes, we haven't had one since your accident. The Main Chamber is off-limits. Those evil spikes rain down a lot more now, especially when anyone goes near the portal."

Evil? That wasn't my sense of them. "I don't think they're hostile, Ari."

He treated me to a dramatic eye-roll. "I'm sure they're very nice little daggers of death once you get to know them. You can explain your theory to Eliasser. He gave strict orders to let him know the moment you wake up, no matter when that is." Ari made a show of yawning. "And in case you're wondering, it's the middle of the night."

I couldn't face Eliasser yet, not after the way I'd read him the riot act. "Before you do that, can you tell me what happened? I mean, were you there when I . . . you know."

"I don't want to talk about it," he whispered.

"Please? It's important. I have a kind of—hunch, I guess—about the purple light."

Ari stared at me for a moment, then shook his head. "I've always been a soft touch where you're concerned." He leaned forward and rested his elbows on his knees. "When you left the Meal Room, Eliasser ethermoved to the Main Chamber. The rest of us followed on foot. We got there just as you shouted at him to move. You shoved him over, the purple spike hit you square in the forehead and you screamed." Ari shuddered. "I've never heard anything like it. The rest of us could tell that you were dead, but Eliasser wouldn't accept it. He sent for potions and the energy channelers. He even tried his version of CPR. Ashara finally had to drag him away. You'd been without a Life Force for close to a half hour."

"That doesn't make sense," I said. "No one can be dead that long and revive with their wits intact. Besides, to me, it was only a few minutes."

Intuition nudged me to ask another question.

"What did the spike of light do right before it hit me?"

Ari grunted. "This will change your benign view. As the purple spike neared your head, it shifted direction like it was aiming for you."

"But it wasn't." I sat up as my hunch took shape. "Nailing me in the forehead was a mistake, not its intention. It was trying to avoid me, but I rolled into its path."

"How can you possibly know that?"

"I'm not sure how I know. I just do." I slid off the stone. "Help me to the Main Chamber."

"Whoa." He held me by the shoulders. "I promised Eliasser I'd get him."

"He'll have to wait." I ducked around Ari and took several faltering steps. "I need to try something. If you won't help, at least don't stop me."

Behind me, Ari grumbled, "Every lifetime, you know that? Every blessed lifetime you have had a stubborn streak that got you into more trouble than—"

"Hello! Recently dead girl walking. She could use your assistance." My knee buckled on cue. Being bedridden doesn't do much for muscle tone, and mine was sorely lacking.

"Okay, okay," Ari said. He swept up beside me, and I threw my arm over his shoulder. "I'll help you. But I'm going to catch hell when Eliasser finds out."

"Not if I'm right."

---

I made Ari wait at the edge of the Main Chamber as I walked the perimeter, hugging the wall while keeping my eyes on the domed ceiling. I'd completed half a lap when a purple spike dropped out of the mist-enshrouded portal. I counted, "One, one thousand; two, one thousand . . ." to gauge the time it took for the spike to reach the Golden Circle. The counting method wasn't very accurate, but it gave me a rough estimate of four seconds.

I continued my perimeter walk. After three full laps, I arrived at the following: The spikes dropped from the ceiling at inconsistent intervals, however, the time it took for them to hit the Golden Circle remained the same—four seconds. What's more, for some reason, I could sense when the spikes were going to appear about three seconds before they left the portal. That added up to a total of seven seconds, enough wiggle room for me to dodge out of the way if necessary.

I went back to Ari. "I'm going to try something. You have to promise not to interfere." Ari refused to comply until I reminded him I'd worked safely with the purple spikes before, and that until we got them out of the vortex, the Reparention was in jeopardy.

"You said it's the middle of the night, so I don't expect anyone to wander through here. But if someone does, you have to keep them away from me. Will you do that?"

He nodded, but I'd never seen him look so nervous. Not that I blamed him. I didn't have a plan, just a gut feeling I'd know what to do. At least, I hoped I would.

I was inching my way toward the Golden Circle, when the rippling fog I'd encountered in my family room appeared on my left.

"Ari, do you see that?"

"See what?"

Curious. "Never mind."

A woman's form took shape within the fog, then she spoke into my mind. *"Wait for the next one to reach the ground, then step beneath the portal."*

Her voice was familiar. She was the one who had spoken to me about love at the Garrammon Lake.

A purple spike came and went. I took a deep breath to steady myself, then walked into the Golden Circle. Ari shouted at me to stop, but his voice was muffled, as though it had to pass through a wall of mattresses. Ignoring him, I looked up. The portal opened like the jaws of a giant shark to reveal a swarm of purple light, rotating feverishly.

*"They want to go home,"* the woman thought to me. *"But they need our help."*

"The purple spikes are alive?"

*"Everything is alive, my Light."*

My throat went thick with feeling at the endearment. Who was this woman?

If she heard my thought, and I was guessing that she had, she didn't address my question.

*"We must do this together. You have the physical body, which I do not, and I know the way, which you do not."*

Her next communication came as a series of images I was certain I misunderstood.

"You want me to go in there?"

Ari shouted again, ran toward me, then recoiled as if he'd hit a force field at the edge of the Golden Circle. Banging his fists on the invisible barrier got him nowhere. He yelled something indiscernible and ran from the Main Chamber.

*"Entering the vortex is the only way,"* my spirit friend said. *"We must blend our Light essences in order to accomplish this. Will you permit me access?"*

I sensed the approach of another purple spike. I was terrified to go into the vortex past the churning purple mass, but did I really have a choice?

She echoed Ashara's words to me once upon a time. *"You always have a choice."*

A single purple spike broke free from the gyrating cloud at the portal opening. Considering what might have happened to Eliasser or Anders, it didn't take long for me to decide.

"Okay. Go ahead. You can . . . um . . . blend essences with me."

It felt like warm liquid poured in through the top of my head, and what I had to do became clear. I slowed the purple light's progress with the same twisting-pulling motion I'd used in my family room and guided it to rest on my outstretched palm. Two voices then spoke as one, as my unseen partner and I moved my mouth to form the necessary words.

***"We wish to help you home. Will you allow this?"***

Their acceptance of our offer surrounded me like the heat of a sauna.

Another purple spike descended and came to rest in my hand. When it joined with the spike already there, a shaft of white light shot down from above and pulled me straight up through portal, transporting me to the center of the vortex in a matter of seconds. Dizzy and disoriented from the near instantaneous travel, I struggled to listen to my spirit woman's instruction.

*"The recent time-shift caused a momentary breach in the side of the vortex. These gentle beings were pulled inside and became trapped within the energy field. The vortex environment is toxic to them, which is why they keep trying to leave through the portals. But our planets are even more deadly to them. By combining our energy signatures, we can create another opening in the wall of the vortex, enabling them to escape and return to their home."*

"The vortex has walls?"

*"It has walls of energy. I will need to lift your vibrations substantially. Stay strong."*

Energy blasted through my body, shaking me so violently that a bad case of vertigo would have been restful by comparison.

*"Oh, God. I can't keep this up,"* I cried.

*"You are doing wonderfully. A little longer."*

She plunged us forward with a spinning motion, drawing the purple vapor in our wake. My body glowed with a bright translucence and white light exploded from my palms at the side of the vortex. I didn't see an opening, but the glowing purple cloud rushed past me and disappeared from view.

In another mind-dizzying rush of instantaneous transport, my unseen companion returned us to the Amoran portal and withdrew from my energy field. I drifted down on a cloud of blue light to the floor of the Main Chamber, then stared up at the closed portal and the normal golden haze curling beneath it. It had all happened so fast.

"They weren't hostile," I said to myself. "They only wanted to go home."

"It is what most people want, is it not?"

My throat nearly closed up. This was the voice I thought I might never have the privilege to hear again.

"And yet, that is what we denied you," Eliasser continued. "How ironic that in our desire to protect your life, we ensured that you would lose it."

"My sweet, sweet king," I whispered. "Can you ever forgive me?"

I gathered up the courage to meet his gaze. It was so full of tenderness, I could barely speak for the likewise emotion it evoked in me.

"When the Elder Foreseer told me I had died, all I could think about besides not fulfilling my Promise was you. To know that I would never again hold your hands or hear you laugh was the most painful thing I have ever endured. There is so much love in my heart for you that I am certain I could not bear another drop to be added. But then I look into your eyes, and my heart expands, and even more love arrives. How can that be?"

He pulled me into his arms, holding me so tightly it became difficult to breathe. I didn't care. I reveled in the feel of his hand stroking my hair, the vibration of his voice saying my name—my real name—over and over. Meirashannar. *Meiri.*

We finally loosened our grip on each other. "I told you I'd turn you into a hug-junkie," I said. "And I'm glad I did. I'll always be an Earth-girl where touch is concerned."

Eliasser smiled. "Then I will confess that when I believed you were dead, I ached for one of your spontaneous hugs that arrive out of nowhere and fill me with an ocean of love. And the feel of your hands when you place them inside of mine. Then there is the sound of your laughter; you are so filled with laughter, did you know that? It makes my heart lighter than a fairybee. And you must have a greater sense of duty than I do, for I dwelt only on my own devastating loss, not the fate of our worlds. Tell me, my Meiri; how can that be?"

We did The Hug, Part Two. I felt such peace wrapped in his long arms that I didn't want to let him go. But my energy level nosedived, leaving me no choice.

"Helping the purple lights took a lot out of me. I need to rest again."

On the way to my room, I filled him in on all that had happened to me from the moment I "died" until the present. I thought he would be concerned, or at least curious, about my spirit friend. But he was more interested in the Elder's comments about gifts I possess, and her repeated assertion that honesty must reign, the implication being that currently, it didn't.

By the time we reached my room, I had to lean on Eliasser for support. He helped me onto my stone and adjusted the sleeping cloths.

"I gave it my special touch," he said, finishing the last panel. "Remedy for a weary soul."

"Is that why I'm so tired? My soul is weary?"

"It would not surprise me in the least."

I sighed. "Sometimes, it feels as if my heart is weary, too."

Eliasser pulled a sleeping cloth over me. "I will summon the next person scheduled to sit with you in the Healing Room and have them come here, just to be certain you are all right."

"Uh-huh." I was already feeling the soporific effect of the sleeping cloths.

"Morning Meal will begin soon. May I relate your story to the rest of the Guardians? They have been waiting for news of you."

I don't remember answering. The vivid dreams Ashara promised me after my party finally arrived. Caught in a web of fantasy, I passed into sleep on the wings of a giant white bird.

———————

For all the complaining I'd done about Makashannar having to child-watch me, there he was, in the chair next to my sleeping stone, doing just that. This time, he'd fallen asleep on the job. As I watched the gentle rise and fall of his chest with each soft breath, I came to the painful conclusion that Megan was right. You don't get to pick who you fall in love with. You only get to choose what to do about it. I'd led an incredibly sheltered life until three Earth weeks ago. Now I was overwhelmed by all that was happening. I guess that's why my soul was weary. But watching Makashannar—Ashi—my heart no longer was. It felt full and alive.

Ashi's eyelids flickered open. "I was merely resting," he said.

"Sure you were. So, how long have I been unconscious this time? Days? Weeks?"

He smiled. "Only a few hours. I relieved Vianna after Eliasser told us what happened to you. I wanted to be here when you woke up." He leaned forward and steepled his hands. "Do you recall when you told us how often you visited the Foreseers?"

I nodded. How could I forget, considering what came afterward? Our moonlit ride across the lake. The way the energy field surrounded us as we lay together in the bottom of the mindsail. How it felt when our eyes almost met at close range.

Yep. I was in big trouble.

"When Eliasser consulted the Foreseers that day, they asked him to entrust me with giving you a specific piece of information about your identity. They conferred upon me the grave responsibility to choose the right time to share this with you. I have delayed this long because, aside from the risk of pentuma, I thought if you knew too soon it would create enormous problems for both of us, and worst of all, threaten the Reparention."

That was a lot of responsibility for a single piece of knowledge.

Ashi let several moments go by. "I would like to have this conversation in my room. I have been saving a special carafe of fairybee wine for this occasion."

The invitation surprised me. Not the fairybee wine part, although I had to smile at the thought of him squirreling away his own private stash of the prized beverage. Ashi was more evasive about where his room was located than Ashara had been. Even more surprising was the way he held my hands with no visible distress as he helped me off the sleeping stone.

"Did Ashara make another shielding draft for you?"

"Yes, thank the Light. A more potent mixture, so I am able to touch you as much as I want without ill effect." He squeezed my hands as if to underscore the statement.

"Oh. Great." A blush rose to my cheeks. Death had done nothing to diminish my attraction to him. In fact, it was growing stronger. I'd have to confess my deep, dark secret soon, then keep the hell away from him for my sanity.

We exited my room. The corridor to the left bent sharply and dead-ended a few feet beyond. Since nothing was down there, I turned right. But Ashi went the other way.

"Where are you going?" I asked.

"Where are *you* going?" he echoed. He smiled and crooked his finger at me in a "come hither" gesture. I changed direction and toddled after him, wondering what was up.

Ashi waved his hand at the corridor's end, and I stared in astonishment through an open doorway. It was a near duplicate of my quarters—sleeping stone, table and chairs, banners, and the long counter—with the addition of a scattering of thick blue throw rugs.

"Your room is *here*? You've been on the other side of the wall from me all along?"

"In a manner of speaking." His smile widened as he guided me inside. "I thought this might surprise you."

"It does. How come I haven't seen you coming and going?"

"I stay at the opposite end of the Mountain when you are on Amoran."

I had a light bulb moment. "To keep us safely apart, right?"

"Yes. So far, we have not had to worry about spontaneous merging. I think your Earth body helps in that regard. It seems to—" He broke off and stared at me. I felt my breath catch at the way his eyes grew soft, tender almost.

Damn. No point waiting. This wasn't going to get any easier.

"Ashi, you're not the only one with a secret. I need to tell you something."

His gaze shifted up. "Ramirra," he called over my head.

I turned around as one of the meal Assistants entered with a tray of food.

"Ashara thought you might like this," Ramirra said. My stomach growled in anticipation as she placed the tray on the table and left. Along with the food were two small drinking goblets, two larger prefilled potion cups, and a carafe of nivinnis juice.

Ashi gave an admiring shake of his head. "I did not ask for this, yet Ashara always seems to know what we need."

"She is rather remarkable that way," I agreed, pondering the fact that she didn't just know what we needed, she knew where we were.

Ashi sniffed the potion cups and handed me the smellier of the two. "We may as well get this over with."

I choked down my stabilizing potion while Ashi consumed another round of shielding draft. Then he moved the tray to a large throw rug positioned in front of a blank wall. With a wave of his hand, a replica of the shallow alcove in Ashara's room appeared. He snapped his fingers and red, blue, yellow, and orange flames erupted from the stones heaped on the alcove floor. They glowed and crackled like a wood fire.

"Well, I'll be damned." I sighed. "It's a fireplace."

"A fire-holder," Ashi corrected.

"Tomato, tomahto. Whatever it is, I want one."

He chuckled. "I do not always understand you, but you make me laugh."

"Don't change the subject. I still want one."

"You already have one. I can show you how to access it."

"Well, okay then. How come I didn't know about this? I love a good fire."

"We only use fire-holders during our cold-time, and that is rare." Ashi shrugged. "I thought the fire might help to warm you. You seem to be shivering."

I chose not to tell him that it was nerves, not the temperature of the room, that set my body trembling. With my momentum broken, I decided to wait until after I had some food in my stomach to make my grand disclosure.

We settled in front of the fire and dug into our meal, washing it down with the nivinnis juice. We made small talk while we ate, mostly about Garrammon. I was using my hands to illustrate a move I'd been practicing, when Ashi suddenly grasped my chin, angled my face toward the alcove, and laughed with innocent pleasure.

"I wish you could see how the glow from the fire dances in your eyes—"

"Stop it," I snapped.

Startled, Ashi quickly withdrew his hand.

On second thought, I pressed his palm to my face again. "What do you feel now?"

"I . . . I do not understand," he stammered.

I gritted my teeth. "Just answer the question."

"Why . . . I feel your face, of course. And . . . your skin . . . which is warm . . . and yet, you are trembling again. Should I increase the firestones? Why are you laughing?"

"Because you are such a babe in the woods."

He looked insulted. "I am hardly a child, and we are nowhere near the forest."

I didn't bother to explain. I had other fish to fry.

"Listen up, Ashi. When you touch me, it makes me want to touch you back in a way that you wouldn't be able to appreciate."

He shook his head like he was confused.

"How about this? I've fallen in love with you, Earth-style."

His expression went blank.

"As in, making love?" I added.

Blanker still. Could he really be that clueless?

"Uh . . . ever heard of sex?"

He gave a strangled cry. "Oh, dear Light. Ari warned us this problem might occur."

Problem? Ouch. "For future reference, a simple 'no thanks, I don't share your feelings' will suffice."

Ashi was contrite. "I did not mean to offend you. But when I tell you the knowledge I have withheld, perhaps you will comprehend why my error in judgment may have allowed this unfortunate situation to develop and jeopardize the Reparention."

Well, wasn't that special. My love had just been reduced to an "unfortunate situation."

Ashi got up, rummaged in a cabinet beneath the back counter, and returned with a carafe. This struck me as the wrong time for sipping wine in front of a fire, even it was only the fairybee wine he told me he'd been saving. But of course, that would never occur to Ashi.

He filled the two small goblets we'd used for our juice, handed one to me, then raised his cup in a gesture of toasting.

"To Twin Lights," he said reverently, and took a dainty sip.

"Down the hatch," I replied, and gulped the entire contents of my cup.

# CHAPTER 25

I wiped my face on my sleeve. "Okay, Mr. Wizard. What the heck are Twin Lights?"

Ashi faltered. "Twin Lights are . . . um . . . they are . . . uh . . ." He peeked inside my cup. "Why did you drink it all at once?"

I laughed. For one thing, I'd never heard Ashi say "um" or "uh" before.

"Back on Earth, Makashannar the Mild, we call that little maneuver 'chugging.' And I do believe I earned the right to chug my fairybee wine, considering what I just had to do. Now," I pointed my empty goblet at him. "It's your turn. What are Twin Lights?"

I meant it was his turn to talk, but he lifted his goblet to his mouth, tipped it straight up and swallowed.

"Like that?" He wiped a few dribbles from his chin.

"Yeah. Like that." I grinned. "You can do shots on Earth with me and my friends anytime." He seemed pleased by that, even though I was pretty sure he didn't know what shots were. "Now, for the third time, what about those Twin Lights of yours?"

He sighed. "In order to fully appreciate what I am about to tell you, you must understand how Twin Lights are created. The explanation is complicated, so I will simplify it as best I can."

*For those of us needing remedial help,* I thought wryly.

"I believe Eliasser has already instructed you in how the One Light came into Being."

"He tried to. I still don't get how the entire universe thought itself into existence out of some great big vast Nothingness. But," I added when Ashi frowned, "I'll take your word for it."

His shoulders relaxed. "If you listen without interrupting, it should make it easier for you to comprehend what I am saying."

Aw, gee. That was the nicest way anyone had ever told me to shut up.

"You are correct, though," he continued. "The concept is hard to grasp, partly because it remains a mystery as to how Consciousness, which birthed the One Light, arose within the formless Nothing. But Consciousness did arise. And at the moment it did so, it somehow knew itself as a part of, yet also separate from, the formless Nothing from whence it came. This miraculous realization, this First Thought—of being a part of, yet separate from—created a spontaneous and phenomenal explosion of energy which we call the One Light."

"Kind of like Consciousness lit up when it discovered it existed," I said.

Ashi just looked at me, then at his empty goblet. I figured I'd said something really stupid and the poor guy was trying not to say so, when he suddenly smiled. "I never thought about it like that, but in a way it is true. Then, in a second great realization, the One Light also contemplated Its existence as a part of, yet separate from, that which came before It. And when It did, It experienced such joy, such ecstasy, that It produced an even greater explosion of energy. So powerful was this explosion, that particles of Itself, like giant Sparks of Light, discharged into space."

Ashi's expression bordered on worshipful, and my pulse quickened as if we shared the same emotion. The man would be my undoing.

"Since these Sparks of Light came directly from the One Light, they were also able to contemplate their existence, their unique Beingness. And in the same manner that the original Consciousness knew Itself as a part of, yet separate from, the formless Nothing, the Sparks of Light knew themselves as a part of, yet separate from, the One Light. And then, another miraculous thing occurred!"

He said it with such enthusiasm I couldn't help mentally adding; *But wait! There's more!*

"The One Light discovered that It could alter the vibrational rate of Itself—Its energy, in other words—to create what we call matter. The individual Sparks of Light, who possessed the same qualities as the One Light, could also generate matter. And for eons, the One Light and Its progeny did just that. They fashioned and explored the cosmos through the building of our physical universe, from the smallest plants and organisms to enormous cosmic systems.

"However, the One Light could only interact as energy with the physical universe. Eventually, It encountered within Itself a desire to broaden Its experience, to explore the physical world as a physical entity. To be consciously inside of the physicality it had created. Put another way, the One Light longed to smell and touch the rose It had brought into existence."

He paused to refill his goblet and took a sip. Then another. Then a long, healthy swig.

And I thought I was the lush.

"My, this is a potent batch," he said. "Would you like more?"

"Hell, yes."

He poured us another round. "Now, where was I?"

"Lights. Lots of 'em."

"Yes, thank you."

"Wanting to take time to smell the roses."

"That is correct, because—"

"A rose by any other name would be hard to smell if you didn't have a nose!" I laughed, then choked it back at Ashi's injured expression. "Sorry. Guess I'm a little nervous." To calm those pesky nerves, I guzzled my wine. They were small goblets, after all. Tiny, really.

Ashi's eyes widened, but he didn't comment on my sudden thirst. "The One Light, and all Its Sparks, in response to their common desire—"

"I know all about desire," I cut in, and hiccupped.

"—to experience physical existence, created bodies that the Sparks could reside in. But the Sparks' vibratory rate was so intense, that in order to dwell inside those bodies without destroying them, each Spark had to substantially lower its vibrational rate. However, when the first

Spark did so, a curious thing happened. It spontaneously became two Sparks of Light."

"It split in half?"

"No." He frowned again. "Well, yes. It did split. However it did not become two halves, but two Wholes of itself resonating at a complementary vibration."

Huh? "So, they were separate but still the same?"

He shook his head. "As energy, they are not really separate."

Sheesh. "The same but . . . different?" As if that made any more sense!

His brow furrowed. "That comes closer."

And then Ashi did. Come closer, I mean. The boy was oblivious. It felt like his energy was swirling all around me, and it made me want him all the more. Honestly, I didn't know if I could make it to the end of his talk without throwing myself at him. Maybe if I relaxed a little more.

I held out my cup. Ashi refilled it, then asked a second time, "Where was I?"

I rolled my eyes and hiccupped again. "Same but different."

Ashi blinked, then sniffed his goblet. "It smells all right, but something is clearly different in this batch. Perhaps it remained in the casks too long. Or maybe the flowers were not fully—"

"Yoo-hoo. Teacher-boy. Back on topic. What about Sparky the Wonder Light?"

He chuckled, then sucked down a generous helping of wine. "When the Spark lowered its vibrations and spontaneously divided, each part of itself could enter a body successfully. But these individual parts were still one Spark of Light, just as each individual Spark of Light was still the One Light. Nothing had changed except the rate at which the One Light was vibrating and the form it was appearing in. Do you understand?"

"Sure." *No.* I was in danger of getting hopelessly lost, so I did a quick mental review while Ashi kept talking.

*After creating the cosmos and playing around in it for a while, the One Light and All Its Children—a.k.a. Sparks—decided it was high time to smell some roses, for which they needed to have a nose. When Sparky the Wonder Light lowered its vibrations in order to safely inhabit a physical body, it surprised the heck out of itself by magically splitting in two. Not two halves, but two whole, complete—*

Wait. How could that be right? I was getting lost again, so I searched for a frame of reference. The only one I came up with was mitosis—cell division—one of the few things I remembered from high school biology, mostly because it fascinated me.

*So, the cell (Spark) divides, and now there are two identical cells (Sparks) instead of one.* Okay. Got it. *I think.*

I tuned back in to Ashi's lecture and drained my goblet, enjoying my fairybee wine-induced relaxation. Any more relaxed and I'd fall over in a dead faint.

". . . And because of a slight variation in their energy signatures after dividing," he was saying, "one part of the Spark is uniquely suited to resonate within a female embodiment, while its complementary aspect will optimally function as male. However, they are free to embody as either gender. Regardless of what body type they choose, these two complementary parts belong with each other because they remain in effect a single Spark."

"Something about this is vaguely familiar."

"That is not surprising. It is similar to what you on Earth call soul mates."

"That's it. A soul mate is supposed to be your 'other half.' Someone who is your ultimate match, the one person in all the world meant just for you."

Ashi shook his head. "What I speak of is different in one important regard. This connection between the two parts is based solely on their complementary energy frequencies and their origination from the same Spark of Light, not an idealized notion of a perfect mate."

"That's not very romantic," I complained. "In fact, it sounds kind of cold."

"Cold?" Ashi went a little bug-eyed. "Not at all. The pure vibration of the One Light is experienced as Love; a Love energy so intense, it—" He stopped for a moment as if he needed to catch his breath. "The essential thing to know is that the connection, the tremendous pull which draws one part of a Spark to its complement is suffused with that very same vibration, that same Love. On Earth, this energy attraction gave birth to the idea of soul mates. But the term soul mates covers a much broader range of relationships, including the extraordinary union I understand is possible with soul-bonding. However, soul mates are not the same as Twin Lights—the name given to the complementary parts of a single Spark of Light."

Ashi poured more wine into my cup without my asking. If I didn't know better, I'd have thought he was trying to get me very, *very* relaxed. He must have been planning on joining me, because he filled his own goblet to the rim, then continued.

"But a Spark wishing to become a Twin Light pair must agree to one condition," he said.

I snorted. "There's always a catch."

"Once the separation occurs, Twin Lights will forever be masters of their own experience, free to travel through space and time apart from one another." Ashi smiled. "But the attraction of their energy frequencies is so strong, they will almost always seek to be together, for they are truly one and the same. And whether they are conscious of it or not, their ultimate desire is to merge back into a single Spark and return forever to the One Light."

Uh-oh. "Ashi, that's how I feel about you sometimes. As though we are one and the same."

"You feel it with good reason, Meiri. We are Twin Lights." He dropped his voice to a whisper. "Yet, we are even more than that."

"More?! What tops being the same person?"

He leaned forward. "Our Spark of Light was not created directly from the One Light, but from the energy of the Vortex. We are Vortex Lights, Meiri. A very rare occurrence."

*It's as though I am the vortex,* I'd told Balthasarre.

Ashi fumbled his goblet to his lips and sucked on it like a straw. I was surprised I didn't have more of a reaction to this news. I chalked it up to the fairybee wine, which was beginning to give me the same thick feeling in my head that real wine did.

"I don't get it. You've acted like this relationship between us is a problem."

Ashi set his cup down with great care. "During the Reparention, you and I will merge back into a single Spark of Light, an ecstatic experience beyond words. The only thing which exceeds that level of ecstasy is when a fully merged Spark reunites with the One Light. But we cannot allow that to happen or the Reparention will fail."

"Is there a danger we'll do that?"

He nodded. But oddly, his expression was once again reverent. "The energetic drive for our combined Spark to rejoin the One Light will be overwhelming, especially because we will merge in the Vortex, which is where our Life began. We are essentially going home, Meiri. But we will have to resist the phenomenal pull to go all the way home. To the beginning. To the One Light."

He sloshed more of the honey-colored liquid into our goblets from what seemed to be a bottomless carafe. In between slurps, I asked, "Why did you wait to tell me this?"

Ashi tried to scratch his nose, missed, and poked himself in the cheek. When he reached for the carafe again, I grabbed his hand.

"Twin-boy. You already refilled our cups. Are you all right?"

His grin went lopsided. "I feel quite odd. And I have the strongest urge to consume more wine."

"I'm feeling pretty weird myself." I threw back my head and chortled. Truth was, we were starting to act like a couple of sloppy drunks. Had we been in our right minds, we would have known to call for help. But we weren't in our right minds, and we didn't call anyone, and by now, I don't think either of us gave a hoot.

"Ashi?"

"Hmm?" There was that stupid grin again.

"Why did you put this off? Get your face out of your goblet and answer me!"

He obeyed. "I was afraid that once I told you, it would activate a part of your subconscious that knows and understands who and what we are. And, that once activated, your energy levels would rise too fast and respond to mine too readily. Your Earth body should be vibrationally dense enough to buffer the effect, but if not? Our energy might then feed off each other and trigger a spontaneous merging."

"Is that why you kept avoiding me for so long?"

"Yes, well that and . . . never mind. I now believe that what I did may have worked against us. Had you been aware of what the risks are, you might have been able to prevent this desire you have. This physical need for me."

I was laughing so hard, I tipped over sideways. "You're priceless. With the right person, these 'desires' and 'needs' are about as easy to prevent as the pull of Twin Lights."

"Dear Light," he cried. "I was not aware. How will you manage?"

"I'll figure something out. I haven't jumped you yet, have I?" I didn't address his baffled expression. "Look. I appreciate that this doesn't appeal to you, but what harm would there be if we were to act on those desires."

*Oh my God. Had I just propositioned Ashi?*

He didn't make eye contact. "I understand it involves a release of energy."

"Hah! You could say that." I giggled into my empty goblet. *Wait. How did it get empty already? I didn't remember drinking it. Oh, well.* I thrust my cup at him, nearly hitting him in the face because I misjudged the distance. "Refill, please."

He poured more wine for both of us. "If it involves a release of energy, could that not trigger a spontaneous merging?"

I lowered my goblet slowly, making sure the floor was under it before I took my hand away. "I suppose so. The feelings evoked can be incredibly intense. The risk of a spontaneous merging would be enormous." *And I'd like to do a little spontaneous merging right now,* I thought, as the harlot-hooch confiscated my morals.

I didn't have to worry about controlling my urges. Ashi bumped my goblet, and we both leaned forward to grab it at the same time, nearly toppling it in the process. Laughing at our clumsiness, we looked up. Only an inch separated us. Not enough distance for us to be protected by his shielding potion. He yelled and tried to move away, but it was too late. Our high voltage connection wired us together as a vision unfolded.

---

Everything was Nothing, rich with potentiality. Then Consciousness arose within the Void, followed by an enormous explosion of awareness. The One Light had birthed Itself into Being.

The One Light pulsed and spun, followed by another explosion of energy. Particles of Its Light—some as large as solar systems, others as tiny as the head of a pin—burst forth from Its center. Drawn to a gigantic ball of Light, we tracked it across the cosmos until it came to "rest" in a far-flung part of a newly formed galaxy. There, the ball of Light pulsed and spun, just as the One Light had done. A single brilliant Spark discharged from its mass, then the ball of Light reformed itself, recognizable now as a vortex. The Spark went inside, pulling us along.

It was the Spark's turn to spin and pulse, increasing in intensity until it split in two. Emanating tremendous Love, the Twin Lights danced around each other, then left the vortex.

Eons passed like seconds. The Twin Lights returned to the vortex and moved slowly into each other, combining in a brilliant flash. The release of Love energy at this reuniting of a Spark was indeed beyond words. We felt our senses stripped of comprehension at the onslaught of pure energy, pure feeling. When the Spark began to separate again, something happened. A small implosion of energy drew the nearly separated Spark back together for a microsecond before it burst forth to completion in an explosion of Love. But now, instead of one pair of Twin Lights, there were two. They exited the vortex, one pair at a time.

It seemed a mere fraction of time elapsed before the second pair of Twin Lights returned to the vortex where they, too, combined in a brilliant flash. When it was time for the merged Spark to separate, the same implosion/explosion occurred, producing yet another pair of Twin Lights.

This last Twin Light pair rushed at Ashi and me, and everything went black.

# Chapter 26

My head throbbed and my mouth felt like I'd been eating paper shreds. I managed to force one eye open a smidge. I was still in Ashi's room, lying on the floor with my head on my outstretched arm. Ashi lay next to me, snoring. Ashara was studying Ashi's special carafe of fairybee wine while Eliasser questioned Ramirra.

"No one approached you on the way here?"

"No one," Ramirra answered.

"And the goblets were never left unattended?"

"They were within my sight or in my hands the entire time."

"All right, Ramirra. You may go."

Eliasser had quizzed Ramirra with zero emotion in his voice, but when the Assistant left the room, his forehead crinkled with worry lines.

Ashara sniffed the carafe, her expression wavering between shock and respect. "This is highly concentrated, with an odd ingredient I cannot place. For Ashi, it would be dangerous enough. But for Meiri? The effects on her Earth body would be unpredictable and might have proved fatal. Yet, they have not been harmed. Someone knows potions and fairybee wine."

"Only you and I know of the Visioning potion's existence. And we would never take such a risk. If neither of us supplied this carafe, who could have brought it to them? And why?"

Moments like this were golden opportunities for me to eavesdrop. My dry throat ruined it. When I coughed, Eliasser and Ashara adopted those inscrutable masks of theirs.

"How do you feel?" Eliasser asked.

I groaned. "Like I've been out drinking all night." I knew the meaning would elude him, so I detailed the splitting headache, nausea, and chalky taste in my mouth.

Ashi stirred. His eyelids fluttered open, then he winced and shut them again. His hand meandered to his head, where he plastered his fingers over his eyes and moaned.

"Maybe you can't do shots on Earth after all," I whispered.

"Not if this is the result."

I grinned. "Do you even know what shots are?"

He split his fingers apart to peek at me. "No. And I certainly will not join you in—"

"Enough!" Ashara knelt beside Ashi. "If you had any idea of the seriousness of this situation, you would not be engaging in idle chatter." She checked the pulse at his throat, held her hand to his forehead and then to his heart. After repeating it with me, she leaned back and sighed. "Tell us what happened."

With great effort, Ashi and I sat up and took turns giving Ashara and Eliasser an abbreviated version of our time together. However, by some unspoken agreement, we left out my declaration of love—and lust—for my Twin. I knew it would have to be dealt with eventually, but I couldn't face it right now. Apparently, neither could Ashi.

"Why did you not contact us when you began to feel something amiss?" Eliasser asked.

"Meiri cannot be blamed for this," Ashi said. "I should have been more cautious. Something was not right with this wine, but I kept pouring it anyway."

"Don't be a hero, Twin-boy. I knew something was wrong, too. But the more I drank, the more I had to have it. And the carafe never seemed to empty."

Eliasser picked the bottle up and studied the design on the side, a swirling pattern reminiscent of the vortex. "Where did this come from?"

"I have had it for a while," Ashi replied. He slid a glance at me and smiled. "I have been saving it for a special occasion."

"I did not ask how long you have had it," Eliasser grumbled. "I asked where you—" The muscles in his face contracted when he looked at the bottom of the carafe.

He tipped the underside toward Ashara, and she gasped. "No! Is the room still secured?"

"Of course it is," Eliasser snapped. "Only you and I have access to it."

They stared at the carafe until Ashara reached out and touched his arm. "That is not entirely true. One other individual is able to enter those quarters."

It took all of three seconds for Eliasser's expression to go from confusion to hope, and then to resignation. "Impossible," he said, with an adamant shake of his head.

"And yet, it would explain the Visioning potion, as well as Meiri's spirit guide."

"Only if we are speaking of a child's fantasy tale! There must be another reason for this. I ask you again, Makashannar. Where did you get this carafe?"

My big, brave, pretend Wizard of Amoran gulped and his bloodshot eyes widened.

"I found it in my room the day after our celebration dinner. There was a note attached inviting me to share it with the person most special to me."

I think even my toes went crimson over that remark, but Eliasser was not impressed.

"You *found* it! And you did not think to mention the appearance of a mysterious carafe of fairybee wine?"

Ashi cringed and rubbed his temples. "I assumed it was a gift from someone."

"You *assumed?*" Eliasser raked his hand through his hair. "It never occurred to you to ask which one of us had presented you with such a gift?"

Ashi shrugged. "I accepted it without question. I do not know why I did, it just seemed . . ." He trailed off and sighed. "You are right. Not coming to you was a mistake."

"One you will not repeat, I trust," Eliasser said sourly.

Ashara's gray eyes grew thoughtful. "Did you understand the vision, Meiri?"

"I'm guessing it was Ashi's and my creation in the vortex."

She turned to Ashi. "And you?"

"I agree that it was our creation. However, I found the other lights puzzling."

Ashara stared at Eliasser. It was the first time I had ever seen something resembling compassion on her face.

"Have you considered, my Light, that you might also have a Truth to share?"

Eliasser's only response to the endearment was to press his hand over his heart as he and Ashara did that eye-to-eye communication trick of theirs. It can be mighty boring to be in a room with two people carrying on a conversation without moving a muscle. I was getting fidgety when Ashara said out loud, "I will check."

She held me steady and blasted her way into my brain with her machine gun eyes. I thought my head was going to fall off. "This is quite amazing," she said to Eliasser, with open admiration as she broke contact. "Not only can the Light Sojourn be safely performed, but you should do it now, as Meiri will be more receptive to it. We can thank our unknown potions expert for that."

"I prefer to thank the Light," Eliasser huffed. He helped me to my feet.

"Good luck," Ashi said. "Is that the right phrase?"

"I don't know," I replied, wondering what a Light Sojourn was. "Will I need luck?"

---

Eliasser and I sat facing each other on floor cushions in his room. The firestones blazed in bright hues of red, orange, yellow, and blue. Igniting them had been my idea. Now that I knew fire-holders existed, I planned on using one at every opportunity.

Eliasser observed me for several moments, then cleared his throat.

"After you and Ashi merge during the Reparention, you will automatically be drawn to the One Light. Indeed, you will feel as if you have no choice but to join with It. You already know why this cannot happen. The Light Sojourn permits you to experience what contact with the One Light is like, albeit in a small way, so that you may prepare yourself."

He held my hands and rubbed his thumbs across my palms with gentle strokes. It wasn't the first occasion that this type of contact with Eliasser, both loving and intimate, made me want to crawl inside his heart and stay there forever.

"I will lead you into this visioning process using my hands to direct energy to specific areas of your body. Soon, it will seem as if your body is gone and you are no longer on Amoran. However, you will never leave this room and your body will remain intact. Is this clear to you?"

I nodded, somewhat distracted by the way his thumbs continued to brush across my palms. My hands were growing steadily warmer.

"To guide you into the Light Sojourn, I must partially merge my energy with you. But the experience will be yours alone to direct."

"You'll stay with me, right?"

"I will not leave you. However, you will need to decide something without my contribution. It will be obvious to you when that moment has arrived, as well as what you are being asked to do. Is this also clear to you?"

"In principle. I take it you can't tell me any more than you already have?"

"That is correct."

"Then it's as clear as it can be, I guess."

"If you have no further questions, we will begin with the meditation on Love."

I had plenty of questions, but none I thought he'd answer, so I closed my eyes and we began our deep breathing. The meditation on Love is so powerful, that when we finished, I think I even felt an itty-bitty dollop of Love for my cousin Camryn.

"Now for the Light Sojourn," Eliasser said. "Until our energies combine, describe each sensation you experience as it occurs. It will help me to know how things are progressing."

He placed his palms on top of mine. "Tell me what you feel."

His lovely energy poured into me with greater strength than usual, rendering me positively blissful. I barely got the word out when his hand went over my heart. Energy throbbed throughout my body. I had more to tell him now. I just didn't know if I could.

"It's . . . I feel . . . I can't . . ."

His other hand settled at the base of my throat. Like a dammed river loosed from captivity, words gushed out of me. "Oh! It's like the entire universe is vibrating inside me!"

He tapped his fingers three times on my sternum. The energy flowing through me expanded so rapidly, and with such feeling, that once more, I couldn't speak.

Eliasser repositioned his hands, one on top of my head, the other over my solar plexus.

My tongue was freed again.

"Okay," I cried out. "I can do this. It's like the energy that makes up the universe isn't just inside me, it *is* me. I'm connected to everything through this energy and . . . oh! . . . it doesn't *ever* stop pulsing . . . I don't think I can . . . it's like . . . it's like . . ."

"Accept me, Meiri," Eliasser whispered.

Excitement coursed through me as his energy blended into mine, producing a unique and exhilarating vibration that somehow belonged to both of us. Even our emotions merged for a short while, which meant my elation over our combining became his, and his elation became mine. And it magnified . . . and multiplied . . . increasing . . . *increasing*—

And then . . . there it was! Pulsating with Life and radiating Pure Love. My physical body disappeared and I propelled toward the One Light at incredible speed, as if the One Light and I were opposite poles of an unbelievably strong magnet.

At first contact with the outer edge of Its blazing energy field, my Soul recognized Home.

*Home. I'm going Home!*

Vibrating with Joy, I did nothing to stop myself, even as I realized that this is what Ashi and I would encounter after we merged. Absolute Love, Joy, and a burning desire to rejoin the One Light. But we couldn't. We would need to resist this most primal of desires in order to repair the vortex, a task that might separate us from any experience of the One Light forever. I understood now that the purpose of the Light Sojourn wasn't just to experience the One Light, it was also a test. I had to prove to myself that I could do it.

*No. Anything but this. I can't leave now. Not when I've finally returned.*

I felt a gentle touch from Eliasser's energy, then he slipped into the background.

The One Light's exquisite vibration caught me up in rapturous arms. The time had come. I knew what I was being asked to do. I simply couldn't.

*This is insane! How could anyone turn away from the One Light? How can I? I'm not strong enough. I don't even want to be. To stay in Light form means no more pain. No more tasks. No more suffering. I'd be done with that. Finished. Finished with physical life.*

Waves of bliss swept through me, met now by a counter-current of sadness.

*Sadness? With all this joy, how can there be sadness?*

I knew the answer even before the question had fully formed in my mind. Because I wasn't finished yet. I had more to do. More that I had promised to do.

But that still that wasn't enough to stop me. Helpless, I melded deeper with the One Light, each moment carrying me further from the worlds I knew and any wish to return to them—until a small kernel of rationality reminded me that the Reparention would fail if I rejoined the One Light.

This had a greater effect. The idea of causing the deaths of billions of people made my spirit heavy with grief and fear, and my connection with the One Light seemed to lessen in response. I clung to the fear, thinking that the weight of it might force me to remain in physicality by default. But the One Light washed me clean of everything but Love. I would have to make my choice without using fear as a crutch.

I mentally cried out—to Eliasser, to my spirit friend, to the One Light—whoever might be listening. *"Help me! How do I do this? How do I do this impossible thing?"*

The response rose up from the depths of my soul in symbolic form. Images of every person, place, and thing that I cherished in both worlds burst into my consciousness, then transformed into identical shining points of light that sparkled like stars. I could no longer tell one treasured thing from another as the dazzling star-lights whirled around me, each one entreating me to rejoin physicality. I could feel their love for me and my love for them, but it *still* wasn't enough. My longing to stay with One Light prevailed.

I was losing all hope of succeeding when my soul reached out in harmonic resonation to one particular star-light. The vibration it set up within me quickened both of us simultaneously.

*This is it. This star-light is why I need to stay in physicality.*

My absorption into the One Light was nearly complete when the love from that single star-light penetrated my heart. If I'd had tears to cry with, I would not have been able to stop as its love filled me with the strength I needed. I was finally able to let go of the One Light, which gradually receded, drawing the star-lights along with It.

*"Wait,"* I called to the star-light I had resonated with. *"What are you? Who are you?"*

I was still processing the answer when I became aware of my body again. As Eliasser withdrew his energy from me, I was beset by a loss so profound, I let myself slip from consciousness to avoid the terrible loneliness of being physical once again.

---

The feeling of loss remained long after I regained consciousness. I begged Eliasser to forsake his other duties and stay with me for the rest of the afternoon and evening. Since his energy was mixed with mine during the vision, I assumed he knew all about my encounter with the One Light, but that was not the case. He only knew that I had chosen successfully. When I tried to share the details with him, he insisted the experience was private and should not be divulged to anyone. I didn't understand, but honored his feelings and kept my silence.

At bedtime, I curled up beneath the sleep cover in my room and waited for Eliasser to bring me my nightly brew. In the Light, everything was connected to everything else. There was no separation, no reason for loneliness. Eliasser had assured me that the feeling of loss and isolation would fade, replaced by the Knowing that even though we reside in the physical realm, we are always in the Light, because we are the Light.

"Here you are, Meiri."

I sat up and accepted the goblet, sipping to prolong the moment before he left my room.

"Meiri?" Eliasser's eyes filled with compassion. He knew from personal experience how the Light Sojourn could affect a person. "Would you like me to stay until you are asleep?"

Truthfully? I wanted him to spend the night, to hold me the same way I hold Kiley when she has a bad dream. But my longing to keep him with me was beginning to feel selfish.

"Thanks, but you can go. I'll be fine."

I handed him the empty cup. Eliasser set it on the table, then stood with his back to me as he ran one long finger absently around the rim.

"If you do not mind," he said at length, "I think I will rest here for a while."

I smiled with relief and lay back on my sleeping stone. "Not at all. Mi casa es su casa."

He didn't ask for a translation, just pulled a chair over and sat down.

"Sleep well, my Meiri." He leaned forward and kissed me on the forehead.

"I will now." I smiled and closed my eyes.

---

Eliasser and Ashara stepped up the number and length of our practice sessions. The Reparention kept moving up due to fluctuations in the vortex, but we couldn't nail down a definite date. Not that it mattered. The vortex could hiccup and throw everything off.

Now that I knew my Amoran name and "real" identity, the gag order around my past was lifted. This permitted Ashi and me an openness with each other that hadn't been possible before, and we spent our spare moments together "catching up." Our favorite time of day was right after Evening Meal. We'd walk to the Garrammon Lake and sit on the hill above the water, talking until the sun disappeared beneath the horizon behind us. My memories were still curiously resistant to surfacing on their own, but as Ashi told me stories about our life before I'd had to leave Amoran, the vivid pictures that formed in my mind made me feel as if I were living it all over again—with one exception. I was still physically attracted to him, an attraction that grew stronger with each passing day. So far, Ashi was the only one who knew about that, and I was hoping I could keep it that way for a while. However, through Ashi's stories, I gained an appreciation of what our nonphysical love relationship had been like. We'd both been incapable of experiencing sexual desire, which meant our love for each other had been purely and simply expressed. Yet it had been richer in a way that was difficult to put into words.

Two days before I was scheduled to return to Earth, Eliasser, and Ashara cornered Ashi and me after morning practice and brought us to an empty room.

"You must have the strongest possible connection before the Reparention begins," Eliasser said. "Starting today, we are resuming Life Force augmentation for both of you. It will amplify your complementary energy patterns and allow your bond to grow even stronger in the coming weeks, something which is necessary and long overdue.

"Because of this heightened connection, you will begin to know each other's thoughts and feelings, and with increasing clarity. It will become a challenge to remain detached, physical or otherwise, while in each other's presence. At the same time, it will be difficult for you to *not* be in each other's presence."

"This means," Ashara said, "that the risk of spontaneous merging will now be extremely high. As a result, when you are together, you must have a fellow Guardian with you at all times."

I smiled at Ashi. "Well, Twin-boy. Looks like we both need child-watchers now."

---

"The days go by far too swiftly, my Meiri," Eliasser said as we stood in the Golden Circle at the end of my visit. "Tell me again what the Elder Foreseer said about a key and a gift."

The out-of-the-blue request surprised me, but I didn't have to work at remembering her words. It was like they'd been permanently etched into my brain.

"She said, 'What you judge so harshly in yourself is the very gift you bring to the other Guardians; it is what they need most from you; it is the key. And the one who holds the key for you has the greatest need of your gift. Indeed, of all your gifts.' Since Ashi held the key to my identity, I assume he's the one who needs whatever gifts I have."

"That seems reasonable," Eliasser said with a vagueness that troubled me. I felt sure he was holding something back, something important. Confirming my suspicion, a cold, premonitory feeling gripped me as we said our goodbyes.

I pressed my hands to his chest. Beneath his tunic, his rapid heartbeat bore false witness to his serene demeanor.

"The Elder also said that *all* truths need to be shared for the Reparention to be successful. That means even the ones you hold dearly to yourself, my sweet king. Please don't wait too long, or you may lose the chance for good."

I'd caught him off guard, judging by the way his face paled and he squeezed his eyes shut.

I didn't look back as I called the vortex. I was holding onto a truth of my own—one I couldn't divulge, according to Eliasser. He was the star-light that drew me back to physicality during the Light Sojourn. He was the reason I was not finished with this lifetime. I was here because of him, and even perhaps *for* him. But I wasn't entirely clear why.

# CHAPTER 27

I arrived in my family room with barely enough time to do the reintegration meditation before I picked Kiley up from school.

"Hey, kiddo," I said as she got into the car. "Bet you're happy to get your cast off soon."

"Moooom." She rolled her eyes. "I only broke my arm four days ago."

Shoot. On Earth, it was still Friday, but I'd automatically factored in the three weeks I'd been on Amoran. If ever there was a time to think before I spoke, this was it.

Of course, it didn't take me long to forget that bit of wisdom.

"I called Dr. Bouchard," John said Saturday morning as he gathered his things for yet another work day at Steven's beck and call. "You were wrong. They're not too busy. I made an appointment for you at 11:45 Monday morning."

I couldn't believe he'd done that! "I can't make it."

"Why not?"

"The appointment will run into my lunch hour and I have things to do."

"Like what?" John snapped.

I glared at him. "Since when do I have to account to you for my every move?"

"This appointment is about you being healthy. Isn't that important to you?"

"Funny, I thought it was about you not getting your needs met," I shot back.

John's face contorted with anger and he stomped out of the room. So much for thinking before I spoke. I could've handled that more diplomatically, but John wasn't the only one whose nerves were fraying.

Sunday night, I crawled into bed and switched off the light, relieved that I'd be heading back to Amoran the next day. Relief turned to repulsion when John slid in next to me and stroked my shoulder. "I don't know what's wrong with us, Kerrin, but can we at least give this a try?"

I knew what "this" meant. I had all I could do to keep from cringing. But I'd come to a decision after our last argument. If John believed things were okay between us, he might not be so angry. When he met with no obvious resistance, he ran his hand up under my nightshirt. The discordant vibration was more pronounced than ever, the "fingernails on a blackboard" feeling nearly unbearable. But I forced myself to turn to him and smile. He seemed so sincerely pleased by my response that I resolved to go through with my plan no matter what it cost me.

I pretended as best I could, but when we were finished, I knew I hadn't fooled him.

We fell asleep with our backs to each other.

---

*The energy in the vortex turned a sickening green, but below the Amoran portal, all was peace and tranquility as Balthasarre walked to the Golden Circle.*

*"Stay here," he said to Anders. "I will not be long."*

*He was right. He wouldn't be long at all. In a few minutes, he'd be dead.*

---

"Balthasarre, *NO*," I shouted. As if I were still dreaming, I could see him in my mind, beneath the portal, unaware of the deadly energy inversion he was about to enter.

I bolted out of bed and took the stairs two at a time. I made a frenzied attempt to open the Earth portal, which would automatically seal the one on Amoran. Nothing happened.

John pounded down after me. I knew I shouldn't let him see what I was doing, but I had to help Balthasarre. I thrust my hands above my head and tried to call the vortex again.

No go. My family room ceiling remained intact. So did my inner vision. I watched helplessly as Balthasarre succeeded in opening the Amoran portal.

"It's three in the morning," John cried out, his sleep-ravaged face alarmed and angry. "Why the hell are you waving at the ceiling?"

"Quiet," I barked, as my mind raced for a solution.

Ashi. I'd felt his emotions before. Did it work in reverse? If I could reach him, maybe he could get to Balthasarre and prevent what was about to happen.

I lifted my palms up and concentrated on my Twin.

John yanked my arms down. "Have you gone insane?"

I shoved him with all my might. He staggered backwards, then just stood there, staring at me with a mixture of shock and disbelief.

"If you touch me again," I hissed, "or say one more word before I'm finished, I'll divorce you." I raised my hands again and silently cried, *"Ashi, please hear me. Balthasarre is in danger. The vortex. Eliasser! Ashara! Someone hear me!"*

A gentle blue fog descended from the Amoran portal and wrapped Balthasarre in cloud of misty light. But I knew what was coming.

In desperation, I called out loud, "Ashi. You must hear me. You *will* hear me. *Now.*"

As if the universe responded to my command, a pathway opened between our minds.

*"Meiri?"*

*"It's Balthasarre . . . danger . . . the vortex . . . he'll die."*

I sank to my knees as a putrid green energy barreled through the portal and dragged Balthasarre sideways into the vortex. Anders's scream of terror echoed in my brain.

Eliasser and Ashara materialized in the Golden Circle and managed to partially reopen the portal. The rest of the Guardians arrived, and the entire group attempted to draw the energy—and Balthasarre—toward them. A turbulent cloud formed below the portal, but the Guardians couldn't move it downward.

*"Meiri."*

*"I'm here, Ashi."*

*"Try pushing the energy with a reverse spinning motion. We will pull from here."*

I didn't see how that would work since my portal remained closed, but I leapt to my feet and thrust my hands up, pushing and twisting them as I "thought" the energy to the other end of the vortex. I couldn't feel any difference in the energy flow, however the picture show in my mind verified our success. The chaotic green cloud burst through the Amoran portal, hit the floor of the Main Chamber, then shot back up.

The Master Technician lay crumpled at Eliasser's feet.

"Oh, Balthasarre, please don't die," I whispered. All I could think about was the terrible thing that had just happened to my friend. I'd completely forgotten about John.

"If you're finished having your nervous breakdown, I'm calling Dr. Bouchard tomorrow to make sure you keep the appointment I made. Something is very wrong with you. I don't know who the hell you are anymore." And he stalked up the stairs.

It didn't seem prudent to go back to my own bed with John so furious. I lay down on the couch, tossing and turning, unable to sleep.

---

The next morning, I canceled the doctor's appointment John had made for me. At work, I sleepwalked through the stack in my in-box, counting the minutes until I could make my noontime trip to Amoran. At 11:30, Dave's assistant came by to say the entire office was "invited" to a working lunch, attendance required. I waited for her to leave, penned a quick note saying I had an unavoidable appointment, left it on my desk, then snuck out the side door to avoid being seen.

I paused beneath the family room portal, the image of Balthasarre crumpled at Eliasser's feet lodged in my mind. I wanted to get back to

Amoran, but was it safe for me to go now? What would happen to the Reparention if I, too, got caught in an energy maelstrom?

I argued with myself over what to do until I recalled Ari's assertion long ago that most energy inversions are short-lived. Hoping I could trust that, I decided to take the risk.

When I entered the vortex, everything was fine. In fact, with the exception of the ever-growing area of Darkness, the vortex looked better than it ever had. The rainbow hues were richer and more vibrant, the swirling patterns larger and better defined.

After a breathtakingly gorgeous ride, I landed in the Main Chamber, both surprised and concerned to find it empty. Hoping no one else had been adversely affected by the energy inversion, I ran most of the way to the Healing Room.

Ashara put down the goblet she was filling and met me at the doorway. Behind her, Balthasarre lay motionless on a healing stone, his pinched-in face the color of ashes.

"I did not expect you yet," Ashara said. "Is everything all right on Earth?"

"Yes," I replied, wondering why she'd asked. Then it sank in. I was at least ten minutes ahead of schedule. "I left work early. I couldn't stand being away from you all. How is he?"

"This energy inversion was far worse than the one you experienced," Ashara whispered. "We were too late to prevent some of the damage that . . . Balthasarre's mind is . . ." She stopped and collected herself. "We have healed his body for the most part, and can sense that his mind is still intact, but we are not certain where his consciousness now resides or if it will return."

A painful knot twisted my insides. "How is Anders?"

"Not well. It is time for Evening Meal here. Eliasser took him away from the Healing Room for a while, to eat and to talk." She glanced at the healing stone. "We have done everything we can, Meiri. Now, we wait."

"Can I stay with him?"

Ashara gave a weary nod. "I will begin stretching time, then fix your potion."

I drank what amounted to a double dose of stabilizing potion, then sat in a chair by the healing stone and held Balthasarre's hands. The coldness of his fingers chilled my heart. I rested my head on his lifeless arm and sent as much energy as I could to wherever his consciousness might be. Then, exhausted by the emotionally trying weekend I'd had, as well as a gross lack of sleep, I tossed aside any concern over the reserved nature of Amoran physical contact and climbed onto the narrow stone. I spooned our bodies so that we fit, draped my arm over Balthasarre, and pressed my hand to his chest.

I didn't plan to spend the night in the Healing Room, but that's where Ashi found me the following morning.

"Were you delivering healing energy?" he asked, after gently shaking me awake. Ashara stood next to him, goblet in hand. "What an unusual position. I would like to learn this method."

I smiled at the idea of Ashi spooning someone.

"Perhaps we can try this later today," he added.

Unable to stop myself, I pictured me as the spoonee, with the predictable somatic results. One look at my reddened face and Ashara's expression turned calculating.

"You are flushed," she said, handing me the cup. "Is it too hot in here for you?"

"No," I mumbled. I slid off the stone and kept my back to her as I downed the potion.

"Yet something has brought a bloom of color to your cheeks." Her mild, curious tone had to be an affectation. "Now, what could do that?"

I was guessing she knew damn well what had "done that." But Ashi the Innocent took her seriously. He planted his hand over my heart to read my energy, seemingly oblivious to what lay on either side. I shuddered and pulled away.

Ashi misunderstood. "If my touch hurt you, then you have developed the same affliction I suffer from. In addition to a calmative for your heart, which is beating unusually fast, you must begin consuming the same shielding draft as me."

"Oh, she needs to be shielded all right," Ashara commented dryly, sounding more like one of my friends back on Earth than the Master

Healer of the Seventh Vortex. "However, I will address Meiri's affliction, Makashannar. I want you to stay with Balthasarre."

She turned to me. "Change into a tunic. You and I are going for a walk."

Ashara rarely left the Mountain, so it came as a surprise when we passed through the Main Chamber and took the corridor to the Outer Grounds. She made small talk along the way, idle chatter really, the kind of conversation she was not normally given to, and because of it, I grew more uncomfortable with each step. Was I about to get a lecture on the birds and the bees from sexless Ashara?

We crossed the stone-walled courtyard and exited through the Main Gate. Too tired for a hike, I was relieved when she halted at the Resting Stones and plunked herself down with an "oof." I propped myself against a slant-backed stone and waited for her to begin. This tête-à-tête was her idea. Unless she had an anti-aphrodisiac in her potion arsenal, I didn't see what good talking would do.

Ashara stared at the ground for a few moments, then leaned over to remove a twig from the path of a little bug that was desperately trying to surmount it. My annoyance with her slid away as I marveled at her thoughtfulness.

"You keep amazing me," I said with genuine affection as the bug proceeded on its way.

She smiled and directed a dreamy gaze at the stream.

"I love this place. Does that also amaze you?" It did and I said so. It was hard to picture Ashara really *loving* anything. "And yet," she went on, "as much as I love the Resting Stones, the Mountain, and all of Amoran, I have known a love that was in some ways even greater."

She stopped to clear her throat. If she hadn't referred to this "great love" in the past tense, her comment would have fallen into the category of a no-brainer. The One Light would certainly fit the bill and was the generally accepted response.

"A great love," she repeated, "for one particular man."

Okay. I wasn't sure where this was going, but she definitely had my attention.

"A *man*," she emphasized.

"I may be from Earth, Ashara, but I'm not stupid. I know what a man is."

"I am certain that you do. However, this man was my husband."

"Your *husband?* You were *married?*"

Her eyes—sharp, clear, penetrating—traveled to my face. "Yes. On Earth."

It's a wonder I didn't pass out from shock. Even when the Earth artifacts decorating her room came to mind, I still had trouble accepting Ashara's pronouncement.

"I don't believe you. You despise Earth as much as Danaeus does."

"Your disbelief does not make it any less true. The details as to how and why this feat was accomplished are not important now. All you need to know is that I was permitted one lifetime on Earth—not in my current body, of course. During that lifetime, I was deeply, passionately in love with my husband. With him, I bore many children, then was forced to stand by helpless as half of them died of illnesses I could have easily cured in my Healing Room. That is one of the reasons I appear to detest Earth. For what I have seen, perhaps unfairly, as its many flaws. Yet there is much to be admired, and yes, even loved about your second home. But life there is so brief, so fragile, so . . . heartbreaking." She shook her head. "While still fairly young, my husband was gored to death by a diseased wild boar, which I then had to shoot as it turned next on the little child of mine who was dearest to me."

I listened in stunned silence. This was an Ashara I had never known, maybe no one here had ever known. I wanted, more than anything at that moment, to be the little child Ashara held dear. To be pulled into her arms and comforted. That desire, more than my attraction to Ashi, shook me to my core. My emotional volatility was bad enough—sadness, tears, anger—I could barely keep myself in control anymore. But the depth of the neediness I discovered within me now was even more dismaying.

"So you see, Kerrin/Meiri," she continued. "I know what it is to be a wife and mother. To love a man—body, mind, heart, and soul. I can only imagine what it is like to feel that way about your Twin Light, knowing you will never be able to consummate that special type of love."

It was already too much kindness for me to bear in my current state, but Ashara drew me into the motherly embrace I'd been yearning for, sealing the deal. The last of my defenses fell under the weight of her compassion, and I broke down.

"Cry, my Meiri," she whispered. "Share your burdens with me. Then we will figure out what to do to keep you sane during the coming weeks, for it is surely only a matter of weeks before we will enter the vortex for what may very well be the last time."

The reminder that I might not live much longer loosened my tongue, and I poured out my worries, great and small. My fear of dying. Grief that I might leave Ryan and Kiley motherless, and without them ever knowing why. Guilt—and not just from the lie my Earth life had become, but also because of my increasing detachment from that life as my connection to everyone under the Mountain grew stronger. And then there was my physical attraction to my Twin.

I saved John for last. Ashara listened with an attentive, sympathetic ear I had not thought she possessed, which only brought my tears harder and faster. It was at the height of my emotional outpouring that Eliasser and Ashi came looking for us. But before they reached the Resting Stones, Ashara waved them away and they retreated to the Mountain.

When they were gone, and I could manage to get the words out, I told her again what happened when John touched me, and how angry he'd become lately. "I know he still loves me, and I must still love him. I just can't seem to feel it anymore. I wish I could pretend, for his sake, but I can't even do that. And now, with how I feel about Ashi . . ."

"That is a complication I had hoped you might be spared. But Makashannar is your Twin Light. I am not surprised that you desire him."

"You might have warned me," I grumbled.

"And plant the suggestion in your mind? That would have been unwise. However, I believe the problem you experience with your husband is due to the energy changes in your body. John must be particularly sensitive to Amoran energy, which you project rather strongly now, whether you realize it or not."

"Can you brew up something to help me with, you know . . . *that?*"

"I can do nothing for you until the Reparention is over. And it will only get worse as the Amoran energy you radiate continues to increase."

Ashara noted the position of the sun, then brought her eyes level with mine once more.

"You have to be strong, Meiri. You straddle two worlds, and must continue to do so while you become more of who you really are here on Amoran. A difficult task, but one you are quite capable of managing," she decreed. "Come now. We must get to Morning Meal."

Ashi stood in the corridor with his back to the wall as I approached the Meal Room. He was the last person I wanted to talk to right now, so I gave him a brief smile and kept on.

"Wait," he called. I turned around. He brought my palms to his chest, wrapped his fingers around mine and stroked the backs of my hands. "Was it I who made you so sad?"

I smiled ruefully. The man was *so* clueless. "No." I leaned into him and whispered, "But you will make me something else if you keep touching me this way."

It took a moment for him to catch on. Then he dropped my hands like they'd burned him and the tip of his nose went pink.

"Forgive me," he said. "It is difficult to know the right thing to do anymore."

"Welcome to my world."

———

Anders was absent from Morning Meal. He insisted on staying by his father's side, which Eliasser agreed to, provided he kept up his strength by eating at regular intervals.

I said nothing during our meal, opting out of what little conversation there was. But word travels fast beneath the Mountain, and my emotional encounter with Ashara was already common knowledge. Danaeus and Ari shot curious looks at me across the table. Ashi joined their ranks, catching my eye and tilting his head as if to nonverbally ask me if I was okay.

I set my fork down. "I appreciate the concern. I'm fine. I just don't feel like talking."

"No?" Eliasser said. "Then perhaps Ashi will speak for you when the two of you visit the Foreseers after Midday Meal."

The room went silent. I stared at my fellow Guardians one by one. Their popped-open eyes had me laughing for the first time in days. "What's the big deal? It's just a visit to the Foreseers."

Danaeus was the first to recover. "No one but Eliasser seeks out the Foreseers, and he doesn't do it on a daily basis like you have."

"But they're so wonderful to be with; why would you ignore them?"

"Ignore them? Hardly," Ari said. "They're very reclusive and next to impossible to find."

"I myself have never been to the Glen of the Foreseers," Ashi admitted.

I was dumbfounded. "Never? How did I stumble across them my first day in the forest?"

"How indeed," Eliasser said mildly. "You will need someone to accompany you."

That's right. Ashi and I couldn't be alone anymore.

"You mean a chaperone," I said. "That's what we call it on Earth."

Ari rose from his seat and executed a magisterial bow. "I would be honored to serve as Master Chaperone to the Twin Lights of the Seventh Vortex on the occasion of their not being able to keep their hands off each other—energetically speaking, of course."

---

Ashi and I stood with Ari on the shaded path outside the entrance to the Glen of the Foreseers. My companions' awed amazement over how easily I located the Glen brought a warm, self-satisfied glow to my heart. I was finally better than them at something.

*"You bring another with you,"* a Foreseer spoke into my mind.

*"Yes. He's here to help Makashannar and me in case we accidentally begin to merge."*

*"We see. Ari's devotion to the Light is appreciated, but he must remain outside the Glen. He need not fear for your safety when you are with us."*

I relayed the message to Ari, then Ashi and I stepped between the trees at the entrance. It was hard for me to believe he'd never been to the Foreseers' Glen, but the way he walked the perimeter, eyes sparkling with interest, confirmed it.

The blue Foreseer wafted through the opening at the far end of the Glen and greeted him. They moved to the center of the clearing and began what promised to be a lengthy conversation, so I sat down to wait for them. After a while, the warm sun made me drowsy, as it sometimes did here in the Glen. My head drooped to my chest.

"He is a beautiful Being, is he not?"

I looked up in surprise, wondering if I'd been asleep. The pink Foreseer had arrived without me feeling her presence.

"He is at that," I agreed, almost wishing she hadn't pointed it out.

"Being near him—this is difficult for you?"

I assumed she was referring to the risk of early merging, and not my attraction to Ashi.

"Yes. Being near him is difficult, as is *not* being near him."

"We understand. Come, Daughter. We must test the strength of your bond."

We joined Ashi and the blue Foreseer in the middle of the clearing, where the pink Foreseer indicated Ashi and I should stand facing one another.

"Recite the Vortex Prayer," she said. "Speak your portion together as one voice. We will say Eliasser's part. However, the transfer of energy is to happen between the two of you. Begin."

I didn't know what prayer she meant until Ashi pushed his hands out to the side and said, "Born inside the spiral of Light . . ." It was the same prayer I'd recited with Eliasser in the Main Chamber. The phrases I thought of as only mine belonged to Ashi as well. When we finished, the energy cycling between us was so intense, I could barely stand. I asked the Foreseer if she could lessen it.

"We are aware of your discomfort, Meirashannar," she acknowledged. "However, we must go forward. Now clasp the hands of your Twin."

I held my hands out to Ashi. As soon as we made contact, the pink mist appeared, spinning furiously around us. Our vibrations skyrocketed and it felt like we shot out of our bodies and off the planet. The state of mutual bliss we experienced was sheer heaven. If the Foreseers didn't return us to the Glen soon, they'd have to drag me back kicking and screaming.

Our vibrations slowed and the Glen came back into focus. But I buzzed with so much energy, I didn't feel "solid." Gripped by a need to prove I still had a body, to physically touch another person, I put my hands on Ashi's chest. His rapid heartbeat drummed against my palms.

"Meiri," he whispered. He slid his arms around my waist and pulled me close. I guess he needed to connect with someone too, but that level of contact put me over the edge. Without thinking, I grabbed his face and kissed him. And I don't mean a little peck on the lips.

The Foreseers slipped between us and their energy gently pushed us apart.

Mortified by what I'd done, I sank to the grass and cradled my head in my hands.

"Meirashannar," the blue Foreseer said. "You still judge harshly your feelings and your actions. Do not. Emotions are essential. Indeed, tremendous power is available to one with a balanced emotional field."

"Vortex Lights," both Foreseers said. "You have shown us the strength of your energy fields and the depth of your Love. Further shielding is required. We leave you now."

The situation must have been serious, because instead of leaving the usual way, they vanished right before us.

To Ari's disappointment, Ashi and I refused to talk about our visit with the Foreseers. The three of us returned to the Mountain, where I pulled Ashi aside for a private word before afternoon practice began.

"About what happened." I couldn't bring myself to say the "k" word. "I don't know what I was thinking." I frowned. "I wasn't thinking, that's the problem. I was just . . . feeling. Anyway, I am truly sorry."

Ashi still seemed dazed by our experience in the Glen. He held his hands out, then must have caught the mistake he was about to make with someone who had trouble keeping her hands—and her mouth—to herself. He redirected his arms, folding them tightly across his chest.

Eliasser came up behind us. "Forgive my interruption, Meiri, but I need to speak with Ashi."

Ashi excused himself and I took my place next to Ashara. My apology to Ashi was sincere and double-sided. I felt terrible about subjecting him to a forced kiss. But I'd also begun to worry that my Earth-style weaknesses might spell disaster for the Reparention. The blue Foreseer had admonished me to stop judging myself, but it was hard not to when I was the only Guardian with self-control issues.

---

Ashara and Eliasser doubled our practices. It was emotionally and energetically hard without Balthasarre, but we had to prepare to do the Reparention without him in case he couldn't rejoin us in time. The possibility that his mind might never return wasn't even discussed. Every moment I could spare, I went to the Healing Room and talked to him—about the garden, Garrammon—anything I could think of that might help our Master Technician find his way back.

Ashara devised a shielding draft to dull my ever-increasing desire for my Twin. Not to be left out of all the potion-producing fun, the Foreseers created one to protect against spontaneous merging. But it wasn't foolproof. Ashi and I still had to be chaperoned, something I was secretly glad about as my liquid anti-aphrodisiac didn't entirely do the job. I no longer trusted myself and steered clear of him whenever I could. In one of those paradoxical twists, this actually made life harder for us thanks to the cosmic drive for our energy fields to unite. When we were apart, my energy surged out from me in a kind of rhythmic pulsing, searching for him, seeking to be with him. I learned through Ari that the same was true for Ashi. But I kept to my plan for both our sakes, all the while hating that I was the Guardians' weakest link.

My last day for this current Amoran visit arrived. I felt queasy at the thought of returning to Earth and the problems that awaited me there. On the other hand, I was grateful for the relief I'd have from the constant pull of Ashi's energy.

Ashara and I said our goodbyes at the edge of the Main Chamber. Our talk by the Resting Stones had transformed our relationship, evidenced by the gentle way she patted my face.

"You will manage," she said. "You always have. You always will."

Homesick for Amoran even before I left, I merely nodded, walked to the Golden Circle, and stepped beneath the portal. Ashi held his hands out, but when I didn't accept the invitation, he withdrew them and they hung limply at his sides. Our bond was now so strong, that as I moved through the portal into the vortex, I was not spared his puzzlement, sadness, and dismay.

# CHAPTER 28

For the next two Earth days, and the ten days I spent on Amoran during my lunch hours, I lived life as an emotional ping-pong ball. John came home early on Monday afternoon. Furious that I'd canceled my doctor's appointment, he wouldn't speak to me. That part was the good news. The great news? He was leaving for an emergency business trip and wouldn't be back until Wednesday night.

He broke the blessed silent treatment just once, to ask if everything was ready for Thursday. The only Thanksgiving preparation I'd done was to pin the shopping list I'd made several weeks ago to the bulletin board. Knowing full well I would have to cram everything into the next forty-eight hours, I sent John off thinking our holiday dinner was under control. It wasn't, but with John gone, the ping-pong ball, still bouncing around like mad, was a lot happier.

Early December was now the current timeframe for the Reparention, and its imminence sobered everyone. Ari rarely laughed and Danaeus turned into Grumpy Gus again. Anders, already depressed about his father, grew sullen and quiet, while Ashara became more demanding and short-tempered than ever. At the other end of the spectrum, Eliasser and Makashannar seemed to be withdrawing.

Thanks to the new ETA, the Guardians, after a firm reminder from the Foreseers that honesty *must* reign, were spilling secrets with abandon. However, most of them didn't seem very important. Anders had manipulated his way out of a turn at nemestes gathering. Ari admitted to cheating occasionally at Garrammon—how, he wouldn't say. I even owned up to kissing Ashi.

I was right about the insignificance of the Guardians' truth-telling. Before long, an actual decree came through from the Foreseers. We were to bare *all* of our secrets. *Now.*

———————

It was the last day of my lunch hour visit on the Wednesday before Thanksgiving. I was heading out the Main Gate when Ari ran up behind me.

"Are you avoiding me?" he panted. "We've barely had a moment alone lately."

"No, silly. I looked for you earlier, but no one knew where you were. I'm on my way to the Garrammon Lake for a quick swim before afternoon practice."

"If you don't mind, I'm going to join you."

"Silly elf. As if I'd mind."

Ari smiled, linked arms with me, and proceeded to fill my ears with Mountain gossip. I was only half-listening until we arrived at the lake and he mentioned Ashi.

"I probably shouldn't tell you this, but you've got our dear Child of the Vortex asking a lot of interesting questions. Hey! Wouldn't that make a great movie? *Children of the Vortex,* starring—let's see, who would we get to play you and Ashi? I'd have to play myself, of course. Being me takes a certain finesse, and I've always wanted to—"

I had to cut him off. "Ari! Stay on topic. It's hard enough for me to follow my own train of thought without having to navigate yours as well."

"Right. Ashi's been asking me to describe what 'physical love' is like."

"You're joking."

"No, I'm not. And neither is Makashannar, Mild Mannered Man of . . . of . . ." Ari scrunched up his nose, searching for the final "m" word for his alliteration.

"Argh. If you don't complete your thoughts in a linear fashion, I'm going to scream!"

He laughed apologetically. "I don't know what's come over me, except that it's very boring around here without you. All Ashi does is mope when you're on Earth."

"He does?" I felt inordinately pleased.

"Yes, lover girl, he does." Ari arched his eyebrows at the satisfied smile on my face. "It's not just that he misses you. He knows you're avoiding him because of that kiss in the Glen."

I sighed. "He's right. I'm afraid to go near him. Afraid of doing something I'll either regret or that will put the Reparention at risk. Or both."

"I realize that. But Ashi's whole frame of reference is life under the Mountain. This kind of thing is purely an intellectual process for him. And as far as 'physical love' goes—a polite reference to sex, don't you think?—I tried to explain what is essentially unexplainable, then gave up and lent him some of the books I collected on Earth."

Uh-oh. "What kind of books?"

Ari's smile held a hint of mischief. "Well, you might call them . . . handbooks? Manuals?"

My face flushed. "Ashi asked you what it was like, not how to do it."

"What difference does it make? He wouldn't know a carnal feeling if it bit him in the butt."

"Knock it off," I snapped. Ari's flip comment shouldn't have bothered me. Yet it did. Never before had I seriously wanted to experience "physical love" with anyone other than John. Now, I ached to with a longing that intrigued me, excited me, and riddled me with guilt. That it could never happen should have made the guilt easier to bear. But it didn't.

Ari chewed on his lower lip and stared at the ground. I had never come down hard on him like that, and with the Reparention edging up over the horizon, this was no time to begin.

"I'm so sorry. I shouldn't have yelled at you."

When he didn't respond, I followed the direction of his gaze. His footwear was new. At least, I hadn't seen these cobbled creations before. I studied the intricate design on the fabric that wound around his foot and up over his ankles.

I elbowed him in the ribs. "Nice shoes, Elf-boy."

"I've always been good with shoes," he said, but without his usual smile.

The "handbooks" he'd lent Makashannar intruded into my thoughts. Before I could stop myself, I asked, "Do you have someone, Ari? A special someone that you—" I cut myself off. What was I doing? Ari had always made it clear that the topic of his love life was off-limits.

"I can't," he said, surprising me by answering this time. "The vibrational frequency of elves makes us unique and allows us ready access to what people on Earth think of as magic. However, it is also a kind of sentence. Elves are only able to mate with other elves."

"But that means . . ." I trailed off before I stated the obvious. As the only remaining elf in existence, Ari's options for a partner were nonexistent.

His expression became distant. "I grew up knowing we elves had to stay with our own kind, but since Elvener had no off-world visitors in those days, I didn't care why." Ari's jaw worked back and forth. "I learned the reason through a terrible accident."

I broke out in full body chills. Ari was about to reveal his secret, and it somehow involved me. Wordlessly taking my hand, he led me up the hill, and we sat beneath our tree.

"During one of your more recent lifetimes," Ari began, "I had to watch over you more closely. By your late twenties, you were widowed with two young children. That's when I positioned myself as a traveling cobbler." He smiled. "I really am good with shoes, you know."

"I can see that." I smiled back. He held my gaze for a moment, then looked away and sighed with such feeling I felt a catch at the back of my throat.

"I loved that lifetime of yours. You were a midwife-healer whose home was filled with the laughter of the girls you were training. I came by often enough that a special friendship developed between us. You insisted that I find a nice girl and settle down. You had already picked out the perfect location for my house, and said, and I quote, 'With your good looks, you need to make lots of babies. I, of course, will deliver them.'"

"Yikes," I said, to ease an amorphous tension. "I was bossy even then."

Ari didn't laugh. "In complete violation of my duty as a Guardian, I fell in love with you. Well, I fell in love with you as Hannah. I never said a word about it to anyone on Amoran. If I had, they would have refused to let me return." Ari shook his head. "You know how it is. You can often tell when a person feels the same way about you in return. You kept joking about hitching me up with someone, but we both knew who we wanted that someone to be."

He leaned his head against the tree and stared up into the lush, green branches.

"I was on my way to your cottage one day when a snowstorm caught me by surprise. 'No problem,' I thought. 'I'll just ethermove and get to see her even sooner.' But as happens sometimes on Earth, my magic deserted me. I had to battle through a mile of icy whiteness and barely made it to your door. You whisked the clothes off of my frozen body, wrapped me in blankets and sat me in front of the fire. 'Drink this,' you said, handing me one of your medicinal teas. 'It will warm you from within.'"

Ari finally looked at me. "Our eyes met then, and you said in the softest voice imaginable, 'Perhaps we should help the medicine along. The children are at my sister's.'"

So far, I'd only had to juggle two lives—Meiri and Kerrin. Now, as Hannah's personality impressed itself into the mix, I recalled that lifetime. And how it ended.

"Oh, Ari. I remember what happened. Even so, it was beautiful."

"Yes, it was. Right up until you died."

Incredibly, I could feel in my own heart the weight of the sadness he carried.

"It's okay. You don't have to continue."

"Unfortunately, I do. There is a very good reason elves can only be with other elves. At the moment that we . . ." He cleared his throat. "That is to say, when you and I reached—" He broke off, his cheeks tinged with pink. "Anyway, it was the release of my elven energy that did it. It was more than your Earth body could withstand. It stopped your heart."

I had to corral a herd of emotions before I could talk. Ari had given me so much in that life—and probably in all of my lives—that I almost didn't know where to begin.

"What did you tell the Guardians about my death?"

"Only that you died of a heart attack. I never told them why."

"I see. Well, I hope you don't regret what we shared, because I certainly don't."

He groaned. "How can you say that? I killed you."

"True. But before you did, you loved me magnificently for what was destined to be my final time anyway. I was dying of cancer, the fast-growing kind. At most, I had a few weeks left. It had been months since you'd been around and I didn't know when, or if, I'd see you again. Traveling craftsman sometimes disappeared for good along the back roads."

It amazed me how strongly I could feel what Hannah experienced before Ari showed up that night; her anguish at having to leave her young family behind; her fear and longing for her absent friend.

"I had to come back to Amoran periodically," Ari explained. "But the vortex acted up and I couldn't return to Earth right away. That's why you hadn't seen me in so long. The wait to get back to you nearly did me in."

I felt Hannah smile at that. She'd been very much in love with her itinerant shoemaker.

"The pain was increasing beyond what I could endure without heavily dosing myself. Just before you arrived, I sent my children to my sister's for a few days so I could end my life in private. I refused to have them watch me waste away, as I had witnessed my own mother do, crying out in an agony that could not be eased."

Ari seemed even sadder at that. I took his face in my hands and kissed his forehead.

"My most wonderful elf, don't you understand what you did? You saved me that evening so long ago. I had expected to die alone, without any way to let the man I loved know he would never see me again. And then, like a miracle, you appeared at my door. 'One more day won't matter,' I told myself. 'Tomorrow's as good a day to die as any.' Had I known the gift you offered me, I would have prolonged our—"

"Gift?" He sounded incredulous.

"Yes, Ari. The gift of a beautiful death. I left that life with a smile in my spirit so broad that the reverberation of those shared moments between us carries forth to this day. And the love you gave to me that night helped to heal the spiritual wounds caused by my first Earth death."

Ari didn't seem convinced. He squeezed his eyes shut and sighed. I took in the gloomy expression gracing his fine features, and decided it was time to put the past to rest. And I knew just the way to do it.

"Hey, Elf-boy. Considering your lovemaking prowess, I could say, 'what a way to go.'"

Ari looked at me like I was nuts.

"Yep," I added. "You gave the 'kiss of death' a whole new meaning."

He frowned. "This confession was heart-wrenching for me, Meiri."

"Yeah? Well it was heart-*stopping* for me."

"Meiri!" he cried. But his frown wavered.

"What can I say, Romeo? You killed me with kindness."

My warped humor finally got him. "Well," he drawled, batting his eyes. "I am to *die* for."

"That's the spirit, you lady-killer."

"Ah, have a *heart* Earth-girl."

"Hah. I needed one after you were through with me."

He was giggling now. "You know what they say."

"No, I don't. Enlighten the dead girl."

"When an elf's been your man, no one else can."

I snorted, "Right. 'Cuz you're screwed in more ways than one!"

Ari slapped his knee. "At least I knew you wouldn't kiss and tell. Oh! Enough already. I can't believe we're doing this."

"Yeah, it's even over the top for me. Or was that on top for me? Either way it was definitely good for—*oof.*" His delicate elf hand shoved me over. When I stopped laughing, I made him an offer he couldn't refuse, seeing as I had him *dead* to rights.

"How about going for a swim with me, Cobbler Boy?"

"It's the least I can do. Besides, when I push your head underwater, I won't be able to hear your sick jokes anymore."

"Like you're one to talk." Then, I shoved *him* over so I could race down the hill and beat him into the lake.

---

Ari and I shared the story of our tragic love affair with Eliasser, Ashara, and Ashi after practice. Then, the five of us walked to the Main Chamber, where I reminded them I wouldn't be back until Monday due to the Thanksgiving holiday weekend.

I hugged each of them in turn. When Ashi made no move to break his hold on me, Ashara intervened, prying his arms away from my back. Breathless from the impact of his energy, I ascended into the vortex.

I could still feel his arms around me when I landed in my family room.

# CHAPTER 29

I t was nearing midnight on Wednesday when I put the pumpkin pies into the oven. I was exhausted, but at least I'd gotten most of the meal prep done.

I sat at the kitchen table to read while waiting for the timer to go off. John was late getting back from his trip, and I was beginning to worry. His route home stretched along miles of highway, beautiful by day, but dark and dangerous on a rainy, windy night. The Guardians had warned me that weather in my area on Earth might be altered by the growing instability in the vortex, culminating in a great storm right before the Reparention was to begin. And here I'd thought climate change was the cause of our recent screwy weather.

Today was no exception. The day had dawned cold and cheerless. By noon, the temperature was seventy-six degrees with the sun beating down from a cloudless sky—not typical New England weather for the day before Thanksgiving. Now, an icy rain battered the house.

When John finally blew through the back door, his mood matched the storm.

"Did you reschedule your doctor appointment?" he growled.

I kept my eyes on my book. "Hello to you, too. I'm fine, thanks for asking."

"Cut the shit, Kerrin. Did you make the appointment or not?"

I glanced up. John's face was marked with irregular pink splotches. "Are you okay?"

"Don't change the subject. Answer me."

I marshaled what little emotional stamina I had left. "I have spent the past two days preparing for Thanksgiving dinner, and I am too tired to—"

"You want me to feel guilty? For what? For busting my ass to keep a roof over our heads?"

"—to fight with you," I finished. "Can you let go of your anger for now? Because our—"

"You think this is all my fault?" he shouted.

"*Because*"—I raised my voice—"our family and friends don't know that our marriage is falling apart, and it would be unfair to expose them to whatever poison is infecting us."

John's rheumy eyes finally registered with me. I stood up, but he quickly tottered backwards. The smell of alcohol reached me anyway and my mouth dropped open in surprise.

"What's the matter, perfect Kerrin?" John yelled in response. "Am I a bad husband because I stopped by Steven's house on the way home for a drink or two? Why should you care? There's nothing for me here." He swayed as his hand sketched an erratic arc in the air.

Damn Steven! "I can't believe he let you drive in this condition."

John barked out a harsh laugh. "I'm only a little drunk." He pinched his fingers together to illustrate 'a little' but couldn't match up his thumb and forefinger. "But you? You're completely fucking nuts. You fucking talk to ceilings!" He waved in the direction of the family room before driving a stake through my heart. In a shrill attempt at mimicking my voice, he screeched, "Balthasarre, please don't die." John lunged forward, grabbed my arms, and shook me so hard my head jerked back.

"Stop it," I cried out.

"Who's Balthasarre? Your new boyfriend? Is that who you spend your lunch hours with? Is that who you're having sex with? 'Cuz you're sure not giving me any."

John smashed his lips onto mine with such force, my tooth cut the inside of my mouth. The painful buzzing was nearly intolerable. I struggled to free myself, but his grip was too strong. I could think of only one thing to do. I kneed him in the crotch.

"Shit," he wheezed, hunching over.

I backed out of reach. "I'm not having sex with anyone."

"Bull," John gasped.

"It's the truth. Do I have a problem having sex with you? Yes. And I'll do something about it as soon as I can." *If I live long enough.*

"You'd better," he hissed. He staggered to the hallway and banged up the stairs.

I gulped at the air, unable to move until the beeping timer pushed me to action. I slid the pies out of the oven, nearly dropping one because my hands were shaking so badly. To calm myself, I took a page from John's new study guide on how to deal with life's problems. I uncorked a bottle of tomorrow's wine, poured a glass, and drained it.

I was still trembling when I got to the bottom. I reached for a refill, but an impulse prompted me to recite the Vortex Prayer instead. A few lines into the recitation, Ashi's presence wrapped around me like a comforter. I heard him—faintly—saying the prayer, too. We continued together, and when we finished, I mentally wished him good night and sent him a wave of Love.

His energy reached me, rich and strong.

*"Thank you,"* I thought to him.

His reply was a warm tickle in the center of my chest.

———————

It was well past noon the next day when John got out of bed to take a shower. The turkey was in the oven, the carrots and potatoes were ready to be cooked, and the salad, courtesy of two children who decided to hold a truce for the day, was in the refrigerator waiting to be tossed. Ryan and Kiley seemed subdued this morning. I dearly hoped neither of them had heard the details of what transpired the previous night.

My stomach tightened when the water shut off in the bathroom. As I arranged blocks of cheese for an appetizer, John made his appearance. He poured coffee from the pot I'd made for him and sat down.

Kiley came in and gave her dad a hug. John held her for a moment, then patted her on the shoulder. "I want to talk to your mom, kiddo."

"Shoot some hoops with me later?"

"With your arm in a cast?"

"It's no big deal," she called over her shoulder as she left. "It doesn't even hurt now."

I placed the appetizer tray on the sideboard, fixed my tea, and sat opposite John.

He ran his fingers through his hair and stared into his coffee mug.

"I don't know what to say, Kerrin. 'I'm sorry' doesn't even begin to cover it. I don't know who accosted you in this kitchen last night, but it wasn't me." He took a long drink, then rested his head in his hands. "Except, it *was* me, and that scares me no end. I never would have believed I was capable of that."

"I think we're all capable of a lot more than we realize, and I guess it must work both ways, the good and the bad." I shrugged. "Let's give each other a little space."

He shot me a look that was equal parts apprehension and defiance.

"I don't mean that kind of space. I don't think we should separate or anything, just . . ." *Leave each other alone,* were the words that came to mind, but I didn't think he'd appreciate that. "I know I haven't been myself lately. If you can just give me another week or so to sort things out, it might take the pressure off both of us."

"Don't you miss us? Us . . . together?"

I tried to be as sensitive as I could. "In all honesty, I feel so strange inside that I'm not able to miss us that way. If things aren't better by Christmas, I'll—"

"Christmas!" His voice rose. "You want me to wait until Christmas?"

"Please, John. Quiet down and listen to me. I'll try to see the doctor on Monday. Let's find out what he suggests."

"He better suggest you see a shrink."

I have only so much patience. "Then I'll demand a marriage counselor."

John sneered. "That's great. You're flipping out and you want to drag *me* to therapy?"

At that opportune moment, Ryan poked his head into the kitchen to announce that the first members of my family had arrived—too early, as usual. Today, however, I considered them to be right in the nick of time.

---

John and I avoided each other while we performed our respective hosting duties. No one seemed to notice anything amiss except for Nancy and Bob, who eyed us with furtive glances. Nancy would never have divulged the details of my talk with her, but I was betting she had at least let Bob know that John and I were having trouble. My suspicion was confirmed when, after pulling John aside to talk, Bob pressed one of Dr. Parks's pink business cards into my husband's hand. John accepted it without argument, which I found interesting.

When dinner was ready, we took our places at the table. Some of our Thanksgiving regulars were missing, including my parents who were visiting friends in the Midwest. But my brother Michael and his wife Diana had made it, as well as my sister Sarah and her new boyfriend whose name I kept forgetting. And, of course, Nancy, Bob, and Robert. As I studied the group gathered to celebrate the holiday, it struck me that, current problems aside, John and I were truly blessed by the life we shared—a life rich with friendships, love, and caring.

Then I had a less comforting thought. At tables across the country, people were giving thanks, unaware that this might be their last chance to enjoy the privilege of breaking Thanksgiving bread together. And even if it wasn't *their* last chance, it could very well be mine. Vulnerability weighed on my heart, spurring me to make an outrageous request. I asked my nonreligious family members currently present if we could say grace.

Michael assumed it was a setup for a joke. "Grace!" he yelled, and everyone laughed. I could have predicted that reaction, but it bothered me anyway. The Guardians took gratitude seriously, giving thanks before each meal, at the start of every practice, upon arising in the morning, and when they lay to rest at night.

"Can't we take a moment to think about what we're grateful for?" I asked.

Michael stopped laughing. "Wait. You're serious? I'm an atheist, in case you forgot."

"Kerrin," John growled. "Our guests are hungry."

"So are the people who have nothing to eat today," I snapped. "I just want to acknowledge what we have. How full our lives are. And the fact that we're all . . . still alive."

John's face darkened. It was crazy of me to push him like this. Like Michael, John disdained all things God-related. But I did it anyway. I closed my eyes and repeated one of Eliasser's favorite blessings. On Amoran it was done as a round, each person saying a line. Since it didn't refer to God, I figured it would be okay.

*"One Light. You are . . .*
*. . . the breath of our existence,*
*the beat within our hearts,*
*the Light within our minds.*
*For this we give thanks.*

*One Light. You are . . .*
*. . . the heat that warms the ground,*
*the ground that grows the food,*
*the food we eat in Love of Life.*
*For this we give thanks.*

*One Light. You are . . .*
*. . . our bodies,*
*our minds,*
*our hearts,*
*our souls.*
*For you we give thanks. So be it."*

This simple recitation was general enough that I didn't think anyone would be put off. I opened my eyes, realizing too late the error I'd made. My fellow diners regarded me with varying degrees of curiosity, shock, and in John's case, red-faced anger. He threw his napkin down, stalked to the kitchen, and returned with another bottle of wine.

"You forgot to thank your *blessed light* for alcohol," he said in a deceptively smooth voice. "I'm going to need a lot of it to get through this meal. Hey there, Michael. How about a little *light* of the grape?"

"I know I've 'seen the light,'" Michael quipped, glancing my way like he expected me to admit this nonsense was just a hoax.

I clenched my teeth to keep from setting him straight, which I was sure would only make the situation worse. But the tense mood in the room, and the confusion on my children's faces, convinced me something needed to be done.

"Let's back this train up," I said. "I'm sorry if I offended anyone; that wasn't my intention. So in the *spirit*—oops, my bad—of *lightening* things up; uh-oh, another bad pun."

Bob grinned. "Is there any other kind?"

I smiled in return. "That *was* pretty redundant. Anyway, I'd like to propose a toast. And for the record, I like my toast *light*." I crossed my eyes at Kiley, who giggled.

"You don't mean that kind of toast, Mom."

"You're right. I don't. But I do mean this." I lifted my goblet and waited until everyone did likewise. "I am thankful for all of you. Please remember that in the days to come. No matter what happens, I love you. I always have and I always will." And since I could no longer talk without giving my emotional state away, I held my glass out and tapped Kiley's, who in turn clinked her glass against Bob's, who touched his goblet to Nancy's, and so on in a circle around the table. When the last glass-tap came home to me, we drank our toast and dug into dinner.

John held his anger reasonably in check until dessert was served. The kids heaped pie and cake onto their plates and headed to the family room to watch a Christmas special. That's when John and Michael declared open season on Kerrin. I wanted to get through dessert without making a scene, so I ignored the barbs they hurled at me or treated them with humor. But it was growing increasingly difficult to do either, because the more they drank, the worse it got.

When dessert was finally finished, my sister and her boyfriend, What's-His-Name, cleared the empty plates and ferried them to the kitchen. I breathed a mental sigh of relief that the evening was drawing to a close—until John and Michael uncorked another bottle of wine. They were totally obnoxious now, and not just to me, although I was still their main target.

"Haven't you guys had enough?" I complained.

They looked at each other and guffawed. "Seems like neither one of us has had *any* lately," John slurred out. Michael tried to slap John a high-five and missed, while his wife, Diana, turned successive shades of red.

"Shut up," Bob hissed. He glared at John. "What the hell is wrong with you?"

John wiped a dribble of wine from his chin and snickered. "I dunno. What's up with you, Bobby Boy? You're awfully preachy lately. Did you get religion at the marriage counselors? In that case, take Saint Kerrin with you."

John's sister snarled, "You're the one who needs a shrink, you flaming asshole."

"Oh, come off it, Nancy Pants," John blasted. "You said the other day you don't know what kinda bug is up Kerrin's butt, she's so weird lately. So don't give me that holier-than-thou shit. That job's been filled by my wife, Little Miss 'I Love the Light but Not My Husband.'"

"You bastard," I choked out.

"Screw you, Kerrin." John's nostrils flared. "You talk about that freaking light in your sleep. What is it? A code name for you and your lover?" He tried to leer at me, but managed only to look like he was about to be sick.

Bob's voice rose threateningly. "I said stop it."

"Or what? You'll make me go to marriage counseling with you?" John shoved his glass at my brother. "Pour me some more vino, bro."

Michael, who was a fraction less inebriated, peered sideways at Diana, who was on the verge of tears. "Uh, maybe Kerrin's right."

"I said *pour*," John thundered. "I want to get obliterated so I don't hear Kerrin talking to her imaginary friends in her sleep. Writing this book of hers has warped her brain."

I shoved my chair back and picked up my wineglass, which had been sitting in front of me virtually untouched since dinner began. I had dearly wanted to imbibe, but I figured one of us had to be the designated human being for today, and it clearly wasn't going to be John.

I was on my way to the kitchen when John again bellowed that he wanted more wine, and he wanted it *now*, damn it!

Something in me snapped.

"More wine?" I said, with syrupy sweetness. "Sure, honey. No problem."

I reversed course and let him have mine—right down the front of his shirt.

---

The wine bath I gave John was like untying the end of a balloon. Instead of erupting in rage, all the arrogant air rushed out of him. He sat there looking lost and confused until Bob pried him up and dragged him out onto the back deck. My brother and sister and their respective partners left soon after. Bob came back inside to say he was taking John to his house for the night—to clean him up, sober him up, and hopefully talk some sense into him. To give them time alone, Nancy and Robert stayed behind and spent the night with Ryan, Kiley, and me.

Bob and John returned the following afternoon. Nancy herded Ryan, Robert, and Kiley into the family room to watch a movie while Bob sat John and me at the kitchen table facing each other as he coached John through his apology. But my husband kept losing his temper. When Bob asked him why he was so angry, John fell back on lack of sex as the reason.

"Bullshit," Bob said. "It hasn't been *that* long. Christ. Nancy and I have gone a lot longer than that. And since when is sex so important that you'll torture your wife nonstop about it?"

John kept silent.

"I know that having Kerrin lose all interest in sex—" Bob turned to me. "Am I right about that?"

I nodded. I saw no point in denying it. John must have told him everything.

Bob looked back at John. "I know that hurts, but your reaction is way out of proportion."

John heaved a sigh. "I can't seem to be in the same room with her anymore without feeling angry. Even when I think I'm okay and I start out trying to be nice—"

Bob cut him off. "Do you hear what you're saying? I've known you both since high school. When have you ever had to force yourself to be nice to Kerrin on a daily basis?"

At John's forlorn expression, I reflected on what Ashara had said, that John might be particularly sensitive to Amoran energy. Could that really be the root of his awful behavior?

"I'm no marriage counselor," Bob went on, "but you guys definitely need one. Call Dr. Parks, or whomever you choose, but do it soon." He glanced at John. "Do you want to stay with me for a few days?" John seemed beyond speech and just shook his head. "In that case, you need to lay off the booze. I don't know what happened to your alcohol tolerance, but it's shot, and you are one nasty bastard when you've had too much. Oh, and no sex."

John and I looked at him in surprise, although mine was mixed with relief.

"I speak from experience. Wait until you see a counselor. There's so much negative charge on this issue now, that even if you do feel like making love, you'll probably screw things up. Oops. Sorry about the pun. That's usually Kerrin's department."

John's cell phone rang. When he made no move to answer it, Bob picked it up off the table, checked the display and rolled his eyes before answering the call.

"Hi Steven. No, it's Bob. How did I know it was you? You mean, aside from caller ID?" Bob held the phone away and mouthed "moron," before saying, "You can't talk to John. He's not at all well. Nooo. I just said you can't. You'll have your work slave back soon enough."

A few seconds went by and Bob smiled grimly. "Tell you what, Stevie. When your inhumane demands on my friend's life destroy his marriage like they did yours, you can have him twenty-four seven. Of course, that's not much different than what you're getting now, is it?"

Bob shut the phone off and dropped it onto the counter behind him.

"John? I forbid you to turn that on until tomorrow morning. Kerrin? We're not answering the house phone for the rest of the day, either. Nancy?" Bob called into the family room.

"Yeah?"

"Can you make some hot chocolate and popcorn? We are going to sit at this kitchen table like we used to and play one of those silly board games we were so fond of. And we are going to have fun. And no one is going to yell or get angry. Except me if I lose."

# CHAPTER 30

The next morning I received two unexpected gifts. John left to fulfill a work commitment he'd made weeks ago that would keep him away until late in the evening, and Nancy took my kids for a day of holiday fun so I could work on my novel.

The minute the house emptied out, I flew into the vortex. When I passed through the Amoran portal, Ashi's pulsing energy engulfed me. My energy swelled out to meet his, then his frequency doubled, mine tripled, and his climbed even higher. I reached the ground so saturated with our mutual vibrations, I had to struggle to stay emotionally and physically balanced.

Ashara and Eliasser stood behind my Twin, but I barely registered their presence as Ashi's emerald eyes found mine. We smiled at the same instant. He raised his eyebrows in question and held out his hands. Tired of swimming against the tide, no longer caring what I might do that I'd regret, I accepted them. Keeping his eyes locked on mine, Ashi brought my hands to his lips and placed the gentlest of kisses on my palms.

Fiery heat licked up my spine, and I gasped. Ashara pushed Ashi away as she pressed a goblet into my hands. I quickly downed the contents, hoping it was stronger than the last batch.

Ashara turned on my Twin. "What is the matter with you? You know that Meiri must have her shielding and stabilizing potions as soon as she arrives. And kissing her hands was . . . imprudent."

Ashi mumbled an apology, but I had the feeling he wasn't at all sorry about what he'd done.

"I wasn't due until Monday," I said. "How did you know I was coming?"

"*I* did not," she grumbled, tipping her head in Ashi's direction. "*He* did."

Ashi smiled again. This did nothing to calm my energy, which pulsed even faster up my spine. *Damn.* At this rate, I'd be throwing myself at his feet before the day was over.

Eliasser seemed oblivious to what was going on. "We have something to show you," he said cheerfully. He opened the Garden Portal, and I stepped through into an array of colors and smells to boggle the senses. *It doesn't get any better than this,* I sighed to myself.

And then, it did. From behind the fountain walked the Master Technician.

"Balthasarre!" I ran down the path and threw my arms around him.

He chuckled as he worked to keep his footing. "Hello, Meiri. Thank you for speaking to me so often while I was in the Healing Room. Your stories anchored me in a reality I could neither feel nor participate in." He shuddered. "It was as if my mind was imprisoned at the bottom of a dark chasm, cut off from the rest of reality."

"How horrible."

"That it was," he agreed. The creases in his forehead smoothed. "I have something to show you. Close your eyes. I want this to be a surprise."

When my eyes were shut, he guided me around the bend in the path.

"Now," he whispered. "Open them."

I obeyed, then stared dumbstruck. The unimpressive rose bed with its sparse, anemic blossoms and zero scent had completely transformed. Now, there were rows of wildly exuberant, fragrant flowers, each one mirroring all the rainbow hues of the vortex. Balthasarre had explained once that the aptly named Vortex Roses only bloomed like this every hundred years, and the last time was half a century ago.

"Aren't they fifty years too early?" I asked.

"Indeed, they are. I would like to believe their appearance now is a favorable sign."

I bent down and cupped one of the delicate blossoms. It gave off a faint glow as I breathed in its spicy-sweet aroma. "At the very least, they're a favorable sight. They're beautiful."

We strolled the length of the flowerbed, chatting about the roses before moving on to our favorite topic, the vortex. I was worried that might prove traumatic for him, but Balthasarre's love of the vortex ran so deep, nothing could shake it.

We eventually made our way back to the entrance, where Eliasser and Ashara were talking quietly. Ashi was nowhere in sight.

"I did not mean to keep you waiting," Balthasarre said.

Eliasser waved it off. "Ashara and I have been enjoying this fine day. But we should practice now that Meiri has arrived."

"Of course. I will inform the others."

After Balthasarre left, I gave Ashara and Eliasser my good news. I had eight Earth hours—nearly six weeks—to spend on Amoran.

"Wonderful," Eliasser exclaimed. "That will allow us to make up for lost time."

I peered through the open portal into the Main Chamber. "Where's Ashi?"

"He went to lie down. Our meeting last night ran late, and he is still tired."

Ashara shook her head. "No one else needed two reviving drafts this morning to recover from a late night."

I felt the shift in Eliasser's energy as he swiveled to face her. "Two?"

She nodded somberly.

Eliasser pursed his lips. "He should be growing stronger, not weaker."

"Yes. He should." Ashara stared at the ground, took a deep breath, then blew it out in a long sigh. "However, I now believe that Meiri's presence drains him of his energy."

"What?" I cried. "You had to double-dose him with reviving draft before I got here today, so how can his low energy be my fault?"

She wouldn't meet my gaze. "Ashi's first bout of exhaustion came right after he picked up your intention to come to Amoran ahead of schedule. When you landed in the Main Chamber, I felt in him a growing dis-ease. By the time we entered the garden, it was significant."

"Did you feel Ashi's presence this morning as well?" Eliasser asked me.

"Not until I came through the Amoran portal." I described how Ashi's energy caught me up as soon as I entered the Main Chamber, and how the pulsations moved back and forth between us. Eliasser seemed pleased by this. It was a necessary occurrence, he assured me, although extra care must now be taken to guard us from an early merging.

*Merging of all kinds,* I thought with chagrin.

And suddenly, it hit me. I had watched—a little smugly, I'll admit—as the Guardians struggled to divulge their secrets. But here I was, still sitting on a big one. I hadn't confessed the whole truth when I admitted to kissing Ashi. Only Ashara knew the full extent of my attraction to him. Telling Eliasser disconcerted me for some reason, but in order for honesty to reign, it would have to win out over embarrassment.

"There's something else you should know. When Ashi kissed my palms—" I broke off, unable to look Eliasser in the eyes. "Let's just say that thanks to my Earth body, you'd have to deaden every one of my nerves for me not to feel a certain way about him, if you get my drift."

Surprisingly, Eliasser did.

He turned to Ashara. "Do you mean to say—"

"Yes."

He gripped her arm. "It is inconceivable that you did not share this inform—"

"Meiri's shielding worked fairly—"

"*Fairly* well? What if she—"

"I no longer know, but if they cannot—"

"It will doom them—"

"Both. I know. All too—"

They stopped abruptly, cast furtive glances my way, then switched their truncated disaster talk to silent mode. They needn't have bothered. I'd heard enough. I might as well paint a skull and crossbones on my chest, because I was like poison to Ashi. Crushed by this latest development, I stalked off to change into a tunic. When I reached my quarters, dismay had turned to anger—with myself, the vortex, and the whole goddamned universe. How were Ashi and I going to save Earth and Amoran when we couldn't save ourselves from each other? Wishing I had a real door to slam open, I stormed through the opening—and smacked right into Ashi.

"What are you doing here?" I cried.

Gasping for breath, he staggered back and collapsed into a chair. I rushed forward, but with an agonized groan, he motioned me to stop. "No," he wheezed. "Do not touch me."

With another loud groan, his head flopped back and he sucked at the air in rasping fits. I didn't need to be a doctor to know he was dying. As his Twin, I could feel it.

I ran to the doorway and screamed, hoping someone would hear me. I didn't want to go for help. I was terrified of leaving him alone.

Almost at once, an Assistant came charging around the bend. Lately, they seemed to roam the corridor outside my quarters on a regular basis. No one had ever said why, but I assumed they were there to guard against unchaperoned visits between Ashi and me. If that was the plan, it had failed.

"Ashi's in danger," I shouted at her. "Get Ashara."

I ran back into the room. Ashi's breathing was even more erratic. I ached to help him, but I had no healing skills. All I could think to do was hold him. But if he wouldn't let me touch him, I couldn't even do that. Powerless, I watched his growing distress with alarm. Then, I did the only thing I could think of. I silently prayed to the Light for help.

Powerless? I should have known better. Yet, with all the magic and miracles I'd witnessed on Amoran, I was still surprised when someone answered.

*"You must balance his energy, or he will perish."*

It was the spirit woman who had helped me with the purple spikes.

*"I'm ready. You can blend your Light essence with mine."*

*"I am unable to do that now. But I can guide you from within using your intuition."*

Pictures scrolled through my mind, their content perplexing. Ashi had just recoiled from physical contact with me, but according to my unseen helper, I needed to touch him to "ground" his energy. This seemed risky. Without proper shielding, my touch caused him pain. On the other hand, if I didn't do anything, he'd surely die. That proved incentive enough to try it her way.

I felt her urging me to hurry. I knelt before Ashi, closed my eyes, and imagined all seven energy centers within my body glowing with light. Then, I pictured the light from each center connecting to form a solid column that rose from the base of my spine to the top of my head. Next, I envisioned the column of light expanding until it extended far out into the room, forming a protected energy zone within which I could safely work.

I opened my eyes. The room was so full of light, all I could see of any substance was Ashi. No longer gasping for air, he seemed almost at peace. A peace I was about to ruin.

I locked our fingers together and held on for dear life as hot, tingling energy flowed back and forth between us. Ashi struggled to free himself, but he couldn't put up much of a fight in his depleted state. I was especially glad about that when I got my next set of instructions. The energy patterns channeling into my brain had to be inserted directly from my mind into Ashi's through eye contact, and his eyes were screwed shut. What was I supposed to do? Pry his eyelids apart?

I nearly laughed at the intuitive flash I received. The fairy-tale implication did not escape me as I grasped his face and gave him a full, passionate kiss. Prince Charming's eyes flew open and I thrust the healing patterns into his mind before he could shut me out. For a moment, our psyches mingled, allowing me access to his thoughts and feelings, even the ones he kept so deeply buried he wasn't aware of their existence. Stunned by what I learned, I withdrew from his mind and sank back in disbelief just as Eliasser and Ashara burst into the room.

"He's okay," I said quickly. "I was able to help him. But he'll need to sleep for a while."

Ashara checked Ashi's vital signs. "We will move him to the Healing Room." She straightened up, looked at me, and her eyelids lowered to half-mast. "What is wrong?"

"Nothing." *Everything.*

I backed toward the exit. I needed time to process what I'd discovered.

Eliasser seemed surprised by my hasty retreat. "Wait, Meiri. Tell us what happened."

I felt the Foreseers calling to me, something they'd never done before.

"Later," I said, and hurried out.

---

The pink, yellow, and blue Foreseers were waiting for me in the center of the clearing. They waved their hands at the ground, inviting me to sit.

"You know why you are here?" the yellow Foreseer asked.

I'd intuited that on the way to the Glen. "You are going to give me further healing for Ashi."

She nodded. "The process is complicated. We will use thought transference."

"First," the blue Foreseer said, "there is something you need to know."

Nothing in her demeanor had changed, yet I felt cold inside.

"Do not be afraid, Daughter of the Vortex," the pink Foreseer said. "All things happen as they must. This we know you accept."

Their calm, ever-peaceful voices then shared a prediction about the Reparention. When they finished, I kept my breathing as steady as possible and asked if it could be changed.

They rose into the air, their luminous bodies shimmering. "Your heart already knows the Truth," they said in unison. "Seek your answer there."

The blue Foreseer spoke next. "We have devised a shielding process which will allow you and Makashannar full access to each other until the Reparention begins."

"Full access?" I blurted out.

A compassionate smile appeared simultaneously on their faces. "Your desires are not unknown to us," the pink Foreseer said. "However, within the physicality of Amoran, sharing love in this manner with your Twin Light would be vibrationally intolerable. We cannot eliminate your desire, but the shielding process will subdue it."

The yellow Foreseer positioned herself in front of me. "We must render you unconscious for the healing and shielding processes to be properly conveyed. The information will be inscribed directly into your Knowingness. When you awaken, go to your Twin and perform the healing. Afterward, there will be no more risk of spontaneous merging."

"The Reparention is almost upon us," the blue Foreseer said. "To ready yourselves, you and Makashannar must further enrich the energy you share."

The pink Foreseer moved to my side. "Spend as much time in each other's presence as possible, day and night. Drink deeply from the well of your Love. Bask in each other's Light."

"Be as much One as you can," the blue Foreseer concluded, coming to rest on my other side.

A final counsel came from the yellow Foreseer. "You are accorded full discretion regarding the Truth we imparted to you about the Reparention. You are to choose what to do with the information."

The pink Foreseer placed her hand on top of my head. "And now, we begin."

# Chapter 31

I stalled outside the Healing Room. I couldn't see any benefit to sharing the Foreseers' prediction, but keeping it under wraps might be difficult. Ashara would be my biggest challenge. If I looked at her too long, she'd be inside my mind, and that would be that.

I steeled myself and opened the doorway. Eliasser and Ashara were busy at the potion table. I sat beside Ashi, observing his calm breathing as if I were witnessing a minor miracle. I wasn't sure what else the Foreseers communicated to me while I was unconscious, but my gratitude meter had edged up a notch or two.

Ashara handed me a goblet. I took a sip and glanced at her in surprise.

"Fairybee wine? Not some potent magical restoring potion?"

She smiled, but then those all-seeing eyes of hers narrowed.

I looked away. "The Foreseers gave me an additional healing for Ashi, along with a new shielding process to prevent spontaneous merging."

"What else did they tell you?" she demanded.

Damn, but she was good. I was in luck, though. Ashi woke up, and Ashara was sidetracked with caring for him. Now that he was conscious, our mutual energy soared. I moved as far away from him as I could, but my body continued to pulse in a way that bordered on uncomfortable. Ashi confirmed similar feelings, so I stayed at the opposite end of the Healing Room where the effect was marginally subdued. As a bonus, it kept me away from Ashara's probing eyes.

"No potions yet," I called out. Ashara stopped pouring. "I need to tell you something first, something I learned when I helped Ashi earlier."

Ashara nodded and set to work propping Ashi up with the Amoran version of a bolster. I paced back and forth, trying to determine how best to approach this issue. I knew Ashi would have a hard time accepting what I had to say. So would Eliasser and Ashara. Hell. The knowledge still blew me away.

I chose to ease in gradually, and began with what I suspected was the initiating event.

"When Ashi used the Integration Link to heal me after my accident in the vortex—"

"You did what?" Eliasser glared at Ashi.

"I had to," Ashi defended himself. "She would have died without that Link."

Uh-oh. I thought this was old news. Guess we could check off another secret.

"Do you know what you risked?" Eliasser cried.

"Of course I do. I risked my life. And you would have done the same in my place."

"Precisely. Which is why you should have sent for me to perform the Integration Link. I, at least, would have understood the repercussions."

Ashi went stone-faced. "There have been no repercussions."

"That's not true," I said. "Besides, whatever repercussions might have ensued were altered when you used it on someone from Earth. All bets were off, as we say on that planet."

I asked for more wine. Eliasser brought it to me, then convinced me to stop pacing and sit with him at the table. I gratefully accepted, drawing strength, as always, from his presence.

"During the Integration Link," I continued, "Ashi absorbed energy from me, energy peculiar to Earth. Unbeknownst to him, it became a part of his own energy field. And that's where the problem lies. This foreign energy has been affecting him adversely ever since."

Ashara's back stiffened as her expression turned calculating. I could almost hear the wheels turning as she tried to work out what this meant. But Eliasser slammed his fist down with such force, our goblets wobbled.

"That is impossible. Ashara and I would have detected something of that nature."

"You weren't able to," I said. "Without realizing it, he suppressed the energy so well that all anyone could perceive, including Ashi, was that he was tired, in pain, or both."

Ashi sighed. "Mostly pain. At first, I thought it was an unusual aftereffect of the Integration Link. When the symptoms continued, I dismissed the Link altogether because the pain would spontaneously disappear."

"Like when I went back to Earth or stayed away from you."

Ashi nodded thoughtfully. "Yes, I believe that is true."

"Which also might explain your inconsistent behavior toward me. However, what you absorbed during the Link was only the beginning. Whenever we are together, you soak up more Earth energy—and the emotions that come with it—which you then automatically suppress, adding to your hidden stockpile. While you aren't consciously aware of these emotions, you are still experiencing them subliminally. Emotions can't go repressed for long without wreaking havoc. Unaccustomed as you are to the intensity of Earth emotions, the effects would be even worse. It's ironic, really. With all the concern about keeping me safe from too much Amoran energy, you suffered daily from the identical thing in reverse. And we never knew."

Eliasser grumbled. "These Earth emotions have been nothing but trouble."

I was inclined to agree. And yet, I sensed there was more to this jigsaw puzzle, something to do with those unruly emotions. I pressed my lips together, squinting in concentration.

Eliasser misread my expression. "I am sorry, Meiri. That was unkind of me."

"I'm not hurt." I placed my hand over his. "We've all decried the shortcomings of my Earth emotions, and Earth body, myself included. And why not? They *are* trouble. They're a royal pain—" I broke off, as the last elusive puzzle piece danced out of hiding and two-stepped into place. "Wait a minute," I whispered. "I think we've had this all wrong."

Insights were coming fast and furious now. I suspected they were a gift from the Foreseers, probably funneled into my brain along with Ashi's healing.

"It was no accident of fate that I died a thousand years ago. The Foreseers said as much to you, Ashara, when you railed at them after my first Earth death. You didn't believe them when they said I was destined to take this path. You lost faith in them that day because you thought they had failed to foresee my death, and were therefore fallible and not to be trusted."

Ashara squeezed her eyes shut, the only indication she'd give that I'd gotten it right.

"But they weren't wrong. I needed to spend the last thousand years on Earth gathering up experiences and emotions that would be necessary, even imperative to repairing the vortex."

Eliasser's face creased with frustration. "This makes no sense."

"It does sound crazy," I agreed. "Like you, I have viewed my intense emotions as a drawback, not a draw. But according to the Foreseers, a tremendous amount of energy becomes available when emotions are properly balanced instead of being repressed. I think that's what they hoped for, maybe even counted on. The rich emotional energy of Earth, partnered with the Amoran energy of my Twin, and balanced by virtue of its being shared between us."

Ashara opened her eyes and sighed. "Dear Light, it does make sense. As a Vibrational, you were the perfect choice to absorb energy and emotion from Earth's environment."

Eliasser frowned. "Well? How do we rid Ashi of this defective energy?"

Okay. That hurt. But I decided to give Eliasser a pass, considering how upset he seemed.

"We don't. For the Reparention to work, Ashi and I must possess the same mix of Amoran/Earth energy. Thanks to my accident in the vortex, and the subsequent Integration Link, that mix—including Earth energy and all the emotions and physical needs that go with it—are now fully available to Ashi."

"All of them?" Ashi squeaked, his eyes wide and round.

"Yes. All of them." Time to deliver the final blow. "Even the kind of desire that needs to be expressed sexually."

Ashara gasped. Eliasser clutched at his chest and sank back in his chair, blinking hard. His mouth opened, but he seemed incapable of speech.

Ashi, however, had plenty to say.

"You are speaking about *my* body. I am not made that way. I know what I feel, and it is certainly not *that*. I would know if—" He broke off, cheeks flushing as his fingers repeatedly gripped and released the sleep cover. "Even if by some chance you are correct, the Mountain's energy should protect me from that kind of thing."

"I can't alter the truth to suit you," I said. "I have no problem experiencing that 'kind of thing,' even with the suppression provided by the Mountain's energy. And when I helped you earlier, I detected what you cannot yet feel at a conscious level. Trust me, it is unmistakable."

"No . . . this cannot . . . I am not . . ." Ashi looked like he was going to be sick. "Even it were true, you do not expect me to—"

"God, no." I let myself have a good laugh over that. "Don't worry. I won't be sneaking into your room at night. It's a moot point anyway. Even if you wanted to, we can't make love due to a vibrational problem the Foreseers didn't bother to explain. Besides, acting on the desire isn't necessary."

He looked so relieved, I wanted to slap him.

"Resisting and repressing that desire is what created your current predicament. But, you do need to experience and come to terms with these feelings." Another insight came to me. "All these months, I have somehow been absorbing your desire for me and holding it in my body along with my desire for you. No wonder my feelings have been so difficult for me to control. It's like I've been doing emotional double-duty. For both our sakes, you've got to accept your own passion."

Ashi grimaced and turned away. Eliasser looked as if he couldn't believe such a terrible thing had happened in his quiet Mountain Sanctuary. Ashara was the least moved by the news. With a simple nod, she asked what had to be done next.

"I need to perform the healing given to me by the Foreseers. In addition to uncovering Ashi's repressed emotions, it will prevent an early merging. It will also subdue our sexual attraction to each other. I'm particularly grateful for that, because the Foreseers require Ashi and me to spend as much time together as possible, day and night."

"Will this be safe?" Ashara asked doubtfully.

"They say the new shielding will completely protect us."

Eliasser finally found his voice. "How will you perform this healing?"

"I don't know," I admitted. "The energy pulsations keep increasing. I'm not sure I can stand up right now without assistance, let alone approach Ashi."

My mind suddenly filled with ingredients and quantities.

"Ashara," I whispered. "Write this down."

When the parade of words through my brain stopped, I asked Ashara if I'd dictated a potion.

She shook her head in admiration as she studied her notes. "A very advanced one. It will not last long, but should allow you to get close to Ashi. How did you arrive at this?"

I gave my full attention to reaching the responsible party.

*"Are you still there?"* I thought to her.

*"Yes."*

*"Thank you for all the help you've given me."*

*"You are most welcome, Meiri."*

*"You know my name, but I don't know yours. Who are you?"*

*"When the time is right, you will know who I am."*

"Ashara asked how you came by this potion," Eliasser demanded, watching me with . . . was that wariness?

I stared back at him. "It was my spirit friend."

Eliasser's expression shifted. He was trying, I think, for impassive. But what I read in those brilliant blue eyes was a hardness I couldn't comprehend. I held his gaze as I tried to ascertain what it was—until I remembered I had to be careful about eye contact.

Ashara quickly made up the potion, and I gulped it down. The effect was immediate. I perched on the edge of the healing stone and put my hands on Ashi's chest. Whatever the Foreseers had placed within me was like a program that ran automatically. Our vibrations lifted, then Ashi's energy signature coincided with mine. I felt his heart lighten as he understood the level of connection we could now have with each other, the sharing that would be possible without pain or restriction.

When the healing was complete, I rose to accept a goblet of reviving draft from Eliasser.

Ashara suddenly marched toward the doorway as if to leave. Surprised by that, I turned my head as she passed by. She stopped, locked eyes with me, and was in and out of my brain with the speed of a lightning strike.

Shock flickered across her face.

I gave the barest shake of my head.

She blinked, a silent acknowledgment of my unspoken request. Then her mask of imperceptibility slid into place.

"Come," she said quietly, taking Eliasser by the hand. "These two need to be alone."

An awkward silence followed their departure. Unsure how swiftly the healing would work on Ashi's repressed emotions, I glanced at him, smiled, and gave a helpless shrug.

He slid off the healing stone and reached for my hands. "I have something to tell you."

"Uh . . . sure . . . okay." My heart began to beat faster in anticipation.

"It is not very Guardian-like of me to say this, but . . . I have never . . . what I mean is . . ." He sighed. "I wish we could escape to another world, just the two of us. A world without a vortex in need of repair. There, we would live a normal life, have twenty children, grow old and die, then merge into the Light forever."

My eyes must have grown as wide as Ether Lights. *This* from the man who looked like he was going to throw up at the thought of making love to me.

"You do realize what we would have to do to conceive even one child."

He smiled, then kissed my palms. Letting his lips linger there for a moment, he slid a glance at me sideways.

Good God. Could the healing have worked that completely? And that soon? Because I was pretty sure Ashi had just given me bedroom eyes.

"I . . . I don't know what to say," I stammered.

He cupped my face with his hands. "Then I will do the talking. I hoped for a thousand years that a miracle would bring you back to Amoran sooner. When you finally arrived, I hoped for you to be as you once were, the Meiri who left here before being changed by Earth experiences." He touched his forehead to mine and brushed my cheeks with his fingers. "Now I find myself hoping for something else entirely."

"Oh, Ashi," I breathed out. Every nerve in my body was tingling, even the nerves I wished weren't. The Foreseers' shielding was better than Ashara's, but not by much. For both our sakes, I needed to lighten up this sexually-charged conversation. "For the record, Vortex-boy? Two offspring would be plenty, unless you plan on having the rest yourself."

He laughed. "There is so much for me to learn about these things."

———————

Ashi and I stayed in the Healing Room for the rest of the afternoon. After my Light Sojourn, we had talked mostly of our life together before I went to live on Earth. Now, we left the past behind and lived entirely in the present, and our symbiosis seemed to grow as a result. It was getting to the point where we didn't need to speak our thoughts out loud, which was a strange, but somehow comforting experience.

Afternoon became evening. We were barely aware of the passage of time when an Assistant brought us our Evening Meal. Then another Assistant presented us with a single goblet and a note in Ashara's scrawl that read: *Share this drink and dream.*

"Mother Healer just announced our bedtime," I said. I put the potion on the table, unable to dislodge the silly grin from my face. I'd been thoroughly enjoying the freedom Ashi and I had to be together. How open we could be now. I turned around, eager for the next step. Spending the night with him. Platonically, of course.

Ashi wasn't smiling. "You have not told me everything, have you, my Twin?"

Oh, God. What an idiot I was. I'd been too open, too free.

"I sense sadness deep within you." He pulled my hands to his chest and pressed them firmly over his heart. "What causes this heaviness in your spirit? Show me."

I didn't realize until that moment how intricately linked we'd become. Without any effort on my part, or ability to prevent it from happening, my visit to the Foreseers played into both our minds like a movie. When it was over, Ashi stared at me in disbelief.

"Why, Meiri? Why would you keep such a thing from me?"

This was it. He had unwittingly removed the last barrier between us. In a way, I was relieved, because now I had nothing left to hide. Now, we could truly be open with each other.

The ache in my throat made talking difficult, but I owed him an answer.

"I didn't want to burden you with this. It can't be changed, Ashi. It is what it is."

It wasn't very brave of me, but I shut my eyes so I wouldn't have to witness his sorrow. I felt the touch of his fingers upon my cheeks, lightly at first, then with more pressure as he held my face and kissed my forehead. Then, he just held me. There was nothing to say, really. Nothing that would matter in the big scheme of things. We had always known that the two of us would be most at risk during the Reparention. What we didn't know until today is that one of us was destined to not leave the vortex alive. And I'd drawn the short straw.

Ashi picked up the goblet of dreaming draft, took a swallow, then offered me the cup. I'd only taken my first sip when I felt the dizzying effect. "I can barely stand," I whispered.

"It is far too strong," he whispered back. He set the cup, still nearly full, back on the table, waved his hand, and the healing stone doubled in size.

We sank down, clinging to each other as sleep claimed us.

# CHAPTER 32

Ashi lay sleeping, facing me. I ran my hand lightly across his chest, enjoying the silky feel of his tunic. I'd worried about dying before, but now that it was a certainty, every moment seemed more precious than the last; each sensation, thought, feeling—a great gift.

His eyelids fluttered open. I snuggled closer to him. "Sorry if I woke you."

"I do not mind at all," he said, his voice still heavy with sleep as he draped his arm over my waist and rubbed the small of my back.

I tried to ignore how his touch made me feel. "Did you dream like boss-lady commanded?"

"Of course. Obeying Ashara is far less painful than going against her wishes. It is strange, though. Dreaming draft usually has a greater effect on me, yet I only recall a single one. In it, the Darkness grew so swiftly we had to begin the Reparention even earlier than our latest estimate."

"That's so weird. I dreamed the same thing."

Ashi turned grim. "Did a voice tell you to prepare as if that day were tomorrow?"

"Tomorrow?" A shiver ran through me. "I don't think it will be that soon. In my dream, I returned to Earth once more before the Reparention began."

Ashi combed his fingers through my hair, held a few strands out to the side, then watched as they slipped from his grasp. "So, with time-stretching we have six more weeks?"

His casual actions and hopeful tone were canceled out by the heaviness I felt in him.

I traced the contour of his cheek. "Yes. But I wish we could make time stop."

With a suddenness that startled me, Ashi pressed his lips to my open hand. The tip of his tongue moistened my palm, and my internal temperature rose so fast, I moaned.

His eyelids went to half-mast. "Maybe we should put the time we do have to good use."

Every cell in my body began to do a little dance. "What are you suggesting?"

"This." He kissed me—an astonishingly skillful kiss. I experienced such an intense longing for more that it frightened me. But that fear paled when a painful shock-like sensation vibrated through both of us. Our heads jerked back at the same moment the Healing Room doorway opened. We scooted apart like teenagers caught pawing each other as Ashara entered, put a tray on the table and began to set out plates and cups.

"If I was worried about what you would do," she said, waving the doorway closed, "I would never have left you alone."

Ashi smiled self-consciously, excused himself and headed to the ancillary. Behind his back, Ashara shot me a questioning look. I didn't need to share a mind with her to know what she was asking. With deep regret, I nodded.

"I thought as much," she said. "It would be difficult to keep something like that from your Twin, especially with your symbiosis growing as it is." A weary sadness crept into her expression. "That is why I want us to take Morning Meal in private. We need to decide when and how to inform the others."

"No need to. The Foreseers say it's up to me what I do with this information. I see no reason for it to go beyond the three of us."

Ashara set a fourth place at the table.

Four? "Oh, no," I said, sick at heart. "Please tell me you didn't."

"The matter was out of my hands." She dropped onto a chair. "I could not hide this from Eliasser any better than you could keep it from Ashi. Your sweet king grieves the loss of you already. I am sorry, Meiri. For all of it."

I left the healing stone and sat beside her. "I'm not angry with you. I just can't bear the thought of causing either of you this kind of pain." I touched her age-worn hand. "I love you, Ashara. You know that, don't you?"

She held my face between her trembling hands and kissed my forehead. A warm glow filled my mind, the effect soothing. "That is my blessing. Remember these words I tell you now. Each of us has the power to alter what some call fate. We always have a choice. Choose well, Meiri."

"What is there for me to choose? I'm going to die."

I am a master of bad timing. The doorway opened again right as I made my declaration of doom. I caught a glimpse of aqua in my peripheral vision and my heart wrenched in two.

"I can't," I choked out in a whisper. "I can't see him. Not yet."

"You must," Ashara commanded, but her voice was full of compassion. "You need this moment as much as he does. Have courage and face him."

Face him? The most I could do was stare at the floor as folds of shimmering fabric advanced toward me. It reminded me of my initial meeting with Eliasser in the Main Chamber, when the first sight I had of him was the hem of his pilea. That memory, and all that had transpired between us since then, paralyzed me with sadness. I couldn't move, couldn't speak.

Eliasser reached my chair, pulled me to my feet, crushed me to his chest and crossed his arms behind my back, effectively pinning me in place. Love energy spilled from his heart into mine, then from my heart into his and back again to me. Round and round it cycled, increasing with each revolution until there was more Love than any two people could possibly contain. Drenched by it, drunk with it, I seemed to float into another reality where all that existed was Light. Pulsing, living Light. And at the center of that Light? Eliasser. I ached to meld into the Light, into Eliasser, into that magnificent heart of his. But the moment I tried to, my consciousness returned to the Healing Room.

For a long while Eliasser and I just stood together, heart pressed to heart. Then he eased me into my chair, and with a gentle squeeze of my shoulder, went to the potion station to mix up my morning brew. Not once did we look at each other.

It wasn't until long after our Morning Meal for four had ended that Eliasser and I finally made eye contact. No one else witnessed our moment of shared sorrow before we donned impenetrable masks to go about our business.

---

The rest of that week was a blur of practice, practice, and more practice. Each day we ran through the seven steps of the Reparention leading up to the point where Ashi and I were to merge. The process was so powerful that we had to rehearse the steps out of order, because to do them in proper sequence carried the danger of triggering the Reparention for real. But once a day we did a "dry run" for timing, reviewing the steps in order without raising our vibrations.

Anders had the lead role in the first step, which was to unite us all in meditation. When we achieved the correct mental state, Eliasser would signal us to begin circling our energy through the group. Ari and Danaeus were to monitor the energy flow, using their unique otherworld energy patterns as counterbalances to keep the frequency from intensifying too fast. They also had primary responsibility for keeping the energy flowing through us until Balthasarre determined the correct moment to begin cycling the energy in an upward, spiraling motion. Then, we would raise our vibrations as a group and enter the vortex.

These first five steps took the longest. The last two happened almost simultaneously. Inside the vortex, Ashara would establish the Mind Link. This would connect us energetically as well as supply a kind of grounding to protect Ashi and me from each other's intense vibrations. Then we had to immediately turn to Light as a group.

It was my job to initiate primary merging—the joining of Ashi's and my Light energy. I couldn't understand why I was granted that key role. Ashi was far more skilled with energy than I was, however, the Foreseers insisted that I must be the one to do this.

Our practice schedule was grueling, yet we managed small breaks for recreation. There was no time for Garrammon, so Ashi, Ari, Anders, and I let off steam by playing tag or hide-and-seek in the garden like little kids. We even coaxed Balthasarre and Danaeus to join us one day, but Eliasser and Ashara would only watch from near the portal.

For reasons she never made clear to us, Ashara moved her base of operations out of the Healing Room, allowing Ashi and me to continue sleeping there. My symbiosis with Ashi had grown to such an extent that we could freely access each other's thoughts and often communicated silently. Sometimes, we didn't even need to "think" to each other. We just knew what the other wanted, needed, or was feeling. Meanwhile, the energetic intimacy of our entire group expanded, making it hard to keep my pending death a secret. But I was adamant that the others not be told. Even though Ashara and Eliasser disagreed, I believed that since the Foreseers gave me the right to choose what to do with their prediction, this was one "truth" that could be kept secret. And I refused to relent.

As the connection among the eight of us amplified, Eliasser grew increasingly distant and distracted. He was fine during practice, but would disappear as soon as he was no longer needed. No one knew where he went until Ashi and I happened upon him in the forest one evening. I no longer visited the Foreseers, sensing that my time with them was complete. However, on this occasion, the Glen appeared in full view. Through the gap in the trees, we saw Eliasser arguing with the Elder Foreseer. We left before he spotted us, but I began to worry about him.

---

At the end of that first week, Ashara and Eliasser brought Ashi and me to a small room lightly scented with cinnamon and cloves. Luminous wall panels, reminiscent of stained glass, gave the space a church-like aura. Four purple floor pillows flanked an oval carpet woven in subtle rainbow hues. Ashara motioned Ashi and me to sit on the pillows across from Eliasser, then took her place beside him. Eliasser's eyes were fixed on the carpet as he began to speak.

"The Foreseers have instructed me to share the following information with you. While I do not believe the time is right, they insist that I must do it today."

*"Do you feel that Meiri? The final Truth is about to be told,"* Ashi thought to me. I knew he experienced the shiver that ran up my spine in response.

Eliasser forged on, his voice heavy with sadness. "My Twin Light was also a Seventh Vortex Guardian. When the Thirteenth Vortex suffered an energy imbalance, the Foreseers selected her to assist them."

*"Did we know her?"* I thought to Ashi.

*"No. It was before our time."*

"Prior to leaving our dimension," Eliasser continued, "the Foreseers asked us to fully merge inside our vortex."

"Merge?!" Ashi and I exclaimed.

Eliasser smiled at that. "I understand your surprise. But it was a different time in our vortex's history, and while the Foreseers would not elaborate, they assured us that we would be able to fully merge our light-bodies without leaving physicality forever. This was such a wondrous gift to receive that when they refused to provide a reason for their unusual request, we did not press them. We simply accepted, and spent days in a blissful energy state that defies words. When the time came to separate our joined Light into our individual light-bodies again, a miraculous thing occurred; something so rare that when it happens, the entire cosmos rejoices. As we lowered our vibrations, an inversion of energy pulled us back together, re-merging us for an instant before we completed our separation in a burst of Light. Only now, we numbered four. Two other Beings in light-bodies had been produced. A new Twin Light pair."

Ashi and I reacted with the kind of trembling that comes from realizing a great Truth. I reached out to hold him, unsure if I was doing it for his benefit or mine. Both, I suppose.

"The new Twin pair," Ashi whispered with reverence. "That was Meiri and me?"

"Yes." Eliasser's voice was suddenly toneless, his expression blank. The rapid change in his behavior—a red flag if ever there was one—made no sense if we were talking about an event over which "the entire cosmos rejoices."

"Hold on," I said as I mentally reviewed what little I knew of Twin Lights. "I want to make sure I have this right. After this happened, there were two pairs of Twin Lights? Two distinct sets of male and female?"

"That is correct," Eliasser replied.

"All from a single Spark of Light?"

He pressed his lips together.

"I'll take that stubborn silence of yours as a 'yes.' So, one merged Light produced four individuals, in which case"—my heart began to race wildly—"that makes you and I—"

"Second Lights," he answered in a monotone. "That is the proper name of the phenomenon."

I couldn't care less what it was called and I certainly couldn't fathom his lack of feeling.

"But . . . if I understand the nature of Twin Lights, doesn't that make me—"

"It makes you a Second Light," he droned.

"Oh, for God's sake. How can you be so . . . ? Damn it, Eliasser! Answer my question. Aren't you as much my Twin Light as Ashi?"

My dear, sweet king, whom I loved more than anyone else in the entire universe, and who, according to Ashara, loved me equally, folded his hands, placed them carefully in his lap and directed his gaze there. And said nothing.

After a silence that seemed to last hours, Ashara said, "Yes, Meiri. While there is a slight difference in frequency, in essence, Eliasser is also your Twin Light."

*Eliasser. My Twin Light. My* other *Twin Light.* I was in danger of turning into a blubbering mess from the sheer emotional impact of this revelation, which made me doubly dumbfounded by Eliasser's brick wall façade. It had to be an affectation, but why would he need to keep his feelings under wraps at a moment like this?

*"Look,"* Ashi thought to me. *"Behind Eliasser."*

Just past Eliasser's shoulder, the silvery energy of my spirit friend vibrated for a brief interval. Before she disappeared, she impressed one word into my mind—and by default, Ashi's.

*Twin.*

*"Oh, Ashi. Can she really be Eliasser's Twin?"*

I felt Ashi smile. *"I believe he will treasure this day forever."*

Ashara and Eliasser didn't seem to sense her presence. I couldn't imagine why that was the case, however, a strong flash of intuition prompted me to proceed with caution.

Ashi read my thoughts. *"I agree. It is not time for him to know."*

*"But, when?"* I was impatient to tell Eliasser about his Twin.

*"We will know when the moment arrives. We will feel it."* Before I could think another word to him, he asked aloud, "What happened to Meiri and me after our creation?"

Eliasser looked relieved to be off the subject of who-was-whose-Twin.

"You remained in the vortex in your light-bodies, as it would be many months before you could manifest embodiments for yourselves. However, my Twin and I . . ." He moistened his lips. "*Elianna* and I remanifested our bodies and left the vortex as jubilant as two people could be. We could not wait to return to the Main Chamber and share our news." A soft smile played at the corners of his mouth. "But Ashara already knew. That is when she told us the story of our own origin within the Seventh Vortex. For you see, Elianna and I are also Second Lights."

I thought of the vision Ashi and I had shared thanks to the doctored fairybee wine. How the One Light created zillions of Lights, one of which formed itself into the Seventh Vortex, which then produced its own Spark of Light. A single Spark of Light which ultimately became—

"Three pairs," I said, making the mental leap. "In our vision, there were three sets of Twin Lights. Who were the third pair?"

Eliasser smiled again. "You mean, who were the first pair. The female Twin of that pair sits beside me now." Ashi and I gaped at Ashara, who regarded us as dispassionately as ever. "Ashara also merged inside the vortex with her Twin Light, Asharren. Their joined Light produced Elianna and me. We are the Second Lights of Ashara and Asharren, just as you and Ashi are our Second Lights."

"Then, doesn't that make all six of us Twin Lights?" I asked.

"In a manner of speaking," Ashara replied. "With each generation the frequency alters slightly, but yes; we are all, in essence, each other's Twins. Male to female, of course."

"Oh. Of course. Male to female," I repeated, feeling suddenly as if the ground turned to liquid beneath my feet. *Male to female.* For the first time, I considered Eliasser and myself in a way that translated into *a man and a woman.* Dear God. If Eliasser was also my Twin Light, what might have happened if he had performed the Integration Link? If he, and not Ashi, had absorbed Earth-style desires. Desires aimed at me. Would I then . . . would I also have . . .

My runaway heart rate pulsed in my throat. Curiously, Ashi seemed not to notice my emotional state as I blurted out a question to derail my thoughts. "Where is Asharren now?"

"We do not know, I am sorry to say," Eliasser responded. "After he and Ashara merged to produce Elianna and me, he departed from Amoran to assist the Vortexes of the Fourth Universe. He has not been heard from since."

"That day was bittersweet," Ashara added. "The creation of Second Lights is indeed a joyful occasion. Yet, Asharren left Amoran, never seeing in physical form the Twin Lights he helped bring into being. And I never saw my Twin Light again." She shrugged. "But such is the life of a Vortex Guardian. You go where you are needed. You do what you must. I was needed here, and here I remained."

Despite Ashara's matter-of-fact manner, an invisible shroud of grief settled over us. Out of respect for what must have been a tremendous loss, I waited a moment before asking Eliasser the same basic question I'd posed once to Ashi. "What you've just told us strikes me as an even more important aspect of our identity. Why did you wait to share this?"

Eliasser's gaze wandered to the stained-glass-like panels. "Three days after Elianna and I learned of our birthright, she left Amoran to help the Thirteenth Vortex. We received word soon afterward that the Thirteenth Vortex suffered a devastating implosion. There were no survivors."

The grief emanating from him was palpable, but I couldn't let my query drop. Not now.

"I am truly sorry for your loss. However, I don't see what that has to do with the question I asked you. Why did you wait to tell Ashi and me who we *really* are?"

Eliasser set his mouth in a grim line as he continued to stare at the panels. When several moments passed without a response, Ashara said, "After Asharren and I merged, we also learned the story of our creation, and that we are Vortex Lights. Until then, we only knew that we were different from others, but not why." She sighed. "Three days after we learned of our birthright, my Twin Light also left Amoran, never to be seen again."

I worked out the common denominator. "Am I hearing right? You've been afraid to tell Ashi and me how we were created, because you're worried that in three days one of us will be gone for good like Asharren and Elianna? Isn't that a bit superstitious?"

"It is not superstition," Ashara said, "but a kind of science you are unfamiliar with. The telling of this birthright sets a unique energy vibration in motion. Once begun, it cannot be altered. We do not know what this energy will bring, but it will bring something, I can promise you that."

I found it hard to accept that merely voicing the story of our creation held that much power, but before I could offer a rebuttal, Ashi thought to me, *"She is back."*

I could now see the faint outline of Elianna's ethereal form as she rapidly "downloaded" information to Ashi and me.

"Oh, Eliasser," I said, thrilled and honored to partake in something so extraordinarily wonderful for him. "It was you all along. You are the Guardian who held the key for me—the key to who I really am. And the Foreseers said that the one who held the key for me was most in need of my gifts."

"As for that"—Ashi stood up and coaxed a guarded Eliasser to his feet—"Meiri will now give herself to you. To you, and to Elianna."

Eliasser's hand flew to his heart. "How can you say this? My Twin is dead."

"Your Twin says otherwise," Ashi said gently. "She was nearing the Thirteenth Vortex when it imploded. The shock wave forced her into a dimensional variance where she became trapped and cannot remanifest her physical body. But she is very much alive."

"You are wrong. I would know!" Eliasser pounded his chest, swayed, and lost his balance. Ashara leapt up to help steady him. The anguished look she directed my way pleaded with me to be sure, absolutely sure, that Ashi and I were not mistaken. Bearing witness to Ashara's pain was no easier for me now than it had been at the celebration dinner. But I swallowed hard, pressed my hand over my heart, and nodded.

"Elianna," she cried softly, covering her face as her shoulders convulsed.

Eliasser eyed her sobbing with alarm. "Ashara! What is wrong?"

I rose up and answered for the Master Healer, since she seemed incapable of doing so.

"Nothing is wrong. I merely affirmed the truth for her, as I do now for you. Elianna is my spirit friend, the one who has been helping me. It was she who spiked the fairybee wine Ashi and I consumed, although I don't know how she managed that without a body; she didn't say. As for why she is here now? The recent time-shift that breached the vortex and brought us the purple light beings also disrupted the dimensional variance she is trapped within, enough so that she can reach me. My Earth emotions have made me receptive to her, and by extension now, to Ashi. But no one else can sense her. That is why you haven't detected her, Eliasser. And it is the only reason Elianna did not come to you instead."

Eliasser's eyes were suddenly moist. I grasped his hands and kissed his trembling fingers.

"There is nothing I would not do for you, my sweet king. Nothing."

*"We must hurry,"* Ashi thought to me, *"or she will lose the opportunity."*

*"I'm ready."*

"Elianna cannot manifest her own body," Ashi said to Eliasser. "However, she can be with you tonight by occupying Meiri's for a short while."

Ashara wiped her tears away and smiled. But Eliasser looked worried.

"I have never heard of such a thing. Will you be safe, Meiri?"

"Completely. The process is a simple one made possible because of my Earth body." I loved that touch of irony. "My spirit and Elianna's will exchange places. It will be my body that you see, but Elianna who is here."

"Meiri . . ." Eliasser's tremulous voice reached deep into my heart. "Are you sure?"

"Am I sure?" I laughed at that, but when I continued, my own voice was none too steady. "You bet I'm sure. I once told you that I feel as if I belong inside your heart, as if that is where I have always belonged. It seems I was right. In a sense, it is where I came from. From your heart. And from hers."

A lovely warm, fluid sensation coated me from the inside out as Elianna's spirit slipped into my body. My vision dimmed to complete darkness, then gradually returned.

I was lying next to Ashi on the healing stone we used for a bed.

# Chapter 33

"Finally," Ashi said. "I have been waiting to tell you about Elianna's visit."

"It's over already?"

He nodded. "Elianna left your body before dawn. She said you must sleep as long as possible. It is well past Morning Meal now."

"But it was only a moment ago that I . . ." I trailed off, feeling a bit disoriented.

"Close your eyes," Ashi said. When I did, like a recording on double speed, a picture show of the previous night was broadcast on the screen in my mind.

"This is amazing. I can see, hear, and feel everything that you did. But slow down, okay? That last memory was too jumbled." I didn't add that it was also confusing to watch myself in his movie playback when it wasn't really me doing the walking and talking.

The memories he shared with me faded as he interlaced our fingers and squeezed my hand. "When Elianna first entered your body, Eliasser would not believe it was her. But Ashara recognized her immediately." Ashi shook his head in wonder. "It was fascinating. Her mannerisms are not at all like yours. She accents her words differently, her tone is deeper, and she uses her hands to gesture while she talks even more than you do." I smiled at that. "When Eliasser was finally convinced that she was alive and within you, he"—Ashi swallowed—"he cried, Meiri. I had only seen him cry once before, when you died after the purple spike struck you."

Ashi's memories downloaded again, blending Eliasser's reaction to his Twin with the memory of my death beneath the portal. The sight of Eliasser in both instances, tears streaming down his cheeks, was too much for me. I burst into tears myself and begged Ashi to stop.

Something like a blackout curtain drew across the window between our souls.

"What did you just do?" I asked.

"There is a way we can shield our thoughts from each other for a short while. Feelings too. I will instruct you, if you like."

"*Yes,* I would like. You've been holding out on me." I toyed with the front of his tunic top. "What did Elianna do when Eliasser cried like that?"

"She hugged him. She also cried. They thank you, by the way, for providing them with the gift of easy tears."

"They think copious crying is a gift?"

Ashi smiled. "They do now. When their tears were spent, they talked long into the night. Talked, laughed, danced. The Love energy that flowed between them was incredible. The same pink mist that surrounds you and I on occasion filled the entire room."

"I guess I'll have to take your word for it."

The protective curtain lifted briefly. I saw Eliasser and me—I mean, Elianna—dancing as the mist spiraled around them.

"Thank you," I whispered. "That was beautiful."

"You are most welcome, my Twin." He kissed my forehead. "As Elianna's time here drew to a close, she asked me to wait outside while she spoke privately with Eliasser and Ashara. She vowed to take good care of your body while I was gone."

"She kept her promise. I feel great! Like I've had weeks of needed sleep."

"When they called me back into the room, Eliasser and Ashara looked happier than I have seen them in quite some time. The four of us came here to the Healing Room so that Elianna could exit your body while you were lying down. She said we can never truly be parted, for we are always connected through the One Light. And then . . ." Ashi sighed. "She was gone."

"The fact that we're always connected in spirit is small comfort when you can't physically be with someone you love." I was referring to Elianna and Eliasser, but the recognition that Ashi and I would soon face our own separation occurred to us at the same moment. And I literally felt his pain. "I'm so sorry, Ashi. I don't want to leave you, either."

He held me tightly. "With all my heart, I promise you this. Even if we are blown to opposite ends of the universe during the Reparention, somehow I will find you. I will know who you are by the Light that you shine, and I will find you. You have my word."

His expression transformed into one of acute longing. "Meiri . . . my Twin . . . my Love . . . I do not know whether I am glad or dismayed that I absorbed from you this desire . . ." He placed a kiss on each of my cheeks. ". . . This desire to—"

"Ashi . . ." I gasped. Our electricity was running at high voltage.

He paused just in front of my mouth. "Yes?" he whispered, and moved in closer.

"We shouldn't—" Our lips made contact, and my whole body reacted like my arm does when I smack my funny bone—only much, much worse. "This is torture," I exclaimed, pushing him away. "The more we are together, the greater my feelings for you become, but so does the energy that prevents us from being able to do anything about them."

He flopped back and flung one arm over his eyes. "Meanwhile, we are slowly being driven pentuma. I cannot think how we will survive the coming weeks." He peeked out at me from under his arm. "What do Earth people do when they cannot be together in that way?"

That was a conversation I was not going to have with Ashi. Besides, our situation was entirely different.

"Earth people haven't had their Life Forces augmented and their energy signatures elevated, so I don't think Earth tactics will be of any use to us."

His groan of frustration made me laugh.

"What is so funny?" he said, testily.

Guess he hadn't bothered to read my mind.

"You. You're becoming more like an Earth person. I'm not sure if that's the good news or the bad news for you."

Ashi grew thoughtful. "More Earth-like. Do you really think so?" I nodded. "Then I will consider that the good news."

"Wow. I did not *ever* expect to hear you say that. Thank you for the planetary endorsement. It means a lot coming from you." I rolled off the stone. "Let's go for a walk and work off some of this excess energy."

---

Ashi and I hiked for miles, and while we did a thorough job of tiring ourselves out, it had no effect on our escalating libidos. With five weeks left to go, we were in big trouble.

We made it back to the Mountain with barely enough time to scarf down Midday Meal before practice. Eliasser and Ashara had skipped the meal altogether, arriving just as the plates were being cleared away. Eliasser seemed to be avoiding eye contact with me. I hoped my stint as Elianna's channel wasn't going to make things weird for us.

When Ashara announced that it was time for practice, the rest of the Guardians filed out of the room.

Ashi and I pulled her aside and requested help for our increasing physical discomfort.

"I will give you something tonight," she grunted. "Now get to practice."

"We'd like something now," I said. "Or we won't be able to make it through practice."

"You will do fine. Tell me if you need anything." And she left the room.

I looked at Ashi. "Didn't we just do that? Tell her we needed something?"

His eyes narrowed. "She is certainly being evasive."

"Then again, when is Ashara *not* being evasive."

Ashi laughed his agreement, and we passed through the doorway together.

Eliasser stood in the corridor, arms folded across his chest as he leaned against the wall, his gaze fixed on the floor. "May I have a word with you, Meiri?"

Ashi went on ahead. For several moments, Eliasser did nothing, said nothing. I waited in the uncomfortable silence until he whispered, "I could try for all eternity to find the words to thank you, but I would never succeed."

He finally looked up, and his eyes, so full of love, made me inexplicably self-conscious.

"Thank me for what? For the privilege of letting Elianna use my body so that you could be with her again? Shouldn't I be thanking you instead?"

He shook his head. "I do not understand. For what would you thank me?"

"Oh, I don't know. For my *life?* If it wasn't for you and Elianna, I wouldn't be here."

His eyebrows lifted. "You know very well that you owe your life only to the One Light."

"Then you should be thanking the One Light, and not me, for Elianna's presence last night."

I cringed at the pompous way the statement came out, but that wasn't what bothered him.

"Meirashannar," he said, sternly. "You have never once accepted my gratitude for anything, as though what you give is not worthy of appreciation. In order to keep giving, you must also allow yourself to receive. The Light cannot drop gifts into a closed hand."

The sting of the remonstration must have shown plainly on my face.

"Oh, my Light," he said. "I did not intend to hurt you. But surely you see that everything has a balance. It is just as important for me to offer you the gift of a grateful heart as it is for you to accept my gratitude and allow it into *your* heart. It is a kind of exchange. In giving, we receive. In receiving, we give. When it flows freely enough, there is no difference between them. Will you promise to think about that?"

I didn't need to. "Can we start this conversation over?"

He smiled, then bowed. "Meirashannar, from the depths of my Being, I thank you for your most precious gift to Elianna and me."

I mimicked his bow. "Eliasser, from the depths of my Being, you are most welcome."

*But it is you who are the gift, my sweet king.*

Ashi and I were preparing for bed when Eliasser entered the Healing Room carrying a carafe and two glistening silver goblets. Ashara followed after him, and as he set the carafe on the table, she flashed us a wide, toothy smile—our first indication that something unusual was afoot.

"I am rather proud of myself," she said, eyeing the carafe with affection. "I have not made this potion in years, yet I must admit it has tempered well."

Eliasser examined the goblets before placing them next to the carafe.

"These, too, have not been used since—"

"Never mind that now," she cut in, waving her hand like she was shooing away a fly.

*"Any idea what this is about?"* I thought to Ashi. He blinked and shook his head.

An Assistant came in carrying a pile of glimmering white cloth. Ashara snatched the bundle out of his hands, then pushed him back toward the opening. The poor guy barely cleared the doorway before she rematerialized the wall.

"These are special tunics with enhanced energy properties," she said to Ashi and me. "You must wear them from now on."

Eliasser took one and proffered it to Ashi like he was bestowing an award.

"There are no words I can say to you, Makashannar, that will do justice to this moment or what is to come. When Elianna suggested—"

"Enough!" Ashara boomed. "That is a private matter."

Eliasser sighed. "Of course." He held the second tunic out to me. "Meiri . . ." But then his voice broke, and he drew me into an embrace that continued until Ashara cleared her throat.

"This is an extremely strong potion," Ashara advised. "Drink it only after you have changed and are ready to lie down."

The ceremonial air seemed out of proportion for the presentation of special tunics and a mysterious potion. I don't know why it never occurred to us to ask them what was going on, but like well-behaved children, we donned our new clothes, sat on the edge of the healing stone, and accepted our bedtime medicine.

"Drink it all at once," Ashara instructed.

I winked at Ashi. "Time to chug."

Ashi's brow furrowed until he read my thoughts. "Ah. We say, 'down the hatch,' right?"

I laughed. I hadn't been thinking it when he peeked into my mind. "You remember that?"

"Yes. Such an odd expression." He sniffed the goblet, scrunched up his nose, and shrugged.

"Down the hatch," we said together and tipped the goblets.

I don't remember getting to the bottom. In the proverbial blink of an eye, we were walking through the forest. It was early morning.

Ashi stopped and looked around in bewilderment. "Are we dreaming?"

I touched a dew-covered vallius leaf and put a drop on his lips. "Seems pretty real to me."

He licked it off. "Yes. Quite real."

Our senses suddenly became heightened—the delicate song of the birds, the vibrant colors of the flowers, the sweet honeysuckle smell that perfumed the air—all saturated to the fullest.

Ashi closed his eyes. "Can you feel them, Meiri? They are waiting for us to perceive them."

"Who?" But then I felt them, too. And as soon as I did, Ashi and I were no longer on the path, but in the Glen of the Foreseers.

One by one, all seven Foreseers moved out of the misty circle and lined up before us. The Elder stood in the center, her luminous face radiating such ancient wisdom, I found it difficult to look directly at her. Then she did something I'd never seen a Foreseer do. Her ethereal form became as solid as our own bodies. She stepped forward and took firm hold of my hands.

"Many years ago, Meirashannar, we relinquished you to the physicality known as Earth. This action caused much pain, to those who love you as well as to yourself. Yet all things happen as they must. You stand before us this day, well-prepared for what lies ahead. In you, we are greatly pleased."

She turned to Ashi. "Makashannar, Child of Light, you have shown great courage, strength and love, yet your greatest trial awaits you. You will be tested beyond measure, but within you resides the wisdom and strength to see the challenge through. And beside you stands your Twin, whose Love will one day guide you out of darkness."

She took a step back and lifted her hands. "Behold these Twin Lights of the Seventh Vortex, who have suffered the pain of separation a thousand-fold. They will enter the vortex on the Day of Reparention to be once more parted from each other. For this, they are honored."

All seven Foreseers bowed their heads. I glanced at Ashi to see if he knew what to do, but he seemed as baffled as I was.

The Elder came forward again. "Makashannar, Meirashannar, we joyously partake in the consecration of your vows and your Promises to the One Light. You have pledged yourselves in service to the Light as well as to one another. Light-to-Light, Soul-to-Soul; in your commitment to this, you have never wavered.

"I beseech you now, give to me the amulets which rest upon your hearts."

We handed them over. She examined them, then regarded us thoughtfully. "You have exchanged them. How came you to do this?"

She seemed genuinely surprised that we'd traded. It was another rare instance in which I questioned whether the Foreseers really did know and see everything.

"I gave mine to Ashi for safekeeping when I went to live on Earth."

"And I gave mine to Meiri when she came back to Amoran."

The Elder tilted her head as she scrutinized the amulets again.

"Was that not allowed?" Ashi asked.

"Allowed?" She seemed to contemplate the idea. "Why did you do this?"

"I do not know," Ashi replied. He tapped the area of his chest where the amulet normally lay beneath the tunic. "It was impulsive on my part, and yet, it felt like the right thing to do."

"Indeed. Wearing each other's amulets provided you and Meirashannar with a strength and connection that would not normally take place until Joining. Unusual to initiate on your own, but certainly *allowed*." She emphasized the word as though it amused her.

"What do you mean by Joining?" I asked.

She looked further amused. "We shall Join you now, and you shall see."

Two silver treasure chests appeared—one in the hands of the red Foreseer, the other held by her blue counterpart. The Elder removed a round, pea-sized object from one of the boxes, then let it rest on her outstretched palm. Her voice echoed throughout the clearing as she spoke.

"Light of the One Light, come now into this sphere. As all lines are unbroken in the Circle of Light, so shall your Love within this sphere be forever whole."

The air crackled and the little ball glowed as its dull exterior transformed into a marbled turquoise and white radiance. The Elder opened one of the amulets, placed the sphere inside, and snapped the cover closed. As she repeated the process with the other treasure chest and amulet, I thought to Ashi, *"I didn't know the amulets could be opened."*

*"I did not know either."* I felt him sigh. *"I am beginning to wonder if I know anything."*

I smiled. *"Yes, well, once again—welcome to my world."*

When the second glowing sphere was safely ensconced in its new home, the Elder handed our original amulets back to us.

"You now have the amulets that were given to you after your creation in the vortex. Put them on, face each other, and recite the Vortex Prayer. I will say Eliasser's part for him."

The last time I recited the Vortex Prayer in the Glen, it had evoked an intense array of feelings. Now was no exception. Moved by a nameless emotion, I stumbled over the words as they shook their way out of my mouth. I was in good company, though. Ashi had the same difficulty getting through the ritual. When we reached the final verse, the energy radiating from our hands produced a brilliant light that made it impossible for us to see each other until we spoke the last line of the prayer and the brightness faded away.

The Foreseers formed a circle around us and began to sing in what sounded like impossible levels of harmony. When the first notes reached my ears, it was as though my soul had been laid bare for all the universe to see. The sheer naked vulnerability I experienced at that moment was both abjectly terrifying and excruciatingly sweet. Ashi and I no longer seemed to have control over the way our bodies trembled or the tears that came freely now.

When the Foreseers finished singing, the Elder said, "My Beloved Lights. We celebrate with you the Union of Spirit which occurred at your creation, and we acknowledge that which *already is.* Soul-to-Soul, you are already One. Light-to-Light, you are already One.

"Makashannar, remove your amulet. Place it over the heart of your Twin and speak these words to her. 'We are Joined in the Light, two Lights returned to one. Always One.'"

Ashi was still crying, which made doing the Elder's bidding a challenge. He gave it his best effort as he slipped his amulet over my head and managed to choke out, "We are Joined in the Light, two Lights returned to one. Always One."

"Meirashannar, you will now do the same with your Twin."

I placed my amulet around Ashi's neck and touched it lightly where it lay over his heart.

"We are Joined in the Light, two Lights returned to one. Always One," I whispered.

"Well done, Beloved Lights. Allow my words to resonate within your body, your heart, your mind, and your Spirit. Soon you will merge your Light essences within the vortex. We have revealed that Meirashannar will experience a death within the physical realm. Know that you are never truly apart, no matter how deeply into darkness or death of physicality you may fall. Have no fear. All things are perfect in their own way."

She stepped back, and the seven Foreseers spoke in unison. "We the Foreseers, who have tended the Third Universe since the Beginning Time, have a gift for Makashannar and Meirashannar in commemoration of their Union of Spirit."

With startling abruptness, morning transformed into evening. We were no longer in the Glen of the Foreseers, but in the clearing where Ashi found me the first time I visited the forest. It looked much the same as it had then. Three red flowers still adorned the base of the wide stone slab. The silver chalice rested on top of the altar-like table. But the lushly overgrown aspect of the trees and plants seemed wilder, almost sensuous in the semi-darkness.

The Elder was now the only Foreseer present. "Know this," she said. "The One Light expresses every thought, desire and emotion within all levels of Beingness. Every manner of expression is to be experienced according to its vibration, and none are to be judged better or worse. The moon blesses all of us with its light, a light that is no less precious because it comes to us as a reflection of the sun. It is, in all ways, a unique and beautiful manifestation of the One Light. When you merge in the vortex, you will be like the sun. But for now, you may revel in the gifts of the moon, and what the moon's light can teach you."

She placed my hands in Ashi's and then reverted to her ethereal body.

"Beloved Lights, this is our gift to you. What has been denied you in the physicality of Amoran, you shall be given this night within our Realm. In its own right, the moon's light is beautiful to behold. Behold, the moon."

A full moon appeared just above the treetops and the Elder vanished.

We stared down at our clasped hands in disbelief.

"Is this gift what I think it is?" Ashi said at last.

"It can't be. We must be dreaming."

His shuddering sigh made my knees go weak. "If this is a dream, may we never awaken." And then his lips met mine, the kiss sweet, soft, and perfect. No jarring energy. No painful vibration. Love and desire seared through me, followed by a commensurate helping of guilt. Until this moment, I'd been able to safely lament that Ashi and I weren't able to make love. Now that we could, I had to confront a more troubling dilemma.

Ashi slowly withdrew from the kiss. "Why do you hesitate, Meiri? Do you not wish to accept this gift?"

"It is a gift, isn't it?" I tried to let that be part of the equation as I struggled to come to terms with what felt like an impossible situation. My Twin Light and I shared a Union of Spirit. That had to count for something. But even if I was Ashi's spiritual partner on Amoran, back on Earth I was married to someone else. How could I ever look John in the eyes if I made love to Ashi? On the other hand, this night was a present from the all-knowing Foreseers. Would they have provided the means for us to be together if it was wrong? Was this one of those things that was "meant to be?"

I was still grappling with my inner demons when Ashi clutched his chest like he was having a heart attack. "Oh! This conflict . . . this . . . this guilt you feel. I cannot allow us to share our bodies knowing the emotional pain you will live with as a result."

We were so in tune that the realization hit us at the same instant.

"I won't have to live with it for long, will I?"

My voice went hoarse on the last few words as a wrenching grief passed through me. It seemed to originate from Ashi, although I couldn't be certain and I guess it no longer mattered. He found my mouth again, his passion now fueled by despair as well as desire. We staggered to the stone slab, losing half our clothes along the way. The other half seemed to melt off of us as we tumbled onto the flat gray surface—which turned out to be as soft as velvet and as cushiony as a down mattress.

Ashi and I heeded the Elder's advice. We reveled in the gifts we gave and received beneath the silvery circle that seemed to hang perpetually between dusk and dawn.

And the moon's light? It was as beautiful as the Elder had promised.

# Chapter 34

*D*amn *alarm clock! It was driving me insane!*

*I banged the snooze button, but the incessant buzzing didn't let up.*

*"No!" I covered my ears. "I need more time."*

*Buzz . . . buzz . . . buzz . . .*

*I punched the clock. It shattered like glass . . . and kept right on buzzing . . . all over my body . . . vibrating . . . painful . . .*

My eyes flew open. Ashi was rubbing his lips like they hurt.

"You were having a bad dream. Your distress was—" He touched his hand to his heart. "I tried to wake you, but when you did not respond, I thought perhaps that kissing you would work."

"I'm glad you did, both the kissing and the waking parts. But why so apologetic? You can kiss me whenever you like." I reached behind his neck to pull him closer.

He jerked back. "You do not understand."

"Silly boy. What's to understand? I love you. You love me. And bless the Light, are we ever good together." In case he needed a reminder of just how good we were, I smiled coyly and danced my fingers down the front of his tunic.

Ashi grabbed my hand and held tight.

"What's wrong?" I asked.

The Healing Room came into focus behind him. Disappointment coursed through me.

"We're back? I don't remember leaving the forest."

"Nor do I. My last memory is—" He stopped and smiled, a smile I felt inside every cell of my body as we recalled our final time together. Judging by our physical reactions now, a night of lovemaking hadn't fully quenched our thirst.

Ashi sighed. "When I could not awaken you from your dream, I decided to kiss you back to consciousness." He rubbed his lips again. "I am afraid that we can no longer share ourselves in that manner. But if we could"—he turned seductive—"I would begin at your—"

"Don't. Not another word out of you."

Here I thought I'd be the teacher instructing Ashi in the pleasures of the flesh, but my Twin had come up with a few tricks on his own, probably thanks to the "handbooks" Ari had lent him. Like describing in exquisite detail what he was going to do to me before he did it. It drove me crazy with anticipation. But anticipation was all we had left now and that just seemed like needless torture.

Ashi pressed his lips to my forehead. "No painful vibration there." His hand wandered to the front of my tunic, his caresses lighting me up from the inside. "What if there are some things we can still do? Some places on you that I can still . . . *kiss.*"

I groaned and pushed him away. "I would never have figured you for a tease."

Ashi's grin went wide. "Maybe we will be allowed to visit the clearing every night."

I wanted more than anything to purchase stock in that fantasy. But we both knew better.

"The Foreseers gifted us one night, Ashi. Only one. Although, they could have waited until my last evening here so we wouldn't have to suffer through weeks of frustration."

It had been a while since I'd experienced a prickling at the back of my neck. I had it now as the doorway to the Healing Room opened. Ashara and Eliasser hovered on the threshold. I'd seen people at a funeral look less depressed.

Ashi and I slid off the healing stone and waited side by side for whatever it was they couldn't bring themselves to tell us. When Ashara finally made eye contact with me, I wished she hadn't. The only other time I'd seen her look so stricken was when she had to reveal the truth about my first Earth death to the rest of the Guardians.

"I am sorry, Meiri," she whispered. "You must leave Amoran immediately."

The room seemed to tilt sideways. "No! I have five more weeks."

"You *had* five more weeks," Eliasser quietly corrected. "We have lost the ability to stretch time. We do not know when, or if, we will get it back."

Ashi's hand gripped mine. "Not get it back? Ever?"

The meaning of my dream came crashing home. I'd grown so dependent on time-stretching, it never occurred to me it might not last.

"How does this affect the onset of the Reparention?" I asked.

"Unknown," Ashara said. "We must recalculate everything now."

"Wouldn't the end of time-stretching move it closer? Maybe I should stay."

"Meiri," Eliasser began, but then he seemed to have difficulty forming words so Ashara took over for him.

"We have just consulted the Foreseers. Your energy moving through the vortex is needed until it is time for the Reparention. As long as the vortex is navigable, you must return to Earth at the end of each visit. And the vortex is, at the moment, relatively stable."

I forced myself to stay calm instead of screaming expletives the way I wanted to. "I've only used up a couple of the eight Earth hours I have for this visit, which means that even without time-stretching, I should have five, maybe six hours left here."

The grim set to Ashara's mouth made my legs go rubbery. "There is a further complication. Time has shifted forward. How far forward is not clear. At the very least, it is hours. Possibly days."

"Days?!" I thought I might be sick.

Ashi's grip almost crushed my fingers. "Leave us. I will say goodbye to Meiri in private."

"Be quick about it," Ashara warned. "Every moment counts."

Ashi's eyes drifted to my face. "I am well aware of that."

He waited until the doorway resealed itself before taking me into his arms. "Do you recall the dream you had where you saw yourself leave Amoran and return once more before the Reparention?" I nodded numbly. "If that is true, then without time-stretching, when you come back we will likely have only a few hours at most."

"Stop it!" I pushed against his chest. "You don't know what you're saying."

"Listen to me," Ashi pleaded. "Do you not see? It is possible that the Reparention will begin soon after you next arrive on Amoran."

"No! You can't base your assumption on a stupid dream."

"I hope I am wrong, Meiri. I dearly hope—" He grasped my face and kissed my forehead, letting his lips linger there for a moment before looking at me. "I will do whatever I can to ensure that we both leave the vortex alive. If we are parted, as the Foreseers say we are to be, then remember my promise to you; somehow, some way, I will find you."

We stole another minute of precious time as we held each other in wordless communion.

---

The rest of the Guardians were in the Main Chamber. They'd arranged themselves in a circle like we did during practice, only now they were waiting to see me off. I was desperately holding onto the belief that Ashi was wrong about my dream, but with a growing sense of finality, I left his side to say goodbye to my friends.

Anders turned beet red, but accepted a hug from me with surprising alacrity.

Balthasarre's generous embrace was solid and wonderful. "I look forward to many more talks with you about the vortex once the Reparention is behind us," he said.

Comforted by Balthasarre's confidence, I moved on to Ari, who played his part well as the court jester. He bent me over backwards in a ballroom dancing move, dropped the pitch of his voice and announced, "Until we meet again, my dear."

Amid a smattering of laughter, I continued on to Danaeus, who crossed his arms over his chest and said gruffly, "A simple farewell is all right with me."

"Oh, no. You don't get off that easy." Stooping down, I hugged him anyway, and then, for good measure, I planted a big, smacking kiss on that furry face of his. Blushing worse than Anders, Danaeus protested, but he didn't stop smiling. This brought another round of laughter, which ended as soon as I turned to Eliasser.

He stepped forward to take my hands, then glanced around the circle. "We have prepared as thoroughly as we can," he said, using his official Master Guardian voice. "When the time comes, we will, each of us, do what we are called to do." His gaze inched downward, as if prolonging the moment before our eyes met. And when they did, neither of us was in a position to talk. I collapsed against him, and we held each other until Ashara reminded us of the urgency in getting me back to Earth.

"May the Light guide you safely home," my sweet king whispered to me. When he let me go, it felt like all the warmth had been withdrawn from my world. But I had no time to process that loss, as an abnormally loud whirring came from the top of the chamber.

"Hurry," Ashara said. She gave me a quick hug.

Ashi walked me beneath portal, then jumped back as the misty light rocketed down and snatched me up. *"I will find you,"* Ashi thought to me as I entered the vortex. *"I will find you . . . I will find you . . ."*

---

"I found her!"

John reached the family room seconds after I landed, eyeing me with astonishment as I lay prone on the throw rug. "It's like she appeared out of nowhere."

I stayed put, observing him warily as he came in followed by our detective friend, Dan.

Dan motioned John to back off and knelt at my side. "Where did you come from just now?"

I shrugged. It was a stupid way to respond, but I had to figure out what day it was on Earth before I could drum up a suitable explanation for my whereabouts.

Dan's face gave nothing away. "Are you all right?" he asked. I shrugged again. "I'd like to check you over, take your pulse, that sort of thing. Okay?"

I nodded. John paced back and forth, increasingly agitated as Dan went about his business.

When Dan was satisfied that I had nothing more serious than an elevated heart rate, he said, "Where have you been all this time?"

All *what* time? I hugged my knees to my chest and shrugged again.

John's expression went from worry to anger. "Kerrin . . ." he growled through clenched teeth.

"Sorry. It's just . . . I'm not really sure about . . . I don't really know how . . ."

"That's it," John shouted. "You're going to the hospital."

"No," I yelled back. "I'm okay. What I meant was—" I caught the view out the window. Dark sky and moonlight. "Uh . . . what I mean is—" I slid my eyes to the media player. It was eleven o'clock. Now I just needed to know what day it was.

My inability to complete a sentence wasn't helping my case. Regarding me with growing concern, Dan tried a different angle. "Rebecca said you thought a man was following you a few weeks ago. Does that have anything to do with your disappearance?"

I pictured Ari in his old man disguise peeking at me from behind a bookshelf in the library and—God help me—I let loose with a gale of inappropriate laughter, the kind that comes from living with unremitting stress. Dan and John reacted to my cackling by jumping in unison like a pair of bad actors in an overly scripted sitcom. Which only made me laugh more.

"Hospital," John barked. "Now!"

"Wait. I can explain. Turns out that the man following me was a friend playing a joke. That's why I'm laughing. It was pretty funny." I gave John a weak smile. "I'm fine. Really."

"Then where have you been?"

Before my panicked brain could invent a story to potentially cover several days' absence, John unwittingly extended me a helping hand.

"The kids have been at Nancy's since this morning! You never called to check on them."

"Thank God it's still Saturday," I mumbled to myself.

*Uh-oh. Did I say that out loud?*

Apparently so. Dan shook his head. "I'm beginning to side with John on this. A visit to the ER is in order unless you can tell us where you've been."

*Come on, Kerrin. Make up a story. Think . . . Think!*

"I . . . um . . . went to the mall."

"The mall?" John's anger continued to escalate. "What happened to writing? That was the whole reason Nancy took our kids for the day."

"I know. But . . . I . . . uh . . . thought I'd get started on Christmas shopping."

"Do you always go to the mall in your pajamas?" Dan asked.

"What?" I tilted my head down. I was still wearing the special energy tunic, although it was no longer shimmering. "Oh, this? It's not pajamas. It's a . . . a kind of . . . yoga outfit. I got it today. At the mall."

"Why didn't you answer your cell phone?" John persisted.

"I didn't hear it. I must have left it at home."

Dan's expression remained neutral. "Your car has been here the entire time we've been searching for you. When did you get back from shopping?"

"I . . . Oh, hell. I don't know. Are the kids in bed?"

John's face went crimson. "They're still at Nancy's, which you would know if you'd checked your cell phone or at least been home to pick up the messages left for you!"

It would probably feed his fury, but I went to the answering machine and hit the play button. I had to know what I was dealing with. Nancy's cheerful voice said she hoped the Great American Novel was progressing well and that she'd like to keep the kids overnight. They were having great fun. No need for me to call back.

The rest of the messages were from John, demanding to know where I was.

In a room electrified by silence, I walked to the couch and sat down.

"I'm guessing you weren't really at the mall," Dan said. "But how did you wind up on the floor of your family room when you weren't anywhere in the house a few minutes ago? And we know, because we checked everywhere."

Another shrug was the best I could come up with. I simply could not make one more lie come out of my mouth.

Dan frowned. "I'm not here in an official capacity, Kerrin. I'm here as your friend, and I don't mind telling you, you've got me really concerned. Either you've become mentally unstable, or you're unwilling to tell us where you've been. Whichever it is, I want to help you. What can I do?"

Dan's compassion got to me. I waited until I could talk past the tightness in my throat.

"I promise you, I'm okay. I don't need a hospital. I just need to rest."

He looked like he wanted to say something else, but changed his mind.

"Are you here for the rest of the weekend?" he asked John.

"No! I have to get back to work early in the morning. Unlike some people, I don't get to wander the countryside without telling anyone where I am."

Dan let John's angry comment slide as he turned back to me. "I'll have Rebecca check in with you tomorrow. All right?"

"Sure. Thanks, Dan."

John walked Dan outside. I crept to the front door and tried, unsuccessfully, to eavesdrop on their murmured conversation. When I heard Dan's boots clunk down the wooden steps, I backed away just as John came in and slammed the door.

"No more crap, Kerrin. I want to know where you've been and who you've been with."

"What is that supposed to mean?" I shouted, as if he were the one in the wrong.

"It means, my dear wife, you've been missing for hours with no explanation. What would you think in my place?"

I knew exactly what I would think. My actions were indefensible.

When I didn't answer, his face twisted in anguish. "What's happening to us?" He reached out for me, but I flinched before I could stop myself.

John stumbled back like I'd turned radioactive. "Are you having—"

"Stop it. Stop it. Stop it!" I yelled to drown out what I knew was coming next. "I told you before, I need time to work this out. And then—"

I choked off, furious with myself. *Then what, Kerrin? You'll make it up to him? In what lifetime?* I deserved every ounce of guilt I suffered and every bit of his anger. Sure, John had been a shit, but if Ashara was right, my Amoran energy had caused a lot of it. Now, even if the Earth survived, I wouldn't! What would John think when I never came back? That I ran off with some nefarious lover? What would he tell our kids? Mommy vanished, whereabouts unknown? And if Ashi's timing was correct, these were the last two days I had with my family.

I held out a faltering hand. "I didn't mean to push you away."

His hurt morphed into anger again. "Too little, too late," he hissed, and went upstairs.

I staggered to the family room and fell onto the couch. Sleep was impossible. An hour later, I got up and made a cup of decaf tea. While I drank, I wrote a letter to John explaining everything. When I remembered I couldn't tell anyone about Amoran, I ran the pages through the shredder. It was just as well. What I'd written would only prove I'd gone off the deep end.

I climbed the stairs to get Ashi's book, the one Ari had delivered to me at the library. John was stretched out on our bed, one arm extended across the place where I usually slept. The place where, had Amoran never entered my life, I would be sleeping right now. A sob escaped my throat, catching me by surprise. Not wanting to risk another confrontation with John, I retrieved the book and went back downstairs.

I curled up on the couch again, clutching Ashi's book to me like it was a beloved stuffed animal. Stuffed animals made me think of my kids, which reminded me that in a few days, I would never see them again. I would have given anything at that moment for one of Ashara's sleeping potions. Instead, I had to settle for crying myself to sleep.

# CHAPTER 35

R ain drummed on the roof, nudging me awake the following morning. John was already gone.

I took Ashi's book into the kitchen and set it on the table while I made tea and toasted four slices of bread. I hadn't eaten since Evening Meal on Amoran, but toast was all the cooking I could handle as I planned how to spend my last twenty-four hours on Earth. First, I would collect Ryan and Kiley from Nancy's. Next, I'd have them use their well-honed wheedling skills to convince their dad to come home early. No matter how angry John was with me, he loved his kids. If they begged him to leave work in time for dinner, he just might do it. I flirted with the idea of cooking John's favorite meal, but if I couldn't manage more than toasting bread, dining-out was the only realistic solution.

The Sunday paper served as my placemat. I hadn't read the headline when I set my plate down on top of it. Now, the letters peeking out from each end—"MA" and "WAY"—caught my eye. After warbling, *"And, I did it myyyyy waaaaay,"* I stuffed the last crust into my mouth, licked my fingers and pushed the plate aside to read the full sentence.

*"MASSIVE STORM ON THE WAY."*

And just like that, my plans, my day, my life—what was left of it—crumbled. A quick scan of the article told me that by nightfall a freak meeting of several storm fronts would cause power outages, flooding, and excessive winds.

I pulled the plate back over the headline, blotting it out as if I could change the truth by not seeing it. Along with prophesying my death, the Foreseers had confirmed that a massive storm—those were their exact words—would descend upon my area when the Reparention was imminent. But what did imminent mean to timeless Beings?

Lonely for my Twin, my hand closed over Ashi's amulet as I wondered where he was.

*"Here,"* he thought-whispered.

Joy bubbled up inside me. My joy. His joy. *Our joy.*

*"I hope you did not need me last night,"* he said apologetically.

A quick impression was all I needed to understand what—and who—prevented that.

*"Ashara gave you a sleeping draft?"*

*"She did not want me to dwell on your absence, or—"*

*"—contact me,"* I finished. Considering what had transpired with John, it was probably a good thing Ashi hadn't been able to reach me. *"What about now? Are we allowed to talk to each other? Or are you breaking the Master Healer's rules?"*

*"I have her permission. She is with me now, and wants to know how the weather is where you are."*

I glanced out the window. The water splashing onto the deck was growing in intensity.

*"It's raining now, and a giant storm is expected tonight."*

Ashi abruptly withdrew. He was only shielding his thoughts, but the isolation I felt at his departure was acute. When he came back, I picked up his emotional state and my heart seized.

*"Meiri. Something has happened in the vortex. Very little time remains before the Reparention. You must return soon."*

One day. That's all I had wanted. I'd accepted losing my own life, but it broke my heart that my family would never know what happened to me. I considered leaving a suicide note to offer them some measure of closure, but it wasn't true and it might even hurt them more.

I'd forgotten to shield my thoughts. Ashi's anguish when he experienced my suffering was too much for me to bear. I blocked my feelings from him, then asked when I should leave.

*"The next opening for safe passage is in two hours,"* he said.

Two hours. Dear God. *"Will we have to remain apart when I come through?"*

*"Far apart, and with the Reparention so close, we must forgo our shielding potions. But once we enter the vortex . . ."* He tried, without success, to conceal his sudden elation.

I sent him a mental hug, unblocked myself and allowed him to feel my own excitement. *"Even though the reason we have to do this is hellish, I'm looking forward to merging, too."*

He sent me such a burst of Love energy, I almost fell off my seat. I was channeling the Love back to him when my doorbell rang. It was probably Rebecca, sent by Dan to check up on me.

*"Darn. I've got company. Don't go, Ashi. I'll get rid of her as fast as I can."*

*"I am sorry, but I must leave. Ashara is calling a practice. She claims we need to keep our skills sharp, although I believe her real reason is to make sure we are busy and distracted."*

He bathed me in multiple waves of energy that had me smiling all the way down the hall. I swung the door open to greet Rebecca, which I wasn't able to do because it was Wretched Cousin Camryn who stood on my porch. She was also smiling, but hers was the shit-eating variety.

"Well, well," she crowed, "for someone who just put her husband through the tortures of hell, you certainly look happy."

I tried to slam the door, but she stuck her expensively booted foot in the way and pushed past me. "Not going to invite me in? Tsk tsk. What would Miss Manners say?"

Camryn sashayed to the kitchen, plunked into a chair and shrugged off her coat. "Sorry I couldn't make it on Thanksgiving."

"I didn't want you there anyway. Just like now, so get to the point."

She pulled off her black leather gloves one finger at a time. "Are you okay?" she lilted in a sickening falsetto. "You seem a little pale."

"I'm fine!" I imagined my ever-lengthening Pinocchio nose poking out one of her overly made-up eyes. "Get to the point."

Her annoying grin went Cheshire-sized. "If you insist. I was in the Tea Leaf Café last night when John and Dan came in. They were looking for you everywhere. John was beside himself. The poor man needed me to console him."

Transparent little phony. "Well, I'm sure you did a fine job of letting him cry on your shoulder. Now, what is it you *really* want? Besides my husband."

She paled slightly beneath that healthy dose of blush, but didn't lose her momentum.

"John was worried sick that something terrible had happened to you. I told him not to worry; you probably found something—or someone—to occupy yourself with while he was working so hard. That's when he asked me if I thought you were having an affair."

Damn my mood ring face. My cheeks flushed as I struggled to think up a quick comeback.

The hesitation was all the perceptive hussy needed.

She smirked. "Guess I hit a nerve. So, who's the unlucky guy?"

A loud whirring in the family room startled us both. Camryn's conniving expression switched to astonishment, then cemented in place as her body went motionless. It was like looking at a figure in a wax museum. One arm, locked in position, pointed behind me.

I whirled around. "We have to start the Reparention," Ari exclaimed.

"Now?" I glanced at my mannequin cousin. "What about her?"

"I froze time for her. Aside from a terrible headache, she'll be okay in a few minutes." He grabbed my hand. "Whatever you do, don't let go!"

We ran to the family room where a booming wind blasted through the open portal and dragged us into the vortex. The air pressure doubled, then doubled again. Every bone in my body felt like it was breaking. I clung so hard to Ari's hand, my fingernails dug into his flesh. But my strength was no match for the wind. It wrenched us apart anyway.

"Ari!" I screamed as he disappeared from view.

Enormous ribbons of multicolored energy thundered by in wild, swooping arcs, then spiraled downward like a giant whirlpool. The tide they created sucked me toward the center of the maelstrom, where the ribbons were transforming into black coils. I clawed at the air with swimming motions as if that could slow my descent. But I sank even faster.

When the first tendril of dark energy licked at my feet, I graduated from panic to terror.

*No! Stay calm,* I told myself.

Calm? Who was I kidding? I was shaking so hard, my teeth kept slamming together. Dark energy slithered up my legs. Fingers of unbelievable cold pressed relentlessly against my skin. I'd experienced this hope-killing cold during my near-fatal trip through the vortex all those months ago. I had to break away from it now or I'd be trapped forever.

*Concentrate. Focus. Find the portal!*

Black clouds thrust into my mind, turning my thoughts into mental sludge.

*Find . . . find . . .*

"Meiri," Ashi shouted inside my brain. *"Do not let Darkness take you. Fight it."*

I labored to form a coherent sentence. *"I can't . . . I need . . . "*

"Meiri," Ashi cried again. *"I am sending you—"*

I couldn't hear the rest. A creeping heaviness made it hard to move as dark energy continued its hostile takeover. My emotions, next in line for extinction, began the slide into deep freeze.

*"No,"* Ashi begged me. *"Resist it. Fight it. You must—"*

He was gone again.

Fight it? How? Confirming the hopelessness of my situation, dark energy played its trump card. Like random injections of anesthesia, paralysis pricked its way through my body.

"Help me," I cried out loud. "Elianna . . . if you're there . . . help me." I gasped, then sucked in a ragged breath. "Someone. Please. Help."

My vision darkened. I couldn't believe it was going to end like this. Cold. So cold . . .

**"Meirashannar of Amoran."**

The male voice reverberated in the air.

**"Bless the Dark and be strong for what the Light calls you to do. All is balance, and balance must be restored. That is your task on this day when you shall once again die to be reborn. Bless and release the Dark . . . bless and release it . . . release it . . ."**

My mind temporarily unfroze. Bless the Darkness? And then release it? How?

**"The power is in your hands. It is *always* in your hands. Embrace . . . everything. Love . . . everything. Fear . . . nothing."**

Fear nothing? Not even the instrument of my pending demise? How could I possibly—

**"Love everything. Every . . . thing."**

I didn't have time to ponder the wisdom of it. I tried to feel actual *love* for the Darkness, but I couldn't manage that emotion for something about to claim my life. With my last scraps of mental acuity, I settled for blessing dark energy for its part in maintaining balance in the universe. Without it, we wouldn't exist. Nothing could exist. It was just as important as the One Light. All is balance, the Voice had said.

*All is balance,* I chanted to myself, keeping my thoughts warm. *All is balance. All is . . .*

The synapses in my brain suddenly seemed to light up.

All . . . *is* . . . balance. The realization impressed itself so potently, I finally did feel something akin to love, followed by a reverent honor for states of Being far beyond my meager comprehension. And with a certainty that surprised me, I did as the Voice suggested. I released the Darkness. I simply *knew* it had no ability to hold me because I spoke from Absolute Knowing and I *chose* to release it. And the revelation I had at that moment was this: I didn't have power over the Darkness any more than I had power over the Light. What I possessed was power over myself. The power to choose and to act.

In that instant of elevated awareness, the fear I'd held onto left me and I spontaneously transformed into my light-body on my own for the first time.

Like a balloon filling with helium, I rose above the Darkness . . . higher . . . higher . . . higher . . .

*"Meiri. Above you . . ."*

Ashi!

In a burst of molecular rearrangement, my physical body remanifested. Unfortunately, so did my pain. Gritting my teeth, I looked up and spied a point of light. My Twin was sending me a homing beacon. The expenditure of his Life Force to create it must have cost him dearly.

*"I see it. I'll try, Ashi."* Working in spite of the pain, I aligned my thought and heart energy, then focused on Ashi's point of light

and willed myself forward. Without the impervious buoyancy of my light-body, the effort was exhausting. I was nearing collapse when I tumbled through the Amoran portal and landed in the Golden Circle with the wind knocked out of me.

Ashara rushed to my side. "I am shielding you with my energy. Eliasser is shielding Ashi. We cannot risk exposing you to his vibrations yet." She lifted my head and held a goblet to my lips, urging me to drink. "This will restore as much of your strength as possible. I am sorry I cannot do more, but we must begin now."

"Ari?" I mouthed to her.

"He was pulled into a counter-spiral that brought him directly here. He was not affected by dark energy." Ashara's eyes softened. She kissed the center of my forehead. "Remember my blessing, Meiri. Keep it with you."

She slapped her stoic demeanor back in place and helped me to my feet. The rest of the Guardians were already in position. Eyes closed, hands out to the sides, the perimeters of their bodies glowed golden-white. Ashi's light was the brightest of all, and that was shielded.

Ashara moved into position. "In a moment, I will remove your shielding. Ashi's energy will feel overpowering, but hold your ground. I love you, Meiri. Choose well."

Choose well? Hadn't I just done that by releasing the Darkness? But I wasn't able to process her last words to me any further. At the same time that the shielding around Ashi and me dropped, the vortex winds blasted through the portal and yanked all eight of us into the vortex's tumultuous interior. This forced us to bypass the first five steps of our carefully rehearsed Reparention. Adding insult to injury, as Ashara struggled to initiate the Mind Link, everyone prematurely turned to Light. Ashi and I were now dangerously exposed to each other without the grounding we needed from the Mind Link.

Six light-bodies scattered as I blasted through their midst like a heat-seeking missile trained on my Twin. I slammed into Ashi's white-hot energy field, then boomeranged off, repelled as if we were the same poles of a magnet. Energetically stunned by the power of his unshielded Life Force, I bounced in and out of physicality as my body made serial attempts to remanifest. Light to solid; solid to Light;

I flip-flopped between extremes. In Light form, I could only perceive Ashi's brilliant energy, but when I switched to physicality, the Darkness reached up, lancing me with pain. I had to regain control of my energy and stay in Light form, and I had to do it fast.

*Flip.* My light-body came back. I propelled myself toward Ashi, figuring it was better to risk merging too soon than the alternative.

*Flop.* My physical form returned before I could reach him. I let out an agonizing cry.

*Flip.* I was in Light form again. I sped forward and was nearly to Ashi when—

*Flop.* My physical body reappeared; the pressure intolerable; the pain indescribable. If I didn't stay in Light form now, I wouldn't have to worry about the Darkness. I'd be dead.

*Flip.* My light-body burst back. Quick as lightning, Ashara lassoed me with her energy. I lost visual on Ashi as Ashara infused me with her own power to keep me from regaining physicality. In rapid thought-speak—a bonus of being in light-bodies—she let me know she'd established the Mind Link with everyone except for Ashi and me. But the effort depleted the group's energy and most of them were exhausted. However, that wasn't the most troublesome part. She'd been able to locate me, but Ashi was missing, and the grounding afforded by the Mind Link made it difficult for the other Guardians to sense where he was.

*"Find him, Meiri,"* Ashara said. *"You are the only one who can."*

She pulled me into the Mind Link. My consciousness reeled from the impact of joining with the Guardians in such a powerful way. During Reparention practice, our group had either practiced the Mind Link or turning to Light, but never at the same time. Now, with both of those accomplished, we were fully connected in a pure energy state. With a kind of cosmic intimacy, I felt the other Guardians simultaneously as if each one were a part of me. Distracted by the power of the communal experience, I wavered.

*"Hurry, Meiri. Find him,"* Ashara urged me on.

*"I'm sorry. I will."*

The Guardians couldn't sense Ashi through the Mind Link, but it seemed to have the opposite effect on me. I turned my attention outward and felt him at once, this time without the shattering vibrational impact. He'd been trying to find me as well, judging by the way his energy raced out to meet mine. *"Wait,"* I thought to him. *"Ashara needs to link you to us. Ashara?"*

My light-body shuddered, then shimmered brighter as the Master Healer moved through the center of me, as if I were a bread crumb she followed on the trail to Ashi. With another shuddering *thunk,* Ashi was linked in.

The eight of us shared a fleeting moment of relief as our group energy stabilized, then began cycling through us. Round and round the energy flowed, gaining speed with each revolution, the power building in gradual increments. We were finally back on track!

And then our train lost its brakes. Ashi's energy doubled every few seconds, even with the Mind Link's grounding. He was spiraling out of control. The other Guardians wanted me to begin the merge, but I had to wait for the right moment. Ashi's and my energy levels had to be in perfect sync or we would effectively cancel each other out.

As the energy continued to cycle and build, I altered Ashi's vibrational rate to get our frequencies in balance. I guess all things do happen as they must, because my brush with dark energy proved a godsend. My own energy signature, much subdued by the dampening effect of the Darkness, acted as ballast for Ashi's volatility. This worked well until his energy suddenly accelerated beyond his capacity to handle it or my ability to modulate it. Ashi was approaching critical mass. I had to hurry or we would lose him. *"Hold on, Ashi,"* I cried. I worked our vibrational rates like the keys of a piano, the energy arpeggios sliding up and down the frequency scales. *"Hold on. Just one more . . ."*

And then I felt it—the synchronization I'd been waiting for. My heart exploded in expectation, my entire Being ignited with Light, and I rushed toward him.

*"Now,"* I thought to everyone. *"NOW!"*

The first edges of Ashi's and my energy fields met, and an upwelling of elation gave way to swells of ecstasy. If this was only the beginning, I didn't think I'd ever want to part from him.

Ashi's energy blended further into mine, producing wave upon wave of fresh euphoria. Each time I thought we achieved the apex of our union, an even greater level of rapturous bliss swept over us. As we melded more deeply, the perpetual ecstasy started to feel like a natural state to me. Then, as our individual identities dropped away, I realized that this *was* our natural state. Ari was right; the physical life I'd considered normal up until now was a kind of window dressing for the soul. Eliasser had said that the Light Sojourn would let me experience in small measure what it would be like to encounter the One Light, but he hadn't put nearly enough emphasis on the word *small.* Would I have enough fortitude to turn away from the One Light when the moment arrived for real?

With the sudden awareness that something was wrong, I realized I'd been so swept up by joy that I lost track of what was happening. Combining two light-bodies requires a gradual advance, and it was my job to monitor that. But Ashi was pushing forward too fast. I had to slow him down, while desiring with all my Being to surge forward into eternity with him.

Eliasser, risking his own life to enter the merging energies of another, slipped inside the last vestige of my unmerged energy field to help keep Ashi at bay. Even with the two of us working at it, we could barely restrain him. Ashi went into distress, his energy in danger of turning in on itself and imploding.

*"I can't wait any longer. It will be too late,"* I thought to Eliasser.

Eliasser held on several moments longer, then left my energy field.

I moved forward at a steady pace, combining more deeply with Ashi. The "you and me" that defined us as two distinct individuals slipped away, replaced by an increasing sense of "we." Our merging continued at a much faster rate than was safe, but I no longer cared. I loved him so completely, and with such connection, that nothing could have stopped our ascent.

And then, in a final burst of Union, we catapulted out of the Mind Link. We were One.

All around us, the One Light radiated Its infinite Love—a Love we returned, vibrating with an ecstasy unsurpassed by any we had yet experienced. Filled with gratitude for our very existence, our Light-Self automatically drew nearer to the One Light, which, never judging, simply accepted our movement. Through the gift of free will, the choice was ours. We could fulfill our destiny, or we could abandon our temporal lives forever by merging into the One Light, where we would remain in a state of perpetual rapture. To never again experience pain or separation. To never again be required to inhabit a physical body; to be born or to die. We had to make our decision quickly, though. The longer we delayed, the harder it would be to leave what some would call Heaven.

"Thinking" is quite different as a merged Being, and is best described as a combination of Absolute Knowing fueled by intent, but without a conscious awareness of either. In that manner, and with the same impartiality shown us by the One Light, we considered our correct path.

Eliasser had said that turning away from the One Light would be a tremendously difficult thing to do. Our own experiences with the Light Sojourn confirmed that. However, the means we had used to turn from the One Light during our individual Light Sojourns now seemed trivial. It was simple, really. Given the choice between eternal bliss for us, or continued life for two planets and billions of people, there was no other choice our Heart could make.

The impression we sent to the One Light was a formality; our intentions had been divined even before *we* knew our decision. We reversed our direction and moved away. We thought that "leaving" the One Light would bring us sadness. Yet, the Light and Love circulating within us increased, followed by a phenomenal explosion of joy.

We had chosen well. Only one task remained.

Our Light-Self sought out, then reconnected with the group through the Mind Link. The effect our merged energy had on individual members was staggering, especially since they were already operating at a deficit. We had to work swiftly or we would risk all of their lives.

Ashara was first to pick up the energy we began cycling. Soon, the entire group was acting like a giant conduit. Energy moved through all of us, faster and stronger with each passing. Half the vortex had been consumed, and the Darkness was swiftly devouring what was left. At the current rate of destruction, the vortex was minutes away from implosion. It had to be now.

We drew the cycling energy back into our joined Self and held it, letting it build until we could release it in a single burst of power directed at the center of the vortex. It was the critical moment when the other Guardians had to break the Link and escape to safety.

Ashara signaled them to disconnect, but only five Guardians moved toward the Amoran portal. Eliasser, after severing his connection with the link, got caught in a downward current. His physical body remanifested and he flailed around, then grew ominously still and sank toward the churning dark area below. Having given up so much of his own Life Force to help us merge, he could no longer withstand the energy inside the vortex. The beloved Master Guardian of the Seventh Vortex was dying, and even with all the power we commanded at that moment, we could not abandon our task to save him. We had to unleash the deadly bolt of energy directly above his motionless body.

Had to, and did.

The impact of releasing the energy blasted Ashi and me apart and sent us hurtling in opposite directions. The separation of our Light-Self was devastating to both of us, something I knew because I could still feel Ashi's emotions. Fortunately, his trajectory would take him within range of the Amoran portal, while mine pushed me in the general direction of Earth. I felt his immense relief that I might make it to safety after all. And then his horror when he realized I had no intention of doing so.

I twisted and turned my light-body, "swimming" through the energy like a fish, angling toward the Darkness. I spiraled downward, once again flipping back and forth between my light-body and physicality, until I found Eliasser. I was close enough to the dark energy that my mind began to slow. *"Not yet,"* I told it. *"I have one more thing to do. Then you can have me."*

Just as Balthasarre had promised, tremendous power was still available to me. Willing myself to remain physical, I wrapped my arms around Eliasser's lifeless body, surrounded us both with a bubble of my Life Force, and fed Love directly into his heart. The buoyancy of that Love caused us to rise up, away from the Darkness, but closer to the center of the vortex where the energy Ashi and I had discharged continued to intensify. Even through my Life Force bubble, heat from the developing "bomb" felt like it was burning my skin. It wouldn't be long before the balancing explosion occurred.

I poured everything I had into Eliasser, thrust every drop of Life Force I could into that incredible heart of his. I was crying now, aching with a fierce grief as I begged my sweet king to come back to life. At last he stirred, reacting with confusion, then despair when he understood where he was and what I had done.

*"Meiri . . . no . . ."* he shouted into my mind.

I shot one last dose of Love into him, boosted his Life Force protection, and shoved him in what I hoped was the direction of the Amoran portal. I prayed he had enough time to make it back safely. As for me? I didn't have the time or the strength to escape; I'd used that up on Eliasser, and I had no regrets. I had chosen well. I waited for the explosion that would end my life with a strange, but calm detachment.

*"I told you I would find you,"* Ashi said.

I was too shocked to react when he spun me around and poured energy into me the same way I'd done with Eliasser, then thrust me away with incredible force. Seconds later, the interior of the vortex erupted. The last thing I felt from my Twin as I spiraled away from him was pain—horrific pain—and then . . . nothing . . . as if he didn't exist. As if he had never existed.

My heart felt like it had been pounded onto broken glass. His complete absence was too agonizing to bear. Death would be a welcome release.

*Light or Dark, you may take me. I am finished.*

It was the Light that answered, infusing me with a sweet, sweet peace. As I prepared to meld into that magnificent brilliance, It unexpectedly transformed into a harsh, pulsing red.

The loss of that pure, sweet Light was the final blow, making me so cold it hurt to breathe.

And then, I couldn't breathe as my Life Force slipped away.

# CHAPTER 36

*I floated above the rain-drenched body of a barely clad woman, what was left of her clothes tattered and town. People spilled out of vehicles with flashing red lights and clustered around her. One of them put a balloon over her face. Air rushed out of it and the woman's chest rose up.*

*I felt a curious pulling sensation in the center of my hazy form.*

*"Don't die, Kerrin," a man said. He buried his head in his hands and sobbed.*

*Kerrin. Why did that name sound familiar?*

*The balloon filled and emptied.*

*My vaporous body began to fade. That's when I remembered who she was.*

*"No!" I swooped down to get their attention. "I want to go home . . . to the Light."*

*But they didn't see me as the balloon filled and emptied.*

*"I told you, NO," I screamed. "I'm ready to go. It's my time to go. I WANT to go."*

*Then there was only darkness. Sweet, sweet darkness.*

---

Voices filtered through the featureless landscape of my mind.

"I've run every possible test, and I don't mind telling you, I'm stumped. Kerrin is suffering from a case of complete physical exhaustion and an unexplainable sunburn. Otherwise, she's okay. I wish I could tell you why her heart and breathing stopped, but it's a mystery to me."

"Something happened, Dr. Bouchard," said the man who wanted Kerrin to live. "I found my wife half-naked on our deck—eyes open, no expression. I don't understand it."

"You and me both. She's not in a coma, per se. It's like she's refusing to wake up. Has anything occurred lately that would make her . . ."

The voices faded away, and I folded myself back into the darkness within.

————————

*Ashi called to me through layers of colored energy, but I didn't have the strength to reach him. I watched helplessly as Darkness blotted out his Light.*

*"Don't go," I begged. "Don't go. Don't leave me . . ."*

"I won't leave you." Fingers gripped my hand. "Please. Open your eyes and come back to me. I need you."

There was a rush of movement. My eyelids were forced apart, and an ungodly brightness stung its way through my pupils.

I struck out at the light. Something clattered to the floor and I slammed my eyes shut.

Dr. Bouchard chuckled. "I may need a new pocket light, but your wife is going to be fine."

————————

Strength slowly returned to my body. I knew I should be grateful I was alive, but I couldn't feel happiness, or even relief, over the fact. More to the point, I couldn't fathom why I hadn't perished in the vortex. And why Ashi had instead. Then there was Eliasser. His fate was still a question mark. I had no way of knowing whether my last-ditch effort to save him had succeeded. And that left as big a hole in my heart as Ashi's death. In some ways, bigger.

Dr. Bouchard prescribed medication for my "depression." Since there was no viable way I could tell him that grief, and not depression, caused my utter joylessness, I pretended to go along with the pill plan. But I had no intention of medicating my sorrow. It was the only thing I had left of Ashi. And so, I got a nurse to tell me which pills were which, and from then on, the only pills I actually swallowed were to relieve physical pain.

John was constantly at my side. I had other visitors, people I was supposed to know, but like a reviving amnesiac, I had to work to remember who they were. Thankfully, the memories came quickly enough and no one detected the difficulty. If they did, they chalked it up to my mysterious "accident," as it was being referred to. It wasn't until Ryan and Kiley arrived for their first visit that I experienced something other than pain and emptiness since leaving the vortex. An aura of wonderfully colored light surrounded them. These two young Lights needed me. I could see it in their eyes and feel it in their hearts. And for the first time in days, I smiled.

---

On a bright, wintry morning, seven days after the vortex expelled my lifeless body onto my deck, I returned home—at least, the only place I'd called home until one Earth month ago. As far as this planet was concerned, the Reparention had been a success. I couldn't be certain about Amoran's fate. I'd reached out with my thoughts while still in the hospital, trying to sense my other world, the Guardians, or even the vortex itself. But I'd felt nothing.

Dr. Bouchard had said a returning home celebration would be fine, but to keep it short, I was still recuperating and would be for some time. My house was decorated for Christmas, thanks to the group of friends who greeted me at the door when I arrived. I tried to look happy, but I wasn't sure I was fooling anyone.

After twenty minutes—that seemed more like hours—John brought me my medication. I told him I needed to use the bathroom first, and went upstairs where I dropped the antidepressant into the toilet.

Watching it spiral down the drain gave me the most satisfaction I'd had in a week.

The house seemed chilly, so I detoured into my bedroom for a sweater. As I pulled open a drawer, a silver object on top of the dresser caught my eye. All the self-control I'd cultivated in the hospital evaporated as a soft moan I wasn't even aware of forming escaped me. I assumed that this particular piece of jewelry had been lost or destroyed during the Reparention. My hand closed over Ashi's amulet, and I fell onto the bed, sobs wracking my body.

When someone came to check on me, I feigned sleep until I heard the soft click of the bedroom door being shut and the welcome sound of footsteps retreating down the stairs.

———

Later that evening, after a quiet dinner and a rented movie, John put his arm around me to lead me up to bed. I managed to back away without flinching.

"I'm sorry. Please don't take this personally, but I don't want anyone touching me yet. I need time to heal."

"And you can't do that with me holding you?" The anger that would have accompanied the question a week ago was gone, replaced by a deep sadness I knew I was solely responsible for. I didn't want to hurt him further by answering truthfully, so I said nothing. Which was stupid, because my silence said it all. That night, I moved into the den.

———

For the next two weeks I did the best acting job I could, but the energy required to live a false life took its toll. Claiming exhaustion, I escaped to the den early each night, locked the door, then held Ashi's amulet to my heart and let my grief spill out until sleep rescued me.

John returned to being the man I had known and loved. He took the better part of those two weeks off from work and we had the kind of family time we'd been missing for the past year. I enjoyed seeing the kids having so much fun, but it was hard for me to be around John, especially when I caught him watching me as if trying to figure out who I was now.

One afternoon, as we waited for Ryan and a now cast-less Kiley to finish ice skating at a local pond, John asked me what I remembered from the day of my "accident." He'd avoided this topic for so long, I thought we were safely past it.

"It's mostly a blur," I said, wishing the time of lies would finally end. "I don't recall much until I woke up in the hospital."

"Well, I recall plenty," John said. He described Camryn's call after waking up in our kitchen with a terrible migraine. I'd disappeared again. It's what made him race home. It's why he found me when he did. Five minutes later and I would have been dead for good, he emphasized. "You don't remember anything before that? Not even Camryn being there?"

I remembered Camryn, all right; especially how she'd deduced I was having an affair. Which made me hate her all the more, even though I apparently owed my life to her.

"What difference does any of that make?" I said. "Can't we move on?"

John's hand closed gently over my jacketed arm. "You tell me, Kerrin. Can we?"

Unable to bear the hope in his expression, I looked back at the pond without answering.

"That's what I was afraid of," he said.

———————

At my insistence, John returned to work full time the following Monday. I spent the day cherishing the empty house and the freedom from pretense I'd lived with for the past two weeks. I even made a full course dinner, complete with our favorite dessert. John told some of his funny stories from his time as an amateur magician during college. Our eyes met while we were laughing and we smiled at each other. Then, a hollow feeling rippled through me and I had to turn away.

When I went into the den that night, I found a note on my pillow. In John's neat printing, it read, *"I'm not giving up on us. I love you and I want you back."* Clipped to the note was a card for a marriage counselor—not Joy Parks—with an appointment date in January.

I tossed the card into the recycling basket.

---

The next morning, I spent several hours at the mall as I half-heartedly selected Christmas presents for my family and friends. On the way home, I slowed down when I got to the Tea Leaf Café. I'd been avoiding contact with people as much as I could, which meant I'd stayed away from my standard haunts in Glenwood Falls. However, the urge for a steaming pot of tea and a fresh-baked scone got the better of me. I pulled into the parking area behind the café.

Doubt crept in as I stood outside the rear entrance. In a small town, where news travels faster than an internet hoax, my accident during The Great Storm—as it was now dubbed—along with my having gone missing the day before, had been grist for the local rumor mill. But when my favorite counterperson looked up from the cash register and waved, I pushed open the glass door and went in.

"How are you feeling after your accident?" Heather asked, her bluntness oddly refreshing.

"I'm okay."

"That was some storm, wasn't it? I guess you're lucky to be alive."

Under the calm scrutiny of Heather's guileless brown eyes, I was instantly humbled and ashamed. So far, I'd only dwelt on my loss. On what I no longer had.

"I guess we're all lucky to be alive," I said quietly.

I surveyed the pastry offerings. "I'll have my usual, thanks."

I chose a table near the back entrance so I could make a quick getaway if necessary—any closer to the door and I'd be in the parking lot. While I waited for Heather to bring me my pot of Earl Grey and a blueberry scone, I engaged in surreptitious people-watching. Two older women, newspapers spread out between them, discussed politics with a passion I wished I still possessed. A couple of college-aged students, camped out in the window seat I normally preferred, played chess, while a few tables away, a group of young mothers, toddlers in tow, were trying to have a conversation and keep their kids from running amok. I almost smiled, remembering what that period of my life had been like. But the sadness I'd lived with since the Reparention had grown even more pronounced after leaving the mall, and it was an effort to keep my expression neutral instead of overtly frowning.

Heather set the teapot, mug, and scone in front of me. "Oh. I almost forgot. There was a man asking for you earlier. I told him that since your accident, no one had seen much of you."

"Was it that reporter?" A journalist was writing a local magazine feature on The Great Storm. The flooding, uprooted trees, property damage and injuries had been covered at the time on TV, the newspapers, and online. Miraculously, my experience had somehow evaded that media blitz. But word had eventually gotten around. This was to be a follow-up human-interest story with the focus on Glenwood Falls, which turned out, not surprisingly, to be ground zero for the worst effects of the storm. While I wasn't the only casualty that day, my tale was the most peculiar. No one else had been discovered half-naked, sunburned, and dead on their deck. So far, I'd managed to avoid the reporter. I intended to keep it that way.

"No," Heather answered. "I've never seen this guy before. He said he'd come back. It was like he expected you to be here."

I lifted the ceramic teapot. "What did he look like?"

"This is the weird part. I can't seem to remember anything about him other than the fact that he was gorgeous. Maybe it's because I didn't pay much attention after I saw the color of his eyes—like a tropical ocean on high voltage." She shrugged and walked away.

My hand shook so much as I tried to pour the tea that I gave up. I knew only one person who fit that description. I glanced wildly around the room, scanning faces for one that seemed familiar, even in disguise. I didn't recognize a soul, but the young moms met my crazed stare with confusion and one of the older women nudged her friend, pointed at me, and whispered.

*Okay, Kerrin. Calm down. You're scaring people.*

I gave the women a smile that felt like it would fracture my face, then took out a book and tried to read so I wouldn't look like a dangerous loony.

I was rereading the same paragraph for the third time when the café suddenly went pin-drop quiet. I looked up and my eyes went wide. Not one person was moving a muscle. But the reason for the tableau of mannequins did not fully sink in until a deep voice behind me said, "May I sit down?"

I jerked my head around. The black turtleneck, khakis, and brown corduroy jacket with elbow patches made him look like a college professor. The finishing touch was his long white hair tied back in a ponytail.

"Please," I breathed out. "Tell me I'm not imagining you."

Eliasser sank into a chair and pulled me into his arms. I was already crying as I burrowed into the front of his blazer. When my heaving shoulders finally relaxed, I blotted the tears from my face and peeked out from the shelter of his jacket.

Eliasser dried his own eyes with a napkin, then felt the ceramic pot.

"Your tea is cold. Would you like me to warm it up?"

I didn't care about tea. My sweet king was alive and well, and here on my world. I could feel the Love radiating from me as I reached up to touch his face. But instead of reacting with equal affection, his expression turned fierce. "What were you thinking?" he demanded, sounding so Earth-like that I nearly smiled. "You should never have risked your life to save mine. How could I have lived with myself if I was responsible for your death?"

"The same way I would have had to live with myself if I hadn't prevented yours."

The piercing glare softened. "Forgive me. What I should have said is thank you. Thank you for your immense bravery. You spared me from a terrible fate."

"Nonsense," I said, flustered by the compliment. "It wasn't bravery. I *spared* you because I couldn't bear the thought of a universe without you, even if I wasn't going to be in it."

Those tropical eyes took on a twinkle. "I believe we had this discussion once before, did we not? I say thank you, and the proper response on your part is—"

"You're welcome." I smiled and pointed at the teapot. "How about a little magic?"

He wrapped those long fingers of his around the pot and used his abundant energy to reheat the tea. I poured a cup, doctored it with milk and sugar, and we passed it back and forth as he filled me in on the health and well-being of the rest of the Guardians. They had made it through the Amoran portal in time to avoid the bolt of energy Ashi and I released, and with the exception of occasional bouts of dizziness, were fully recovered from the effects of the Reparention. All but one, of course.

"Can you tell me what happened to Ashi?" Eliasser asked.

This was the question I most dreaded. I had replayed our final moments in the vortex all too often. I couldn't even escape it when I slept. Thanks to the vividness of my dreams, I got to experience, over and over again, Ashi's suffering when the explosion occurred.

I poured more tea and cradled the cup in my hands, trying to take comfort from the warmth. Then, adopting Ashara's flat, unemotional tone to get me through the ordeal, I told Eliasser how Ashi found me and pushed me to safety, and the terrible pain I felt from him when the vortex erupted. And after that, how I had felt nothing from him at all.

Eliasser squeezed his eyes shut, waves of grief crossing that beautiful face.

I lost it. "I was supposed to die, not Ashi! How could the Foreseers lie to us like that? Now I see why Ashara turned her back on them. They're nothing but sneaky, manipulative—"

"Meirashannar!" Eliasser looked shocked. "Even Ashara would never speak that way about the Foreseers, and neither should you. Besides, you know very well that the Foreseers cannot lie. There must be another explanation."

I brought the mug to my face and drank so Eliasser wouldn't see how bothered I was by his scolding. But he seemed lost in thought as he tapped his fingers on the little round café table. "Perhaps," he said at length, "our task is to consider what that explanation might be." He tilted his head to the side and caught my eye. "Tell me about your encounter with the Darkness just before the Reparention began."

I related my tale from the moment Ari's hand was pulled from mine after we entered the vortex to when I freed myself from the Darkness and landed in the Main Chamber.

Eliasser stroked his chin, considering. "The Voice that spoke to you in the vortex; you are certain it was male? Not female?"

"Definitely male." I guessed he was asking because of Elianna.

"And you believe you know this . . . individual?"

I frowned as I tried to put it into words. "No. Well, kind of. It's more like the Voice seemed familiar, but I don't know why. Do you have any idea?"

"Not a one." Taking the mug from me, he swirled it around like a potion goblet, then narrowed his eyes. "What did the Foreseers tell you about your death that you believe constituted a lie? Their exact wording may be important."

I had to suppress my anger with them in order to consider his question. "The first time the Foreseers mentioned it, their precise words were that I would 'not leave the vortex alive.' And at Ashi's and my Joining, they said I would 'experience a death within the physical realm.'"

Eliasser's snowy eyebrows lifted in a silent "ah-ha."

Crap. I can be such a fool at times. "So, they didn't lie, technically speaking. When John found me, I had no pulse and I wasn't breathing." I clenched my fists. "I'll give the Foreseers this much; they're good at their game. They can't engage in outright deception, so whatever they do tell us has to be the truth. But they clearly don't tell us everything. A friend of mine calls that a sin of omission. With the Foreseers," I spit out angrily, "it's just business as usual. They could've told me I would survive my death in the vortex, they chose not to. They manipulated and betrayed me. I don't care what you say, Eliasser. How can I ever forgive them?"

I would have thought Eliasser would be equally angry with the Foreseers in light of the grief he experienced because of their careful selection of Truth. However, his response was the opposite. Studying me with that affectionate attentiveness that made me go all squishy inside, he coaxed my fisted hands into relaxing, slid his palms over mine, then did what Eliasser was so remarkably good at. I accepted the tranquilizing effect of his Love, trying not to dwell on whether it, too, constituted a form of manipulation.

"What else did they tell you at your Joining, Meiri?"

I droned on with as much enthusiasm as I would have devoted to reciting the times tables.

"They said I was well-prepared for my part in the Reparention. That I would experience a physical death. That Ashi's greatest challenge was yet to come, but that he had the courage to meet it. And that I would guide him—"

I straightened my spine. "Oh, my God! Ashi's not dead. He can't be. The Foreseers specifically said that I would guide him out of darkness. I haven't done that yet, which means Ashi is alive and waiting for me to find him."

"I dearly hope you are correct," Eliasser said, "in the way that you imagine it."

"Imagine it? What other explanation can there be?" I didn't understand his grim expression. "And if I'm the one who has to rescue him, I probably have to do that from Amoran. Has time-stretching been restored? If not, I can work with the normal timeframe, but it will be easier—" I broke off, chilled by the sudden, impassive look on Eliasser's face. "What's the matter?"

Eliasser doubled the energy channeling into my hands, probably to inoculate me against the impact of what he was about to say. But my intuition kicked in before he could speak. I snatched my hands away as my stomach turned over. "I can't come home?"

"You can. Eventually. However, you must fully reenter your life here first."

"My life?" I snapped. "What life? Kerrin Scott's? It's too late for that. You're the one who wanted me to be Meiri. Well, here I am. And you know what? Now I can't be anyone else."

I was so upset that when he tried to take my hands again, I knocked them away. "Stop it. I want my anger. It's a gratifying change from the overwhelming grief I usually feel."

Based on the color spotting his cheeks, the tight hold Eliasser had on himself was slipping. He pulled in a long, slow breath, pressed his lips together, then blew out a sigh.

"You are Meiri, that is certain. But you are also Kerrin. In truth, you are a wonderful blend of the two. For now, though, you must live only as Kerrin. On Earth."

"Oh, no," I moaned. "Please, Eliasser. Don't leave me here all alone."

"I cannot change what must be. I wish that I could," he whispered regretfully. "But this is the best course of action, according to the Foreseers."

"The Foreseers!" At the stony look on Eliasser's face, I bit back a pile of negative sentiments. "What about Ashi? I'm his ticket out of hell. Do we just leave him hanging until I can return? Is that a 'best course of action?'"

Eliasser answered a question with a question, never a good sign. "Did the Foreseers give you a timeframe for when Ashi would be rescued?"

"Oh, yeah," I said sarcastically. "They were quite specific that my love will *one day* guide Ashi out of darkness. I guess we can take our pick out of all the days left between now and the end of time! Well, screw that. I'm coming home whether they like it or not. They can't stop me. Now that the vortex is restored, I can open the portal whenever I want."

My defiance brought another tinge of pink to Eliasser's face. "It will take several months for the vortex to regain its normal stability. Until then, travel between our worlds will be too dangerous. I took a great risk coming here today. To ensure your safety, the portal will be sealed after I return to Amoran. And, at the risk of increasing your resentment of the Foreseers, I share the following in hope that it will temper your need to leap into action and save your Twin. They made it clear that where Ashi is concerned, everything is happening as it should. They trust you will look into your heart and see the wisdom of this path."

My response to that would have singed Eliasser's ears.

I stared at the human statues dotting the café. "Did the wise Foreseers have any tips on how I can fully reenter my life here? Because I'm sick of living one filled with lies and pretense."

"Are you referring to your husband?"

It was a perceptive call on his part. "I know you can't relate to this, but I made love to someone other than the man I'm married to. I can't undo that, and I can't seem to live with it."

"Would it make a difference to know that when you and Ashi 'made love'—what a curious phrase that is—you were not in a physical state; at least, not as you know it on Earth?"

I shook my head. What Ashi and I experienced had certainly felt physical to me.

He sighed again. "Then consider one important fact. You believed you would soon be dead; that you would never again have the opportunity to share yourself in that way. Will you allow that to absolve you of guilt?"

I tried to think about it rationally, but it still wouldn't wash. "I can't. And it's not only that. I think the worst part of this is that I don't know if I love John anymore."

Eliasser smiled. "You do love him, Meiri. I can feel it within you now. And Ashara claims that the energy which disrupted your relationship should no longer be a problem."

I thought back over the past two weeks. John had respected my wish to forgo physical contact, except on one occasion when he held my face and gave me a good solid kiss. I pulled away out of habit, but not before noticing that his hands no longer felt like sandpaper on my skin and the kiss was actually nice. I hadn't wanted to admit it to myself then, as if by doing so I was now being unfaithful to Ashi.

Resigning myself to my current fate, I asked, "So, how long is my prison sentence for?"

"I inquired the same thing of the Foreseers, although not in those words. They did not affix a date to your return. 'When it is time' was all they would say."

"How surprising. The Foreseers wouldn't give you a straight answer."

Eliasser granted me a smile, but then he sobered. "I must go, my Meiri. I am only able to stay on Earth for a limited time."

He stood up and I did likewise. Not wanting to make this parting any more difficult than it already felt, I even tried to smile as I pointed at the mannequin-people. "What about them? Are they all going to have killer headaches when you unfreeze them?"

Eliasser's forehead crinkled, then relaxed. "Ah. You are referring to what happens when Ari stops time for an individual. I have not stopped time, but have taken us completely out of it. When we reenter the current timeline, it will be at the precise moment we left it. And they"—he indicated the café customers—"will be none the wiser."

"Wow. How many more tricks do you have in your magic bag, Master Guardian?"

He laughed. "Seven." He dug inside one of his blazer pockets and withdrew a handful of tiny vials. "Ashara brewed a series of potions to help reintegrate you to your Earth life. She calls them reverse shielding drafts. You are supposed to intuit what that means."

I studied the miniature bottles, each one a color of the rainbow. "I think I understand."

"She thought that you might." Eliasser drew my attention to the bottom of one of the vials. "They are numbered. Begin with the first one tonight just before sleep. Then follow suit with the others for the next six nights."

Seven vials. Seven nights. I'd swallow the last potion on Christmas Eve.

"One more thing. You must also perform the meditation on Love each day or the potions will do little good. It is Love, after all, which works the greatest magic."

And with that, Eliasser slipped out the back door, waved his hand to restore the normal time continuum, and vanished.

# CHAPTER 37

The vials contained a highly concentrated form of potion. I was guessing, more than intuiting, that as a reverse shielding draft, they would undo some of the energy changes in my body, making my "Kerrin self" more accessible. Every evening I performed the meditation on Love, then downed the contents of that day's vial. When I arose each morning, it seemed as if parts of me had been knit back together during the night.

On Christmas Eve Day, I sat alone in the family room, staring out the window at the gathering grayness. After a long stretch of bitterly cold, dry weather since The Great Storm, snow was finally in the forecast.

Ryan and Kiley had gone for a walk in the woods and were due back any minute. I heard the back door open and yelled out, "Wipe your feet, guys." When no one answered, I headed toward the kitchen, bumping into John as he rounded the corner carrying a large, gift-wrapped box. Something tentative was happening between us, and I blushed like a teenager when our bodies collided.

"Weren't you going to be at Nancy's for the afternoon?" John asked, as he struggled to put the bulky package behind his back.

"We came home early. The kids wanted to go for a hike before it snows."

John shifted back and forth. I got the impression he was holding something heavy.

"I bet that's my Christmas present you're doing a bad job of hiding. And I bet you'd like me to get lost so you can stick it under the tree."

To underscore what I thought of that idea, I folded my arms across my chest and grinned.

John laughed. "You are, without a doubt, a hard woman, Kerrin Scott."

"Yeah, but you—" I broke off, hyperaware of the usual conclusion to that line.

His eyes glinted, his voice was soft with regret. "Go ahead. Finish it. Even if it isn't true for you anymore, it's still true for me. And it will always be true for me."

I had to clear the lump out of my throat before I could say, "But you love me anyway."

"Always and forever. Now get out of here. This present of yours is breaking my arms."

I tried to get a peek at what he was holding as I skirted around him, but he about-faced, backed into the family room, and kicked the door shut.

I was putting water on to boil when John came into the kitchen and sat down.

"I'll take a cup of that while you're at it."

I added more water to the kettle, then joined him at the table.

"By the way," he said, "I found your journal."

"My what?"

"Your journal." He tipped his chair back and reached behind him to the shelves that held my cookbooks and assorted kitchen knickknacks. "I found it on the table after your accident. Sorry I didn't mention it earlier. I just stuck it on the shelf and forgot about it."

He pulled a plain white volume from behind two ceramic geese and slid it across the table.

Willing myself to breathe normally, I picked up Ashi's book, the one I'd held like a teddy bear the night before the Reparention. I don't know why I hadn't thought about it until now.

"Everything okay?" John asked.

My face must have given something away. Not trusting myself to speak, I merely nodded.

John tilted his head, thinking. "Didn't you get this back in October? How come you haven't written in it yet?"

I decided not to remind him that at the time, I thought it was a library book. When I spoke again, my answer was oblique as well as true. "I haven't felt much like writing for a while."

"That might change when you're feeling better."

Kiley burst through the back door. "It's snowing! Come *on!*" And she ran back outside.

First snow is always special. On Christmas Eve, even more so. John took my hand and we went out together to watch the soft white powder renew the landscape.

---

It had been John's and my special tradition every Christmas Eve that no matter how late we were up putting toys together, no matter how tired we were, we always made love. But this Christmas Eve was different, and we both knew it.

John approached me after the Christmas preparations were completed, his expression a question. I couldn't believe I was about to break what we once thought of as inviolable, but I shook my head. I just couldn't. Not yet. He nodded, but I knew I'd hurt him.

I went into the den, relieved to hide away from my problems. I performed the meditation on Love, then held the final tiny vial in my hand, sensing that this was the most important potion. I removed the stopper and tipped the bottle up, depositing what amounted to a few drops onto my tongue. My head swam and I plunged into darkness.

---

"Mommy, wake up. It's Christmas," Kiley yelled through the closed door. The doorknob jiggled and I heard her ask, "How come she locks it?" John's reply wasn't discernible.

I didn't remember anything after downing the potion. I was especially grateful for the lack of dreams. For the first time in weeks, I hadn't been forced to relive Ashi being ripped from existence. Something else was different, too, but I couldn't quite tell what.

Kiley's impatient yells reached a crescendo. I threw on a robe and joined my family.

Even though I'd been so detached from the holiday spirit, it was one of our nicest Christmases. My extended family gathered at Michael and Diana's, and I brought along John's present to me: a small laptop, something I'd wanted for ages, but hadn't been in our budget. There was a note taped to the lid; *Why not make every month November?*

I would never want to repeat this past November, but I knew what he meant, and his support for my dream of writing touched me.

I guess there was one good thing to come out of my accident. Everyone was on their best behavior, even Camryn. Lucky for me, there was a small gap in her memory from the day of the storm, which meant she'd forgotten how I'd inadvertently confirmed her suspicions about my "affair."

---

We arrived home from our festivities late that evening.

"It was a nice Christmas," John said.

I nodded, unable to speak for some reason.

"Look, I'm sorry if you felt pressured last night. I want you to be happy, Kerrin. Whether that's with me or without me . . ." Leaving the sentence unfinished, he climbed the stairs and turned the corner toward our room without looking back.

I stared up into the deserted hallway, wondering if John was offering me an exit to our marriage. Was that really what I wanted?

I went into the den and picked up Ashi's book—my "journal." I placed it on its spine and let it fall open. No writing appeared on the pages, no secret messages or instructions. I hadn't really expected anything, but the presence of those blank sheets set in motion a chain of events that put my Earth life back on track.

I filled one of the empty pages with a letter to Ashi, telling him how much I loved and missed him. I also promised to find *him* this time, just as he had promised, then succeeded, in finding me. He hadn't let me down. I wouldn't let him down, either.

I lifted the pen to add something, but the words I'd scribed into the book disappeared. At first, I was surprised. Then it occurred to me that the vanishing verbiage was a kind of message in itself. I searched my heart, a move the Foreseers would have applauded. And when my heart answered, I set pen to paper one last time, asking Ashi's forgiveness for what I was about to do.

Those words vanished, too. I closed the book and removed Ashi's amulet—I'd worn it since the day I came home from the hospital. I put them both into a wooden treasure box I'd received as a Christmas present from my mother, then stashed the box at the back of my file cabinet.

I went upstairs, opened my bedroom door, and slipped inside. John was in bed, reading. The look of surprise on his face quickly became guarded. "Did you forget something?" he asked.

"I think so." I stayed where I was, my back to the open door.

"Do you need help?" John asked uncertainly.

"Yes. Yes, that's exactly right. I need your help."

John swung his legs over the side of the bed and took a few hesitant steps forward.

"Okay," I said. "This is what I need your help with. I will never be able to explain what happened to me, why I seemed so . . . different . . . for a while. If I tried to, you would have me committed, and I wouldn't blame you."

I took a deep breath, looked him straight in the eyes and told him the Truth the same way the Foreseers had told me the Truth. Very carefully worded.

"On this planet of—I don't even know how many billions of people there are now—you are the man I love. I think that's what I forgot. And you are the only man on Earth I have ever made love to. I know I've made things terribly difficult for you, but I'm going to be all right. And I think *we* can be all right, too, on one condition. I never want to talk about the past two months again. Ever. That means no marriage counselor, either. Can you live with that?"

John pulled his lower lip between his teeth. It felt like my entire future was hanging in these moments empty of sound. My plan would only work if he agreed.

"Yes," he said at last. "I can live with that."

I smiled—with relief as well as anticipation. "Want to pretend it's Christmas Eve?"

"Oh," John whispered, "I thought you'd never ask."

And with unaccustomed shyness, he reached behind me to shut our bedroom door.

# Author's Note

Do you Cootie?

I've been part of a Cootie group for over twenty years. The adult version of the children's game is, like Bunco, played with paper, pencil, and dice. Food is present, as is wine and plenty of chocolate. But it's the friendship, support (and hilarious shenanigans) of twelve women that have met monthly (or as nearly as we could) since 2003 that mean the most to me—and I wanted to honor something that is such an important part of my life by giving it some "airtime" in the Amoran Chronicles.

In much earlier drafts of both the *Amoran* and *Elvener's Legacy*, the grown-up version of Cootie figured more prominently. Sadly, in the interest of moving the story forward, most of those scenes wound up on the "cutting room floor," and Cootie only appears "off-page" in *Elvener's Legacy*. I am hoping to include a few Cootie scenes in the third or fourth books, but will have to see if that fits well with the storyline.

In the meantime, if you'd like to learn more about the grown-up version of Cooties, and/or you'd like to start your own Cootie Group, the directions are on my website: www.debrakoehler.net

Happy Rolling!

# Acknowledgements

First, I am forever indebted to Chris Baty, one of the founders of NaNoWriMo (National Novel Writing Month). It is because of that contest that this series exists. Thank you, Chris, not just for starting that crazy writing challenge, but for the pep talks you gave us fledgling writers in the early days when you helmed NaNoWriMo.

Second, to Peg Donovan and Marlene Cullen—good friends and first fans—for feedback, love, and support along the way. You propped me up all those times I felt like switching to something less daunting than writing a series—like skydiving or mountain climbing! Marlene, also a writer and editor (who had the first crack at helping shape Amoran) hosts TheWriteSpot blog, a treasure chest of gems for writers.

To my early readers, writing groups, and critique groups—you have all helped make me a better writer. Special thanks to Rebecca Patrascu, an excellent writer and poet, and Maria Ade, who read one of the first drafts of Amoran and said she especially liked it because it had no "monsters, dragons, or evil beings." That was my goal, and I'm so glad that I reached it.

I am so grateful to Raquel Brown (RaquelBrown.com) for her excellent editing. Any mistakes are mine alone, as I am prone to continuous tinkering with the text until I am finally forced to hit SEND.

Many thanks to the Authors Guild forums and the wealth of information and support offered there.

Last, but certainly not least—to my family, who suffered frozen meals each November while I penned the beginning of yet another novel.

# About the Author

Inspired by her elementary school English teacher, who read Edgar Allen Poe to a batch of fourth-graders, Debra Koehler penned her first story at the age of nine riddled with words like "eerie" and "utterly dreadful." (Fan fiction, anyone?) Horror quickly went by the wayside, but her love of writing remained.

In addition to *Amoran* and *Elvener's Legacy*—the first two books in her four-book fantasy series *The Amoran Chronicles*—Debra has been published in the anthology *Vintage Voices* as well as the poetry anthology *And the Beats Go On.* She has also given presentations on Honoring Your Unique Writer's Journey, and Paths to Publishing, and is a member of the California Writers Club, the Authors Guild, and the Alliance of Independent Authors (ALLi).

Debra lives in Northern California with her husband, daughter, and three rescue cats, one of whom bangs on her bedroom door at five every morning demanding to be fed. The early start gives her plenty of time for writing contemporary fantasies with cozy vibes, epic stakes, humor and a touch of romance.

The second book of The Amoran Chronicles, *Elvener's Legacy*, is now available, and the third book, *The Amelea Variance,* is in the works! To receive information about release dates—or just to say hello—visit Debra at www.debrakoehler.net

9 798990 742901